THE WORST FUGITIVES IN THE STAR NATION

DUMB LUCK AND DEAD HEROES, BOOK SEVEN

SKYLER RAMIREZ

eBook ISBN: 978-1-964457-18-5

Paperback ISBN: 978-1-964457-17-8

Cover design and illustrations by: Persephone Entertainment Inc.

Printed in the United States of America

Published by Persephone Entertainment Inc.

Texas, USA

For anyone ever separated from someone or something they love
(especially if it's tacos)

Don't ever miss a new release!

Sign up now for Skyler's newsletter and get access to new release updates, free content, and great deals.

Just go to www.skylerramirez.com/join-the-club

CONTENTS

WHAT'S HAPPENED UP TO NOW

I thought my readers might benefit from a brief recap of everything that's happened up until this point. Feel free to skip this part and go straight to the Prologue if you feel you remember most of the storyline from the first six books. Otherwise, I hope this helps. Warning: Tons of spoilers here if you haven't read the books before this one.

BOOK ONE: THE WORST SHIP IN THE FLEET

After making an impossible decision in the line of duty that killed 504 civilians at Bellerophon, Brad Mendoza has hit rock bottom. He's drunk and recently divorced, and he feels he has nothing left to live for. But he's still a captain in the Royal Promethean Navy, and he was cleared of any actual wrongdoing. Because the admiralty can't kick him out of the Navy, they decide to force him to quit by sending him to the backwater system of Gerson to take command of the worst ship in the fleet: HMS *Persephone*.

Brad can immediately tell something is off when he arrives to take command of *Persephone*. On his first day, an enlisted man, Petty Officer Nedrin Jacobs, talks down to him and practically threatens him. Then, he meets Lieutenant Commander Jessica Lin, his new executive officer (XO), with whom he is immediately smitten. However, Jessica appears to have secrets of her own, and Brad surmises she might be in a relationship with Jacobs.

After a confrontation with Jacobs and another with Jessica, Brad learns, to his horror, that there is, in fact, a relationship, but that it's not consensual. He further learns that *Persephone's* former captain, Clancy Jessup, was also assaulting Jessica. Despite his efforts, she refuses to talk about it or condemn the two men. Just as Brad is resolved to learn the details and take action anyway, they encounter an enemy ship from the Koratan Confederacy sneaking about in Gerson's outer system.

Outgunned, outmatched, and with a blown engine, *Persephone* has nowhere to run. Brad enlists the help of his crew, especially Jessica, to devise a daring plan. They pretend to have a high-level government agent on board (a member of the King's Cross), betting that the Koratans will prefer to capture the agent alive versus destroying the ship outright.

They lure the Koratans in close and plan to self-destruct *Persephone* to destroy the enemy ship. Brad offers to be the one to stay behind and blow up *Persephone*, sending the rest of the crew out on escape pods first. He loads a message into one of the escape pods with video proof that Jacobs and Jessup have been assaulting Jessica, hoping to at least get justice for his XO before his death.

However, at the last minute, one of his officers knocks him out and takes Brad's place, destroying *Persephone* and the Koratan ship.

Brad awakens later in his escape pod to Jessica's frantic

calls. The entire crew is rescued shortly thereafter and taken back to Gerson Station. There, Brad encounters a real high-level agent of the Promethean government, assassin and Agent of the King's Cross Heather Kilgore. She informs him that the Koratans were in the system to find an extremely valuable and recently discovered deposit of stellarium, a metal used to make impregnable warships. She then reveals that Nedrin Jacobs is the King's nephew and that the King will likely order Brad's and Jessica's deaths to cover up the scandal that will result from Brad's message.

Taking pity on the two officers, Kilgore arranges for them to fake their deaths from injuries supposedly sustained in the battle and then gives them a ship on which to make their escape.

BOOK TWO: THE WORST SPIES IN THE SECTOR

Brad and Jessica flee Gerson on their new light freighter, *Wanderer*. At Jessica's insistence, Brad gets sober, and they start looking for work to pay for their new lives on the run. But when they attempt to secure a paid cargo to haul, bureaucracy gets in the way, and they end up having to take a job from a sketchy man named Owen Thompson, who is traveling with several 'friends'.

En route to the Fiori system to pick up Owen's cargo, Brad and Jessica get to know each other better, and Brad admits to himself that he's fallen in love with his former XO. But he believes she'll never feel the same. Meanwhile, Owen and his friends are scheming against them, and they take over *Wanderer*, putting an explosive implant into Jessica's head so that Brad will do their bidding.

They force Brad and Jessica to help them locate a

defector from the Promethean Navy on the Rishi Paradise Casino Orbital. Owen claims the deserter has valuable intelligence his employers want and that they need Brad to use his intimate knowledge of the Navy to help them locate their man. Brad and Jessica reluctantly agree but have little luck at first.

Finally, Jessica manages to find their target, George Peterson. Brad pretends to be an agent of the Promethean Security Service (ProSec) and forces George to take them to an abandoned asteroid mining facility where he's hidden the intel he stole.

The intel George Peterson stole ends up being the exact coordinates to the stellarium deposit in Gerson, which he plans to sell to the Koratans. Once they are at the asteroid and have recovered the intel drive, Owen tries to kill Brad and take the coordinates. Through skill and a lot of luck, Brad manages to kill Tucker, Owen's enforcer, and then Owen himself.

At that point, Heather Kilgore arrives to recover the intel from Brad, revealing that she hired Owen and suggested he use Brad and Jessica to help find the coordinates. Brad is angry but focuses on saving Jessica. He boards *Wanderer* again and finds that Jessica has already somehow subdued Owen's two other soldiers. They convince one of them, Harris, to disable the explosive implant in her head. Harris then decides to join their crew, and they leave the final mercenary, Jules, alone to die on the asteroid's surface.

While flying out of the Fiori system, *Wanderer* is stopped and boarded by a Leeward Republic battlecruiser, *Dauntless*, which is carrying Jessica's estranged father.

BOOK THREE: THE WORST PIRATE HUNTERS IN THE FRINGE

While Jessica has a meeting on *Dauntless* with her father, Brad is interrogated in a friendly fashion by Admiral Walters of the Leeward Republic, who unsuccessfully tries to learn from him what the Promethean King is hiding at Gerson. Before she releases Brad and Jessica, she convinces them to take on a mission to save a small, independent planet, Carter's World, from a pirate siege. She introduces them to Kayla Carter, daughter of the planet's president, who offers to lead them back to her home and pay for their help.

Desperate for money, Brad and Jessica agree. En route to Carter's World, Kayla starts to flirt with Brad, making advances that he rebuffs at first. But he hears Jessica say something that makes it nearly certain she will never return his feelings. Distraught, he starts to succumb little by little to Kayla's flirtations.

When they arrive in Carter's System, the pirates are waiting and almost capture them. Only some fancy flying through the atmosphere of a gas giant allows them to escape. Kayla guides them to Carter's World, where they land at her father's farm out in the countryside, away from the eyes of pirate spies. There, they meet her father, President Carter, and members of his government.

Brad agrees to train the Carter's World militia to attack the pirate base, using weapons given to them by Admiral Walters. During the week of training, Kayla continues to make advances toward Brad, but he rebuffs her again, realizing that he's still very much in love with Jessica.

Training complete, Brad and Jessica take the militia members, President Carter, and Kayla to the pirates' asteroid base. There, they confront the pirate boss, Poulter, and kill him and his crew. Afterward, they split the spoils of war with President Carter, giving him much of the pirates' stolen loot and keeping for themselves a small warship, which they name *Persephone II.*

As Jessica and Harris fly *Persephone II* out of the system and Brad flies *Wanderer* to ferry Kayla, her father, and their people back to the planet, Brad is having second thoughts about the entire mission. Suspecting there's more to things than meets the eye, he calls the planet and discovers that the real President Carter is there and doesn't have a daughter named Kayla. He's about to call Jessica and warn her when Kayla intervenes, revealing herself as a mercenary hired by unnamed forces to get the stellarium coordinates from Brad. He learns that the mission against Poulter's pirates was both a way to gain Brad's trust and a way for Kayla's organization to use him to take out an increasingly annoying ally in the process.

Kayla takes Brad prisoner, and he watches helplessly as a bomb she planted on *Persephone II* explodes, supposedly killing Jessica and Harris.

But Harris discovers the bomb just in time, and Jessica manages to get it into the airlock to jettison it. However, the bomb explodes before she can shut the hatch, and the ship is damaged while Jessica is badly burned and almost killed.

BOOK FOUR: THE WORST RESCUERS IN THE REPUBLIC

Kayla tortures Brad for the stellarium coordinates, believing he memorized them from George Peterson's intel. Meanwhile, the real President Carter, grateful for the removal of the pirate threat, agrees to help Jessica go after Kayla and save Brad. He patches up *Persephone II* and provides her with a crew from his now-defunct system patrol fleet.

Jessica leaves the planet with her new ship and crew but has little idea where to start looking for Brad. She decides to head back to the Fiori system to confront her father there, suspecting he had something to do with Kayla kidnapping Brad.

In the Fiori system, Jessica hires Gunnery Sergeant Quinn Boyd and his team of mercenary soldiers. They help her storm Skytran Orbital, making it to her father's executive office and confronting him there. We learn that Jessica's father once betrayed her, using her to get valuable Promethean intel for the Leeward Republic, resulting in the deaths of 57 members of the Promethean Navy. Jessica has never forgiven herself, and Nedrin Jacobs and Clancy Jessup used knowledge of the event to blackmail and assault her on *Persephone*.

Jessica also confronts her father about Brad's kidnapping, and he admits to working with Kayla in return for part of the windfall from the stellarium deposit. Under duress, he gives her a comm code and a dead drop location in the Kate's Hope system to make contact with Kayla.

Taking her ship and crew, Jessica flies to Kate's Hope, but a stakeout of the dead drop location yields nothing. About to give up, she encounters an odd woman named Hayley Uvalde, who claims to be an intelligence officer for hire. Uvalde uses the comm code to trace Kayla to the Capaldi system.

Meanwhile, Brad has been barely holding up under weeks of Kayla's relentless torture. He finally gives her a set of fake coordinates for the stellarium, and when she sends a ship to Gerson to investigate, it's followed back to

Capaldi by Agent of the King's Cross Heather Kilgore. But Kilgore's ship is captured by pirates allied with Kayla before she can rescue Brad, and she joins Brad as Kayla's captive.

They soon learn that Kayla's employers are officers of the Jutzen Collective, a star nation of neo-Nazis who want the stellarium to build an unstoppable fleet of conquest. The Jutzens provide Kayla with a truth serum, which she uses to enhance the interrogation of Brad and Kilgore.

Jessica and her crew take *Persephone II* to Capaldi, but they're ambushed by the same pirates who captured Kilgore. They narrowly escape and destroy the pirate ship. But then, they encounter a Jutzen battleship, whose admiral tells Jessica that Brad is already dead and warns her to leave the system.

Uvalde finds the exact coordinates of the station where Kayla is holding Brad. Escaping the Jutzens, Jessica and her crew fly to the coordinates and undertake a daring space jump to assault the station and rescue Brad. They find him and Heather Kilgore alive but learn that Kilgore gave up the stellarium coordinates under the influence of the truth serum.

During the rescue, still under the influence of the Nazi truth serum, Brad confesses his love for Jessica. He's overjoyed when she reveals that she loves him back.

The Jutzens, intent on not letting Brad, Jessica, or Kilgore escape, come to the station to chase them. Once again, the scrappy crew of *Persephone II* manages to outwit the enemy, but the ship is too damaged to continue, and they take escape pods down to the system's inhabited planet. The Jutzens pick up Kayla's pod and then leave the system to take the coordinates back to their fleet.

On the surface of Christos, Uvalde finds where Kayla

stashed *Wanderer*. Some of the Carter's World crew decide to stay with Brad and Jessica, as do Quinn Boyd and Hayley Uvalde. Together, they set off in *Wanderer* to build lives as both mercenaries and legitimate freight haulers. But on their first stop back at Kate's Hope, they encounter Brad's ex-wife, Carla, who has an urgent mission for them.

BOOK FIVE: THE WORST DETECTIVES IN THE FEDERATION

Carla hires Brad and Jessica to find a missing Promethean Navy task force, Task Force 32. Her new boyfriend, Horace Clarington, was with TF32 when it disappeared at the opposite end of Promethean space. Somehow, Clarington managed to get a cryptic message out to Carla asking for Brad's help and suggesting he find Admiral Ricardo Jimenez, an old quasi-friend of Brad's and an officer in the Koratan Navy.

They travel to Hudson, a contested planet claimed by both Prometheus and Koratas, taking cargo with them and almost getting captured by poachers and then by pirates in the process. When they finally arrive at Hudson, they find an ex-cop named Timothy Gentry, recommended to them by Heather Kilgore. He agrees, for a large fee, to help them find and question Ricardo Jimenez.

After escaping a kidnapping and assassination attempt by an unknown agent, Brad and Jessica, with Gentry's help, finally find Jimenez at a high-stakes underground poker game. Brad makes contact, but ProSec is also there to see what Jimenez knows about TF32. In the ensuing chaos, Jimenez is shot by a hidden sniper and dies, but not before confessing to Brad that he knows where TF32 is being hidden in the XB-411 system.

Captured again, this time by ProSec agent Kat Henderson, Brad's old XO, our heroes barely escape yet another assassination attempt. This time the danger comes from a traitorous member of Kat's own team. Capturing one of the traitor's colleagues, they learn that the Jutzens are behind everything, planning to use the ships of TF32 to attack Koratan ships in the Hudson system, with the goal of starting a shooting war between Prometheus and Koratas. By doing so, they hope to force the King to leave Gerson and the stellarium deposit undefended.

Unable to convince the arrogant Promethean admiral at Hudson to believe their circumstantial intelligence, Kat Henderson enlists Brad, Jessica, and their crew to help her take a top-secret stealth ship, HMS *Vampire,* tc XB-411 to gather the proof she needs. At XB-411, they search for days and finally find both the ships of TF32 and a massive Jutzen dreadnought, the *Bismark.*

Our heroes sneak onboard *Bismark* and rescue the small number of surviving crew of TF32, leading them to freedom. At great cost of life, they manage to steal back one of TF32's destroyers, HMS *Bainbridge,* to use in their escape. Before they leave, they set off a nuclear bomb inside *Bismark* that destroys the Jutzen ship, but not before it manages to shoot down *Vampire* with Jessica on board.

Luckily, Brad is able to rescue Jessica and the others with her before they run out of air. They take *Bainbridge* back to Hudson, but the Jutzen-crewed ships of TF32 beat them there. Brad, Jessica, and the rescued Promethean officers of TF32 arrive at Hudson expecting to find a war broken out. However, in their absence, Carla managed to call in favors owed to her and Brad from Duke Laraby Garrison of Kipling, the Promethean Federation's second most powerful man behind the King. Duke Garrison and his fleet destroy the ships of TF32 before the Jutzens can carry out their attack, stopping the war before it starts.

When Brad and Jessica arrive at Huston Station, the Navy attempts to arrest them, but Duke Garrison intervenes and arranges for them escape *and* take *Bainbridge* with them. In return, he asks Brad to undertake a mission to rescue his little sister, Larissa Garrison, who he believes has been kidnapped by revolutionaries and taken into Koratan space. Brad and Jessica agree and leave Hudson with their crew on board *Bainbridge*.

A few days into their journey, however, they learn that Hayley Uvalde is a traitor, secretly working as an agent for the Koratan Confederate Guard, an organization of deadly assassins and spies.

BOOK SIX: THE WORST TRAITORS IN THE CONFEDERACY

Brad and Jessica continue their mission to rescue Larissa Garrison in Koratan space, but they worry about what to do with the knowledge of Hayley Uvalde's betrayal. Knowing they will need all the help they can get, they set out in search of Quinn Boyd's old team, who took a mission at his direction in Koratan space.

Finding that Boyd's team inadvertently took a job for Koratan drug lords, Brad and team interrupt a high-level meeting of crime bosses on Santa Maria Station. They are briefly taken captive, but Hayley Uvalde reveals her true colors and takes out the cartel soldiers, allowing Brad, Jessica, Boyd, and his old team to escape on *Bainbridge*. They leave the station listening to a litany of threats from Baron Dexter Hornsby, a well-known Promethean mob boss who was part of the meeting they interrupted.

Shortly thereafter, *Bainbridge* is disabled by a ship of the

Koratan Confederate Guard. Nido, Hayley's old boss, boards their ship and offers to pay them a substantial amount if they are successful in removing Larissa Garrison from Koratan space. She believe the girl is there to foment more rebellion within both star nations and is willing to share her exact location. The only catch is that Nido insists that Brad and Jessica have to keep Hayley with them, despite also revealing that Hayley suffers from multiple personalities, including a ruthless assassin named Lola.

Along the way, Brad and Jessica pick up more crew in the Santo Domingo system, including two teenage twins, Tina and Sam DeJong, whom they save from pirates. *Bainbridge* must then play a game of cat and mouse with a Koratan Navy destroyer before finally arriving at the Serenidad system, where they expect to find Larissa Garrison.

Brad, Jessica, and a troublemaking Tina DeJong infiltrate the fortress Larissa is being held in by crashing a charity auction there. Searching the manor house, they find Larissa, who claims to be there against her will. But on their way out, Tina disappears, and the rest narrowly evade capture by stealing an antique car, a 1964 ½ Ford Mustang from Earth, worth billions of credits.

Brad drives the Mustang with Jessica and Larissa to where Quinn Boyd and team can pick them up. Jessica and Larissa get to safety, but Brad stays in the car to draw off pursuit so they can escape. He crashes the priceless car and is taken back to the manor house as a prisoner.

There, he discovers that Laraby and Larissa's mother, Duchess Charlotte, is behind the efforts to gain Koratan support to depose King Charles. Charlotte hates Brad for twice before foiling her plans while he was still in the Navy (outlined in *The Brad Mendoza Chronicles*) and promises to torture and kill him. But he escapes when Tina DeJong, still hiding in the manor house, pops out of an air vent and leads him to where Hayley Uvalde has infiltrated the compound to rescue them.

Hayley, operating as her ruthless Lola persona, mows through the manor house's guards to get Brad and Tina to safety. She leads them to a safe house to await the rest of their crew. There, they are ambushed by Nido and other Confederate Guard agents, who confess to manipulating Brad for their own purposes and must now kill him to cover their tracks. In the scuffle, Hayley, Brad, and Tina are all knocked out and taken prisoner, but not before Hayley fights her own organization attempting to save Brad.

However, when Brad, Hayley, and Tina wake up, they find that they've been rescued by the personal security detail of none other than Koratan President Nanette Fournier. Fournier confides in them that she has been fighting traitorous elements in her own government, including Nido and her colleagues. She thanks them for exposing both Duchess Charlotte, who died resisting arrest, and Nido, and grants them safe passage out of Koratan space.

Meanwhile, Jessica is back on *Bainbridge* and must use strategy and cunning to defeat two Koratan warships loyal to Duchess Charlotte. After the battle, she returns to the planet, threatening to bombard it if Brad, Tina, and Hayley are not returned to her. With the cooperation of President Fournier, she picks up her three lost friends and they leave the system together on *Bainbridge*.

Halfway back to the border with Promethean space, Larissa Garrison reveals her true colors, betraying them and calling in support from Baron Dexter Hornsby, one of her mother's sponsors and financiers. Hornsby ambushes *Bain-*

bridge in the Helgatha system, where a third of the crew dies in the ensuing battle against his boarding forces. Only Hayley, acting as her Lola persona, manages to save the day by killing enough of Hornsby's soldiers to scare them into retreat.

Now aware that Larissa was a fully willing participant in her mother's treason, Brad and Jessica decide to return her to her brother, Duke Garrison, anyway. They deliver the rebellious teenager to agents of the duke and then proceed to a shipyard in the independent Jewel system to get *Bainbridge's* damages from the fight with Hornsby repaired. On the way, Jessica proposes marriage to Brad, and he naturally (and very ecstatically) accepts.

While waiting for their ship to get fixed, Brad, Jessica, and the crew take a well-deserved vacation at an all-inclusive luxury resort on Jewel's surface. All is perfect until Jessica gets a mysterious call and must leave abruptly without telling Brad.

A SUPER IMPORTANT LIST OF PEOPLE WHO WANT BRAD DEAD

Wow, that was a lot! I mean, seriously, what more could possibly happen to Brad and Jessica at this point? In reality, quite a bit more. Because there are many, *many* people in the galaxy who still want Brad Mendoza dead. In fact, I thought it might be helpful to compile a non-exhaustive list of everyone who wants to kill Brad:

1. Fleet Admiral Terrence Oliphant
2. Captain Wainwright
3. Petty Officer Nedrin Jacobs
4. Commander Clancy Jessup
5. King Charles of Prometheus

6. Approximately 4,328 members of the Koratan Confederate Navy
7. Owen Thompson's third cousin, twice removed on his mother's side
8. Kayla 'Carter'
9. Vizeadmiral Heinrich of the Jutzen Collective Navy (along with all his Nazi friends)
10. Several poachers on the planet Jocelyn
11. Admiral Christoph Turly
12. 'Baron' Dexter Hornsby
13. Agent Nido of the Koratan Confederate Guard
14. Oswaldo Heraldo Hernandez Guadalupe (because Brad crashed his priceless Mustang, which frankly infuriates me as well)
15. Duchess Charlotte Garrison (deceased)
16. Larissa Garrison
17. A concessions vendor at the Royal King William Memorial Stadium, home of the Promethean Navy Knights.

Unfortunately, with everything still left to write about in the sordid history of Brad Mendoza and Jessica Lin, I'm afraid we will likely never get to the story of #17 on the list above. However, should Brad ever again come face to face with this specific concessions vendor, he will be wise to turn around and run away as fast as he can. Hopefully, he can escape before the vendor can lay hold upon a foam finger or other deadly weapon to strike down our hapless idiot of a captain with the mad, righteous fury that is unique to stilted concessions vendors and middle-school physical education teachers.

Hmm. Maybe I *will* have to write that story one day.

'The Worst Concessions Vendor in the Stadium'. It has a nice ring to it, doesn't it?

But, for now, all of the above leads us to the opening of book seven, *The Worst Fugitives in the Star Nation*, which starts in just a few pages. It's a very good book, but unfortunately, it features exactly zero angry concessions vendors. Please try to enjoy it anyway.

Skyler Ramirez

BRAD & JESSICA'S CREW

Here's a helpful reminder of the members of Brad & Jessica's crew, as constituted at the beginning of book seven.

CREW OF THE MV *BAINBRIDGE*

Captain Brad Mendoza (M) – Everyone's favorite idiot.
Commander Jessica Lin (F) – Brad's XO and better half. Seriously, she's more like 7/8s of this relationship, if we're being honest.
Lieutenant Commander Francis Illian (M) – Tactical Officer. Joined the crew from Carter's World initially just to help Jessica save Brad in *The Worst Rescuers in the Republic*, but he's stuck around ever since. Likes to shoot at other ships and date unstable assassins with multiple personalities (Hayley Uvalde). Otherwise, a pretty boring guy.
Lieutenant Commander Kelly O'Malley (M) – Chief Engineer. Was with Brad and Jessica in the beginning on the original HMS *Persephone* in *The Worst Ship in the Fleet*.

Rejoined the crew in Hudson after the events of *The Worst Detectives in the Federation*. Everyone likes Kelly.

Lieutenant Hayley Uvalde (aka Agent Sparrow) (F) – Intelligence Officer and undercover member of the Koratan Confederate Guard. Has multiple personalities, and we're never quite sure which one is going to show up or what color her hair is going to be. But extremely good at her job. Favorite pastimes include toppling planetary governments, ruthless assassinations, and making her boyfriend (Francis Illian) uncomfortable in public settings. Joined the crew in *The Worst Rescuers in the Republic*.

Petty Officer Harris (M) – Who knows? One day, he's a makeup and disguise expert. The next, he's a tailor sewing extra pockets on Brad's uniform. Sometimes, he's an incredibly talented hacker. But always introverted and generally a bad dresser. Joined the crew at the end of *The Worst Spies in the Sector*.

Karen O'Malley (F) – Ship's Cook and Kelly's wife. The only person on the crew who can order anyone around, even Brad. At least if he wants dinner.

Lieutenant Laia Gammon (F) – Sensor Officer. Was part of Jamie Durkin's crew, which all joined Brad and Jessica during *The Worst Traitors in the Confederacy*. Enjoys long walks on the beach and designating sensor contacts for Brad to shoot at.

Chief Petty Officer Saki Hashimoto (F) – Helmswoman and MV *Bainbridge*'s senior enlisted spacer. Also formerly part of Jamie Durkin's crew. No-nonsense personality.

Petty Officer Toshi Ishii (M) – Engineer. Also formerly part of Jamie Durkin's crew.

Spacer 1st Class Pilar Moya (F) – Engineer's Mate. Also formerly part of Jamie Durkin's crew.

Spacer 2nd Class Max Vealer (M) – Gunner's Mate. You guess it! Also formerly part of Jamie Durkin's crew.

Doctor Damien Bean (M) – Ship's Medical Officer. A mad scientist type who joined the crew to escape the law during the events of *The Worst Traitors in the Confederacy*.

Spacer 3rd Class Tina DeJong (F) – Engineer's Mate. Seventeen-year-old girl rescued from pirates by Brad and Jessica during the events of *The Worst Traitors in the Confederacy*. Likes to hide in air vents and listen to other people's private conversations.

Spacer 3rd Class Sam DeJong (M) – Helmsman. Tina's 16-year-old brother. Can't really fit in air vents like his sister.

SHOOTERS

Gunnery Sergeant Quinn Boyd (M) – Gunny. Joined the crew to help Jessica rescue Brad during the events of *The Worst Rescuers in the Republic*. Big, scary ex-Marine, but really a teddy bear once you get to know him. I mean, don't you just want Gunny Boyd to give you a warm hug… right after he vanquishes your foes?

Corporal Heddy Rodriguez (F) – Gunny Boyd's original number two. Don't get on her bad side. Trust me on that. My ribs are still healing.

Private Drake Forbes (M) – Original member of Gunny Boyd's team. Has a secret crush on Jessica, but you didn't hear that from me.

Private Edgar Kluth (M) – Looks like a marshmallow; can kill you six different ways with a toothpick. Originally part of Jamie Durkin's crew.

Private Daren Beck (M) – Also originally part of Jamie Durkin's crew. Likes checkers over chess.

PROLOGUE - SAND GETS EVERYWHERE

TWO WEEKS AGO - JESSICA LIN

"Hey, idiot! Give it back!"

Brad regards the tanned teenage boy looming over us, the one who just sprayed us with sand from his poorly thrown football… for the fourth time. Brad frowns but doesn't say anything; instead, he throws the ball. It sails over the teenager's head and lands about ten meters beyond him and well into the surf.

The kid says a not-so-nice word and runs toward the surf line to retrieve his wayward football, his friends hooting and hollering at him to hurry.

Stretched out on my stomach across the large blanket I'm sharing with him, I turn my head to look over at my fiancé. "That wasn't very nice," I chide.

Brad sits back down and watches the kid awkwardly flail about in the water while the waves pull his ball farther out. "Really? I thought you would appreciate it."

I lever myself up onto my elbows, feeling the warm sand shift under the blanket, and use one hand to shield my eyes against the bright sunlight so I can frown at him. "Why would I appreciate you messing with some kid?"

He raises an eyebrow and gives me a skeptical look in return. "Really, Jess? Come on, do you think that the ball landing near us *four* times was a coincidence? That boy just wanted an excuse to come and check you out up close."

"No," I say in disbelief, twisting to look at the group of adolescent boys egging on their friend as he tries to retrieve the fleeing football. Sure enough, a couple of them are staring right at me. When they catch me looking, they avert their gazes quickly and pretend to be studying the sand in front of their feet.

"Of course," Brad confirms, stretching out on his back, his hands interlaced behind his head for a cushion. "I mean, you look good in just about anything, Jess. But in that swimsuit? Let's just say the words 'devastating beauty' come to mind."

I regard him wryly. "Devastating, huh? I think I like the sound of that. Makes me sound dangerous."

He grins, tipping down his sunglasses so I can see his eyes. "Trust me, right now, 'dangerous' is an under-statement."

I laugh and swat him playfully. "Okay, Captain. You're making me blush." Then I lay my head and chest back onto the towel to keep sunning my back, still chuckling.

He laughs along with me, and it feels good. We've been on the planet Jewel for two weeks now while our destroyer, *Bainbridge*, undergoes repairs in the orbital ship-yard overhead. The latest report is that in four weeks, five at the most, all of the damage we sustained in our battle with Baron Dexter Hornsby in the Helgatha system will be completely fixed. And while we're still mourning the members of our crew lost in that battle, I also have to admit it's been incredibly nice to just relax on the beach and not worry about anything more than clumsy teenagers for a while. I believe this is the longest stretch of time without anyone shooting at us since we left Gerson six months ago.

"So, what do you think of a spring wedding on a planet like this one?"

Suddenly, all the relaxation of the last two weeks leaves my body. I turn to regard my fiancé with a frown. "Uh, I guess that could work," I reply awkwardly.

He sits back up, regarding me. "You okay?"

"Of course," I say, trying to sound unbothered. "Why wouldn't I be?"

"Well, it's just that every time I bring up a wedding date, you start to look like I'm proposing we attack a battleship head-on in an unarmed freighter. Having second thoughts already?" He asks the question in a casual, light manner, but I can see the worry lines on his forehead even though I can't see his eyes behind the sunglasses.

"No, nothing like that," I say quickly. "I just... I don't know. Can't we just enjoy being engaged right now? It's only been a few weeks. Planning the wedding this soon, it just feels rushed."

His cheek twitches once, but otherwise, nothing disturbs the false smile he's wearing. "Sure, Jess. Didn't mean to rush you. We can talk about it later." He lies back down, pretending to be content in the sun, and I do the same, turning my face away so that he won't see the moisture in my eyes.

The worst part is, I can't explain to him why talk of a wedding date throws me into a near panic attack every time he brings it up. That would require sharing a part of my past with him that I've tried very hard not to think about for three whole years. Every time I consider telling Brad the truth, my throat seizes up, and I can't bring myself to say the words.

We lie there on the beach in relative silence for another 15 minutes before he says something inane about the weather, and then we talk for a while like nothing happened. But we both know better.

PART ONE
SEPARATE WAYS

ONE
THE MESSAGE
PRESENT DAY - JESSICA LIN

"Hurry back!"

Those are the last words I hear my fiancé say before I'm forced to leave him behind, possibly forever.

The day started out normally enough. Breakfast on the beach. Surfing lessons—Brad is much better at it than I am. Yoga in the exercise center—Brad does yoga the same way he flies ships: too fast, too hard, and not all that pretty to look at. Cooking class for lunch—we're both hopeless as chefs. Then, we lie out by the pool, Brad eating tacos and me reading a book while our crew either plays in the water or tours local attractions on the planet's surface. Everything is *perfect*, just as it has been for the four weeks we've been at the resort. It's almost enough to make me forget we're wanted fugitives in just about every star nation we've ever visited.

Then Doctor Damien Bean interrupts me with a reminder that it's time for my scar treatment. The daily visits with the quirky doctor are a little tedious and sometimes painful, but the scars are almost entirely gone, and I recognize the old Jessica in the mirror once again.

I bid Brad a quick farewell at the pool. I don't even kiss him goodbye because his mouth is full of tacos. I just reach out and squeeze his hand. That's it. It's funny the things you reflect on when your latest interaction with a loved one might very well have been your last.

But I'm getting ahead of myself. It only takes me two minutes to get back to my room, where I plan to change into loose clothing for the scar treatment. As I reach out to open the door, the ring on my finger catches the light. I smile to myself. Brad insisted on buying it, not even waiting until we were settled at the resort. He said it was a 'requirement' to make our engagement official. He's oddly old-fashioned like that, and I love him for it.

Of course, he wanted to buy a *really* big diamond, recklessly spending some of our remaining funds from the mission to rescue Larissa Garrison. I talked him out of it—I had to threaten to make him review a budget spreadsheet with me if he wanted to spend that much—and convinced him to buy a modest ring instead. I get a thrill every time I look at it on my finger, but the feeling is mixed with… something else.

I shove the darker thoughts aside and enter my room, tossing my towel onto the bed and heading to the dresser to grab something to change into. A flashing red light on the bottom edge of the room's viewscreen catches my eye, stopping me short. A message? Who at the resort would be sending me a message? And why not just use my comm? Curious, I query the viewscreen with my implant.

Then I gasp and drop the shirt I was in the process of pulling out of its drawer as a painfully familiar face fills the screen in front of me.

"Jessica," the man says somberly. "I need you. I've

attached coordinates to this message. Come alone or…
well, you can probably guess."

The image on the screen changes to what looks like a
live shot of the pool I just left. By the angle of the video
and the image quality, it's almost certainly from a drone
hovering just over the line of trees that ring the swimming
area. In the live feed, I can see Brad still lounging poolside,
holding a plate of tacos in one hand and laughing at something one of the crew has said. Then, superimposed on the
image, right on top of Brad's head, red crosshairs appear.
Whoever is in control of that drone wants me to know,
without a doubt, that they can and will kill Brad in an
instant if I don't do as they say.

I'm too stunned to do more than watch as tears start to
cloud my vision.

The live feed of the pool disappears, and the familiar
man's face is back on the screen. "We're monitoring all
signals in your area and, as you can see, watching your
crew. We have people all over the resort. *Any* attempt to
communicate with or warn your friends, and they have
orders to eliminate Brad Mendoza." As if the crosshairs on
my fiancé's face didn't already send me that message quite
loudly.

"You've been reactivated, Lieutenant Commander Lin.
This is not voluntary. Your orders are to proceed to the
designated coordinates immediately. You have eight hours
to arrive. Failure to comply will be met with swift action."

Tears are falling in rivulets down my cheeks now, and I
start letting out great, choking sobs.

"Jessica." The man's voice stays hard, but there's a
slight catch to it when he says my name again. "Don't test
us on this. Trust me when I tell you that this is the only
way. I'll be seeing you soon."

The message ends as abruptly as it began, replaced by a dark screen. I fall to my knees on the room's carpet, still sobbing, as my implant pings and the promised coordinates are delivered to it. The AI helpfully informs me that they lead to a mining station on an asteroid in the outer system. With only eight hours to get there, I need to leave now.

I only briefly consider running back to the pool to tell Brad what's going on. The enemy will be expecting me to try and they'll know if I do. A sniper or drone operator can pull a trigger much faster than I can shout a warning to Brad and our crew. I can't even risk leaving a note; knowing these people, they likely have eyes and ears *everywhere*.

Which all leaves me with absolutely no choice. I mechanically start to change my clothes and then quickly throw some extra clothing into a small bag.

I have no idea if I'll ever see Brad or any of our other friends again, but I don't like my chances at all.

TWO

TACOS BY THE POOL
BRAD MENDOZA

Tacos by the pool. If I could sum up all my hopes for eventual retirement and independent wealth, it would be in those four words. The last month here at the Chalinga Resort, waiting and vacationing while the shipyard in orbit high overhead fixes the damage to *Bainbridge*, have been some of the best days of my life. And not just because people are bringing me unlimited tacos by the pool, though that is pretty great. Spending this time with Jessica has been amazing. And with the crew. It's awesome.

"Captain, got a minute?"

Well, except for maybe one part.

"Francis," I say, looking up and shielding my eyes against the sun to look at my dour and serious tactical officer standing over my lounge chair. "How many times do I need to tell you? We're not on our ship; we're on vacation. Just call me Brad."

Lieutenant Commander Francis Illian grimaces. "Uh, sorry, sir. It just doesn't come naturally."

I roll my eyes. "Fine. Have a seat and tell me what's on that rigid, puritanical mind of yours."

He ignores my entirely accurate characterization of him and settles awkwardly into the lounge chair Jessica vacated a few minutes ago. The guy is pasty white and covered in so much sunscreen that I'm not even sure I'm seeing his natural color underneath it, not that there's any real difference.

"What's up, Francis?" I press when he doesn't immediately start talking. He's working up to something, and I wish he'd just spit it out. My tacos will get cold. Sure, they'll bring me new ones, as many as I want. All-inclusive means all-inclusive. But it's the principle of the thing! Letting a good taco go to waste is like jumping out of a perfectly good spaceship, something I've had to do a few times and never really enjoyed.

"I wanted to talk to you about my future on the crew," Illian says in a voice so low I have to strain to hear him, but the solemnity of the words immediately grabs my attention.

With a last forlorn look, I set the pork al pastor taco—my latest conquest and my favorite—down on the plate, which is balanced on my stomach to keep the food close. Then I give my tactical officer and friend my full attention.

"Go on," I prod him.

"When I left Carter's World to help Commander Lin rescue you from the mercenaries and the Jutzens, I was only supposed to be gone a couple of months. Now it's been almost five, and I've started getting messages on the Net asking me—more like *ordering* me—to come home."

"Well, that's not great." My tone is more serious than it typically has been during our time at the resort. This really is a conversation between a captain and one of his officers, as hard as it may be to treat it as such when we're both shirtless and sitting by a pool, and my sensor officer just did a backflip from the diving board in my peripheral vision. "What are you going to do?"

"That's the problem, sir. I don't know."

I raise an eyebrow at him but otherwise stay silent. He'll keep talking when he's ready.

He takes a deep breath. "If you'd asked me a couple of months ago, I wouldn't even have hesitated; I would have caught the next starliner or freighter berth toward the border systems and made the best possible time to Carter's System. They want me to take over the entire system patrol, which has always been my dream. Or, at least, *was* my dream."

"And that dream has changed?" Would he notice if I snuck another bite of that taco? Serious conversations like this make me hungry.

He nods. "Yes, sir. I mean, I think it has... changed, that is." He breaks eye contact with me and looks at something across the pool.

I follow his gaze to see Hayley Uvalde sunning herself on another lounge chair, her neon-blue hair clashing with her neon-green swimsuit and a pair of ridiculous pink sunglasses that cover half her face. She looks relaxed, but knowing her, she's probably scanning the nearby resort building rooftops and evaluating them as potential sniper nests.

"I see," I say slowly. "Do you think there's a future there? Given who—what—she is?" I mean, I'm rooting for Illian and Uvalde as much as anyone else. In my head, I call them 'Frankly', a mix of Francis and Hayley. I think it's the best couple name in the history of the Fringe, but I haven't gotten it to catch on with the rest of the crew yet.

I've considered ordering them to use it, but that's probably overstepping my authority as captain.

However, despite my enthusiasm in choosing their amazing couple name, I've never truly thought that a deadly and very mentally unstable assassin is a great fit for the stodgy system patrol officer sitting next to me. I think we all figure it's just a matter of time until she either breaks his heart or literally puts a knife in it. But I try not to dwell on that second possibility. So far, she's only killed people who are trying to kill us.

Illian frowns and lets out a long sigh. "I don't know, Captain. For the first time in my life, I have no idea what the right decision is. There are no guarantees with a woman like Hayley. Frankly…" I so badly want to point out that he just used their couple name, but now is probably not the time. "…there are no guarantees at all in our current situation."

He's got me there. One day, we're battling pirates; the next, we're blowing up a Nazi dreadnought; then, we're trying to 'rescue' a traitorous teenage girl who turns out to be the bad guy. After that, we're fighting off a mob syndicate and losing a third of our crew. And then we're here, enjoying a well-deserved vacation but all knowing that it will eventually have to come to an end. I don't even know what next *month* will bring, much less the next year. If Illian is coming to me looking for guidance and wisdom, he's probably searching in the wrong place. I've never claimed to be smart—much the opposite, in fact.

My mind races, searching for the right thing to say to the man. "Commander, do you know how great my old life was?" Hmm. Maybe that wasn't it.

He looks at me and cocks his head in confusion at the change in topic. "Uh, sir?"

I swear I'm going somewhere with this—or at least I'm pretty sure I am. "Well," I continue, "it was great, terrific even. I was the youngest captain in four generations in the Promethean Navy. Five years, ten at the most, and I would have made flag rank. I had a wife—you've met her, but she was a lot nicer back then—and a pretty good life with her on Prometheus when I wasn't out doing my two favorite things, flying a ship and shooting at stuff. Which was my actual job! On top of all that, I really felt like I was making a difference, you know? Like I was part of something incredible."

I turn and look him in the eyes. "You could have all of that on Carter's World. Find a nice Carterian... Carteranian—whatever—wife, settle down, have kids, and train the next generation of a legitimate system patrol. Maybe even run for political office one day. You'd be good at that. The best politicians have no sense of humor."

He doesn't laugh at that, and I mentally smack myself. I need to take this conversation more seriously. It's just hard to change from vacation mode back into captain mode. I lick my lips and take the plate of tacos from my lap and place them on a small side table next to me. Maybe I'll focus better without pork al pastor and grilled pineapple right under my nose.

"You could have all that by going home," I continue, more solemnly now. "You'd have what we call the Promethean Dream: a house with a white picket fence, two and a half kids, and a robot dog." I shudder a little at that last part. I've had bad luck with robot dogs. One saved my life once, when I was just an ensign. But the whole experience was incredibly creepy, given that the entire station we were on was trying to kill me at the time, so I've really tried hard to forget it.

Illian nods slowly. "We call it the Carter Promise, but I get the gist. I don't understand, sir. Shouldn't you be trying to convince me *not* to go home?"

I shrug. "I can't convince you of anything, Commander. But what I *can* tell you is that as great as my old life was, I wouldn't trade it in a million years for what I have now."

"You mean life as a fugitive mercenary on the run with the entire Fringe trying to kill you and never knowing where your next payday is coming from or who is going to shoot at you next?" he says dryly, and I give him a wide smile. Illian just made a joke; we're *finally* starting to get this guy a sense of humor! But he doesn't return my smile, so maybe he was being serious. Hard to tell.

I shift in my chair and cast a longing glance at my plate of tacos just in time to see one of the ever-present resort attendants swoop in, grab it, and take it away, probably figuring I was done with it. I resist the urge to leap to my feet and chase it down and instead turn my full attention back to Illian.

"You're right. Our current life is very stressful sometimes, and there are no guarantees. We lost a lot of good people at Helgatha, and losing Chief Perry at XB-411 still hurts."

We share a brief frown and moment of silence. As much fun as we've been having at the resort, the thoughts of those not here with us are ever present.

"But despite all of that," I tell Francis, emotion creeping into my voice even though I try to keep it neutral, "I still wouldn't go back to my old life for anything. Truth is, Guns,"—he smiles briefly at the once-hated nickname—"I can't even explain to you why. My entire childhood, I dreamed of joining the Navy and having *exactly* the life I eventually built. But now that it's gone, I don't even miss it.

"I've been thinking a lot about that lately, and I really believe it comes down to the people we surround ourselves with. You see, I loved Carla, and I liked my friends and colleagues in the Navy. I *hated* my in-laws, but that was mostly bearable. Now, I have a new group of people I love, and I'm starting to realize that it almost doesn't matter what happens *to* us or what we *do*. What matters, I'm convinced, is who we go through it all with."

I pause, waiting for him to process my words and respond. For an off-the-cuff speech, I think I'm nailing this.

"So, you're saying that I should stay here because the people here are better than the ones back on Carter's World?"

I frown. Okay, maybe I'm not doing as well as I thought. I've never been good at psychobabble. "No, Francis. What I'm saying is that you can find happiness here *or* back on Carter's World. You just have to decide if you'd rather find that happiness with Hayley Uvalde—for as long as that lasts—and the rest of us, or if you want to find it with the people you left behind at home. There's no wrong choice, you see. Either can lead to some pretty great things for you."

He looks down at his hands in his lap and doesn't respond. The air between us is thick with emotion, which, of course, is making me horribly uncomfortable. So, I do what I always do when faced with emotions I don't know how to process. I say something glib and inappropriate.

"But, let me also remind you that only one of those life paths leads to tacos by the pool."

For a moment, he frowns, but then he lets out a small snicker. Illian pretty much *never* laughs at my jokes, so I'll take the win. I'm wearing him down! Or maybe it has nothing to do with me; perhaps it's Hayley who's forcing him to loosen up. A guy has to be willing to loosen up a little and maybe even surrender some of his sanity to date a woman who has multiple personalities, one of whom is a remorseless super-assassin, and all of whom have different hair colors and seem to speak different languages.

Illian sighs loudly. "I appreciate the perspective, Skipper. It helps. Unfortunately, it doesn't make the decision any easier."

I smile. "Well, Commander, that's how you know both paths are good—when they're so hard to choose between, like a good al pastor taco and a carnitas taco. Now, both are pork, of course, but one has pineapple, and the other has this great citrus taste, and—"

He's opening his mouth to either reply or interrupt my soliloquy about tacos when another voice shouts across the pool, drawing all of our attention.

"Captain Mendoza!" Doctor Damien Bean storms around the perimeter of the pool and stops right at the foot of my chair, blocking my sun. "Commander Lin was supposed to meet me at the resort clinic 20 minutes ago! I'm a busy man, and the least she could do is show up for her appointment."

I smirk at the doctor as a few of our crewmembers in the pool laugh at his tirade. Just like always, he's wearing an anachronistic pair of thick glasses, and the white tufts of hair on his head and his customary white lab coat—he wears the thing even in Jewel's stiflingly hot climate—make him look like a mad scientist from just about every low-budget movie I've ever seen. But he's a good doctor, and he comes cheap. I get the feeling that some government out there wants him dead almost as badly as my old star nation wants to kill me and Jessica.

"Relax, Doc," I admonish him. "I'm sure Jessica just got sidetracked or lost track of time. I'll call her now."

I use my implant to connect to the resort's Internet and ping my fiancée. No response. So I do it again. No response.

"Don't you think I already tried calling her?" Bean yells, flapping his arms like he might take flight at any second. "No courtesy at all! She won't even answer her comm."

I'm barely listening to him now. I try to call Jessica a third time. No response. I use my military implant's command overrides and try to track her implant, but it returns a no connection message. Either she's out of range, or she's shut off her transmitter. I look over at Illian, who's watching me with a concerned and questioning gaze.

"I can't find her implant," I say soberly, jumping to my feet. "I'll check her room. You go to the main resort building and see if she's in any of the shops on the way to the clinic."

We both run from the pool area, not even bothering to grab our shirts, towels, or sandals.

"The nerve!" Doc Bean shouts after us. "Does *no one* on this crew pay attention to me?"

By the time I reach Jessica's room, Quinn Boyd has gotten out of the pool and is only a few meters behind me. Without waiting for him to catch up, I bang on Jessica's door and then press my ear to it. I can hear no movement inside.

"Gunny," I say, nodding to the door. It would take my implant at least a few minutes to hack the lock; Chalinga serves high-income vacationers, and the resort's security is state-of-the-art for civilian stuff. But I don't need to hack the lock when I have a Gunny Boyd instead.

It only takes him one try to shoulder open the flimsy obstacle, and I rush through behind him. After that, it only takes us about two seconds to confirm that the room is empty. On the bed is a bathing suit, the one Jessica was wearing out by the pool. The drawers are open, and clothes have been flung onto the bed and the floor at random, like someone packed in a hurry.

I move quickly to the open closet and look inside, immediately noticing two things: first, that about half the hangers are empty, and second, that Jessica's duffel bag is missing.

She's gone. She left me.

THREE
WE FIND NOTHING

BRAD MENDOZA

Nothing in Jessica's room gives any hint as to where she might have run off to. By now, Harris and a few other crewmembers have joined us in searching every square centimeter of the room while others are canvassing the resort in a well-organized grid pattern assigned by Gunny Boyd. Uvalde is off on her own somewhere, doing whatever it is she does to get information.

We're searching every nook, cranny, and drawer in the room, looking for any clue to my fiancée's disappearance. Clothes are flying everywhere as eager and distressed crewmembers grab individual pieces from each drawer and throw them aloft to discover what might be hidden underneath.

Then I hear a grunt of shock and surprise. I look over with excitement to see Gunny turning red at something he's found, but my hopes are dashed when I see the source of his consternation: Jessica's underwear drawer. Normally, the sight of the big, indestructible ex-Marine turning red at the sight of a woman's unmentionables would make me laugh or at least say something snarky. Not now.

Saki Hashimoto, our crew's chief enlisted spacer and *Bainbridge's* navigator and helmswoman, shoves the much larger Boyd out of the way with one hip and quickly searches the drawer, shaking her head to tell us there's nothing helpful in it.

"Captain," I hear over the shared comm channel. "We've cleared the shops, and we're moving on to the restaurants in the south wing."

"Roger that, Heddy," Boyd answers for me. "Keep us posted."

"On it, Gunny."

"No luck at the beach," Laia Gammon, our sensor officer, transmits next. "I've been showing her picture around, and no one has seen her here in the last few hours."

I swear loudly, kicking at an open drawer that slams shut and then rebounds right into my shin, making me swear again. I look up to see that the room has gone quiet and still, every eye riveted on me. I expect judgment in those gazes; how can the captain be losing his cool when it matters most?

But I don't see any of that. All I see is fear and pity, and it suddenly makes me angry in a way I can't explain.

"Listen, people!" I snap, both to those in the room and on the comm. "We don't stop looking until we find Jessica. Once you've checked everywhere, check it again. Heddy, forget the restaurants for a moment. You and Beck get down to the port. Buy a ticket to any shuttle that will get you past security and start looking for her there. On the double!"

Gunny's number-two shooter acknowledges my order, and I turn to Harris, who's fiddling with a data pad and frowning at the blank viewscreen in Jessica's room.

"Harris, tell me you found something."

He looks up in surprise as if just noticing he's not alone in the room. In his loud, red-and-yellow floral shirt and green-and-black-striped swim shorts, he's a sight to behold. But what really draws my eye right now is the frustrated set to his mouth.

"Sorry, Skipper," he says in a voice that seems to be on the edge of a full meltdown, and I have to remind myself that he's known Jessica for almost as long as I have. If this is killing me, then it must be doing the same to him. He views Jess like a little sister.

"It's okay, Harris," I say, fighting to keep my own voice in check. "Just tell me what you have so far."

He looks back down at the pad, his lower lip quivering like he might start to cry at any moment, but he blinks away the tears and starts talking. "I can see that the room got a message just a few minutes after Jessica left the pool, but it's been deleted clean. I can't find it on the viewscreen's memory or even on the hotel servers." He hacked the latter within our first few days here just because he was bored. Well, bored and trying to impress Pilar Moya, one of the engineer's mates we picked up in Koratan space.

His words surprisingly fill me with both frustrated anger *and* an overwhelming sense of relief. Jessica got a message. That means whatever was in that message is what caused her to leave. And it means she didn't plan this; she didn't plan to leave me. But that still gets me no closer to finding her and making sure she's safe.

"What about the resort's vid feeds?" I ask.

Harris shakes his head. "Sorry, Captain. Security vids

are stored on a separate server with a different encryption schema from the hotel's main systems. I guess they take guest privacy pretty seriously. It would take me another hour or two to hack my way in."

I stifle another curse and turn to Gunny Boyd. "Quinn, you're with me."

He falls into step as I stride out the still-broken hotel door. "Where we headed, Skipper?"

"To the front desk. We're going to get those vids."

"How?"

"We're going to threaten someone."

FOUR
LEAVING IN A RUSH

JESSICA LIN

I leave the Chalinga Resort behind mere minutes after hearing the message that ripped me from an ideal vacation with Brad and dashed my dreams for a future with him. As I take the robotaxi from the resort to the port, I almost ask it to turn around a dozen times, fuming that I should be forced to leave without even saying goodbye.

But I can't turn around because someone at that resort has my fiancé in the sight of a very powerful rifle—certainly more than one—and I very much prefer Brad *with* his head. I've grown to like his face.

The knowledge that I have no choice doesn't stop me from spiraling out of control, alternating between red-hot anger and the deepest despair for the 30-minute ride. When the taxi finally drops me off at the port near my shuttle's gate, I have a new emotion: fear.

The timeline the message gave me is tight, and if I miss even a single connection on the journey to the designated coordinates, I won't be there in time. Leaping from the taxi almost before it rolls to a stop, I sprint toward the security line, which is thankfully short. Minutes later, I dash through the open gate leading to the shuttle that will take me to the station in orbit above, making it onboard seconds before the attendants announce boarding has ended.

Ten minutes later, we're rocketing up through the atmosphere, pressed into the backs of our seats as the shuttle's engines propel us toward Jewel Orbital II, the main commercial hub for this part of the planet.

I close my eyes, fighting back more tears, shutting out the curious looks from other passengers around me as I start to cry again. Every meter we rise toward space is that much farther from Brad—and that much closer to what-ever awaits me.

"Miss, are you okay?"

I look over at the man seated next to me. He's fit, though he's probably 30 or 40 years older than me, with a face worn by lines and gray hair. His eyebrows are knit together in concern as he studies my tear-streaked cheeks.

"I'm fine," I say, my voice ragged with emotion.

He reaches out a hand and pats mine lightly, surprising me with his fingers' rough, callused skin. "Sure you are, miss. Everything will be okay. You know what I do when I'm nervous about shuttle flights?"

I shake my head, not to answer his question, but because I don't trust my voice to tell him that the flight has nothing to do with my current state. He leans toward me anyway, almost like a grizzled old grandfather about to comfort a small child.

"When I'm scared like this, I stop making a scene that might get the people I love killed," his voice, suddenly very hard and stern, hisses in my ear.

I recoil, but he shakes his head at me, motioning toward a data pad sitting in his lap. I look at it now, shocked to see an image of the interior of my hotel room back on the surface, multiple members of my crew visible in the camera feed searching the room.

"Just sit back and relax now, Lieutenant Commander Lin," the old man says with a smile that doesn't reach his eyes or color his voice in the least. "Everything will be okay if you just hold it together and do exactly what you're told. But don't force us to make an example of any of your friends down on the surface. You wouldn't like that, I'm sure."

I nod despondently, reaching up and doing my best to wipe the tears off my face.

"Good," he says, patting my hand again and not reacting when I jerk it away from him. "Just a little while longer now, and everything will be fine."

FIVE
THREATENING EVERYONE
BRAD MENDOZA

"I'm sorry, sir, but resort policy is very clear. There is no way I can share our video logs with you unless you have a warrant or a subpoena. Now I'm going to have to ask you to—"

I lean across the desk, and the thin man wearing a suit and way too much hair gel involuntarily recoils from me. I should just have Gunny hit him over the head, but I'm actually worried that the clerk's spiky hair might be just hard enough to impale the big man's fist. Besides, we've already drawn the looks of a couple of the resort's security guards across the wide hall, which is lined with shops and help desks like this one just off the main lobby.

So, it's time to try a different tack.

"Do you follow the news?" I ask him, trying to sound friendly and conversational.

"Excuse me, sir?"

"Do. You. Follow. The. News?" I repeat.

"Uh… yes, sometimes."

"Have you ever heard of the Butcher of Bellerophon?"

He looks confused and shakes his head.

"Look it up. I'll wait."

After a moment's hesitation, he types a few things into the console in front of him. I'm a paying customer—paying a *lot* for a month and a half for a crew of 21—so he's automatically programmed to do what I tell him to so long as it doesn't go against 'resort policy'.

It takes about ten seconds—every one of them ticks by like a death knell as Jessica gets farther and farther away from me—but I can see the moment the clerk realizes who he's talking to. His eyes go wide, and he looks from the console up at me, then back at the console, and then back at me again.

"You're…"

I nod and hold his startled gaze. "A mass murderer who killed 504 civilians? Yes, I am. And I've killed a few dozen more people since then. Most of them deserved it. But do you know what the best thing about being a mass murderer is?"

He gulps and shakes his head while Gunny shifts behind us to block the view of the distant security guards.

I lean toward the hotel clerk once more, and he flinches but doesn't shy back this time. He's rooted to the spot, like a mouse hypnotized by a deadly viper. When I speak again, I don't shout or raise my voice. I almost whisper. "The best part is that one more murder on my record isn't going to do much when they finally catch up to me."

He gulps again and turns a shade of white even paler than Illian covered in sunscreen. "You just need to find one video, right, sir?"

"That's it, just one. I just need to find out if and how my friend left the resort."

He hits another few keys and then turns the console screen toward me. The vid he's pulled up is of the resort's front drive, where a line of robotaxis waits to take guests to the port or to whatever sightseeing destinations they'd like. He runs the video at high speed until I spot Jessica.

"There! Stop."

He complies, and the vid returns to real time. I watch Jessica walk to the robotaxi attendant, fidgeting nervously as the next cab moves forward to pick her up. I memorize the taxi's number so Harris can double-check the drop-off location, but I'm fairly certain it's the port. Nothing else makes sense.

After she gets into the cab and drives off, the clerk stops the video.

"Play it again," I order him.

He instantly complies. Amazing the type of service you get when you threaten someone with death.

"Pause it, right there! Now reverse two seconds and play it again, but zoom in here." Too impatient to wait for him to do as I ask, I reach out, swipe the screen, and then reverse pinch the image to zoom in on the indicated frame. I play the video again at half speed.

"Gunny, you seeing what I'm seeing?"

I see him nod out of the corner of my eye as I reverse the video and replay it a third time, focusing on Jessica's fingers tapping against her leg in a way that most might dismiss as nervous twitches.

"Flash code," he rumbles. "All numbers?"

It's my turn to nod. "Coordinates." I capture them in my implant and ping them over to him in case something happens to me.

"Will that be all, sir?" the nervous clerk asks.

I ignore him and turn to stalk away. Gunny has to jog a few steps to catch up to me.

"What's at those coordinates?" he asks, and I realize

that my implant is Navy issue, but his is from the Republic Marines. So, it probably doesn't have all the fancy astrogation apps mine does.

"Outer system. Some no-name asteroid with a mining station," I tell him as we near the main lobby. "Comm Heddy at the port. Tell her to take Beck and get to that asteroid as fast as possible, and that we'll be right behind them."

"Aye, Skipper."

I'm opening my mouth to say more but stop in my tracks as a shock of bright blue hair appears in front of me out of nowhere.

"Hey, boss," Hayley Uvalde says, though with none of her customary cheerfulness. "One of the security hombres saw the commander walking through the lobby. Said she was crying, but when he asked her what was the matter, she just shook her head and walked right by him."

"Okay," I say, though I'm not sure what that tells us other than to reinforce the almost ironclad certainty that Jessica didn't leave of her own free will.

"There's something else, boss," Hayley says, leaning closer to me and lowering her voice. "We're being watched."

"You mean by the hotel security cams?"

She shakes her head. "Someone else, chico. There are stealth drones hovering over the property and following members of the crew, especially you. Pretty sure they're armed, too. And they're good; even my implant almost missed them."

"Huh. Any in the building?" I fight the urge to look up at the vaulted ceiling.

"No. But there are a few hombres who have been *very* interested in you since you entered."

31

I nod, again resisting the urge to look around and see if I can spot said hombres.

"What do you suggest, Lieutenant?" Subterfuge and spycraft are her specialties.

"We need to stay here until we know what they intend, boss."

I open my mouth to argue, but she holds up a hand to forestall it. "I know, boss. But we can't save the commander if you're dead. Like I said, those drones are armed. Cuidado."

She's got a point there, even if I don't like it. Whoever is watching us is almost certainly connected to whoever forced Jess to leave. But maybe this also gives us an opportunity.

"See if you can isolate one of them," I tell her.

Hayley smiles, though there's no joy in it. "De cierto, Capitán. Give me two minutes." Then she's gone, disappearing around the corner and into the main lobby. Quinn and I wait before following, listening in our implants as Hayley fills us in on her plan and calls in a few other crewmembers to help.

When we arrive in the lobby, I see her almost immediately. And not just because of her blue hair and bright clothing. It's also the fact that she's standing right in the middle of the ample open space, arguing loudly with a plain-looking man in cargo pants and a gray T-shirt. By his build, he looks military.

I start to move closer to hear what they're saying, but suddenly Hayley screams, a bloodcurdling, high-pitched sound that hurts my ears and draws every eye in the spacious lobby to her and the suddenly very flustered military guy.

"He grabbed my butt!" she yells, pointing at the man. "Help! He's assaulting me!"

Mr. Military holds up two hands as if to ward off an evil spirit and starts backing away from Hayley, looking frantically around for an exit, but two beefy resort security guards appear on either side of him, each grabbing an arm.

They lead him away, asking Hayley to accompany them to give her statement. Boyd and I follow at a discrete distance.

The security office is outside of the main building, across a big open courtyard with a fountain at its center. As the guards are about halfway across it with the military man, more screaming breaks out nearby. Everyone looks to the courtyard's edge to see two women trading blows and trying to gouge each other's eyes out with their nails.

"You knew he was mine!" one of them yells at the top of her lungs as she delivers a hard, open-hand slap to the other's cheek.

"He loves me more!" the other retorts, kicking the first woman in the shin.

The flummoxed security guards spend a second looking back and forth between the two fighting women and their prisoner. At some unspoken agreement, one of them releases their captive and makes his way over to separate the women. With the other watching the scene and not paying attention to his surroundings, it's a simple matter for Hayley to sidestep closer to him.

She produces a small stunner in one hand and presses it to the remaining security guard's neck. His eyes roll up into the back of his skull, and he slumps to the ground. Before Mr. Military can react and escape, Hayley uses the same stunner on him.

Gunny and I jog forward and help her drag Mr. Military toward the other side of the courtyard and a wall of bushes and trees there. I risk one quick look upward to see if I can spot any of the watching drones, but if they're using active camouflage, I probably wouldn't see them even if they were right above me.

Moving quickly and avoiding cameras where we can, we take our prisoner to my hotel room, down the hall from Jessica's. We get our prisoner tied to a chair just as there's a knock at the door. Hayley stands on her toes to check the peephole and then opens it. Laia Gammon and Pilar Moya walk in, hair askew and clothes torn in a few places but both smiling grimly.

"Any trouble with security?" I ask the two women.

Laia shakes her head. "No problem, Skipper. Once we stopped fighting, the guy was way too freaked out by finding his comrade passed out and their prisoner gone. He barely noticed when we left."

I study their battered appearances. "You both okay?"

It's Pilar who answers this time. "Sure, Captain. It's not every day an enlisted grunt like me gets to slap around an officer. 'Sides, Laia really did steal my boyfriend once, so I owed her." She sobers up, looking past me at the tied-up man, who's starting to stir in the chair. "Think he knows where Commander Lin is?"

I frown. "If he does, we'll get it out of him. If he doesn't, he's in for a world of hurt either way."

SIX
AN UNEXPECTED COURSE CHANGE

JESSICA LIN

"**S**tay close," the older man says in a low growl so the other passengers can't hear as the shuttle docks and we prepare to disembark.

I don't reply, but he obviously takes my silence as agreement and walks behind me all the way off the ship, through the airlock, and into the docking corridor. His hand is on my lower back the whole time, and it makes my skin crawl.

We quickly find ourselves on Jewel Orbital II's main concourse. "Docking port A23," the old man says in my ear. "Try to run or draw any attention, and your friends on the planet die."

I nod to show I understand and try to ping the station's Net to see where gate A23 will take us. Unsurprisingly, he's jamming me. So, instead, I search with my eyes for one of the big viewscreens showing departures and arrivals across the station. Finding one, I locate the entry for A23, expecting to see the asteroid's designation next to it.

What I see instead stops me in my tracks.

"What are you doing?" my companion hisses, trying to shove me forward again.

"I… That ship is going to—" I stammer, but he cuts me off.

"What, you thought that asteroid was the real meeting place? What do you think we are, stupid? You probably found a way to signal that loser Mendoza with the coordinates. No, we need to get you far away where your crew can't find you. And if you value their lives, you'll keep on walking."

Numb with despair, I allow him to prod me forward. I *did* manage to signal the coordinates to Brad, tapping my fingers on one leg in flash code where I knew a resort camera would catch it. So long as it seemed my captors were planning to keep me in the Jewel system, I held out hope that somehow, he and our crew would find me. Now that I know where we're actually headed, that hope disappears.

There's also a second reason I reacted with such shock. The destination listed for the ship at A23 is a place I'm intimately familiar with but one that I swore I'd never return to.

SEVEN
I REALLY HATE SPIES

BRAD MENDOZA

"**B**oss, I found three cameras in the room," Hayley reports as we wait for our new guest to wake up. "Super sophisticated ones. Had to look hard to find them, even with my Guard implant. Sorry, I missed them all before. It was sloppy."

I sigh loudly. "Don't beat yourself up, Hayley. None of us thought we'd be in this situation. But we'd better move quickly, since they doubtlessly know where we are." I decide not to share that I already have a strong suspicion about who our prisoner works for; let's see if I'm right first.

I walk over to the tied-up military man, reach back one hand, and slap him hard against the jaw. He jolts awake, eyes fixing on me and arms straining against his bonds. I ignore his frantic and short-lived efforts to free himself. With Gunny on one side of me and Hayley on the other, I'm about as protected as a man can be in this galaxy.

Crouching down in front of him, I look him in the eyes, keeping my expression as impassive as possible. "Name, rank, and serial number?" I ask evenly.

By the way his eyes go wide for a mere fraction of an instant, I know my suspicions are true, which is highly unfortunate.

"Listen," I tell him. "I'm in a hurry. Normally, I'd let you stew for a bit, and it would be at least a few hours until I'd resort to cutting off appendages. But you and I both know that I don't have that kind of time today. On top of that, I know who you are and who trained you, so I also know anything short of severe physical pain isn't going to get you talking.

"So, you can tell me what I want to know now and still be in one piece when your friends get here, or you can start losing fingers and... other things. Do you have a preference?"

"You're mad!" he spits out. "I'm just a tourist. I have no idea who you people are!"

"Okay." I shrug. "If that's how you want to play it." I reach out a hand to Gunny Boyd, who places in it the hilt of a 20-centimeter tactical knife. By the way our captive is watching, with half a smirk, he thinks I'm bluffing. But the very fact that he doesn't look all that afraid is further confirmation that he's no simple tourist.

Gunny puts a massive hand over Mr. Military's mouth to muffle his startled scream as I reach down to cut off his little finger. Maybe you think I'm cruel for not giving him more time to come around before I head straight on to torture, but our time really is short. Plus, he can definitely live a long and happy life without his little finger. I should know. Kayla Carter cut mine off in the Capaldi system, and I've done just fine without it.

But just as the blade makes contact with his skin, we're interrupted by a knock at the door. I nod to Hayley to go and answer it, turning to watch. From out of nowhere, Gunny produces a pistol. I don't know if he somehow smuggled it onto the planet through customs or procured it here, and I don't care. I feel better knowing he has it.

Hayley looks again through the old-fashioned peep-hole on the door and then calls back to me. "Capitán, I think this guy's boss is here."

I look over to Gunny, who nods, then to Laia and Pilar, who both magically produce knives from somewhere in their torn clothing.

"Why do you think it's his boss?" I ask Hayley cautiously.

"He just looks bossy, boss. Plus, he's got four other big guys with guns standing behind him."

"Well, open it and invite the boss in," I tell her, and she swings the door wide to admit a tall, wiry man with black hair, a square jaw, and gray eyes. He steps into the room, arms raised just enough to show us he has no weapons but still low enough to look lazy and disrespectful. He takes us all in at a glance, frowning as he sees me still holding the knife to his man, though now I have it at the guy's throat as a sort of insurance.

He motions for his men behind him to stay back, and Hayley shuts the door in their faces. The newcomer turns back to face me.

"Now, now, Captain Mendoza," he says in a voice that gives me the impression of tar oozing across hull metal. "There's no need for violence. I just want to have a conversation."

"Skipper?" Gunny rumbles next to me, his tone equal parts a question toward me and a threat toward the unnamed interloper. Behind the man, I can see Uvalde ready for action, her hair already starting to lose its color.

If those other guys try and break down the door, they're in for a big surprise.

I wave both of them down. "At ease, folks. Let's hear what my old pals in Promethean Naval Intelligence have to say for themselves. *Then* we can decide if we need to kill or maim them."

EIGHT
AND I REALLY HATE LACROSSE

BRAD MENDOZA

The boss man's name is Commander Jake Traeger, and if a name like that has you picturing a finance guy in a fleece vest, you're not far off. By his accent, he attended the King's University of Prometheus and graduated with full honors and probably a few lacrosse trophies. By his clean and unbroken nails attached to soft hands, he hasn't practiced hand-to-hand fighting since joining the Navy. And by the way he looks around my high-priced resort room distastefully, his mommy and daddy probably have some fancy words ahead of their names that make them—and him—feel more important than us normal folk.

I would hate this guy by pure instinct, even without knowing that he's Promethean Naval Intelligence *and* that it's his fault Jessica is gone.

"Were you really going to go straight to cutting off his fingers?" Traeger asks me, studying his still-tied-up man with a disapproving frown.

"Why, you like his fingers?" I ask casually. "Which one's your favorite? Say the word, and I'll box it up for you to take home as a souvenir."

He looks for a moment like he might either snicker derisively or throw up, but then thinks better of both. "Calm down, Captain. I assure you that I mean you no harm. I can also give you my personal guarantee that Jessica Lin is alive, well, and perfectly safe. And she'll stay that way so long as things remain civil between you and me, and as long as you do exactly what I say from here on out."

I take a step forward, looking him dead in the eye. He's a centimeter or two shorter than I am, and I see a brief flash of anger in his gray eyes when my proximity makes him look just slightly up at me. This is a man who is conditioned to look down his nose at *everyone*.

"You see," I say coldly, "when you say things like that, it really makes me want to test how much I can hurt you before you squeal like a little pig. My guess is you're some desk jockey, and you'll cry at the first cut. Care to test my theory?"

"Such talk, so unbecoming of a King's officer," he chides, though there's a hint of raggedness to his voice now that tells me at least some of my words got to him.

I smile, showing my teeth. "But I'm *not* a King's officer anymore; the King himself saw to that. So spare me the games and just say what you came here to say."

He shrugs. "It's quite simple, really. Your star nation has need of you, and we knew you wouldn't agree to help us of your own accord. So, we arranged a little vacation for your former XO as insurance that you'll do what we need."

I hold up a hand to stop him. "Uvalde, I'm sick of this conversation. You can gut him now. We'll torture what we need out of the other guy." I turn away from him and start to walk back toward his tied-up subordinate, who stares at me with wild eyes.

"Before you do anything so rash, Captain," Traeger says, speaking quickly now, betraying his fear. "I would suggest looking down at your chest."

So, I do, and I let loose an involuntary groan. Right over my heart, there's a nice, neat, bright little red dot—a laser sight. I look up and out through the broad sliding glass doors at the far end of the room to see if I can locate the source, but no luck. It's either one of those stealth drones Hayley detected or someone far enough away that I can't see them or their sniper rifle. Most likely the former, given the angle.

I turn back to Traeger. "All right, you have my attention. Start talking," I order, keeping my voice stern. Despite his threats, I know that if he truly wanted me dead, I would have never seen the bullet coming. But I'd rather not call his bluff quite yet, at least not until I have a better idea of the cards he's holding.

"We," he starts, clearly referring to his wonderfully shadowy arm of the Navy, "know all about the little dustup you had with Dexter Hornsby last month in the Helgatha system."

I frown. "Dustup, huh? I lost nearly half my crew in that little 'dustup'."

He frowns back. "My condolences." Something tells me he's not being sincere about it. Maybe it's his tone of voice, like he's sending back an overcooked steak. Or maybe it's the arrogant and dismissive expression on his stupid and very punchable face.

"As I was saying," he continues. "We know about that battle. And we also know why you were in Koratan space to begin with. Duchess Charlotte's little rebellion reached our attention some time ago, but until now, we didn't know who her sponsors were."

"And now you do?" I ask, not wanting to reveal any information in case he's fishing.

Traeger nods. "We do. The so-called 'Baron' Dexter Hornsby, though we suspect there's another party backing *him* as well. We just need to find out who."

"So, what does that have to do with me?" I ask. "Send the Navy to kill Hornsby and be done with it. I won't argue. He and I aren't exactly best friends."

He shakes his head. "Would that we could, Captain. Unfortunately, Hornsby has chosen not to return to Promethean space since his battle with you and your ship. Had he done so, he would even now be in our custody, I assure you."

Now, it's my turn to scoff. "Sure, and I've got a water-logged moon in the Orcan system that I'd be happy to sell you cheap. Face it, Traeger, if the King's government wasn't so busy looking the other way whenever Hornsby has someone killed, you might notice that he's a little hard to track down no matter what part of space he's in. Plus, he's got his own little fleet. I should know; I destroyed a quarter of it."

His smile in reply is *so* arrogant that now I *really* want to let Hayley start slicing and dicing him, but I hold back for the moment, at least. "Quite well said, Captain. Which is why we need *you* to go and get him for us."

I about triple the force of my earlier scoff into a full-fledged laugh. "Yeah, right. Me, go back into Koratan space? Good luck with that. I'll take my chances with that little popgun you have hovering outside and your four gorillas in the hallway. Thanks for stopping by, Traeger. Don't let the door hit you on the way—"

"You'll do it, or Jessica Lin dies," he says coldly, all earlier veneer of civility gone. "Besides, Hornsby isn't *in* Koratan space; you made things too hot for him there. He's here in the independent systems somewhere, and *you* are going to smoke him out and capture him for us if you want to see your girlfriend alive ever again."

You know that condescending look I described on Jake Traeger's face earlier? Well, I now have the grim satisfaction of seeing it wiped away when my fist connects with his jaw. He goes down hard, and I flinch, waiting for the bullet to slam into my back. It doesn't.

Traeger groans and sits up, rubbing his jaw and glaring at me.

"You get *one* of those, Captain Mendoza. Next time, I send the message that kills Jessica Lin. Understood?" I notice that he's not even bothering to threaten *my* life anymore. Unfortunately, he knows that as long as he has Jessica, he doesn't have to.

Still, I don't let my anger and despair show through. Instead, I grin at him. "Sure. Got it out of my system now. You'd better start talking, though, or I might get bored and want to hit you again. And you should know by now I don't take threats to my friends lightly. So how about you drop those and just tell me what Naval Intelligence is going to extort me into doing?"

So, he does. And based on what he's asking, I almost wish he'd go back to just threatening my life. Because what he's proposing—no, forcing me into doing—is pure suicide.

NINE

THE RETURN OF NINJA LIN

JESSICA LIN

The fast naval transport that greets us at Jewel Orbital II's gate A23 is disguised from the outside to look like any other light freighter. But a cursory glance at the interior just beyond the airlock is all it takes to know that the ship is nothing of the kind. I imagine the engine room contains an oversized main drive and reactor and a more advanced jump drive than what graces even most Navy warships.

It's a ship built with one purpose only: to get its passengers from point A to point B as fast as possible without being too obvious about it.

"Strap in," the old guy orders me, practically shoving me into one of the seats at the front of the otherwise empty passenger compartment. The accommodations are spartan, like those of any other Navy ship, just rows of seats like a shuttle's and a single head at the rear that has a full-body disinfectant and deodorant sprayer in lieu of a shower. I've been on dozens of transports like this over the years, so it doesn't bother me.

What *does* bother me is being flung around like a piece

of meat. This old guy is quickly rising in the ranks of my least favorite people, and his treatment of me doesn't bode well for the rest of the journey. If the silent crew of the transport—none of them in uniform—are anything like him, I'm in for a rough time.

I try to think of what Brad would do in my situation. He'd no doubt work hard to throw this guy and the crewmembers off their game or force them to reveal something new about the situation. He would do it using snarky and sarcastic humor, digging at them until they each broke in some way.

I'm not nearly as good at talking my way out of situations as he is, but I do have one skill set that he lacks.

I don't strap in to the seat like the old guy suggests. Instead, I stand up and start to move around him.

"What are you doing?" he demands, reaching out and grabbing my arm tightly. "I told you to sit down and strap in."

"I have to use the head," I reply, not raising my voice.

"You can do that *after* we're underway."

"I'd rather not wait." I still don't let my anger show through my tone, fighting to keep it flat.

"I said, after we're—"

He doesn't get to finish his sentence. My hand lashes out and jabs into his nose, not hard enough to break it but enough for him to choke off his words. Then my knee takes him in the crotch. As he releases his grip on my arm and starts doubling over in pain, I slam the tip of my elbow down and into the back of his head, flattening him to the deck, face down.

Two of the crew rush at me from behind, but I hear them coming, and in the narrow aisle between the seats, they can't both attack me at the same time. I whirl and kick one of them hard in the stomach, knocking him back into the second crewmember, a woman. They go down in a pile of limbs, the woman thrashing helplessly underneath the man's weight.

Calmly turning my back on them, I step over the old guy, still moaning on the floor, and make my way, without looking like I'm rushing, to the back of the passenger area. Once inside the head, I shut and lock the hatch and then start to hyperventilate.

Did I really just do that to the men and women who have a sniper somewhere aiming his weapon at Brad's head? I did, and the next few minutes are going to be crucial in making sure this has a chance of ending the way I want it to and not very, very badly.

I don't actually use the head, but I do flush it for their benefit. Then I step back through the hatch to find all three of them waiting just outside for me, angry-looking and holding pistols aimed right at my chest.

"Gee," I say, using the words I briefly rehearsed before emerging, "can't a girl use the facilities in peace? Or does the remit of Naval Intelligence now extend to watching defenseless women on the toilet?"

"You're going to suffer for that," the old guy growls, not even flinching at the revelation that I know who he and the others are working for; they haven't exactly kept it a secret. "And your boyfriend is going to die."

I raise my eyebrows at him, keeping my expression calm even though my body is practically trembling with fear and adrenaline. "I don't think so."

"What?" he demands.

"You won't kill Captain Mendoza, because the second you do, you lose any and all leverage over me. Not only will I not tell you whatever it is you want to know when we reach our destination, but I will also do my best to kill each and every one of you at some point in the journey. Which I think I've just demonstrated is a threat you shouldn't take lightly. However, if you treat me with the respect due to any other human being, then I believe you will find me to be quite cooperative."

All three of their mouths drop open in surprise.

"Now," I quickly add before the old guy can figure out another threat to throw at me, like killing another member of my crew. "If I'm not mistaken, you asked me to take my seat and strap in. If you'll excuse me?"

Done talking, I shove my way through the three of them, who don't make any effort to stop me. When I reach the row the old guy initially threw me into, I sit and fasten my restraints. I make them tight enough to hopefully keep my body from shaking so badly that I'll fall right out of my seat.

It will take two full days to traverse the stars to our destination in Promethean space. Two *long* days cooped up with hostile Naval Intelligence officers reporting to a man with more reason to hate me than almost any other in the galaxy. Still, perhaps, just maybe, I've made my captors a little more wary than they were five minutes ago. Even if I didn't, it felt really good to hit that old guy.

TEN
EXTORTION

BRAD MENDOZA

"What about the coordinates Commander Lin left for us on that video?" Illian asks as I gather the crew together to tell them about our new mission.

"Our Naval Intelligence friends would have us believe they were a false flag and nothing more," I reply. "But Heddy and Beck are halfway there by now to check things out, just in case." I feel comfortable saying that aloud. We're in one of the resort's conference rooms—yes, even paradise has boring meetings, apparently—and Hayley assures me that she's found and killed every listening device Traeger and his people planted here before letting us use it.

Traeger himself wanted to be in the room for this discussion along with half his men, but I think between me looking like I wanted to punch him again and Gunny Boyd literally growling like an injured bear, he thought better of it. So we're alone without any listening ears. Not that they should be worried; so long as they have Jessica, they have all the leverage.

"Why did they take her, Captain?" asks Drake Forbes,

one of Gunny's original shooters and a good friend to Jessica.

"Simple," I tell him. "Extortion. They're holding Jessica —Commander Lin—hostage because they want to force us to do something for them."

There's grumbling all around the massive, real-wood table we're gathered at.

"Force us to do what?" Laia Gammon asks.

"To do what we were going to do anyway," I admit. "They want us to go after Baron Dexter Hornsby."

The room breaks out into moans and angry invectives. I wait a few moments for them to get it out and then wave my hands to calm everyone down.

"I know—ironic, right?" I almost punched Traeger a second time when he told me he'd kidnapped Jessica just to force me into doing something I already wanted to do. But there's a catch. "Except for one thing. *We* were going to find and kill Hornsby. *They* want us to capture him."

Now the room really erupts, with a dozen different shouted conversations drowning out anything I try to say next.

"Everybody shut up and let the captain speak!" a loud, firm voice yells across the room with an authority that reminds me of my own command voice. All eyes turn in shock to its source, a very angry-looking Francis Illian.

Huh. I didn't know he had that in him. I take advantage of the stunned silence.

"Listen up, people, because this next part is important. *Bainbridge* can't be ready for at least a week and a half, and I have zero intention of just sitting and waiting while they do who-knows-what to Commander Lin. Luckily, or unluckily, depending on your point of view, Naval Intelligence already thought of that. The spooks have brought us a Q-ship to use to go after Hornsby."

There is a little bit of dark laughter as I use the derogatory term, 'spooks', for Naval Intelligence.

"Uh, sir? What's a Q-ship?" Pilar Moya asks, raising her hand and casting a quick look over at Illian as if seeking permission to speak.

"Glad you asked," I answer. "A Q-ship is a warship designed to look like a civilian ship. In this case, it's a Promethean heavy cruiser class dressed up like a bulk freighter. She's in orbit above us now, just waiting for us to crew her."

"But why us?" Kelly O'Malley asks from the opposite end of the table. "If they want Hornsby, why not go after him themselves?"

It's the question I was expecting—and the one I was dreading, because the answers Traeger gave me when I asked him the same thing were less than satisfying. "They say it's because they can't operate openly in the independent systems. Prometheus has a lot of trading partners in this sector, and they don't want to lose them or push any of them to form stronger alliances with Koratas."

It's a legitimate concern, given that the independent sector sits in a sort of V shape formed by the borders of the Promethean Federation and the Koratan Confederacy, with Jewel at the bottom of the V and several dozen inhabited star systems filling in the rest. Most of those are single-system star nations.

"Sir, how are we supposed to crew a heavy cruiser and capture Hornsby with just ourselves?" Kelly presses. "Operating a destroyer with a skeleton crew is one thing. But a heavy cruiser? And we've only got a few shooters. We'll be seriously outmatched in any boarding action. No offense." He says the last part with a nod toward Gunny Boyd.

"You're right, Kelly," I tell him. "Plus, I don't think Naval Intelligence would trust us to go alone. They have to know I'd just take the ship and go looking for Jessica. So they're augmenting us with a crew of Naval Intelligence officers and enlisted. On top of that, they're sending us with a platoon of Marines to help capture the baron. Apparently, they think that so long as the ship's *captain* isn't formally part of the Promethean Navy, it gives them plausible deniability if we're caught."

More grumbling around the room. Yeah, I had a hard time believing that part, too, when Traeger told me. He's holding something back, some *other* reason why the Navy is so dead set on me being on this mission.

"Why is everyone so grim about it?" demands Doc Damien Bean. "Weren't we planning to go after this Hornsby character anyway?"

"Sure, Doc," Saki Hashimoto replies. "But we were just gonna kill him. Find whatever ship he's on and blow him out of the sky. But capturing him... that's a whole lot of complicated." She looks to me for confirmation.

"Saki is right," I admit. "Capturing Hornsby won't be easy. Which leads me to the next part." I pause, taking a deep breath, knowing that what I'm about to say is necessary but also realizing what a monumental risk it is. "We have to vote on whether or not we're going to do what they say. There's a chance, however small, that if we refuse, they'll let Commander Lin go because she won't be leverage against us anymore."

I'm lying, of course. There's not a chance that Naval Intelligence lets Jessica go. In fact, I'm fairly certain that they won't even honor their end of the deal if we *do* capture Hornsby for them, but I'm hoping to play for time and leverage of my own. Still, I can't force my crew into going on what amounts to a suicide mission.

I look around at the room, about to call the vote, but I'm interrupted by Laia.

"Skipper, exactly why are we voting?"

The question takes me off guard, and I stammer for a second. "Well, Lieutenant, you all signed on to this crew voluntarily. We're not the military. I can't force *any* of you to go on this mission."

"No, sir, I get that," she presses, "but in what universe would any of us *not* do whatever it takes to save Commander Lin?"

The room erupts again, but this time with sounds of agreement and support. I have to reach up and wipe moisture from my eyes; there must be dust in the air vents or something.

"I think we just took our vote, sir," Illian says, loudly and firmly enough to quell other conversations in the room.

I look around at all of them, resting my gaze on each of their faces and seeing the mix of anger, support, and determination on all of them. A real tear falls down one cheek, and I quickly wipe it away. "Thank you all," I say, voice hoarse. Several of them nod in response.

"What about Heddy and Beck?" Boyd asks. "Do we need to recall them?"

I shake my head. "Traeger is insisting we call them back. Gunny, think you can send them a recall notice with a coded message to ignore it and keep searching for Jessica instead?"

The big man smiles in a way that reminds me of the

piranhas in the resort's lobby fish tank. "Aye, Skipper. I think I can arrange that."

"Good. Tina, Sam," I call out to the two teenagers we rescued from pirates in the Santo Domingo system. They're trying very hard to hide from me behind the adults in the room. No answer. "You both know I can see you, right?"

"Uh, yes, Captain?" Tina says in a small voice, peering around from behind Edgar Kluth. But before I can say more, she starts talking loud and fast. "Don't make us stay behind. We want to help! We love Commander Lin just as much as the rest of you do."

The protest almost brings a smile to my face. "Sorry, Tina, but the mission is too dangerous. I've convinced Traeger to let the two of you stay here at the resort with a single adult crewmember to chaperone." I turn to look at Karen O'Malley.

"No, you don't, Captain," the matronly woman—our crew's chef—says sternly. "Where Kelly goes, I go. You try to make me stay behind, and I think you'll find your next meal full of something that will hurt your stomach for a week."

I nod, having expected as much. "Fine, Karen. Pilar." I turn to face a very surprised-looking Pilar Moya. "Sorry, Spacer Moya, but we'll have plenty of engineers on the ship. I need someone to watch over Sam and Tina and keep them safe—"

"We don't need a babysitter, Captain!" Tina shouts over me. "And we won't just sit around the resort while everyone else is out risking their lives. We won't do it!" At the last, she literally clenches both hands into fists by her sides and stomps one foot on the floor.

"That's good," I say before she can go on. "Because I

don't expect you to just sit at the resort. I have a mission for the three of you."

I see Pilar raise her eyebrows questioningly.

"I want you to wait a day or two and then sneak past the spooks on guard. You'll get passage to Hudson and find our old freighter, *Wanderer*. Harris will give you all the command codes, documentation, and funds you need to get her out of whatever impound yard they've got her in there. Then you'll bring her back here, pick up Heddy and Beck, and start searching for Jessica in nearby systems."

It's a long shot, and maybe more to keep the DeJong twins—they hate it when we call them that, given that they were actually born a year apart—busy, but something also tells me we might need another ship before this is all said and done.

Pilar, Sam, and Tina reluctantly agree. There are a few more questions about logistics, and then everyone starts to file out of the room to go and pack their bags to meet our Q-ship in orbit. I stop Laia before she can leave.

"What's up, Skipper?" she asks when we're alone.

"You didn't have to do that, Laia," I tell her. "You and the others who came onboard with Jamie Durkin owe us nothing. On the contrary, we owe *you* for getting you all involved in our crazy lives and getting a bunch of you killed, including Jamie, at Helgatha. No one would blame any of you if you wanted to take your back pay and walk away now."

She frowns and actually looks offended and angry, forcing me to take an involuntary step back. "Skipper, are we part of your crew now or not?"

I nod, not trusting my voice.

"Then there's no debate. We're going with you. And if

you're worried about the others, then don't be. We took an informal vote after Helgatha. We like you, and we like *Bainbridge.* And it would feel wrong to abandon you and make Jamie's death and the others not mean anything."

Her voice softens, and she smirks at me. "Besides, we all know just how hopeless you are without Commander Lin. We owe it to the galaxy to get her back so she can keep an eye on you."

I bark a small laugh and wipe another tear from my cheek. I'm going to have to lodge a complaint with management over these dusty air vents.

ELEVEN

A WOLF IN SHEEP'S CLOTHING

BRAD MENDOZA

My second command in the Promethean Navy was the heavy cruiser HMS *Queen's Pride*. I remember the day I first boarded her. Compared to my first command, the light cruiser HMS *Farragut*, the *Queenie* felt absolutely palatial. She also felt tough enough to take on the entire galaxy.

The experience the first time I step foot on HMS *Odysseus* is very different. From the outside, she looks like any other bulk freighter, essentially barbell-shaped. The front sphere holds the bridge, combat information center, comm shack, and crew quarters. The rear one contains engineering, more crew quarters, and the drive nozzles. Between the two spheres is a deceptively thin-looking spine with cargo containers attached radially around it all along its nearly half-kilometer length.

Odysseus's landing shuttle docks against her port forward airlock, and we disembark. Inside, at first, *Odysseus* still looks like a standard bulk freighter; the bulk-heads and deck are spartan and utilitarian and even show some no-doubt carefully painted lines of rust. It's not until we go through a few hatches that we start to see evidence that she's not what she appears to be.

"About a third of the containers attached to the spine are real so that we can be seen dropping off and taking on cargo at each port of call," Jake Traeger explains as he leads me and my command staff deeper into the ship while the rest of our crew gets settled. "The other two-thirds are fully integrated with the hull and house weapons, sensor arrays, and even extra quarters and an armory for the Marines. Most of the containers have a false front that slides open to reveal the missile tubes and laser emitters underneath. So long as those are shut, even the closest scans won't be able to tell she's a warship."

I nod along, actually somewhat impressed by the ingenuity but unwilling to show that to the Naval Intel spook and wannabe professional lacrosse player.

"There's a false bridge in the bow right where it normally would be," he goes on. "It and the corridors to it from the forward airlock all look standard for this type of freighter. That's in case we get boarded by a system patrol or need to take on a pilot for navigational hazards." He speaks with evident pride. "But the real operational bridge is in the middle of the forward sphere, the most protected part of the ship. We're heading there now to meet the rest of the command officers."

I grunt. I'm *not* happy about having to take on a bunch of Naval Intelligence people as part of my command staff, and I've made that very clear to Traeger. I'm even less happy about the fact that *he* is going to be my executive officer. I'd be surprised if the guy has seen an iota of actual combat. In my experience, most spooks like to sit at desks on stations or in underground bunkers and tell each other how smart they all are over tea and crumpets.

Still, there's not much I can do about it. When Traeger told me I was to be the captain of *Odysseus* for the duration of the mission to capture Baron Hornsby, I was skeptical. I still am. He might be satisfied with the fiction of it all, but I fully expect he and his Naval Intelligence crew will take full control of the ship the first time he disagrees with one of my orders.

Which puts me in a tough position. I'm highly motivated to find Hornsby, not just because Naval Intelligence is forcing me to, but also because I still owe the crime boss for killing a third of my crew at Helgatha. But let's just say my style of command is a little different from that of most captains—I'm willing to take risks and throw out the book whenever necessary. It served me well in my Navy career, except for the many times it upset various admirals. But I'm positive it's going to give Traeger and his people major heartburn, and I can't find and capture Hornsby with them tying my hands behind my back.

Which means I need to establish dominance quickly. Otherwise, the mission will fail, and I'll definitely never see Jessica again.

We reach the true bridge, which looks like it could have been cut out of *Queen's Pride* or any other regular Navy heavy cruiser. All the stations are where they should be, though there's an extra control console in the back, probably to oversee the functions of the ship that mimic those of an actual freighter.

Waiting for us in the center of the room are four officers, none of them in uniform but all unmistakably military with their close-cropped hair and ramrod-straight postures.

"This," Traeger says, beginning the introductions, "is Lieutenant Commander Fara Lipton, your new chief engineer. Lieutenants Senior-Grade Cory Hanson and Opal Winston are your tactical and comm officers. And finally," —he motions to the biggest of the bunch—"Marine Captain Bryan Shultz, commander of the platoon of Marines we have on board to help capture Dexter Hornsby when we catch up to him."

I shake my head, ignoring the outstretched hands of greeting. "Sorry, but I have my own chief engineer and tactical officer. I know my people, not yours. Comms, fine; ours died at Helgatha, but the rest of you will be subordinate to my people—including you, Captain Shultz."

They all frown at me, the Marine looking like he might break me in half. Next to me, Traeger sighs loudly, and I brace myself for the coming fight.

"I have no problem with your Commander Illian filling the role of tactical officer," he says, surprising me. "Lieutenant Hanson can be his second down in the CIC if that's acceptable to you." He pauses and looks at me for confirmation.

Holding my tongue, I nod. He gave in way too easily to that demand. What game is he playing?

"But I would highly recommend you reconsider keeping Lieutenant Commander Lipton as your chief engineer. Unless your Commander O'Malley knows the ins and outs of a Q-ship exactly like *Odysseus*, you're going to need her expertise."

Before I can open my mouth to argue, Fara Lipton speaks up. "All due respect, Captain Mendoza, but Commander Traeger is right. The *Oddie* can be a little temperamental. I've been spending the last several months learning all her quirks, and there are a lot of them. But I've read Lieutenant Commander O'Malley's file, especially what he managed to do at Gerson, and I'm impressed. If it suits you, I'll keep him as my second and train him up on everything he needs to know."

I frown, realizing that I've been had. Traeger must have expected me to come out of the gate shooting and making these kinds of demands. By phrasing the order to keep Lipton as my chief engineer as a perfectly well-reasoned *request*, he's painted me into a corner. Fara Lipton's equally well-reasoned and conciliatory words on top of that mean that I either have to accept the very logical recommendation or reject it and look like I'm doing so just to be obstinate.

I look at Traeger in time to see the corner of his lip twitch up ever so slightly, confirming that he knows exactly what he's doing. I may have underestimated the lacrosse player.

"Very well," I say, keeping my tone neutral. "But I have—"

Before I can finish my sentence, Bryan Shultz steps forward aggressively.

"There is *no* chance I'm putting my Marines under the command of whoever you have leading your pathetic bunch of shooters, Mendoza," he snaps, and I see Traeger wince out of the corner of my eye. This obviously wasn't part of the Intel spook's script for this first meeting.

Behind me, I can hear Hayley shift from one foot to another as if the tension is making her nervous. More likely, she's just putting herself into position to kill every one of my new officers if I tell her to. I love that little psychotic assassin.

"And my shooters won't answer to some Promethean cake eater," Quinn Boyd growls. "The Republic doesn't bow to the Proms."

Shultz's face turns red at Quinn's use of the derogatory

nickname. "You mean *ex*-Republic. You're not even a Marine anymore."

Quinn takes a step to close the distance, and the two big men are suddenly nose-to-nose. "Once a Marine, always a Marine," my friend says calmly, which usually means he's about to hurt someone.

Just as Shultz is starting to open his mouth again and I think Traeger is going to pee his pants, I take command of the situation. "Gunny! Step back!"

Instantly, without any sign of resentment toward the order, Quinn steps back and stands at attention, eyes straight ahead. "Aye, Skipper."

I turn and glare at the Promethean Marine. "Captain Shultz, you just ably demonstrated why I *won't* be putting my shooters under your command. Gunnery Sergeant Boyd will continue to report directly to me. As will you. When the time comes to engage Baron Hornsby, *I* will decide how to deploy both your units to maximum effectiveness. Is that understood?"

Shultz bristles and casts a look over at Traeger, but I step forward and grab his attention again. The man towers over me, but I look him in the eye and use every ounce of my command voice. "I asked you a question, Marine! Are you going to have a problem with the chain of command on this ship?"

Human beings are like computers in many ways. We all have our programming—heuristics, if you will. It goes all the way back to when people lived in caves and hid from big freaky cats and lizards. If a predator arrived at the cave door, the occupants didn't stop and debate how they should respond. They picked up their spears and their guns—I think they only had single-shot muskets back then, but I've never been all that proficient in Earth history—and defended their homes. They followed their programming, gained from hard-earned experience.

Any military uses this human characteristic to maximum advantage, leveraging training in place of experience so that when the bullets start flying, and the lasers are burning into the hull, their officers and enlisted men and women don't stop and debate solutions but automatically do what needs to be done, even if it's their first time in battle.

Right now, my tone and the wording of my question are like sending a keystroke command to the military-honed computer that is Bryan Shultz's brain. Without even thinking, he straightens to attention and barks, "Sir, no, sir!"

I nod once. "Good." Then I throw my own little smile over at Traeger, who nods almost imperceptibly. Game recognizes game, I suppose.

"Very well," I continue, stepping back and turning to regard the rest of the assembled officers, including my own from *Bainbridge*. "We'll be getting underway in 18 hours. I expect each of you to come to me with a plan ahead of that for how you'll integrate the two crews into one, respecting the individual ranks of each man and woman. Dismissed!"

I catch the Naval Intel folks quickly eyeing Traeger, who nods before they hasten to leave the bridge to follow my orders. *That* is going to be a problem. This first of many battles for command between myself and the Naval Intel commander was a draw, but I'm under no illusions that worse fights aren't yet to come. All Traeger has to do is threaten to kill my fiancée, and I'll have to do whatever he says. Not to mention that he'll have Shultz and 40 Marines to back him up.

As they all leave, I grab Harris, who was trying to stay unnoticed at the back of the group, and stop him from following.

"What's up, Skipper?" he asks, but I hold up a hand to shush him until everyone else is off the bridge.

Once they're gone, I lean in to put my lips close to Harris's ear. I have to assume that Naval Intelligence has bugged every centimeter of this ship. To be extra safe, I turn on my implant's jamming field as well.

I softly whisper to him, describing exactly what I need him to do. When I'm done, I pull back and look him in the eyes. He nods once, both to acknowledge my order and to tell me he can do what I've asked—I hope—and then departs the bridge, leaving me alone.

To say that this mission is going to be a minefield fraught with peril and personnel issues is an insult to most minefields. None of the ones I've ever seen were *this* bad. To make things worse, I doubt there's a single taco on board this tub.

TWELVE
UNDERWAY AND ROYALLY UPSET

BRAD MENDOZA

"**D**ocking clamps are released, Captain," Saki Hashimoto announces crisply from the helm.

"Very well. Helm, thrusters at 10 percent to move us away from the station."

Next to me, I can see Jake Traeger stiffen in the XO's chair. The standard rule for separation from dock is no more than 5 percent thruster power. Back on HMS *Persephone*, I ordered 10 percent to mess with my then helmswoman, Junior Lieutenant Petra Yesayan, having pegged her as a stickler for the rules. I'm pleased to see it working just as well on Traeger.

Of course, I'm not only doing it for the personal satisfaction of tweaking the man's nose. If he argues with me on something so small, it will immediately shatter his carefully constructed fiction of me being in command of this mission. I'm banking he's not ready to do that quite yet. But by *not* fighting me on it, he's establishing a pattern of acquiescing to my orders even when he disagrees with them, starting with this one small thing.

My grandpa used to tell me that if you put a frog in an

already boiling pot of water, it will immediately jump out. But put a frog in room-temperature water and slowly turn up the heat, and it will happily remain until it's well cooked and dead. I'm not actually sure why anyone would ever want to cook a frog—sounds disgusting—but it's a good analogy for our situation here. I'm just hoping that Traeger is the frog and not me.

Of course, I immediately have to turn the heat way up and engage in the next battle. And this one is quite a bit bigger.

"Lieutenant Uvalde," I say, turning in my command chair to face the young Latina, who is thankfully sitting at a secondary weapons station instead of her usual spot cross-legged on the bridge deck. "Have you finished going over the intel reports on Baron Hornsby?"

We've only been on board *Odysseus* for a day as we integrated the crews and took on supplies to get underway, but my guess is the undercover Guard agent only needed about an hour to go through the sparse intel Traeger and his people presented us with.

"Sure, boss," she says in her infuriatingly casual manner, though it's a lot of fun watching Traeger stiffen again at her tone. "These Prometheans don't know their elbow from their—"

"Without the color commentary, please, Lieutenant," I admonish gently; no need to give Traeger an aneurism quite yet.

"Okay, boss. The intel reports are sketchy, and their conclusion that Hornsby is in the Decker system doesn't add up. I think we need to start looking in the Valle de Oro system."

"Based on what intelligence?" Traeger barks, his professional pride allowing him to stay silent no longer.

"Every report points to the Decker system as being his new base of operations. We've found shipments heading there with his fingerprints all over them. We've even intercepted communications from that system to his top lieutenants back in Federation space. Why..." He trails off when he sees me glaring at him, his hand subconsciously rising to rub his jaw where I hit him two days ago.

"Continue, please, Lieutenant," I say calmly to Hayley without taking my eyes off Traeger.

"All that intel is suspect, boss," she says with a little half grin I can see out of the corner of my eye. "Hornsby wants these chicos to *think* he's in the Decker system, so he planted a false trail. The clue is that it's all way too easy to find."

"Too easy?" Traeger explodes, standing up from his seat. "We had to burn a good agent in Hornsby's organization to get that intel. It wasn't easy at all!"

Hayley doesn't react beyond just cocking her head to one side and meeting the spook officer's angry gaze. Even sitting in the chair, she reminds me of a little girl about to listen to story time from her grade-school teacher. Traeger can have no idea that he's currently challenging one of the galaxy's most deadly assassins. Under other circumstances, it would make me laugh.

"Sit down, Mr. Traeger," I say in a low voice. "Let her finish her analysis, and *then* you can argue with her."

For a moment, I think that the time has come that he will choose to assert his authority over me. But he considers my words for only a short time before doing as I ask. I'm almost disappointed. I'd much prefer we have it out over the chain of command now rather than later when it could get us all killed.

"As I was saying, Capitán," Hayley continues, thankfully imbuing her tone with just the slightest hint of professional decorum. "The trail to Decker is too clean and easy. It's a false flag. But I found some evidence that one of Hornsby's top lieutenants was sighted in the Valle de Oro system a few days ago. Seems he's got a chica there he likes to visit. So, I figure we go there and capture him and get the baron's true location from him. Entiendes?"

I nod, ignoring Traeger's silent fuming next to me. Deciding maybe it's time to extend a small olive branch, I turn to him. "Thoughts, Commander?"

"It's insane," he practically growls, but then he sees my expression and tacks on, "sir. We vetted that intel a dozen different ways. Hornsby *is* in the Decker system."

I nod slowly, pretending to consider his words. Given he doesn't know who Hayley really is, I have to sympathize a little with his incredulity that she would so blatantly disagree with the conclusions of dozens of trained agents and analysts. Still, I'd be mad to ignore her and go with the official intel just to assuage his hurt feelings, even if he is holding the figurative gun to my head and Jessica's.

So, I decide to compromise. Surprised? Hey, every once in a while, I can be diplomatic. It's rare, but it does happen.

"Valle de Oro is just one jump out of our way to Decker," I say evenly. "We'll stop there on the way and check out this man who Lieutenant Uvalde says is there. If it's a bust, we'll continue to Decker."

Traeger chews on this for a moment but then reluctantly nods. Apparently, he can be diplomatic as well when the situation calls for it.

"Chief Hashimoto," I order, "as soon as we're clear of the inner nav beacons, take us to two-thirds power toward the Rincar jump point. We'll transit the system there and take the next jump point to Valle de Oro."

"Aye, Captain," she replies, and starts working the math.

"Comms," I say next. Opal Winston looks up. "File a flight plan to Rincar with station control, but leave out the part about continuing on to Valle de Oro."

"Aye, sir."

I turn my chair back to watch the plot on the forward viewscreen, silently considering. Given the placements of the jump points—relatively close together—in the Rincar system, it will be a two-day journey to Valle de Oro; it would be shorter if I took *Odysseus* to full military power, but that would be like raising a beacon to everyone in the sector that says, 'Hey, Q-ship over here! Totally not a lame and boring freighter!'. So I don't order it. Even though every *second* it takes me to find and capture Hornsby is one more second that my fiancée is essentially in prison.

Out of the corner of my eye, I study Jake Traeger. He looks uncomfortable and out of place in the XO chair and keeps squirming to adjust how he's sitting. Naval Intel spooks don't often do rotations as ship's officers, so I imagine this is all a new experience for him: both being on the bridge of a warship and taking orders from a regular Navy—well, ex-Navy—officer. But he'll have to get used to it. At the speeds we can safely fly *Odysseus* without blowing our cover, we're *all* going to have to get used to things the way they are for a long while until we catch ourselves a crime boss.

Assuming, of course, that we can even find him.

THIRTEEN

ARRIVAL TO MY DOOM

JESSICA LIN

The transport exits jump space into the Lightman system, our final destination, and I let out a long, frustrated sigh. My captors have been a little more respectful, if not more sullen, since I beat them all up when I first boarded. They've even let me connect my implant to the ship's systems, though in a strictly controlled, read-only mode. As a result, I'm able to use that connection to peer through the transport's external cameras as we resume our voyage in normal space.

A familiar yellow star greets me in the distance, and I flash back to five years ago when I first saw it. It portended doom to me back then as well. I was at one of the lowest points of my life at that time, fresh off the events of Hothan and Yolandra, where my dear father manipulated me into giving him intelligence that allowed Leeward Republic privateers to ambush a weapons convoy and kill 57 of my Navy colleagues.

I should have been tried for treason and probably put in prison for the rest of my life or even executed. Back then, I might have welcomed that outcome for all the guilt

I felt for getting those spacers killed. But the Navy, in all its wisdom, didn't agree. Specifically, Naval *Intelligence* 'saved' me.

They wanted to keep me in the Navy and leverage me. They thought I might be useful in passing false information along to my father and the Leeward Republic. But the admiralty staunchly refused to put me on a warship, even if my treason was a secret to all but them. So, a compromise was struck: Lightman Station.

Station duty is just about the most boring thing any Navy combat officer can be asked to do, which is why most station assignments last for only three to six months. But the Navy put *me* on Lightman Station for two whole years. There, I was given the most menial of duties that they could justify for my rank of lieutenant senior grade. They also assigned me a Naval Intelligence handler, whose day job was to stop Koratan smugglers and spies trying to infiltrate Promethean space through the independent systems.

I landed on Lightman Station a beaten-down, ragged shadow of the woman I'd once been. I wasn't much better when I left two years later after the Navy *finally* saw fit to assign me back to combat duty. And the two years in between were… interesting.

I sit back in my seat now, shutting off the visual feed in my implant and sighing again. When I left Lightman Station behind three years ago, I swore I'd never return. The place has far too much baggage for me and is a reminder of all my failures, not just those at Hothan and Yolandra.

Now I have no choice, and if I want Brad and my other friends to survive, I'm going to have to face the past, no matter how much that terrifies me.

FOURTEEN
BAGGAGE
JESSICA LIN

I'm escorted from the transport by Chief Petty Officer Gilliam, the same mean old guy who forced me onto it two days ago. As he grips my arm so tightly that it hurts, my only comfort is his bruised nose from when I hit him.

He manhandles me down the station docking corridor and into a larger compartment sometimes used to greet visiting flag officers. For my arrival, it's devoid of furniture and decoration, just a slightly wider part of the corridor for all intents and purposes.

Standing in the middle of that space, waiting for us, is the man from the recorded message in my hotel room.

He's tall, a bit taller than Brad, but the similarities between the two men end there. He has fair skin and almost bleach-blond hair above icy blue eyes. His hair is perfectly combed, and there isn't a trace of stubble on his square jaw. His uniform is tailored to fit in a way that isn't Navy standard issue, and he stands with a naturally straight back that almost always makes it look like he's about to return some lesser officer's salute.

Everything about him screams unapproachable and

unattainable. When I first met him upon starting my exile here five years ago, that's certainly how I viewed him. But then... everything changed.

"The prisoner, as ordered, Captain," Gilliam says, practically flinging me in front of the tall blond man and releasing his iron grip on my arm. "I'd watch out for her, sir. She's a feisty one."

The tall officer's cheek twitches slightly as he looks me up and down. "I'll take that under advisement, Chief," he says neutrally. "You're dismissed."

"Are you sure, Captain? Maybe I should—"

"You're dismissed, Chief," the blond man says, more sternly this time.

Gilliam grunts an acknowledgment and sets off back the way we came toward the waiting transport, no doubt flying on to exciting new systems where he can harass people and ruin their vacations and lives as he did mine.

When he's gone, the perfectly groomed captain frowns tightly at me. My first reflex is to shrink under his gaze. But it passes quickly, and the ordeals of the last six-plus months well up inside me and straighten my spine so that I return his stare without flinching. His cheek twitches again.

"Jethro," I greet him coldly.

"That's Captain Jensen, if you will, Lieutenant Commander Lin."

I stop myself from letting out a big, frustrated breath. "Fine. *Captain* Jensen. What gives you the right to kidnap me and threaten my friends?" I don't even try to keep the hot anger from my tone.

Jethro Jensen—yes, his name is an alliteration, and yes, it annoyed me even back when I knew him under better circumstances—was my old Naval Intelligence handler here at Lightman. Now, he's the man set on destroying my life. He actually takes a small step back at the vehemence in my words, but his face hardens before he replies.

"The *right* I have stems from the fact that you and your crew are criminals, and *you,* Lieutenant Commander, are a traitor to the Crown twice over and a deserter from the Navy. You have no rights. And whether or not you *ever* have any rights again, or even a crew to go back to, is going to depend entirely on you telling me everything I want to know while you're here. Is that understood?"

I stare back at him defiantly for several tense moments. Then I shake my head. "Jethro, if you wanted information, all you had to do was ask. Contrary to what you and your ilk believe, I never betrayed the King, nor did I ever want to. He and his family betrayed *me.* But everything I've done since has *helped* Prometheus. So ask whatever questions you want, but don't expect me to make the answers easy, because now you've just pissed me off!"

I punctuate the last part by literally shoving past him and stalking down the corridor toward whatever fate awaits me. Behind me, I hear him sputter.

"Lieutenant Commander Lin, stop this instant!"

I don't slow down or look back.

"Jessica!"

Now, I do pause and turn back. "Yes, Jethro?"

He frowns and stalks toward me. Out of nowhere, I feel hands grip both of my arms. I try to struggle for only a moment, mostly out of surprise, before I register the visages of two stone-faced Marines who appeared from a side passage to restrain me.

I look away from them, no longer fighting their grips, and back toward Jethro, who stops a meter away and glares down at me.

"It's like that, then?" I ask acidly.

He nods, and I see his eyes flash down to Brad's ring on my finger. He suddenly looks like he's sucking on a lemon. "It's like that. Marines, show Miss Lin to her quarters, and see that she does not leave for any reason."

I shake my head as the Marines start to drag me away. Out of sheer anger and frustration, just before we round a bend in the corridor that will put Jethro out of sight, I yell at him. "You weasel, Jethro! I've never been so glad I didn't marry you!"

PART TWO
THE HUNT

FIFTEEN

COWBOYS AND MARINES
BRAD MENDOZA

W hen I was in the Promethean Navy, back before I became a mass murderer and a worthless drunk, I would often amuse myself by studying up on the history of any system my ship was about to enter. Now that I'm on the *Odysseus* and surrounded by the energy and cadence of a naval ship underway, some old habits return to me as if they never left.

Valle De Oro was named out of its founders' overwhelming and ultimately misplaced optimism. In the early days, when this part of space was being settled by colony ships from Earth's South American continent, a small ship from somewhere called Uruguay settled on a recently terraformed and still largely unexplored world way out in the middle of nowhere, even by Fringe standards. One of the original colonists' first discoveries was a rich gold vein in the valley they chose for their founding settlement. Expecting it to be the first of a number of wealth-creating finds, the colonists named both the planet and the system after it. Hence the name Valle de Oro, or 'Valley of Gold' in English.

By the time that first discovered vein ran out a decade or two later, they still hadn't found any other deposits of anything worthwhile across the entire planet. And when the majority of the other Spanish-speaking colonies banded together to form the Koratan Confederacy, Valle de Oro was too far away from the main body and too resource-poor to even be considered for membership. That drove the final stake through the heart of the economic hopes of its citizens.

Today, the planet is only truly known for two things. The first is a particularly bad rash called gold fever, which is highly contagious, very annoying, and otherwise mostly harmless. The second is a lawless landscape where the authorities will turn a blind eye to just about anything short of murdering a local. You want to kill another off-worlder? Sure! Go ahead, but be sure to clean up the mess afterward.

Valle de Oro is so lawless, in fact, that it's become a refuge for petty and not-so-petty criminals from across the Fringe. It makes a great place to lie low after committing all sorts of infractions in either Promethean or Koratan space, given its proximity to both. Not surprisingly, the planet has a reputation for resisting any extradition requests.

The result is that the entire planet is often overrun with seedy types and thus attracts the sorts of businesses and establishments those types like to frequent. Like Betty's Run, where a certain girl named Chastity, of all things, often entertains one of Baron Hornsby's lieu-tenants.

"Skipper, target is coming up the street now," I hear Gunny Boyd say in my implant. We're not close enough to each other for a direct head-to-head connection, but we've both routed our handheld comms through our implants so we can talk privately.

"Uvalde," I ask through the same connection. "You ready?"

"Sim, Capitão," comes the even reply. I choose not to ask or wonder why she's suddenly speaking Portuguese. I'm sure I don't want to know.

"Shultz," I ask next, "are your Marines in position?"

"They are, Captain Mendoza," the Marine captain answers, the frustration in his tone evident even in my implant. "But I protest again that you've kept us so far away on the perimeter."

Protest all you want; I'm in charge, is what I want to say, though I almost lost this argument, and only Traeger's surprising and reluctant backing of my plan won the day. But what I actually say is, "Understood. Just be ready if the guy rabbits."

"Yes, sir."

I peek around the corner of Betty's Run. It's a squat, one-story building with a narrow front on Carson City's main thoroughfare, if a barely paved two-lane road can be called a thoroughfare. But the building is much longer than the front suggests, extending well back from the street. As I spot our target ambling his way down the street toward the establishment, I duck back and start to run along the alley between Betty's Run and the next building over, a dentist's office.

Nearing the alley's end, I look for the chalk mark on the wall that Hayley left for me. I take a small device, courtesy of Naval Intelligence, out of my pocket. It's shaped like a handheld comm, though a bit smaller and without any speakers or a touchscreen. I press the single button on the top and am rewarded when a small light blinks green.

Then I hold it up to the chalk mark on the wall and let it and my implant do the rest.

It takes another few minutes before I hear much, the listening device easily translating the minute vibrations making their way through the wall so that I can hear everything going on inside. A door practically slams open, and I hear a man's voice say, "Sweetheart, I'm here!"

There's the sound of the door swinging shut and footsteps across the wooden floor. I hear a whoosh, like someone just yanked the sheet off a bed, followed by a semi familiar female voice saying, "Olá, garoto. Chastity is sorry she can't make it today. I'm Victoria."

A buzzing noise is followed by the sound of a heavy body thudding to the floor. I remove the box from the wall, satisfied that Hayley doesn't need the cavalry, and make my way to the back door of the building. There, I only have to wait a moment before someone pushes it open from the inside.

"Hey, boss," Hayley says with a big grin. "Come and give me a hand. He's a heavy hombre."

Drake Forbes appears from the other side of the building and enters with us; two minutes later, we drag the limp, stunned body of our target out through the back door and into the sunlight. A truck pulls up behind the building, an old-fashioned pickup on actual tires instead of repulsors, and we heave the knocked-out mobster into its bed. Edgar Kluth, one of the shooters who used to work for Jamie Durkin, is driving. I take the passenger seat while Hayley takes the middle seat between us on the single bench. Quinn is already in the bed with the body, and Drake joins him there.

Kluth hits the accelerator, and we start speeding away and onto a dusty back road. So far, the plan has gone perfectly, and we make it an entire block and a half back toward the shuttle waiting to return us to *Odysseus* before disaster finally strikes.

It comes in the form of two other pickup trucks, both loaded with armed men in the seats and the beds, who pull out and block each side of the road in front of us just as two more trucks, similarly loaded, pull out to block the road behind, boxing us in.

"Edgar!" I cry, but he's already a step ahead of me. He yanks the wheel to the right, turning us away from the town's center, and the truck leaps a curb and then bounces across what could loosely be described as someone's front yard, only it's so overgrown that it's hard to tell.

At first, we're heading straight toward what looks like an abandoned house, just as I hear bullets start to thud into our truck. Kluth deftly turns the wheel, first one way and then the other, and we find ourselves running full speed in the narrow gap between two houses. Ahead of us is a wooden fence that's seen better days, marking the end of their backyards. We blast right through the fence and find ourselves on another dirt road, where Kluth spins the wheel again to get us headed back in the direction of our waiting shuttle.

"Sorry, boss," Hayley practically shouts next to me over the road noise. "His implant must've had an automated distress signal."

"Didn't you jam it?" I call back, and she nods.

"Sí. Must have been a continuous all-clear signal to his people. When it cut out, they knew something was up."

I grunt loudly just as the truck hits a bump and I bang my head on the cab's hard ceiling. Then I grunt again when Gunny taps on the back window and I look behind us to see that at least two of the enemy trucks are in hot pursuit.

"Shultz!" I call through my comm. "We're headed toward you. Hostiles in pursuit. Be ready!"

The Marine gives me a two-click acknowledgment, and I turn back to see that our pursuers are even closer. Bullets start whizzing by Gunny and Drake, who are both exposed in the truck's bed as they attempt to fire back despite the bumpy ride.

I hear a loud pop, and the ride suddenly becomes even rougher.

"Lost a tire!" Kluth yells as the truck fishtails across the road, Gunny and Drake holding on for dear life.

I see the utility pole coming before Kluth does, but my cry to watch out isn't enough, nor does he have the control to do anything about it. The truck slams into the pole at speed, and only the cabin's airbags prevent us from being tossed out the front windshield or slammed into the dash.

Our two shooters in the back aren't so lucky, nor is our unwilling passenger. Gunny Boyd sees the collision coming and leaps out of the truck bed, hitting the ground hard but rolling to absorb some of the impact. Drake flies over the truck's cab and rolls across the hood at an angle, just missing the utility pole and landing in a heap on the gravel beyond.

Our target, prone in the bed, flies hard into the back window, shattering it with his head. As the airbags retract and free us, it only takes a short look to see that Hornsby's lieutenant is dead from the impact.

Great. There goes our one and only lead to the self-proclaimed baron!

"Captain!" Kluth yells. "We need to go. Now!"

I unfasten my restraints after fumbling with the catch

for a moment and then follow him and Hayley as they exit the truck and sprint toward a decrepit building at the side of the road. Gunny is already dragging a moaning Drake in that direction. We reach the front door just ahead of him, and Hayley thankfully finds it unlocked and barely hanging on its one remaining hinge. The place is obviously abandoned.

I help Gunny drag Drake inside just as the two trucks pursuing us skid to a stop in front of the building, disgorging armed men and women who start immediately shooting our way.

We collapse inside, where Kluth and Hayley help us finish dragging Drake into the center of the open space. It looks like this might have once been a mechanic's garage. There's a lift to one side, but otherwise, the place has been picked clean by scavengers, and there isn't a single thing that might help us. But at least the walls are thick cinder blocks and the bullets that miss the barely-there door or the few windows thud harmlessly against the building outside.

Gunny tosses Drake's assault rifle to Hayley, and they both move to take position under two of the windows, soon joined by Kluth. They start popping up, returning fire while I call in the Marines.

"Shultz! We're pinned down. We need you to come to us at these coordinates!" I ping over our exact location.

"ETA four minutes," comes the reply.

"Hurry!" I yell back into the comm. "We might not have four minutes!"

I don't wait to hear his response, dropping the comm and grabbing the pistol strapped to my belt. I just saw a shadow move where there shouldn't be one.

"They're flanking us!" I call to Gunny and Hayley, but

either they can't hear me or they're too busy with the enemy still at the front, because neither reacts. Nor does Kluth, who's reloading his rifle.

It's up to me. I crabwalk to the rear window and reach it just as bullets shatter the dust-coated glass. I wait for a tick, then peek over the sill and immediately duck back down as more bullets fly through. In the brief instant before my move for cover, I saw four or five figures standing brazenly out in the open—there's nothing but a flat field out in that direction—shooting at the rear of the building.

I wait another second. Then I pop back up, this time bringing the pistol up with me, and quickly trigger off a few shots in their general direction. I must have hit at least one, because I hear a scream of pain just as I duck back down again to avoid their return fire.

"Skipper, catch!" Gunny yells, and I turn as something skitters across the floor toward me. I stop it with a knee and see that it's a fragmentation grenade. Leave it to Gunny to pack explosives on what was supposed to be a quick, covert, surgical capture mission. I've never loved the man more than I do now.

I set the fuse for three seconds and pull the pin. Briefly exposing myself, I throw it out the window straight at the remaining enemy. I duck back down, my back to the wall and my hands over my ears, letting the pistol fall into my lap.

A loud thud follows, and a few more screams behind me. Just a second later, two more dull thuds sound from the front of the building, where grenades thrown by the rest of my team landed.

"Any more of those?" I shout to Gunny, but he shakes

his head and pops up again to fire at the remaining enemy out front.

I lift my head cautiously to peer out the rear window, my gun back in my hand and tracking. I needn't have bothered. I won't describe the sight that greets me, but needless to say, the enemy at the rear of the building is no longer a threat. I'm about to breathe a sigh of relief when I hear a bone-chilling sound of screeching metal, and suddenly, the interior of the building gets a lot brighter.

We missed an entrance, and as the giant garage door closing off the fourth wall of the former mechanic's shop slides open, I see three men quickly shimmy under. I lift my pistol and shoot one of them, but the old lift blocks part of my view of the other two, and they evade my fire.

"Gunny, incoming!" I scream, but just then, the front door blasts inward off its single remaining hinge, filling the room with dust and debris.

It takes a second for my ears to stop ringing and my eyes to stop stinging. When they do, I feel someone wrench the pistol out of my grip, and I look up to see two men standing over me, assault rifles aimed squarely at my face.

A quick glance shows Gunny, Kluth, and Hayley being similarly handled. I briefly expect Hayley to let Lola out to take the enemy down, but a quick look around shows there are far too many for her to fight before they shoot us all. There's even an enemy soldier standing over the still unconscious Drake, with a gun pointed at his head, in case he wakes up and tries anything.

A couple of the men turn to face the now fully open garage door, and I turn to look in that direction as well. A man walks in, at first just a silhouette in the dust. He's tall and thin, wearing a cowboy hat, of all things, and boots.

He has a gun strapped to his thigh and walks with a rolling stride that reminds me of some of the seasonal farm hands on my grandparents' spread.

Seriously? A cowboy?

He stops in front of me and looks down. His face is lined and weather-worn like he spends all his time outdoors on sunny planets. He gives me a little smirk and then claps one of the other men on the back. "You know who this is, Clyde?" he says almost playfully. The other guy shakes his head. "This here is Captain Brad Mendoza. Baron put quite a price on his head. What say we collect?"

Clyde grins. "Sure, boss."

The cowboy crouches down in front of me, balancing on the balls of his feet. "You know, for someone with your reputation, I expected you to put up a lot more of a fight," he says, still smirking at me. "As it is, I can't say I'm all that impressed. Listen to the baron talk, I thought you'd be breathing fire and farting nerve gas."

What a weird thing to say. My grandpa used to make me watch old Western movies with him and had a bookshelf full of the stories of gunslingers and the like. I always expected a *real* cowboy to be significantly cooler than this guy.

"I don't know." I try and respond in a similarly casual manner. "We killed a good chunk of your guys, including *your* boss,"—I wave toward the crashed truck outside—"and we're still all here."

A flash of anger crosses his face, but it's quickly replaced by the same infuriating smirk. "Well, you got me there, partner. But in the end, I'll be the one taking you into the baron. So that evens the score, don't it?" His voice is a lazy drawl, and he winks at me to emphasize his words. Is this guy for real?

That's when I hear two little clicks on my implant comm. Since I can see my handheld comm in several pieces on the floor where I dropped it, that can only mean that the sender of those clicks is close enough for a direct connection.

I smile up at the guy. "I don't think you'll be taking me anywhere, *partner*."

"Oh, and why's that?" There's a slight laugh to his tone.

"They won't let you."

You know how, in the movies, the hero says something really cool right before the cavalry comes in and helps him save the day? I remember one movie where the hero said, "Not today, Doctor," just before the bad guy's—he was a mad scientist, doctor, whatever—front door was blown in, and the hero's friends came in with guns blazing.

This is like one of those moments. As soon as I finish my pithy, 'They won't let you', line, I hear, "Drop your weapons!" Suddenly, the cowboy boss and his remaining dozen or so men and women are surrounded by 40 Marines with a variety of instruments of death all pointed straight at them.

I'm expecting the smug little smirk on the cowboy's face to fail, but to my surprise, he barely even looks bothered. Which is a shame, because the combination of my line and the Marines' sudden appearance is incredibly cool and *should* have left him in awe. Instead, he reaches out and grabs something off the belt of his closest foot soldier, then casually tosses it into the center of the room.

"Grenade!" someone yells, but it's too late. A loud crash hits simultaneously with a flash of light so bright that it blinds me completely.

Gunfire erupts around me again, as do the screams of the injured and dying.

SIXTEEN

ADMITTING I MESSED UP
BRAD MENDOZA

"So let me get this straight," Jake Traeger says as Doc Bean bandages my side where a bullet grazed my ribs. "You went down to the planet following *your* plan, found your target, got your target killed, and then almost died yourself, relying on Captain Shultz to rescue you but, in the subsequent fighting, you lost five Marines?"

He's shouting at me now. At least we're in my ready room and not in the med bay where the rest of our injured are being treated. I refused to take a bed that could go to a hurt crewman or Marine.

I knew he and I would eventually get into a full-blown argument about chain of command. I just didn't expect it to be because I made such a monumentally stupid mistake. It really puts me on the defensive, not to mention I already feel horrible for the deaths of those Marines.

Marine Captain Bryan Shultz is here as well, glaring at me murderously. And Hayley and Gunny aren't even here to back me up. They're down in the med bay being treated for minor wounds. Same for Drake Forbes, who, other than a nasty concussion, escaped surprisingly unscathed.

Illian has the conn, leaving me alone with a very pissed-off Naval Intelligence officer and a nearly apoplectic Marine captain.

Well, except for Doc Bean, but I kind of doubt he'd be much good in a fight.

"Yep, that's the long and the short of it," I say simply, wincing as Doc wraps another bandage around my bruised torso. "I made a mistake."

I look up in time to see both men's eyes practically bug out of their sockets. I can tell that my agreeing with them was the last thing they expected. I take advantage of their temporary speechlessness to continue.

"Look. You don't trust me, and I certainly don't trust the two of you or any other Prometheans on board. My crew and I aren't exactly on this mission of our own free will and choice. But the simple fact is that, for now, we're essentially behind enemy lines together. Today, we saw what that lack of trust can do to us when we're face-to-face with the enemy. It's a disaster."

I'm not overstating things. Today's foray really *was* a disaster. Not only did we fail to capture the man we came to find—we killed him instead—and not only did we lose five people, but that weird cowboy got away, and something tells me he might have been even more important to capture than our original target.

Shultz finds his voice before Traeger does. "Mendoza, if you'd just listened to me, all this could have been avoided. Or better yet, if we'd just gone to Decker like Commander Traeger first said to."

I turn to him and change my expression from one of contrition to anger. "See, that's the problem, Shultz. Either I'm in charge of this mission, or I'm not. Which is it?" I turn my angry gaze to Traeger, who involuntarily flinches back.

"How am I supposed to trust either of you when you so plainly don't trust me? The straight answer is that I can't. Would having your Marines closer in have made a difference today? Probably. But I couldn't afford to do that because I was legitimately worried about you using them to take over the mission the second you didn't like how it was going, and I couldn't have *my* people at risk like that. Understand?"

Shultz opens his mouth to argue but then seems to think better of it. I press harder. "Today was a dry run. Because now, Hornsby knows we're coming. Uvalde doesn't think they could have figured out what ship we came in on, so we still have some element of surprise, but otherwise, we're blown. Wherever Hornsby is—and I'm almost certain it's not the Decker system—he's going to be marshaling his forces, digging in deep, and getting ready for us. Our mission just went from hard to nearly impossible. And the *only* way we're going to stand a chance is if we work together and under a unified command."

I haven't raised my voice, not even once in the conversation. But I'm using my old command tone, and it, along with my words, is driving the message home to them.

"What do you suggest, Captain?" Traeger finally asks, his voice low.

"Simple," I say, standing as Doc finishes the last of the work on me and beats a hasty retreat. "As I said, a unified command. How many combat missions have you commanded, Mr. Traeger?"

He looks ruffled for a second, but my matter-of-fact tone, without any challenge in it, seems to defuse any defensiveness. "Zero," he answers frankly.

"Which is to be expected," I soothe, again playing the diplomat. "It's not part of your job description. But that's my point. This *is* my job. This is what the same government that trained the two of you trained me to do. And before the King decided to declare me persona non grata for blowing the whistle on his rapist nephew, I was deemed one of the best at this kind of thing."

I look each of them in the eye, daring them to disagree. Traeger winced when I called out the King and his nephew, but Shultz didn't even bat an eye. I'm sure he doesn't believe me. So, I have to double down.

"Mr. Traeger, you have access to my file, correct?"

"Yes," he says cautiously.

"My unredacted file?"

"I believe so."

"How many King's Stars does it say I earned?"

For a moment, he cocks his head, and his eyes go out of focus as he checks his implant. When they come back into focus, they're a bit wider than before. "You earned *two* King's Stars?"

I nod. "The real number is four, which means you don't actually have my fully unredacted file. Two of them are so secret that only the King, a few of his top advisors, and a handful of flag officers know about them. But regardless, that should tell you that I used to be a very good ship commander."

I pause, knowing I have to play this carefully. I'm on the edge of coming across as a braggart, which isn't my intention. I just need them to know that I'm good at my job, and for better or worse, the awards I received in my career are a common language we speak. If *any* of this is going to work, I can't just be in command of this mission because they want plausible deniability if we're caught; I have to be in charge because they feel I'm the best man for the job. Otherwise, we might as well quit now.

I soften my tone. "I may not be here willingly, but believe it or not, I want what you want. Baron Hornsby killed seven of my crew and almost killed the rest of us. Even if you hadn't shown up, our plan was to go after him as soon as our destroyer was repaired. I would love nothing more than to see him brought to justice for his many, *many* crimes. And whatever plot he's part of against the King, I don't want to see my old star nation brought into a costly war. So, what I'm saying is that if you'll trust me to do my job, to go after this man, then I'll trust the two of you to help me do it."

That was a pretty good speech, if I say so myself. Unfortunately, it only worked on Traeger. Shultz is still fuming from the death of his men. The spirit of King William, founder of the Kingdom of Prometheus himself, could descend from a cloud of light right this second and anoint me his holy champion, and Shultz would still scoff at it. Unfortunately, the only thing I can give the man is time to come to his senses.

In the meantime, I'll take the half win of convincing Traeger, even if it did come at the cost of five lives I would very much like to have back. I always liked Marines, even if they sometimes sweat too much and smelled bad and knocked my spacers around in station bars.

"Now," I resume, "Lieutenant Uvalde has informed me that our mysterious cowboy friend left a trail of bread-crumbs on his way out of the system. I suggest we cautiously follow them and start contingency planning if there's a trap at the other end."

"Let me guess," Shultz says with a triumphant glare, "the trail leads to Decker?"

I shake my head, keeping my expression neutral. "No, the trail leads to Pointon. Mr. Traeger, please take the conn and move us out at two-thirds speed toward the Pointon jump point. I'm going to check on the folks in the med bay and will join you on the bridge shortly."

Shrugging on a loose tunic over Doc Bean's bandages, I walk from the room before either of them can respond, but I'm gratified to see Traeger start to move toward the opposite hatch, the one leading to the bridge, almost certainly— hopefully—to carry out my orders.

SEVENTEEN
LOLA PAYS A VISIT
BRAD MENDOZA

As we exit jump space in Pointon, I get to see a new capability of the Q-ship that I didn't know about. When we left Valle de Oro, our transponder identified us as the bulk freighter MV *Yates*. But on arrival in Pointon, we're now the MV *Benning's Hope*. A rotating transponder, on its own, isn't all that impressive. Harris jury-rigged one on *Bainbridge* in a day's work.

What's impressive is that the visual profile of *Odysseus* has *also* changed, along with its name.

Whoever designed the Q-ship installed inflatable bladders that can be extended through purpose-built doors in the hull and then filled from compressed air tanks to add realistic-looking wings, blisters, and even entire new sections to the ship—all fake, of course. Better still, they're woven with metallic fibers that return active sensor pings, the same as hull metal would. So, for all intents and purposes, no one viewing us through a station window or a ship's sensor array would ever guess we're the same ship that left dock at Valle de Oro just a day and a half ago.

"Captain, we'll dock at Pointon Station One in 12 hours

and 53 minutes," Chief Hashimoto reports from the helm. That's the largest station around Pointon, and the one Hayley tracked the cowboy's ship to.

"Comm traffic is clear, Captain," chimes in Lieutenant Opal Winston. "Nothing to suggest anyone recognizes us or is taking an undue interest."

"Sensors?" I ask, and Laia answers quickly.

"Only active pings are from the planet's array, sir. Strength and frequency suggest regular traffic control sensors, and we're still well out of range. There are four other ships within our sensor range right now, none on anything approaching an intercept course and none that show weapons signatures."

"Thank you, Lieutenant. Any sign of the ship our cowboy friend was on?"

"No, sir, not yet," she answers, a hint of worry to her tone that I can't help but share. I've come to fully trust Hayley's almost preternatural means of gathering information in any system we enter, but a little independent confirmation would have been nice.

"If he didn't just transit the outer system to another jump point," Traeger observes from the XO chair.

I look over at him sharply, but his expression is thoughtful rather than challenging. I begrudgingly admit to myself that he's only doing his job as XO to provide feasible alternative explanations and not let me simply see what I expect and hope to see.

"You're right," I tell him. "But until we check for him here, we can't know Lieutenant Uvalde is wrong. And if we can somehow get access to the planetary sensor logs, then we might be able to track where he went from the station.

He nods. "Yes, sir." Since our watershed chat in my

ready room yesterday, he's been surprisingly amenable to just about any order I give him. He still has a very punchable face, and his upper-crust accent reminds me of all the self-entitled jerks I served with who were fortunate enough—in their own eyes, at least—to have grown up on Prometheus itself. I have to keep reminding myself that I'm now *engaged* to a native-born Promethean, but Jessica is the exception, not the rule.

Regardless, I do have to admit I don't hate Trager quite as much as I did 48 hours ago. He's slowly growing on me, except for the fact that he's part of the group that's holding my fiancée hostage somewhere. I'm totally going to make him pay for that, though I may feel a twinge of guilt now when I do it. Whoever heard of a mass murderer with a conscience?

If only Marine Captain Shultz were so easy to bring over to my side.

I get up out of my chair. "Commander Traeger, you have the conn. I feel like visiting Marine country."

He looks up at me in surprise but doesn't argue. "Aye, sir, I have the conn."

"Come on, Uvalde," I say to the short Latina in her cross-legged seat on the deck—her professionalism didn't last beyond the first day, nor did her willingness to sit in a chair. She leaps to her feet and follows me out of the hatch.

"Why we visiting the Marines, boss?" she asks cheerfully as she almost jogs to keep up with my longer stride through the ship's corridors. It's a long walk down the spine to where the Marines are housed. I may lose a few kilos on this mission.

"You up for a little sparring practice?" I ask her.

She grins up at me. "Sure, boss, but you think maybe you oughta be asking Gunny Boyd to do this instead?"

Smart woman has already picked up on exactly what I'm intending to do.

"Just go with me on this, Hayley," I urge, and she nods briskly.

"Okay, boss."

It's an eternal truth in every Navy since time immemorial that if you have a contingent of Marines on your ship, they'll invariably find a place to fight each other. They call it training, of course, and declare it to be their Providence-given right to keep their skills sharp, even if it drives ships' doctors mad with the number of broken noses and bruised knuckles they need to treat during any given voyage.

Odysseus is no exception. On this ship, the Marines have converted one of the fake storage containers, which doubles as their armory, by putting a mat down in the middle of the deck and throwing each other around on it. Hayley and I head there now. As we near it, I hear shouting and grunts through the open hatch, but as soon as we enter, the compartment goes deathly silent. Even the two Marines stripped to the waist on the mat step back from each other and regard us suspiciously.

"Captain Mendoza, can we help you?" Shultz asks, stepping forward and regarding me with a hostile glare. Even if he didn't hate my guts, it's a breach of unwritten protocol for the captain of the ship to intrude into Marine country without giving any notice, even if the Marines on board are under his command. It's a rule born of tradition, if not any official decree, but is no less sacred in its import.

"Just visiting, Major Shultz," I reply. A ship can only have one captain, so by another tradition, I've given him a verbal promotion in rank for the purposes of avoiding confusion. "Actually thought we might join you for some light sparring."

He looks at me incredulously, and there are several snickers behind him as his Marines take in my words. "*You* want to spar with one of my Marines?" he asks, his voice full of dangerous delight.

I shake my head. "Nope. I'm all thumbs when it comes to hand-to-hand combat. Give me a 35cm laser any day over a fistfight. But I was thinking more that Lieutenant Uvalde here might like to have a go." I step aside to reveal Hayley behind me, short and thin, her face full of wide-eyed innocence as she takes in the Marines and their training space.

The compartment fills with laughs, including a dark one from Shultz himself. "No, seriously, Captain, why are you here?" His tone and the question border on insubordination. Traditions aside, a captain never need explain himself on his own ship. Luckily, Hayley saves me from a potentially embarrassing confrontation over the intentional slip.

She steps forward. "No, seriously, chico. I want to spar. Pick any of your Marines. Give me a challenge."

More laughter greets that, but Shultz shrugs. "Sure. Patty!" A trim but tall woman built of iron cords steps into the center of the compartment. "Why don't you show the lieutenant here how Marines spar?"

Patty smiles in anticipation and removes her uniform shirt, revealing ripped muscles and a sports bra underneath. It's another breach of protocol with the ship's captain present, but I choose to let it slide as well. In fact, the more arrogant and disrespectful the Marines are leading up to this, the harder my intended message will land.

Hayley slips off her combat boots and shrugs off her customary red leather jacket, which she hands to me for safekeeping, but makes no other sign of preparing for the fight. She steps slowly, almost tentatively, onto the mat to face Patty.

"Marine sparring rules," Shultz barks. "No broken bones if you can avoid it, and no hitting the crotch. Otherwise, anything goes. Fight until one of you taps out or loses consciousness." He says the last with a smirk at Hayley, clearly expecting Patty to knock her out cold early in the fight. He steps back. "Fight!"

Patty, unsurprisingly, strikes first, leaping forward and lashing out with a straight jab to Hayley's face. With her body's momentum behind the punch, it should be a devastating blow, enough to break the smaller woman's nose and probably end the fight. Except when Patty's fist arrives at where her opponent's face is supposed to be, it finds nothing but empty air.

"Nice hit, chica," Hayley says with a grin from half a meter to the right, her hands clasped behind her back innocently.

Patty doesn't stop and gawk; she's too well-trained for that. She instantly recovers and launches a roundhouse kick at Hayley's left kidney. But once again, her strike finds only empty air as the purple-haired girl steps back smoothly, and Patty's foot misses her by centimeters.

The Marine follows up her missed kick with a two-punch combo—a feint with her left followed by a right-hand jab. Both fail to find their target as Hayley, her hands still clasped behind her back, deftly dodges this way and that. The next four attacks similarly fail, the little woman dancing around the perimeter of the sparring pad, managing to dodge each blow by the barest of margins, the infuriatingly wide grin never leaving her face.

The Marines watching are in a frenzy now, eagerly calling out advice to Patty and booing and jeering every time Hayley evades yet another hit but refuses to fight back.

Finally, I admonish her, forcing my voice to sound as bored as possible. "Hayley, stop messing with her."

She throws me a wink and sounds cheerful when she responds. "Sure, Skipper!" Then she moves like lightning, springing toward the frustrated Patty and delivering a blindingly fast punch to the taller woman's kidney, following it up with a crouch and a sweep of the leg that knocks the Marine down on her back, hard. Hayley is instantly on top of her, delivering two fast jabs to her nose, which sprays blood. She jumps off just as Patty is going to try a grappling roll.

The Marine gets to her feet slowly, her now wary eyes on Hayley, who stands casually, not even breathing hard, just two paces away. She lets Patty stand fully and even lets her take the first swing at her, which she once again dodges expertly, moving inside the punch and sinking a fist into the other woman's stomach.

Patty doubles over, and Hayley finishes her with a fierce uppercut that snaps the Marine's head back and makes her eyes roll back into her skull as she slumps to the mat, unconscious.

For a long moment, the entire compartment is deathly silent. Then Shultz whirls on me. "You hustled me! You made it sound like she didn't know what she was doing so I would send out one of my weakest fighters." He levels a finger at my chest threateningly, though a few of the

Marines behind him wince at his disparaging remark about the unconscious Patty.

I shake my head. "I made no claims whatsoever about her fighting ability. *You* made an assumption, Major. But, if it'll make you feel better, pick your best fighter for the next round. You don't mind, do you, Hayley?"

"No, boss, that was fun!" my intelligence officer answers as she helps two Marines drag Patty off the mat.

"Kittridge!" Shultz snaps. "Get up here and show these squids how it's done!"

"Oorah," comes the deep reply as a huge Marine wearing sergeant's stripes steps forward, peeling off his uniform tunic and the shirt underneath. Kittridge is as tall as Gunny Boyd but probably weighs an additional 30 kilos. His muscles have muscles. I gulp. I've seen Uvalde take down men nearly that size—some of Duchess Charlotte's guards on Serenidad came close—but never a trained Marine. For the first time, I actually start to doubt my clever plan.

I watch as Kittridge air boxes for a second to warm up. Not only is the guy massive, but he's fast. His fists move through the air so quickly that I can't tell where one punch ends and another begins. He bounces back and forth lightly on his toes, almost like a dancer, moving in a way that no man with his build has any right to do.

When I glance over at Hayley, she must see the doubt in my eyes, because she throws me another wink, still grinning like a madwoman. I half expect her hair to turn white as she channels her alter ego, Lola, the ruthless assassin, but it stays a bright purple. Which is probably smart, because there's no way the Marines would miss her hair changing color right in front of them. But none of them seem to notice her eyes shifting from brown to gray, and I suppress a shudder.

Lola *is* here. Just like that, all levity leaves my friend's face, and I'm staring at a cold-blooded and extremely lethal killer. I only hope that Uvalde knows what she's doing, channeling her deadliest personality now. For this to work, I need her to win but not to *murder* her opponent.

This time, when Shultz calls a start to the fight, Hayley —Lola—moves first. Like a snake, she lashes out, diving under the larger man's reach and delivering two fast punches to his stomach. It barely even phases Kittridge, who slams down both fists to pound Lola in the back, but she anticipates the move, hitting the mat and rolling away, coming back to her feet two meters away in a defensive stance. Then she's back on him, springing forward and delivering a kick to the Marine's right quadricep.

Kittridge grunts but shows no other sign of being the least bit hurt by the blow. Then he moves, fast as lightning, feinting a right hook and then ringing Lola's bell with a left jab to her face. It connects, and the surrounding Marines cheer, except for Shultz. Standing next to me, he only grunts; he noticed what I did, only visible from our angle. Kittridge's blow was ineffective, glancing off the side of Lola's head as she dodged at the last possible instant, turning a punch that should have shattered her jaw into nothing but an annoyance.

Still, she retreats as if the punch did more than that. Kittridge, sensing blood, follows her, his huge stride moving him across the mat and pushing Lola to the edge. But just as he's lining up for another shot to her face, she ducks and rolls between his legs! Really? I thought that only happened in cheesy B-grade movies, but she actually rolls through his legs, twisting and coming up behind him.

She kicks hard against the back of his knee, causing it to bend, and forcing the big man to half kneel down on the mat.

Before Kittridge can get up, she delivers two quick rabbit punches to his right kidney from behind, and he roars in pain and anger. From there, she leaps on his back, putting a forearm around his throat and locking it into place with her other arm.

He does the natural thing and tries to reach back for her, finding her face with one massive mitt and trying to stick his thumb in her eye, but she turns her head and evades his desperate grasp. Then he stands, Lola still riding his back and cutting off his air supply, and everyone in the room can see what he intends. As he jumps up and back, aiming to land on top of her and probably break most of her ribs, she digs her feet into the small of his back and pushes off, releasing her grip on his throat and propelling herself out of the way so that Kittridge crashes to the thin mat on the hard deck, knocking out his own wind—what's left of it—instead of hers.

Lola lands better, rolling once and springing to her feet. She's quickly back in the fight, this time wrapping her legs around his massive neck, yanking one of his arms upward and holding it with both of hers to take it out of the fight as the other struggles to pry her off him so he can breathe.

Kittridge's weight works against him as he struggles to get back to his feet. Every time it looks like he might get his free arm under him to lever himself up, Lola jerks her legs tighter around his neck, forcing him to rethink things. Having already had the air knocked out of him by his fall and never having had the chance to regain it in any significant measure, he starts turning purple almost immediately.

Finally, he weakly taps the mat to his side with one big hand.

Next to me, I can practically feel Shultz tense up. This may be a no-holds-barred fight, but Lola is going to kill Kittridge if no one stops her, and he's already technically conceded the fight to her. But we can all see the murder in her eyes, which have an almost gleeful look in their gray depths as the life of the big Marine slowly leaves him. Finally, having pushed it as far as I feel comfortable doing, I bark out an order.

"Hayley, that's enough!"

Instantly she blinks, as if just waking up from a long sleep, and releases the big Marine, who sucks in a great, sputtering breath and then chokes on it and starts coughing violently. Several other Marines rush to his side and help him sit up and get more air into his lungs. Hayley—her eyes are dark again—leans forward and pats him on the shoulder from behind.

"Sorry, chico. No hard feelings?" She doesn't wait for a response but practically skips across the mat over to where I stand with Shultz. "That was fun, boss. Can we do it again later?"

Despite her tone, I can see something flash in her eyes: genuine fear. She's confided to me in the past that she hates letting Lola out; the white-haired, gray-eyed assassin is an aspect of Uvalde's psyche that scares even her. And when Lola takes control, the only thing that can often stop her is someone calling Hayley by her first name, as I just did. We both know what would have likely happened if I hadn't. Unfortunately, I saw no other choice than to release Lola. I just have to hope my plan worked.

"How did you do that?" Shultz demands angrily, glaring down at her.

She shrugs but doesn't respond.

"You switched fighting styles against Kittridge," he presses. "No one is that good with two different styles against bigger and stronger opponents. How?"

I reply for her. "Gunny Boyd taught her." It's a lie, but it's one that will serve our purposes quite nicely. In fact, this very conversation is the entire reason I brought the undercover Guard agent down here to Marine country to beat some of them up.

"No kidding?" a woman's voice asks, and Patty steps around from behind Shultz, offering her hand to Hayley; she must have woken up sometime during the fight with Kittridge. "I've never seen anyone move like that, and I've never seen *any* woman who could take down a man that big and well trained."

Hayley smiles, grasps the Marine's hand, and shakes it.

Then Patty turns to Shultz. "Sir, any chance we can get Lieutenant Uvalde and Gunny Boyd down here to show us a few things?" she asks eagerly.

Shultz, still glaring daggers at me, frowns tightly while I try very hard not to shout for joy at the woman's question. I was going to suggest the same, but Patty doing it for me is so much more effective. I could kiss this woman... you know, if I wasn't already engaged to Jessica and if Patty wouldn't break me in half for even suggesting it.

"Sir," another voice adds. "I'd love to learn some of those moves."

We all turn to see a still-gasping Kittridge being supported by two other Marines. He smiles weakly at Hayley. "That was incredible. Took me down a few dozen notches, but it was a real thing of beauty." Several other Marines mutter in agreement.

Shultz, still angry but helpless in the face of so much

enthusiasm from his men and women, surrenders. "Fine. We'll get Gunny Boyd and Lieutenant Uvalde to come down after we leave Pointon and train with us." He turns back to me, and I can tell the next words out of his mouth cause him almost physical pain. "Assuming that's alright with you, Captain."

I nod. "Of course, Major. I'm sure they can learn more than a few things from your Marines as well. In fact, I'd suggest bringing the rest of Gunny's team down, too. Private Kluth could pick up a few things from Patty and Kittridge here.

For the barest instant, Shultz's face softens in silent acknowledgment of the face-saving bone I just threw him and his Marines, but it's only an instant. Then he's wearing the same hard mask as always around me. "Thank you, sir. We look forward to it."

EIGHTEEN
A REALLY COOL GUN
BRAD MENDOZA

This time, when we hit the planet's surface, we do so as a unified force. A scan of the ships docked at the orbital above Pointon reveals no sign of the cowboy's escape craft. But a close scan of the planet's surface finds a likely candidate at a spaceport in the southern hemisphere. Laia gives it a 75 percent chance of being the ship we're looking for. Hayley has to admit she was actually wrong; apparently, our quarry *didn't* stop at the station.

You would think that a party of nearly 30 would draw some attention landing on a backwater planet, but Pointon, unlike Valle De Oro, has had better economic success than most independent systems in this part of space. So, the place to which we follow Laia's lead is a proper city in its own right. Sure, it's nothing like the cities one would find in the Federation or the Confederacy, but with almost a million citizens, we blend in just fine.

Or would, if the blasted Marines didn't stand out like sore thumbs no matter how you dress them up. I could practically feel Harris twitching as they passed to board *Odysseus*'s shuttle. He *really* wanted to get his hands on them and fix up their so-called disguises. But I have a feeling that they wouldn't have appreciated his ministrations.

What they *do* seem to appreciate are the sacked lunches the galley packed them for the trip down to the planet. Our intrepid cook, Kelly's wife Karen O'Malley, has done far more to earn the loyalty and love of the hungry Marines than I could ever do. I swear that even Shultz seems to like her, though I heard she chewed him out when he tried to suggest a menu change. She's done a much better job of making her authority in the galley absolute than I have on the bridge.

Harris was equally upset that I didn't let him disguise me for the mission. Our plan calls for the cowboy to recognize me. At least we might have a name for him now... probably. Hayley's deep search of the intel files on Hornsby revealed that the baron has a fixer—a man he sends to do his dirty work—only known outside the organization by the name of Merl. The name reminds me of an accountant, not a man who dresses like a cowboy, wears a pistol slung low on his hip, and works for the biggest crime boss in the Fringe. But hey, we can't all have cool names like Brad.

If the cowboy really is the mysterious Merl, then Traeger's other intel suggests he's much higher placed in Dexter Hornsby's organization than we thought after encountering him on Valle de Oro. So even though we lost our target there, we might have clued in to a much bigger fish. I'm willing to bet that if we capture Merl, he'll lead us to the baron.

"Shultz," I say into my comm as I walk down the open boulevard, this one a true thoroughfare with middle-grade shops lining each side. We've agreed not to use ranks while on the surface in case someone manages to hack our comms. Not only do we have to worry about Hornsby's people, but the police on Pointon are notoriously invasive in their techniques, and we have to be wary of someone in the government discovering us running an illegal operation on their planet. "Any sign of our friend?"

"Nothing," the Marine captain responds sourly. "There are only six hotels within a few kilometers of where he landed his ship, and I've got a man in each one. No sign of him."

Which means he's not there. The Marines, for all their inability to blend in, are highly motivated to find the man who killed five of their brothers and sisters. If they say the cowboy isn't in those six hotels, then he's not. I imagine more than a few clerks have been threatened in a similar manner to how I forced the resort employee on Jewel to show me the security vids. I just hope they were subtle enough not to get the police called—never a given for Marines.

"Hayley, how about you?"

"Nothing, boss," she says, echoing Shultz. "If he's here, he's not leaving any electronic trail. And the guy at the landing field hasn't seen him. Trust me, he would tell me if he had."

I switch to a private comm channel with her. "What are you talking about, Hayley? What did you do?"

"Nothing, boss," comes the innocent reply. "Victoria thought the guy at the landing field was cute. So she flirted with him a little to get him talking. And maybe they kissed a little. No big deal."

"Uh, Hayley. What would Illian think if he found out about you kissing some other guy?"

There's a long pause on her end. "What do you mean,

Capitán? Illy's dating me, not Victoria. Sure, he likes her, too, but he's *my* boyfriend."

I shake my head rapidly like a dog trying to shed water, drawing some weird looks from nearby pedestrians. "Hayley, I'm not sure Illian will appreciate the difference between you and Victoria." I'm thinking of the conversation I had with him about possibly leaving us and going to Carter's World. The *last* thing I need is for him and Uvalde to get into a fight in the middle of a mission where I need them both at the top of their games.

"Maybe you're right, boss," she replies slowly. "I never thought of it like that. Victoria won't like it, but I'll tell her no more men until we check with Illy."

I sigh, half-relieved and half-wanting to stop walking and bang my head against the brick siding of the closest building. "That's good, Hayley, but maybe don't mention *any* of this to Illian until *after* we're safely on our own ship and have Commander Lin back."

"Sure, boss!"

As we've been speaking, I've been doing my best to casually meander down a city street, hoping that some member of Hornsby's organization or even some AI in the planet's robust surveillance systems will recognize me and tell the cowboy, Merl, I'm here. Then he can come and confront me, the Marines will encircle him, and all will work perfectly.

But I'm a little preoccupied with worrying about my tactical officer and his extremely weird girlfriend. So when I hear a woman's scream from an alley opening to my right, I don't stop and think, *Hey maybe this is a trap!* Nope, I just go to rescue the poor damsel... like an idiot.

"Captain, where'd you go?" Shultz demands on my

comm as I sprint into the alley, turn a corner, and stutter-step to a stop.

It's empty, terminating in a high brick wall. Only one door leads into an adjacent building, and there isn't even a handle on this side of it.

I turn to retreat, only to find Merl standing behind me, blocking my way out of the alley, a giant grin underneath his stupid cowboy hat.

Okay, fine, the hat is *really* cool, and I want one just like it. But he doesn't deserve it!

"Mendoza," he says, just loud enough to hear. "Heard you was looking for me. Well, you found me."

My hand is already on the gun at my waist, hidden by my coat from the Pointon authorities but still loaded and ready. Merl's hands are both hooked in his belt, his long coat thrown back to reveal the pistol strapped to his thigh. By all rights, I should be able to get my gun out first, but the gleam in his eye as he watches me makes me think that he's playing with me the same way Hayley played with Patty.

"I just want to chat with your boss," I say to keep him talking. If I can stall long enough, Shultz's Marines or Gunny Boyd will surely come looking for me. I should be happy, right? My plan worked.

"Sure," he drawls, "and I'm sure he wants to talk to you, too. But something tells me it won't be a friendly chat either way."

I shrug, my hand still on my gun. "Well, last time, he killed a good chunk of my crew, so you're probably right about that."

His smirk turns into a grin. "I like you, Mendoza. You've got a certain style. Too bad I've gotta kill you."

"Why?" I ask, trying to keep my voice steady. "Because

you keep a conscience under that ridiculous hat?" Ugh. I shouldn't have said that. He'll know I'm lying. *No one* would honestly disparage that piece of headwear.

"No," Merl says with a chuckle. "It's a shame I gotta kill you because the baron really wants to do the honors himself. He'll be right upset if he doesn't get that chance. But oh well, he's not here right now, is he?"

"So why not take me prisoner? Take me back to Baron Hornsby, and you can watch while he murders me like the coward he is."

He doesn't take the bait but just chuckles again. "Like I said, a certain style. But no, I think I'll just save him the trouble now."

Sensing my death coming, I tighten my grip on the pistol and start to draw it from its holster. Before I can get it even halfway out, his hand moves in a blur, and there's a loud crash. A bullet slams into my chest, knocking me back and onto the hard concrete of the alley floor.

I lie there, gasping for breath, and watch helplessly as the cowboy walks slowly toward me. I try to raise the gun in my hand, but he casually kicks it away, as if swatting at a gnat. He stands over me, his pistol pointed at my head, the open borehole looking for all the world like the eye of a malevolent cyclops as it stares down at me.

"Pity, really," he says, almost to himself. "Would've been fun for it to be more of a fight. But I guess your reputation is a little overblown."

"Wait!" I cry, my eyes fixed on the gun. "Is that a revolver? Like an actual six-shooter?"

He looks at me like I'm crazy. "You can see it, can't ya?"

"Well, yeah. But... Look, I've never seen one of those

outside a museum. Why do you even have one? Just six shots?"

"So, what of it?" he demands, looking annoyed.

"You know modern pistols can hold several dozen rounds, right?" I ask.

He furrows his eyebrows together. "Of course I know that. I'm not an idiot; I just like this gun! 'Sides, a good shooter don't need more than six shots!"

"That's a really good point," I admit, still lying on my back with the gun pointed at my face. "Plus, it really matches this whole old-timey cowboy thing you've got going on here."

He frowns at me like he's not sure if I'm being serious.

I keep going. "I mean, I think it's super cool. If I have to die of a gunshot to the face, at least it'll come from an awesome gun. Say, you think I could hold it first? You know, just for a minute? I want a closer look before you kill me with it."

"Uh, thanks, I guess…" he starts, clearly still confused. Then his face turns angry. "No, you can't hold it!"

I shrug as best I can, lying there on my back.

"Captain Mendoza!" a voice yells from the direction of the street.

I watch as Merl's finger tightens on the trigger, and I close my eyes tightly, waiting for the bullet to come.

But when I open them after a moment, the cowboy is gone, and I'm looking up at the concerned faces of two Marines whose names I can't remember. They're shortly joined by Gunny, Drake, and even Shultz. The latter just scowls down at me.

"You okay, Skipper?" Gunny asks.

I nod while I reach up and open my shirt, revealing the light ballistic armor they all insisted I wear underneath, the bullet from Merl's first and only shot embedded right above my heart. It's a miracle that he never fired the second shot into my head, distracted by my banter about his gun. I can't believe that worked. That should *not* have worked.

"He got away," Shultz growls. "Not sure how he got out of the alley without being seen, but he's probably out the other side of one of these buildings by now and half a block away."

I'm not sure if I should feel supremely relieved that I'm not dead or ticked off that we failed our objective again. Two planets, two chances to catch one of the baron's lieutenants, and two botched missions, both because of my own stupidity.

Maybe I've gotten too used to my crazy plans working, and I've gotten sloppy. Or maybe my luck has finally run out. Though I did just talk my way out of being shot in the face, so who knows? Either way, we're no closer to completing this cursed mission.

NINETEEN
STRANGE BEDFELLOWS
BRAD MENDOZA

"Captain, have a minute?"

I look up from my ready room desk to see Francis Illian poking his head through the hatch from the bridge.

"Sure, what is it, Guns?" I ask, grateful for the break from obsessing over where to go next. We're still in orbit over Pointon, ostensibly so we can take on some new cargo, but really because we have no idea where to continue our search. The cowboy, good old Merl, somehow slipped off the planet without leaving any trace of his passage, or so we think. He hasn't resurfaced since almost killing me in that alley, and we've searched *everywhere*. Nor has the ship he arrived on moved.

My gut tells me he's long gone, and we missed our opportunity.

Illian swings the hatch open all the way and enters with Uvalde and Traeger on his heels. I raise an eyebrow. This is an odd threesome to come to see me.

"Sir," Illian starts as they all line up in front of my desk.

"We've been working together to try and figure out where Hornsby is."

"Okay?" I draw the word out into a question. These three? Working together?

"Yes, sir," Traeger answers for the trio. "We know you ordered us to focus on his man Merl, but we thought we might be able to cut out the middleman, so to speak."

"We decided to focus on the members of his organization in this part of space that we know about," Francis says excitedly, talking faster now. "Not just Merl, but the dead lieutenant we went after on Valle de Oro and every other known associate. Then we had Harris hack into police bulletins down on Pointon for us."

I raise my other eyebrow. That was an incredible risk; as good of a hacker as Harris has proven to be, infiltrating the servers of a paranoid police state sounds like a recipe for disaster. But I'm more worried that it may have taken too much of Harris's time from the assignment I asked him to work on the moment we boarded *Odysseus* at Jewel.

"I know what you're thinking, boss," Hayley chimes in, mostly misreading my fleeting look of concern. "El extraño was very careful. I don't think anyone noticed his hack."

"But he found something," Illian says before I can argue. "These may be the independent systems, but their various law enforcement agencies have formed a sort of loose affiliation. They share information on local criminals as well as those that visit from other star nations and sectors in the Fringe. Once Harris got us into those files, it was a treasure trove."

"Look." Traeger takes up the narrative, using his implant in share mode to project a 3D rendering of the local area of space so that it appears to all of us to hang in the air over my desk. The various systems are labeled, and there's a green dot where we are in the Pointon system. Then, a flurry of red dots start appearing, peppering all the other systems as they multiply and form large concentrations of red in each. "These are reported sightings of the men and women we know are part of Hornsby's organization. See a pattern?" he asks eagerly.

I nod slowly. "Sure. The biggest concentration is in the Decker system. Looks like you were right to—"

Traeger waves me off before I can finish. "No, no, no, Captain. Look closer."

I grunt. I've never seen the man so excited or animated. Both Illian and Uvalde have similar looks of nearly uncontained anticipation as I turn my gaze again to the star map. I study it closely, not seeing what they see until it suddenly clicks.

"One of the systems has almost no red dots," I observe, starting to understand.

"Exactly!" Illian practically shouts, then has the good sense to look momentarily embarrassed by his outburst. "It's the Zepha system, Skipper. There have been reported sightings of Hornsby's people there, but not nearly in the same volume as every other system in the region."

Hayley jumps back in. "And the sightings they do report, boss, follow a more or less fixed schedule, like someone is controlling the reports to make sure they come out just often enough not to raise suspicion."

They all stop talking and look at me intently. When I say nothing, Traeger frowns. "Captain, do you understand what we're trying to tell you?"

"Of course I do," I say, probably sounding a little defensive. "You think Baron Hornsby's base of operations is in the Zepha system and that he's got control over local law enforcement and they're not reporting on his activities or people there. Instead, he's got his own people doing it just enough not to raise suspicion of anyone who goes looking. Uh, right?"

"Exactly!" All three of them shout the word in unison.

"But, Commander," I say to Traeger, "what about the big concentration in Decker? Maybe you were right about him being in that system."

"No, sir. I'm convinced now that you and your people were right all along. Decker was a false flag; the evidence of Hornsby being there is too neat and too strong. No way he's that sloppy. But *this*, this could be the break we need!"

He suddenly stands to attention. "Sir, I recommend we burn with all haste to the Zepha system. It's two jumps away from here and should only take us two and a half days at two-thirds thrust."

I chew on it for a moment, trying to ignore the hopeful looks on Illian's and Uvalde's faces. Then I relent. "Make it so, Commander. Let's go see if you're all right, and maybe we can catch a baron. Perhaps if we're lucky, we'll bag a cowboy as well."

The three of them leave excitedly through the hatch to the bridge, with me frowning after them. As soon as they're gone, I use my implant to summon another crewmember to my ready room.

Harris arrives about five minutes later, looking like he might have been asleep, though he's so sloppy all the time that it's hard to tell. What he's wearing might constitute pajamas or could just as easily be his idea of formal wear.

"What's up, Skipper?" he asks after the hatch closes behind us. He looks around the room meaningfully, and I give him a quick nod. Hayley sweeps my ready room and quarters for bugs four times a day. At this point, the spooks on board have stopped trying to listen in, obviously having figured out that we can find and disable the bugs faster than they can plant them.

"When you hacked the servers on Pointon, did you…" I trail off, prudence preventing me from saying the words out loud on the off chance that the spooks have installed a bug that even Hayley can't detect.

Harris, luckily, gets my meaning but then ruins the entire effort at discretion by giving me his unedited answer. "Sure, Captain. Pilar says they had a little trouble, but they managed to get *Wanderer* off Hudson like you asked. They're on their way to pick up Heddy and Beck, and then they'll go look for Jessica."

Deciding not to chew him out for his lack of prudence, I nod gratefully. "And the other thing?"

This time, it takes him a second, but then his eyes go wide in recognition, and I'm half expecting him to blurt out every secret we have right then and there. To my relief, he's more careful this time. "Almost, boss. I need a few more days. But I found something else."

He reaches into a pocket, removes a small piece of paper, and slides it across the desk to me.

I pick it up and read what's on it. It's a container number, D14, meaning it's the fourth container clockwise around the central spine of the ship, 14 rows down from the command sphere. I raise an eyebrow at him.

"Not sure, Skipper," he replies to my unspoken question. "But whatever's in there, they *really* don't want us to know about it. So, I thought it might be important."

I nod and slip the piece of paper into my own pocket. "Good work, Harris," I tell him sincerely, and then shoo him back to his quarters to continue working on the job I gave him.

TWENTY
NEVER ENDING QUESTIONS
JESSICA LIN

"So, you had dinner with Vizeadmiral Heinrich on his flagship?" Jethro Jensen asks incredulously.

It's day six of my captivity on Lightman Station, and this is at least the *seventh* time he's asked this same question. For the first couple of days, I refused to answer any questions from him or the other Naval Intelligence officers sent to interrogate me. But around day three, I had a change of heart, mainly because I figured that the truth might actually help me *and* Brad.

After all, everything we've done since our 'deaths' in Gerson over six months ago has been to *help* Prometheus. So, I've explained everything to Jethro and his colleagues.

I told them how we captured the deserter George Peterson and stopped him from giving the stellarium coordinates to the Koratans.

I related how Brad held out for weeks under torture and refused to disclose those coordinates to Kayla Carter and the Jutzens. I've left out the part about him never knowing the coordinates in the first place, and I also don't tell Jethro or the others about Heather Kilgore being the one to actually give up the location of the priceless metal deposit.

After that, I explained how Brad and I saved Prometheus from a major shooting war with Koratas by foiling the Jutzen plot at XB-411 and Hudson.

In all, as I've explained to them repeatedly, Brad and I have undoubtedly done more to help our star nation *after* our so-called betrayal of it than we ever did before as officers in its Navy.

But now I'm thinking that telling the truth may have been a colossal mistake. It seems that no matter how I answer their questions, Naval Intelligence twists my words around to put Brad and me in a negative light.

"As I told you already," I say, frowning across the small metal table at Jethro, "Heinrich essentially ordered me to meet him on *Brandenburg* so he could convince me that Captain Mendoza was already dead so that I'd stop looking for him."

Jethro momentarily looks like he's sucking on a lemon. "Then he just let you go? And you'd have me believe that you then managed to somehow escape from his battleship in nothing more than a tiny corvette?"

I let out a long, frustrated sigh, mostly to buy myself time to think. It's clear that Jethro and his colleagues have a very biased view of events, and little I say is going to change that. So I decide to try a different tack.

"I felt terrible, you know."

He looks up from making notes in his data pad and cocks his head inquisitively. "About escaping from the Jutzens?"

I shake my head. "No, about leading you on as long as I did. I never should have accepted your proposal, and I definitely shouldn't have waited four whole months before telling you I couldn't go through with it."

His face hardens into an impassive mask, and he licks his lips. I push onward anyway.

"Look, Jethro, I'm not saying I bear all the responsibility in this, but what I did wasn't fair to you. Ever since then, I've wanted to—"

"Lieutenant Commander Lin," he interrupts, his voice stiffly formal, "please keep your remarks to the matters at hand. Now, let's move on. Tell me again how you and Brad Mendoza managed to steal the top-secret stealth ship, HMS *Vampire*, at Hudson."

I slump forward and rest my forehead on the table in front of me, mostly so he won't see my silent scream of frustration. After a moment to compose myself, I look up at him again. "As I said before, we didn't *steal* anything. We were working with ProSec Agent Katherine Henderson, who had command of HMS *Vampire* as a ProSec asset. Then we…"

We talk about things for another four hours, breaking only once for a quick lunch. By the end, I've made exactly zero headway on convincing my former fiancé that me and my new fiancé aren't the dastardly traitors he and everyone else believe us to be. And with every scoff and disapproving frown, I feel the hope of ever seeing Brad again fade further and further away.

TWENTY-ONE
I GET TO SHOOT STUFF

BRAD MENDOZA

I n my dream, I'm chasing Jessica through a space station. I can't actually see her, but I can hear her cries for help, always just around the next bend or through the next hatch. But no matter how fast I run, I can't seem to get any closer. The dream ends with me running into a section of corridor that suddenly starts flashing red because I'm too late to—

I jerk awake, the red flashing lights and sound of klaxons bringing me to instant alertness.

"General quarters, general quarters. Set Condition One throughout the ship. Dog all hatches and man battle stations! Captain to the bridge." It's Traeger's voice, and there's an undercurrent of panic in it.

I practically jump into my skinsuit, still zipping it up as I charge out of my quarters and down the short corridor that leads to the bridge. I'm there less than 30 seconds later.

"Report!" I bark before the bosun—another Naval Intel transplant—can announce my presence.

"Unidentified ship on an intercept course, sir," Illian

replies crisply, his voice carrying none of the panic that colored Traeger's moments before. "Estimate light cruiser class; no transponder."

I settle into my chair, frowning at the white-as-a-ghost Traeger in the XO's seat to my left, his eyes switching from the battle plot to me and almost pleading. It's the same look I used to see on shiny new ensigns the first time they went into combat; it's the face of an officer unbloodied by battle. In the real Navy, he never would have made it to the XO's chair without having been in at least a handful of skirmishes, but now he's about to get a crash course.

"Range?" I call out, and Laia Gammon gives me a number.

"Captain," Traeger starts, "aren't we going to take evasive action?"

I fight the urge to roll my eyes. "No, Mr. Traeger, not yet. That ship, whoever they are, was running cold, waiting for us to happen along. Even now, they're hiding their drive plume behind them. If *Odysseus* were the civilian freighter she appears to be, we still wouldn't be able to see them. If we react too soon, they'll have a pretty good idea that we're not a helpless freighter."

He opens his mouth, possibly to argue, but can't seem to get the words out. I ignore him and call back to Illian. "Guns, ready all missile tubes and charge laser capacitors, but don't open the outer hatches yet." Opening the outer hatches on *Odysseus* involves sliding back the false container fronts and hull plates that hide our missile tubes and other weapons. Doing that now would give us away even faster than disclosing our military-spec sensor range.

"Do you think it's Hornsby?" Traeger asks next to me, talking over Illian's acknowledgment of my order.

I turn to him. "Could be," I admit, "especially given

we're only one jump now from the Zepha system, but I think it's unlikely he'd just stumble upon us like this. Probably just pirates or commerce raiders. They're pretty common in this part of space, and we look like a nice, fat, juicy target."

"I see," he says stiffly. "And remind me of the difference between a pirate and a commerce raider. I know the theory," he hastens to add, probably trying not to sound as ignorant as we all know he is, "but not the practical difference."

Stifling a sigh—I wasn't planning to have to teach an Academy course during our first space battle—I reply as patiently as I can. "Commerce raiders tend to be sponsored by an enemy star nation to disrupt the economy of their foes. They typically disable your ship, board you, then steal or even destroy your cargo. But they don't kill anyone unless they have to, and they almost always let you go on your merry way after they've robbed you blind.

"Pirates, on the other hand, work only for themselves and their own greed. They don't care how much they damage your ship so long as your cargo stays intact for them to pillage. When they board, they kill anyone who gets in their way and often those that don't. Those that survive they often take as prisoners either to toy with or sell as slaves in one of the lawless systems. You *don't* want to be on a ship taken by pirates; trust me when I tell you that death would be infinitely preferable." I choose not to describe the aftermath of pirate attacks, something I witnessed all too often during my time in the Navy. I'm sure he's seen pictures, but until you see it live, you can't really know how bad it is.

I can see Traeger actually gulp as he nods his understanding. "So, how does that inform our strategy... if they're pirates or raiders?"

I shrug. "No real difference for us today or even in the eyes of interstellar law. We're well within our rights to defend ourselves using deadly force. We don't even have to wait for them to fire first if we can prove they were trying to board us. In our case, we can't afford to leave any witnesses, or the entire sector will know about this Q-ship and Baron Hornsby will have even more warning than he does now. If that happens, mission over."

"So, you're just going to kill them all?" If it's even possible, he loses more color in his face.

This time, I do sigh. "Only if they continue to act hostile. But then, yes, I will destroy them completely. It's standard practice. Once we know another ship is the enemy, we don't do half measures. Those who try usually end up dead."

I don't wait to watch him process that. "Anything on comms?"

"No, sir," Opal Winston reports, her voice not quite as shaky as Traeger's.

"Okay, coordinate with Lieutenant Gammon. Once they get in range of standard civilian passives, wait a minute and then send a query. Try and sound scared." That won't require much effort, I'm sure.

"Skipper, all weapons manned and ready. It'll take about 30 seconds to clear the hatches before we can fire."

"Thanks, Guns. Start working up firing solutions as soon as they're in range. And prep all countermeasures."

"Aye, sir."

"Commander Lipton," I call out, and the ship's AI routes my voice to engineering. "How are my engines?"

"Ready when you need them, Captain," comes the reply. At least her voice is steady. Either she's seen combat, or she's so focused on her drives that she isn't even thinking about the battle. Both are equally likely.

Just to be safe, I still send a private message to Kelly O'Malley. He replies almost instantly, assuring me that both the engines and Commander Lipton are ready. I relax marginally. Taking an untested ship and crew into battle for the first time is always nerve-racking, but things are as ready as they can be. All we can do now is wait.

Twenty minutes pass quickly. Opal sends out a message querying the approaching ship's intentions. She definitely manages to sound afraid, possibly even over-playing it. As expected, there is no answer, which points toward pirates. State-sponsored commerce raiders would be ordering us to heave to and prepare to be boarded, working with us to minimize damage and casualties by ensuring our cooperation with their demands. Pirates, on the other hand, work primarily via fear. Not responding or stating their intentions is calculated to instill in their victims a terror of the unknown.

"Time to weapons range?"

"Fifteen minutes 34 seconds, Skipper," replies Illian.

I nod but otherwise stay silent. We continue to wait. A few times, I almost rebuke Traeger, who is fidgeting so badly in his seat that I'm worried he's going to put the rest of the crew into a panic. But when I catch Laia glancing over at him and stifling a laugh, I stop worrying about my crew. Even Opal, the only other Naval Intel officer on the bridge right now, seems to be taking her queues from Laia and Illian and doesn't look nearly as nervous as her commander.

When we finally enter weapons range, things start to happen quickly.

"Vampire, vampire." Illian announces the launch of enemy missiles in an almost bored voice, in sharp contrast to Traeger's wide-eyed, panicked look hearing those words. "Two light ship-to-ship missiles, Captain. Both appear aimed at our drive nozzles."

That's no surprise. The first thing any pirate will do is try to put their quarry dead in space. It makes boarding a lot easier. And warshot missiles are a much cheaper way to do that than scramblers. Even for a freighter as large as *Odysseus*, two of the lighter missiles would normally do enough damage to our drive to cut our acceleration.

"Open all tubes and covers," I order. "Launch interceptors and fire a full port broadside at the enemy ship."

As I wait the 30 seconds for the false hull plates to retract so we can fire, Traeger looks over at me questioningly. "A full broadside, sir. Isn't that overkill?"

I frown at him. "Is there a missile shortage I'm unaware of, Commander?"

"Uh, no, sir," he replies, still looking confused.

I sigh again. "That ship is a light cruiser analog. It means that they probably have enough defensive weaponry that we'll be lucky to get one missile out of five through to strike them, even if they don't know what they're doing and just let their AI have control. Since we don't have ship killers on board, we'll need to hit them with at least three or even four missiles to destroy them. And we have to destroy them fast enough that they can't get to escape pods, or they'll tell everyone we're out here. Understand?"

He nods. "So, it's a numbers game?"

"Basically. Our full broadside is only two dozen missiles. If the pirates are well-trained—never a given—we might get a maximum of five or six through. It'll be a bit more than we need, but it gives us a margin of error if any miss or if they can take out more than I expect. If they're not well trained…" I shrug, leaving the rest unsaid. I fully expect the pirate ship to disappear completely with just our first salvo, though I won't count on it.

We watch the plot as a series of small green dots separate from the larger green dot representing *Odysseus* and fly toward the large red dot, signifying the pirate ship. A few of those green dots converge with the two missiles the pirates fired at us, which wink out as we destroy them.

"They're firing again," Illian says, still sounding almost like he's about to yawn.

"That's a lot of missiles," Traeger says with awe as a flurry of new red dots lance out from the pirate ship.

"They know we're a warship now," I tell him. "Guns, launch a full spread of interceptors and ready point defense turrets. Take over helm control and be ready to roll us on our z-axis so we're always presenting charged weapons toward the enemy." It's more instruction than Illian needs, but I'm overexplaining for the sake of Traeger. No use having a panicked XO on the bridge in the middle of a battle because he doesn't know what's going on.

"That math works both ways, doesn't it?" Traeger asks, almost in a whisper. "Some of those missiles are going to get through, aren't they?"

I nod but don't elaborate. No use giving him false hope.

We watch the plot, and I start counting down to myself in my head. A few minutes pass, and I watch as our missiles converge on the enemy ship.

"Eight direct hits," Illian reports, a small measure of excitement now entering his tone. "Enemy destroyed."

Traeger gives a small but very unprofessional yelp of triumph, then looks sheepish when we all stare at him like he's crazy.

"Seventy-eight percent of enemy missiles destroyed by interceptors. Launching second wave and readying defensive lasers and gatling guns," Illian says next.

"Lipton, get ready to give me everything," I call down to engineering. Then I look over at Saki Hashimoto. "Helm, go to full military power on my mark."

I wait ten more seconds, watching the incoming missiles carefully on the plot and letting my implant calculate the vectors and timing as a backup to my own intuition. Two seconds after my implant declares the timing right, I yell, "Mark!"

A surge of acceleration presses us back into our seats as *Odysseus's* inertial compensators struggle to catch up to our sudden change in power. I keep my eyes glued to the plot, where I see with satisfaction that a portion of the enemy missiles aren't able to change course fast enough to account for our leap forward and look set to fly harmlessly behind us.

The space around *Odysseus* fills with invisible fire as our lasers and gatling guns lance out their destructive energy and projectiles. The remaining missiles drop like flies from the plot, but then the ship shudders underneath us, and we hear the distinctive sound of an explosion aft.

"Direct hit starboard aft," Toshi Ishii calls from the damage control station at the rear of the bridge. "It took out one of the legitimate containers, sir. Full of auto parts."

I grunt, looking back and seeing Hayley Uvalde sitting on the deck next to Toshi, a wicked, gleeful grin on her face. It's probably a good thing she's sitting where Traeger can't see her; she looks scarier right now than any pirate.

"All other missiles destroyed or out of range," Illian reports, and I watch as Jake Traeger practically slumps in his seat in relief.

I ignore him. "Helm, bring us about to search the wreckage for survivors and escape pods."

"So you can kill them?" Traeger asks, horrified, and we all turn to regard him incredulously. "You said," he continues, voice going higher, "that we couldn't leave any survivors. But… but…"

"Pull yourself together, Commander!" I bark harshly. His antics have gotten on my last nerve by now. "Of course we're not going to kill the survivors."

"But you said—"

"I know what I said," I snap back. "But that was when the pirates were in a warship trying to disable and board us. Now they're either in escape pods or a tumbling derelict. The rules change in that situation, and we *don't* kill helpless survivors."

He looks monumentally relieved, but it disappears when I lean over to him and growl under my breath, "Get off my bridge, Traeger. Confine yourself to quarters until we're done here. These kinds of hysterics are dangerous in battle."

Nodding numbly, he doesn't argue. He quickly retreats from the bridge, leaving me and Illian both frowning after him. Only a small part of me is glad to realize that the Naval Intelligence commander is now completely conditioned to follow my orders. I should be happier about that, but this whole situation is still just the worst.

Two hours later, having found no sign of survivors from the would-be pirate ship, we resume our original course toward the Zepha jump point. We're bruised but not damaged in any significant way, and now everyone on our crew has seen combat together. I'm not sure it will be enough when the time comes to fight Hornsby, but it's better than where we started.

I still think we're in way over our heads.

TWENTY-TWO
NEEDLE IN A HAYSTACK
BRAD MENDOZA

"Where do we start?" I ask as I gather my officers all together in *Odysseus*'s wardroom for a conference just hours before we're set to exit the jump into the Zepha system. "I need recommendations on how we find Baron Hornsby once we arrive in system."

"Uh, Captain, what are you wearing?" Traeger asks, staring at me.

I look down. "It's a uniform, sort of, for my mercenary company. It's what I wear when I'm commanding *Bainbridge*."

He cocks a head. "Why does it have so many pockets?"

I frown tightly at him. "I'll have you know, Commander, that it has exactly the *right* number of pockets. Now, please focus! How do we find Hornsby once we're in the Zepha system?"

"Isn't this a Q-ship?" Kelly O'Malley asks from the other end of the table. "I mean, shouldn't we use it like one? Let's find the wannabe noble and blast him out of space before he even knows we're a warship!" It's a surprising show of anger from the ordinarily cheerful man and reminds me of his reaction when he first learned Jessica was missing on Jewel.

"What if they know we're coming?" Opal Winston asks. "They've seemed to be consistently one step ahead of us. And if that Merl fellow got here before us, then Hornsby knows we're after him."

"Maybe, but they won't know we're on this ship," retorts Lieutenant Commander Fara Lipton, Kelly's temporary boss. "We've altered our configuration again and changed the transponders *twice* since leaving Pointon. There's absolutely no way they've been able to track us here."

I don't buy in to her optimism on that point, but I choose not to argue. In fact, I choose not to say anything, letting my subordinates hash things out before I speak up as the captain.

"All we need to do is find where Hornsby is hiding, and my Marines will do the rest," Bryan Shultz says firmly, and unhelpfully.

"A system is a big place," Francis Illian argues. "We're not just going to happen upon the baron, and if we fly the ship around obviously looking for something, then they'll have zero trouble flagging us as not being the freighter we appear to be, no matter how many times we change our configuration or transponder." He looks meaningfully across the table at Fara Lipton, who opens her mouth to argue back.

"Maybe we should just go to the planet and look for clues on the stations and on the surface," Laia Gammon chimes in before Fara can speak again. "Maybe we'll find something or someone who can lead us to Hornsby."

Quin Boyd shakes his head. "Again, too obvious. If we're in orbit or docked too long without a legitimate reason, they'll clue in to us being there under false pretenses. They know to watch for us now, and this whole thing fails if Hornsby runs before we can find him. He has to think he's still safe in Zepha until the last possible moment."

At least no one is arguing anymore that Hornsby isn't in Zepha. At first, much of the crew was skeptical about the conclusions drawn by Traeger, Uvalde, Illian, and Harris. I think in the end, the only thing that convinced them was that people from both sides—my crew and the spooks—were involved in the analysis.

Surprisingly, Shultz was among the first to agree. Ever since Gunny and his team started training with the Marines—Uvalde has even joined in a few times to share some of her moves, though none of Lola's—there's been a noticeable thawing between the Marine captain and myself. It's exactly what I hoped would happen when I set up the first sparring match, but it feels good that it actually worked. He still hates my guts, but he's a little more polite about it now.

"Alright, everyone, that's enough," I finally say, jumping in just as Fara Lipton and Illian start to argue about the best way to keep *Odysseus* disguised while we search the system. To my surprise, they all immediately shut up and look my way. I wasn't really expecting that to work, and it takes me momentarily off guard, so that I pause a little too long before speaking again.

"Listen up," I say at last. "Commander Illian is right. We can't just search the system. Gunny Boyd is right as well; if we're stationary too long over the planet, they'll start to get suspicious real quick." I cut off Illian's triumphant glare at Fara with my next words. "But Commander Lipton is right as well. They likely won't recognize us when we enter the system, and we have a few more configurations we can use to fool them into thinking we're different ships."

I take a deep breath. "So, here's what we're going to do. We're going to fly directly from the jump point to the inhabited planet. There, we'll exchange some cargo. Then, we're going to fly directly to the jump point to Innes on the other side of the system. When we get there, we'll jump out."

They're all looking at me incredulously, and I have to fight to keep from smiling.

"Uh, Skipper?" Illian asks, a bit more timidly than before. "How are we supposed to find Hornsby if we just jump into the system and then leave without even looking?"

"Because, Commander, we're *going* to be looking that entire time. I want every sensor, every receiver on this ship to scan the system around us the entire time we're in transit to the planet and then to the Innes jump point. While we're docked at the cargo transfer station, Lieutenant Uvalde will lead a small team aboard the station to see what they can learn. Then we'll leave, go through every scrap of intel we can find, and when we get to Innes, we'll hopefully have a better picture of where Hornsby is hiding."

"But we won't be there anymore to do anything about it," Shultz argues, though not forcefully. He seems to understand I'm going somewhere with this.

"Correct, *we* won't be. As soon as we arrive in Innes, we'll change configurations and transponders and jump back to Zepha as an entirely different ship. But this time, we'll be able to target our search based on what we learned the first time. From there, we'll do the whole journey again in reverse. And then again, as many times as it takes us to find Hornsby."

"But that could take us days or even weeks to locate him," Illian argues. Like me, he wants this over as quickly as possible. Every moment spent dragging out this mission is a risk that we'll never see Jessica again, despite Traeger's constant assurances that she'll be okay.

I nod. "That could be, but until we have a better plan, this is the best way to find the baron without being too obvious about it." I look at them all in turn. "Unless someone has a better idea."

There are frowns, but no one speaks up.

"Very well. Commander Traeger and Lieutenant Uvalde will coordinate the intelligence gathering. You'll all take your orders from them once we're in system. Dismissed!"

TWENTY-THREE
HARRIS SAVES THE DAY

BRAD MENDOZA

Our first pass through the Zepha system takes a day
and a half. We dock at one of the largest orbitals
around the inhabited planet, where we offload some cargo
and take on a few new containers, apparently full of
cotton, one of the planet's chief exports, along with
murderous cowboys and bloodthirsty crime bosses.

Now we're on our way out of the system toward the
Innes jump point. So far, the trip has yielded just about
nothing.

I've had every member of the crew who's not busy
doing other things enlisted to gather intel the entire day
and a half. Even the Marines have joined in, listening live
to comm chatter throughout the system, straining to hear
anything that might indicate where Baron Hornsby is. The
ship's AI will double-check their work, of course—Harris
has already fed it the search parameters—but it's good to
have a human ear as well. Besides, it's keeping everyone
busy during what would otherwise be a whole lot of
waiting.

And on a ship that's probably always just one step away from mutiny, waiting and thinking isn't something I want any of those Marines doing.

Of course, they're still Marines. And it's not too long before a few of them discover that *Odysseus*'s massive computing power really does mean they can find and listen to just about *any* comm traffic in the system. Luckily, I don't have to intervene. Shultz, in a typical profanity-laced chewing out, informs them that they are highly unlikely to find Baron Hornsby's location in the love letters between miners in the outer system and their girl-friends and wives back on the planet.

Up until now, we haven't picked up a single sign of Hornsby in the system: no comm traffic, no reports of piracy or burgeoning crime, not even oblique references buried in the dark web. Nothing.

Until four hours out from the Innes jump point, when Harris sticks his head through the hatch of my ready room.

"Captain, got a second?" he asks tentatively. I look up from a piece of incredibly boring comm traffic I've been dissecting to look for clues about Hornsby. This one is from a horticulturist in one hemisphere of the planet talking to a zoologist in the other hemisphere; the AI thought the Latin names of the plants and animals they're talking about might be hidden codewords. I think the AI is full of it, and the horticulturist is trying to hit on the zoolo-gist, though it's all buried in nerd speak, which is hard to decipher. Still, there are one or two lines I might need to try on Jessica when we find her again.

"Sure, Harris, come in."

He closes the hatch behind him.

"What's up? This about your special project?" I ask hopefully.

He sits down in the chair across from me and balances his ubiquitous data pad across his knees. "No, Captain. That's going just fine; almost there. But I have a question about something else."

"Shoot," I tell him.

"Why aren't we flying toward Baron Hornsby's hideout?"

I look at him and snicker a little. This guy is so clueless; he has no idea what's going on in the ship around him. "Well, first, we have to find the baron," I tell him wryly.

"Oh." He looks surprised. "You mean that isn't him in that compound on the planet's northern continent?"

I stare at him in shock. When I find my voice, I manage to eke out, "Harris, what are you talking about? What compound?"

He shrugs. "The one in Landing City. You know, big place, lots of guards, high walls?"

I shake my head at him, not giving in to the sudden urge to slap my forehead. "No, I have no idea what you're talking about."

"Huh." He looks mildly surprised. "I thought you knew. That's why I couldn't figure out why we were flying *away* from the planet. I just figured it was one of your plans, Captain. But thought I'd ask just to be safe, you know?"

"Okay, Harris." I lean across the desk. "Tell me everything."

In the end, it's so simple that it makes me want to cry and laugh at the same time. Here, we've been reviewing every single comm message that came through the system, dissecting their contents via AI and human review. And while none of them read anything like a crime boss communicating with his people, we missed one fundamental thing: the encryption schemas.

You see, *Odysseus*'s AI was capturing the comm messages and very helpfully decrypting them for us to read. Spook AIs are built for that sort of thing. It's all been pretty impressive, really, and it proves to me that Naval Intelligence often gets the cool toys before the regular Navy. But *Odysseus* and its super advanced AI weren't with us and *Bainbridge* at Helgatha when we fought Hornsby. Harris was. And while he was idly analyzing some of the Zepha comm traffic on his own, he noticed that the encryption schemas of a few messages matched up with the schema we saw Hornsby use when we fought him at Helgatha.

From there, he backtracked the messages to their source, a compound on Zepha's surface, and from there, he pulled the government blueprints on file, hacked nearby traffic cameras to steal their feeds, and pretty much learned everything possible about Hornsby's hiding place. All while he waited for his code to compile for the other little project I'd given him.

That he waited six hours *after* that to bring all this to my attention is infuriating, but in his typically absentminded way, he was just playing. He thought that surely the Navy spooks on our ship had already figured all of this out; plus, he got distracted by his other project and forgot all about Hornsby for a few hours. It wasn't until he noticed we were burning *away from* the planet that he decided he'd better check with me just to be certain.

"Harris," I say to him, shaking my head. "Sometimes, I

don't know if I should kiss you or throw you out of an airlock."

"Um, I don't think Jessica would appreciate either one," he says, clearly confused.

"Never mind. Petty Officer Harris, how'd you like to be a *Chief* Petty Officer?"

"Is that good?"

TWENTY-FOUR
PLANNING THE LONG CON

BRAD MENDOZA

T he next morning, after Harris's revelation of Hornsby's whereabouts, I gather all my mixed command staff in the wardroom. I shared Harris's findings with them electronically last night, but now I have Harris relate it all to them live.

"How did you recognize a 432-qubit encryption schema just by sight among all that traffic? Didn't the organic algorithm scramble it enough to make it unrecognizable?"

All heads turn to see the speaker, a young woman with short, dirty-blond hair and an anachronistic pair of glasses on her face, shoulders slumped forward, and her expression excited at all of Harris's technobabble.

"And who are you?" I ask, fairly certain I've never seen this particular Navy spook before.

"This is Evelyn Spencer," Traeger says helpfully. "She's one of our top civilian analysts. We brought her along for this sort of thing."

"Okay." I nod. "Harris, want to answer that?"

"Sure," he says, his voice sounding strange. "I recognized a pattern in the final sequence rotations that looked familiar. After that it was a simple matter to compare it to the records I had from Helgatha and verify the blah, blah, blah, blah, blah."

Okay, maybe he doesn't actually say 'blah' that many times, or even once, but that's about the point where I tune out, and his words just all run together. And not just because what he's saying is *so* boring and technical, but also because I'm distracted by the look on his face.

Have you ever seen a puppy and its master? Or a pig and its food trough? How about a Zagorian bathawk and a weevil colony? If you've seen any of those, then you can picture how Harris is looking at Evelyn Spencer.

While the two trade more techno-nonsense, I lean over to Quinn Boyd, who is sitting next to me and watching Harris's face with the same rapt attention. "Is that how I look at Jessica?" I whisper to him.

He turns and gives me a dubious look. "Do you really want me to answer that, Skipper?"

"Okay, fair enough." I clear my throat loudly and address the table again. "Um, as interesting as this all is, the real question is what we're going to do with this knowledge. Major Shultz?"

The Marine nods at me from the other end of the table. I sent him a note last night asking him to workshop various scenarios for taking Hornsby's compound.

"What we have," he begins, throwing up a schematic in share mode so we all see it hovering over the table, "is a classic hardened target with multiple layers of security, each stronger than the one before. From the satellite images Mr. Harris provided,"—he nods to my odd crewman—"we estimate manpower in the compound at somewhere between 40 and 60 able fighters. Normally, that would be no problem for a platoon of His Majesty's Marines, except for this."

The image zooms in to show a picture of a really big and mean-looking turret gun. "This," Shultz explains, "is a Gorendi X-900 point defense turret from a capital ship. We believe that there are eight of them encircling the compound and that they draw power directly from a reactor hidden underneath the place, completely independent from all external power sources. So, cutting the power to them is out. They have nearly spherical fields of fire and pack a punch big enough to take out a ship killer missile.

"In other words, nothing we have can withstand even a single shot from one of these, and Hornsby has them at strategic points along the outer wall that provide overlapping fields of fire. There is nowhere we can attempt to infiltrate on the ground or in the air that is not covered by at least two of these monsters, and the city sewers don't extend underneath the compound, so going *under* is out as well.

"In short, this is a target I don't believe we can crack."

There are frowns around the table and a few mutters. I wave them all silent. "Thank you for the analysis, Major," I say sincerely. I much prefer an honest Marine to one who is so gung-ho he thinks he could take on Hades with a bucket of water. "We need other ideas, people. Since a frontal attack on the compound isn't feasible, how do we draw Hornsby out so we can take him?"

"They're not throwing any charity galas any time soon at the compound, are they?" Laia asks with a slight grin.

"No, why?" Shultz asks in confusion.

"Never mind," I say. "Inside joke. Seriously folks, how do we lure a ruthless and paranoid crime boss out of his impenetrable stronghold so we can kidnap him—excuse me, take him prisoner—and escape before his goons can come after us?"

There are a lot of blank looks all around. Even Hayley shrugs helplessly at me. I'm about to open my mouth to start some brainstorming when Evelyn Spencer speaks up again.

"Uh, Captain, I might have something."

All eyes turn to the mousy analyst, and she physically shrinks under the scrutiny. "What do you have, Mrs. Spencer?" I ask.

"Uh, sir, pardon, but it's *Miss* Spencer. I'm not married."

I look over at Harris and mouth, 'You're welcome', then turn my attention back to the analyst. "Go on, Miss Spencer, tell us your idea."

"Well, now that we know what messages in the system are from Hornsby and his people, I've been running an algorithmic search—"

"Heuristic or multidirectional?" Harris interrupts, sounding excited and a little nervous.

"Both, actually, along with a standard NLP."

Uh oh, Harris is in love. It's clear as day on his face. I may never get him to focus on anything ever again.

"Miss Spencer," I interrupt. "What's your point?" I try to sound gentle, but she shrinks a little more into her turtleneck.

"Well, they're talking in code, Captain. They don't trust their encryption, and with good reason. There isn't an encryption schema in the Fringe we can't crack, except for the ones in people's implants, of course, so—"

"The point, Evelyn?" Traeger prods, not sounding nearly as gentle as I tried to.

"Oh, I think they're building something. A lot of some-things, really."

The collective eyebrows in the room rise a little bit higher.

"Explain, Miss Spencer," I say gently.

She sits up a little straighter. "It all started with pota-toes, sir."

"Potatoes?"

"Yes, sir. I found a freighter manifest outlining the delivery of 54 sacks of potatoes supposedly going to a research station on the seventh moon of Romana, one of the system's gas giants."

"And why is that unusual?" Shultz presses. "People buy potatoes all the time."

Evelyn shrugs. "But do they pay a hundred thousand credits per bag? Or send them to a desolate ice moon that has no inhabitants or research stations on any records I could find?"

Anyone not paying attention to the mousy analyst before is now giving Evelyn Spencer their full and undi-vided attention. Harris never stopped, and the guy is prac-tically drooling now. Someone needs to tell him to close his mouth. If this is even *close* to how I look at Jessica, I'm surprised she doesn't slap me every time we're in a room together.

"Isolated event?" I press.

Evelyn shakes her head. "No, Captain. There are two to three incoming shipments every week to that same import/export company that follow the same pattern: a shipment of women's clothing last week for two million credits; a cargo of anti-diarrheal medicine after that for 24 thousand per bottle. All going to that same moon."

"That's a lot of diarrhea," someone quips, and I have to fight not to laugh. The captain needs to be stoic, right?

"What do you think the true cargo is? And why do you think it involves Hornsby?" Traeger asks.

Evelyn frowns. "Not sure about the first. For that, we'd have to know what the manifests are hiding. As for the second, Mr. Harris solved that for me."

"I did?" Harris asks, wide-eyed, looking at her like she just proposed marriage.

She nods. "Once you identified Hornsby's encryption schema, I went back and checked on these manifests. They all were sent with the same schema. It has to be the baron."

There are mutters around the table. I let it go on for a couple of seconds before clearing my throat to silence the compartment.

"Miss Spencer," I start, "now that you know what to look for, any chance you could find the manifest for a shipment that *hasn't* been delivered yet?"

By the smile that breaks out on her face, I know the answer before she gives it. "Yes, sir! In fact, there's one that says it's carrying 64 bushels of apples for two million credits. It's going to arrive on a freighter called the MV *Hassan* that's due in the system the day after tomorrow."

I smile and shake my head. "No it's not."

She looks confused and consults the data pad in front of her. "I'm sorry, sir, but I have the manifest and schedule right here. MV *Hassan* is due to reach Romana's seventh moon at 1100 hours two days from now."

I shake my head again. "Nope. Because someone's going to steal that shipment."

"They are?" she asks in amazement. "Who?"

Hayley and Traeger both roll their eyes, and Shultz frowns at the analyst's innocent gullibility.

"We are," I announce, almost giddy considering the situation. "It's time to play commerce raider. Harris!" I turn and regard the man, who reluctantly takes his eyes off Evelyn Spencer and meets my gaze. "Time to make some uniforms." Then I turn and grin at Traeger before continuing. "And Mr. Harris, make sure they have a *lot* of pockets!"

TWENTY-FIVE
ROYAL INTRIGUE

JESSICA LIN

"So, the Duke of Kipling just *gave* you a destroyer?"

I study Jethro across the interrogation room's table. It's day 12 of answering his never-ending questions. And I still feel no closer to convincing him that anything I'm saying is the truth. I'm also seriously questioning what I ever saw in him that made me convince myself I was in love with the man. How much of my infatuation then was simply because I was just happy *someone* wanted me after Hothan and Yolandra? It's easy to forget, in all that's happened since, just how desperate I was for any kind of external validation in the years immediately following my colossal failure and betrayal.

"No, not just the duke," I reply in a longsuffering tone. "He and Admiral Pettigrew *both* felt that interstellar salvage laws dictated that—"

He cuts me off. "Salvage laws that no judge would ever interpret as allowing a civilian to abscond with hundreds of millions of credits of military hardware and weaponry."

I just shrug. We've already had this argument multiple

times. The more I insist, the more he digs in his heels and tells me why I can't possibly be telling the truth.

He frowns again—it's been his most common expression the entire time I've been on Lightman Station—and refers to something in his notes. When he looks up at me again, there's a new intensity in his eyes, and I get the unmistakable impression that something has changed.

"Now, what *exactly* did Duke Garrison tell Brad Mendoza when he supposedly hired the two of you to go and 'rescue' his sister from Koratan space?" The way he says 'rescue', I know he doesn't believe that's what our mission truly was.

I take a moment to consider my response, surprised to suddenly realize that our latest mission into Koratan space to rescue Larissa Garrison has barely come up in the almost two weeks of questioning I've undergone. It's as if he and the others have been building up to this.

Which means I need to be incredibly careful about how I answer his questions from here on out. At least until I can figure out their game.

"I wasn't there when they spoke," I tell Jethro honestly. I *don't* tell him that Brad recorded the conversation and played it back for me word for word. "But according to what Brad told me, the duke felt his little sister left Kipling unwillingly, captured by rebellious elements to be taken to Koratan space in an attempt to leverage her to foment some kind of action against the Crown. Our mission was to follow her trail into the Confederacy, find and rescue her, and bring her back to her brother. Which is exactly what we did."

He nods along and makes rapid notes on his pad, another signal that he's far more interested in my answer to this question than the myriad of others he's asked me before.

"And, in your opinion, did Duke Garrison know it was his own mother, ex-Duchess Charlotte, who had kidnapped his sister, Larissa?" He leans forward slightly as if to better hear my answer.

Here it is. I suddenly realize that this is the real reason that he effectively kidnapped me from Jewel to bring me here. The last dozen days have been softening me up so that I'll tell them what they *really* want to know.

They're trying to figure out if Laraby Garrison was involved in his mother's treason. This entire thing, ripping me from my fiancé and friends, threatening me with their deaths and my own, and locking me in this tiny room for days on end, is all because of the King's paranoia about his own family betraying him.

I'm here because of Royal Family drama!

"To my knowledge," I start, speaking carefully, "Duke Garrison was as surprised as we were to learn that Duchess Charlotte was behind Larissa's kidnapping. Frankly, I think it surprised him that she was even still alive."

That's not strictly true, of course. The duke never came out and said as much, but Brad and I are both pretty certain that he knew, or at least strongly suspected, his mother's role both in Larissa's kidnapping and the growing voices in Koratas calling for war against Prometheus. In fact, we're also pretty sure that the reason he chose Brad to rescue Larissa was so that, if we failed and got captured, Laraby Garrison could mend fences with the duchess by delivering her Brad, the man she hated almost more than the King himself. After all, Brad foiled her family's plans for a coup against King Charles... twice! I guess three times now.

I can tell that Jethro doesn't believe me, but at least he moves on from that question. It takes *six* hours and a lot of coffee, but we go through, in minute detail, my version of events from our mission to Serenidad, our recovery of Larissa Garrison there, and our flight from Koratan space, including our battle with Baron Dexter Hornsby in the Helgatha system, another part of the story that Jethro seems very interested in.

I'm careful to leave out anything about Larissa's very real and willing participation in her mother's rebellion, her betrayal of us at Helgatha, and anything else that might cast suspicion on the duke and his surviving family. Brad and I may be upset about Duke Garrison using us the way he did, but we've also both decided that we can't afford to burn our bridges with the second most powerful man in the Promethean Federation.

At times, especially as I outline our run-ins with Baron Hornsby, it's clear that Jethro already knows a lot of what I'm telling him. So it's hard to discern if he's trying harder to fill in the blanks he doesn't know or to catch me in a lie when I contradict something he already does.

It makes for an incredibly nerve-racking day, and by the end, I'm practically shaking from all the adrenaline and caffeine in my system. I want to slump in relief when he finally declares we're done for the afternoon.

When a couple of Marines deliver me back to the simple bachelor officer's quarters that is my off-hours prison, I fall onto the bed and scream into the pillow, punching the mattress underneath me several times to release the pent-up frustration and energy from the day's ordeal. All of this because our King is an insecure child of a man who wants me and Brad dead for revealing his nephew's dirty secret and is now using us to figure out his own cousin's loyalty. If King Charles were here on the station, I'd find a way to throw him out of an airlock.

Practically shaking with rage, I turn on the room's small viewscreen—its only concession to my comfort—and cue up the next episode of *The Adventures of Firebrand's Marauders*.

I've seen every episode before, of course; Brad made me watch them all with him… twice. And they're just as ridiculous and over-the-top now as they were then. But having the show on is comforting and immediately helps me relax by degrees—it reminds me of Brad and almost makes me feel like he's here with me. As the opening credits roll with absurdly large explosions, unrealistic space battles with ships full of windows shooting at each other from just meters away, and the hero with his ridiculous mustache and two very attractive women on each arm, tears start to stream down my cheeks.

TWENTY-SIX
COMMERCE RAIDERS
(DEFINITELY NOT PIRATES)

BRAD MENDOZA

The trouble with being a wanted crime boss trying to smuggle expensive goods past multiple system governments is that you can't be too obvious about it. This is probably why MV *Hassan*, the ship carrying whatever it is that Hornsby is trying to get his hands on next, is traveling without weapons of its own or even an escort.

At first, I worried it was all an act—that *Hassan* must be a Q-ship just like *Odysseus*. But deep sensor scans have pretty much proven that's not the case. The fact that we've even gotten close enough to do those scans without so much as a twitch from *Hassan* is another clue that she is what she appears to be.

Stupid, right? Well, not so much, really. Who would honestly suspect a dumpy tramp freighter like *Hassan* of carrying potentially the most valuable cargo within four parsecs? If I were a pirate captain, I wouldn't even want to waste my time with such an obviously down-on-its-luck ship.

"MV *Hassan*," Traeger says stoically into the camera when the freighter is just three hours away from the jump point to Zepha. My temporary XO is wearing the white-on-green uniform of a Leeward Republic Navy Auxiliary. Harris really outdid himself; there are even extra pockets. "This is Commerce Raider LRS *Duncan*, operating under the remit of the Congress of the Leeward Republic. We have reports that you are transporting illegal Republic weapons. You will heave to and prepare to be boarded, or we will fire on you."

"Guns," I tell Illian as soon as the message is sent. "Put a laser blast right off their bow. Might as well show them quickly that we mean business."

"Aye, sir. Firing one across their bow."

I imagine the panicked argument happening on the *Hassan's* bridge right now. I have no idea what their cargo really is—it's almost certainly *not* Republic weapons—but I'm sure it's illegal and very expensive. So right now, they have to be debating whether it's worth incurring Baron Hornsby's wrath by surrendering without a fight or if they're more afraid of the heavily armed commerce raider that just put a laser blast within a few hundred meters of their nose.

As it is, it only takes one or two more transmissions from Traeger and a few close shots from Illian before MV *Hassan's* captain surrenders. Imagine his surprise when, instead of a boarding party in Leeward Republic Greens, he's faced with a bunch of Promethean Marines wearing street clothes and trying very hard *not* to look like Marines —and failing very hard at it as well.

TWENTY-SEVEN
DANGLING THE BAIT
BRAD MENDOZA

"Zepha Station, this is MV *Williamsburg*. We need to report a derelict ship back in the Cochran System. Freighter by the name of MV *Hassan*."

We wait several minutes for Traeger's message to reach Zepha Station and several more minutes for their response to reach us as we fly along in the outer system.

"Roger, *Williamsburg*, did you report the encounter to Cochran Station?"

Traeger records his reply. "We did, Zepha Station. But given the nature of the situation, they asked us to pass along the warning to you."

Another long wait.

"Roger, *Williamsburg*. Why did they want you to warn us?"

"Looked like pirates, Zepha Station. But they only took part of the cargo. We found a hidden compartment in the hold with more in it. Highly unusual stuff—military-grade goods. Ship's manifest suggested they were bound for this system, but there's no final destination or recipient beyond that."

The minutes tick by.

"Roger, *Williamsburg*. What kind of military goods? And where are they now?"

"We have them in our hold, Zepha Station. As to the nature of the goods, probably not something to put over an open channel. Just letting you know that we've declared salvage rights. We're going to stop at the outer system fuel depot, and then we'll bring them straight on in for inspection, and you can decide whether or not the system government wants them."

Tick, tock. Tick, tock.

"Negative, *Williamsburg*. We'd like you to just come straight here. You can top off your tanks on station."

"Negative, Zepha Station. We burned our reserve responding to *Hassan*'s distress beacon. If we don't get fuel fast, we'll hit you ballistic."

The conversation goes back and forth a few more times, all over an open channel as is standard for communications between stations and legitimate merchant ships. Now, we just have to hope the right people are listening.

TWENTY-EIGHT
SETTING THE HOOK
BRAD MENDOZA

"Captain, new sensor contacts bearing oh-four-one mark seven on an intercept course," Laia Gammon calls across the bridge. "They're trying to hide their drive plumes, but our sensors picked them out."

I feel my body relax a little in relief. We took our sweet time at the outer system refueling station. It was fully automated, so there was no one to question why we filled up with so little fuel after telling the system traffic controller we were low or why we spent several more hours than necessary to do so.

But we left the station an hour ago to start our slow, meandering journey toward the inner system and the inhabited planet. I was beginning to think *no one* was going to try and kill us and take our cargo today. That would have been terrible!

I turn to Illian. "Guns, work with Laia to find out everything you can about those ships. I want to know weaponry, crew complement, and what the captains had for breakfast."

Traeger breaks in before Illian can acknowledge my

order. "The bearing implies they're coming from the planet. You think it's Hornsby?"

I shrug. "I'm hoping. We broadcast in the clear, so it could be another opportunistic parasite coming to take our unspecified military-grade cargo. But I'm willing to bet that anyone else who would normally try is getting waved off by the baron. I'm also willing to bet no one else in this system has three warships they can call upon."

Traeger nods. "One thing about this entire situation still bothers me."

I look over at him, raising an eyebrow, which he takes as permission to continue.

"What's he doing out at that moon that requires the 64 focusing lenses we liberated from the MV *Hassan*?"

I shrug. "Ask your pet analyst."

"I did. Miss Spencer says that only two things use those exact lenses: one specific and rare type of industrial mining laser and military-grade jump drives."

Turning in my seat, I look at him sharply. "Really? Nothing else?"

Traeger shakes his head. "Nothing else she could find, at least. So either Hornsby has a rather large and unique mining operation on that ice moon, or…"

"Or he's building military-grade jump drives. But why would he do that? Jump drives are expensive, but not so much that it's worth the trouble and secrecy of setting up your own manufacturing facility and smuggling in the components."

"That's what worries me," he replies. "None of it makes sense. And you don't get to be as wealthy and powerful as Dexter Hornsby by spending money where you don't need to."

"So, unless that moon is just a waypoint in his supply

chain—and let's assume it's not—then he's building something out there. Did Miss Spencer happen to say where he's shipping whatever finished product he's building?"

He frowns and his eyes go out of focus as he checks Evelyn's report on his implant. "Interesting," he finally says. "The outgoing manifests list a variety of systems, but she traced them all to the Reynolds system, to the galactic southwest."

I lick my lips and nod. A quick check of my implant shows Reynolds is a very small independent system just outside the Promethean Federation. There are not nearly enough people there to use specialized mining lasers *or* military-grade jump drives. No, the true destination must be elsewhere in that direction, and I start to suspect I know where it must be.

I blow out a long sigh through pursed lips. Why does it always have to be so complicated? It seems that every time I get involved in something, it turns into some grand conspiracy. Sometimes, I feel like I'm a character in a TV or book series, and the writers *really* have it out for me. What did I ever do to them? Jerks.

"Well, one thing's for sure," I tell Traeger.

"What's that?"

"We'll have the opportunity to ask Hornsby in just a few hours." I nod toward the forward viewscreen where Laia, not wanting to interrupt our conversation, has put up the latest sensor feed. On it, I can see three ships: a destroyer and two *very* familiar-looking frigates. The last time I saw ships of that class was in the Helgatha system. It certainly appears that Baron Hornsby has come out to recover his stolen shipment.

TWENTY-NINE
REELING IT IN
BRAD MENDOZA

"Captain, the lead ship is hailing us. Would you like me to put it on the forward viewscreen?" Opal Winston asks.

"Please do, but make sure our feed is limited to Commander Traeger," I reply.

Jake Traeger is out of his fake Leeward Republic privateer uniform and is now dressed like a typical freighter captain in a plain gray skinsuit with a utility belt adorned with random tools. He even took my advice and hasn't shaved since the Cochran system. He has a passable shadow of whiskers on his face—not enough to look unprofessional for a freighter, but enough to lessen the Navy in his appearance.

Opal does as asked, and an image appears on the screen of a man I've never seen before, wearing clothing very similar to Traeger's. I feel a flash of disappointment that it's not Hornsby, but I also didn't expect him to reveal himself quite this soon—assuming he's even *on* one of the approaching ships. I'm hoping he is, but I'm a lot less

165

confident about it than I led everyone to believe when I told them my plan.

"MV *Williamsburg*, this is Captain Trask of the *MV Sisko*. I believe you are in possession of a cargo that belongs to us, and I wanted to save you the time and fuel of heading to the planet and instead conduct our transaction out here. We're willing to pay what we'd agreed on with MV *Hassan*, of course, plus a finder's fee that I think you'll find quite generous."

Okay, so the guy doesn't beat around the bush. That's good—saves us time.

Traeger gives the response we agreed upon. "MV *Sisko*, this is Captain O'Reilly. I appreciate you trying to save us the trip, but we've already committed to delivering the cargo to Zepha Station. I'm sure you can sort out proper ownership with them. But we wouldn't mind an escort on the way in if you're willing."

I bite the inside of my lip as we wait for the transmission to hit the enemy ships and for their reply to come. Traeger isn't much of an actor; he's sort of managed to mask his accent, but his diction still screams aristocratic officer. I just hope the baron and his people are too excited about getting their lost cargo to notice.

"Sorry, MV *Williamson*," the reply finally comes, "but you should know that if you deliver to Station Control, they're likely to hold any payment in escrow pending a full investigation. Might end with you not getting paid for several months, if at all. Likewise, we wouldn't get our goods very quickly that way. I was hoping we could work out some sort of deal to avoid all that. I believe it's in both our best interests, wouldn't you agree?"

"Sorry, MV *Sisko*, but we're looking to avoid any issues with the authorities. Let us deliver the load to the station as promised, and you can negotiate with them on the particulars after that."

The response that comes next is predictable. Gone is Captain Trask's nice-guy routine. His face is hard. "Listen, Captain O'Reilly, I've been polite and tried to find something we can do that benefits us all. But if you're not willing to be reasonable, I'm afraid we're going to have a problem."

"Skipper," Illian reports from the tactical station. "They've locked on to us with active sensors."

"Thanks, Guns." Just as expected.

I won't bore you with the words of the next couple of messages back and forth. It's enough to say that Captain Trask goes very quickly from conciliatory and gracious to outright pirate, threatening to fire on us if we don't heave to and prepare to be boarded.

Traeger, for his part, does a passable job of playing the indignant role of a captain about to be set upon by pirates intent on stealing his very valuable cargo. I could have done better, sure, but Hornsby would have recognized me instantly. Same likely goes for any member of my crew. Maybe if Traeger had spent less time on the lacrosse field or the polo grounds, he could have taken a theater class.

"Talk to me, squints," I say quietly into my comm so that I don't distract Traeger as he orders the ship to stop acceleration and, in all respects, be ready to surrender and be boarded.

"Captain, I really don't like that nickname," Evelyn Spencer replies.

In the background, I hear Harris arguing with her and telling her to just go with it. He's doing so in a very timid fashion, but it's nice to see his irrational fear of me is still stronger than his obvious crush on her.

"Sorry," I respond. "Tell me we have him."

"We think so, Captain," Harris comes back. "We can't be sure, but the message traffic between the destroyer and the planet does hint that Hornsby himself is on board."

The knots in my shoulders relax just a bit. This was the biggest risk of the operation. I thought I knew Hornsby well enough to guess that he would want to personally oversee an act of piracy like this one—his reputation in Promethean space is of a man who likes to pull the trigger himself—but I couldn't be sure in this instance. Now, it sounds like I was probably right.

"Terrific. Thanks to you both. Keep listening in; tell me the instant you get firmer confirmation."

"Yes, sir," they reply in tandem, and I cut the connection. Two meters away, Traeger is still talking to Captain Trask, his tone one of dejected surrender.

I check my implant's connection to the ship's AI and see that the enemy flotilla is an hour away from weapons range with *Odysseus*. I turn and leave the bridge to head back to Marine country. Time to get the grunts ready to shoot at things.

THIRTY

BEATING IT WITH A STICK
BRAD MENDOZA

"Captain, I'll need 30 seconds to retract the false container sides, expose the weapons, and fire," Illian reminds me.

I nod, not even wanting to whisper as the destroyer—it's an honest-to-goodness Koratan Scimitar class—draws close. Why is it *always* a Scimitar that's trying to kill me?

"Sir, are we sure we want to let them dock with us?" Cory Hanson asks over the intercom from the CIC. "Why don't we just hit them now with a few scramblers and then board them at our leisure?"

I frown. We've been over this several times, but from the tone of his voice, it's the nerves talking, so I humor the Naval Intel lieutenant and my backup tactical officer.

"Because the only thing we've got going for us right now is the element of surprise," I explain calmly. "That destroyer has a crew of a hundred if he has it fully staffed. And, knowing Hornsby, he's got a few mech troops mixed in with his normal ones; he hit us with those at Hegatha. If we disable them, they'll have all the time they need to prepare to repel our boarding action, and a lot of Marines will die—maybe all of them."

He doesn't argue the point.

"Twenty seconds to contact," Laia whispers from the sensor station. It's amazing how we all default to staying quiet, as if the enemy might hear us through two thick hulls separated by vacuum. It's ridiculous, especially for those of us who have lived most of our adult lives in space. But it's hardwired into the human psyche to be as silent as possible when you're being hunted, and I've known few seasoned spacers who have ever overcome that instinct.

"They've docked," Illian announces.

"Shultz," I say into the intercom. "Be ready."

I get two clicks as acknowledgment. Despite my personal issues with the Martine captain, I've really missed working with professional Marines. I almost start to feel bad for Hornsby... almost.

"Airlock door is being hacked," Harris says from the secondary tactical station at the back of the bridge. "Whoever they've got is okay, but I've told the AI to let them in easily so they won't realize this ship has military security."

I nod. All according to plan so far. I watch the forward viewscreen, which is currently showing a security feed of Traeger waiting at the airlock, still playing the character of Captain O'Reilly of the merchant vessel *Williamsburg*. By the terrified look on his face, I can even believe he's nothing more than a freighter captain waiting for a bunch of pirates to board his ship.

The inner airlock door finally clangs open, and three men and a woman with assault rifles rush through. Two of them lower their guns and grab Traeger by each arm, while a third roughly frisks him, and the fourth scans the surrounding corridors with her rifle.

We can hear them talking, demanding he take them to the bridge, which he reluctantly agrees to do, leading them through the corridors toward the false bridge set up to look like a true freighter's command center. Waiting there will be Opal Winston and Fara Lipton, playing the parts of two of Captain O'Reilly's officers. There will also be a squad of Marines hidden just outside.

Another squad of enemy soldiers comes on board, turning to go in the opposite direction toward the cargo containers and engineering. Unless they take a wrong turn somewhere, they'll get all the way to the containers before they realize this isn't a standard freighter, and I'm hoping by then, it'll be far too late for them. We have Marines waiting in that direction as well.

Four more enemy troops come through the airlock and take up guard positions on either side of its hatch. Their presence is a minor complication but not an unanticipated one. We wait a minute more to ensure no more of Hornsby's people are planning to board our ship. They must figure an even dozen is enough, because no one else appears through the airlock. Satisfied, I give my secure comm to Shultz the two-click signal. A false bulkhead near the airlock slides aside quickly, and the four enemy soldiers standing guard don't have time to do more than look surprised before they slump to the ground and Marines with smoking, silenced weapons move past them.

On the vid feed, Shultz himself leaves the hidden compartment with more than two dozen of his Marines, all heavily armed and in ballistic armor. After the five we lost on Valle de Oro, this represents his full effective fighting force, less the eight he's leaving behind to take out the other enemy troops already on board *Odysseus*.

Silently and efficiently, Shultz and his Marines move through the airlock and onto Hornsby's ship. At least, I *hope* it's Hornsby's ship. My resident squints—Harris and Evelyn—haven't been able to find any further confirmation that he's on board the destroyer. But either way, we're committed.

"Guns, now," I tell Illian, and he presses a button on his console that slides back the false container and hull covers spread across our ship. I imagine that the sensor officer on that destroyer is frowning at his screen right now, trying to figure out what's happening. He's probably calling over Captain Trask or even Hornsby to tell them that something is wrong, probably at the same time they're getting panicked reports of Promethean Marines on board.

I smile as the two small frigates escorting the destroyer start to fire their thrusters to take evasive action. It's too late.

"Fire!" I yell my single favorite word, and Francis Illian gleefully complies.

Lances of energy spear out from *Odysseus*'s heavy cruiser–size laser projectors, slicing into the two frigates like a hot knife through butter. At such close range, the lasers hit with their full force, and I watch with a predatory grin as the running lights of both ships flicker and the frigates start uncontrolled tumbles through space, one of them breaking into two pieces where one of our shots severed its spine.

As whoops of triumph echo across the bridge, I start to get reports from across the ship. The Marines who stayed behind have successfully taken out all of the men and women Hornsby sent to board us. Now, the only thing left to do is take over the destroyer and capture the crime boss and his top people.

"Encountering heavy resistance!" Shultz shouts through the comm. "They were ready for us!"

"They knew we were looking for them," Illian observes solemnly from the tactical station. "Must have suspected a trap."

I nod. "But at least they didn't suspect a Q-ship." Then I turn to the comm. "Gunny, go!" I watch on the vid feed as Gunny, Kluth, Forbes, and Hayley rush through the airlock to support the Marines.

It's over in less than 20 minutes. Hornsby's people, criminals and mercenaries for hire, can't withstand an assault by trained Marines. When it's done, I see Quinn and his team return through the airlock to guard it against any counterattacks from Hornsby's remaining people, just as Shultz calls me with a mix of good news and bad from the enemy ship's bridge.

"Captain, we've secured the bridge and engineering. There are a few pockets of resistance, but nothing that threatens our control of the ship. Unfortunately, there's no sign of Baron Hornsby on board, and the crew maintains that they've never heard of him."

I slam a fist down on the arm of my command chair. Then, another voice speaks up in the comm. "Captain Shultz, Captain Mendoza, this is Lieutenant Porter. My team has successfully taken the engineering compartment, but there's something odd going on down here."

"Spit it out, Porter, what is it?" Shultz orders.

"We're not exactly sure, sir. The controls here are all locked out, which is normal for when a ship gets boarded, but there are some weird spiky energy readings from the reactor. And everyone down here seems real nervous."

"Lieutenant." A new voice breaks in. "This is Commander O'Malley. Look at the consoles around you. What else do you see?"

"Uh, not much, sir. Most are blanked out except for what looks like a loading bar, like someone rebooted them. But it's red; I wonder why the Kories use red for that."

"Captain Shultz, get your Marines off that ship now!" Kelly practically screams into the comm. "That reactor is going to blow!"

I listen in stunned silence—nothing I say will do more than distract the Marines—as Shultz tries to organize his men and woman and get them off the Scimitar-class destroyer. Before Porter and his Marines leave engineering, O'Malley has them set up a small camera and comm repeater so he can watch the progress of that red 'loading' bar, which he confirms grimly is a progress indicator for the reactor going critical.

In all the chaos, I have two thoughts. First, I can't risk letting any of the doomed sailors from Hornsby's ship escape to mine; we'd be overrun. Second, we're not going to get all our own people off in time.

"Kelly, how long?" I ask as I watch the camera feed of the first squad of Marines that crosses over and exits the airlock back onto *Odysseus*. Gunny, Beck, Uvalde, and Forbes, guarding the hatch, wave them through while they fire beyond them, doubtlessly to keep some of Hornsby's crew from rushing in after the Marines.

"Four minutes, Skipper. Maybe five if we're lucky."

"There's no way to reverse it?"

"Not without the command codes."

I slam a fist onto the arm of my chair in frustration and rage.

"Captain," Illian reports, his voice flat. "If we don't

undock and get going now, we won't reach minimum safe distance in time."

I shake my head, refusing to hear what he's saying but knowing that he's right. In fact, it's almost certainly too late. Ironic that I'll be killed by a self-destructing Scimitar the same way I killed its sister ship by self-destructing *Persephone* at Gerson.

"Captain," Illian pleads, his voice growing insistent. "We have to go now!" I can hear the pain behind his words, but I curse his callousness in my mind nonetheless. So many Marines are still on that ship. We have to—

"*Odysseus,* go!" Shultz yells over the comm, having reached the same conclusion as Illian.

I open my mouth to refuse but can't make the words come. Without waiting for my orders, the latest two Marines to come through the airlock hatch turn around and close it behind them, sealing it tight. Even on the camera feed, I can see the anger and tears on both of their faces.

"Captain, we have to go!" Illian repeats, practically shouting.

"Saki, full military power! All crew, brace for impact!" I shout, my voice hoarse. I feel the ship lurch underneath me as it separates from the destroyer, and then I feel it surge forward, pressing me into the back of my seat. In our wake, the Scimitar spins out of control when our main drive exhaust hits it.

Less than a minute later, the enemy ship explodes, and *Odysseus* lurches again. We find ourselves thrown against our restraints in virtually every direction as our ship begins to tumble through space. Klaxons sound and red lights flash across every console as the AI reports damage throughout the ship. My vision blacks out for a second as the blood rushes to my feet, and then my head pounds as blood rushes back to it.

Over and over again we tumble until the AI finally brings us back under some semblance of control using the surviving thrusters. I check my console, my mouth dropping open as I see the damage reports scrolling past.

"Sir," Laia says from her station, sounding drunk and slurring her words. "There's another ship, sir. A shuttle. Looks like it detached from the destroyer a few minutes before it self-destructed. Must have kept them between us, sir. I missed it."

"It's okay," I say, my own words almost unintelligible as I struggle to find my equilibrium again. Just a few seconds pass before I feel better—one of the advantages of so much time in space and in combat—and then I start barking orders, mostly about where to send the surviving Marines as damage control parties. There are far too few of them.

THIRTY-ONE

THE BIGGER FISH ESCAPES
BRAD MENDOZA

"Sir, that shuttle isn't headed toward the planet," Illian reports. "Its vector will take it to Romana."

"The moon," Traeger practically whispers beside me. He rejoined me on the main bridge after we got our mad tumble through space under control. He has a cut over one eye and dried blood going down one side of his face but seems otherwise unhurt. The same can't be said for some of the other crew. Several of them weren't strapped in when the blast from the self-destructing Scimitar hit us, and they took nasty falls.

"Well," I say to him, "I suppose we'll get to find out what he's building out there after all."

He looks over at me sharply, his eyes wide and stricken. He's taking the loss of Shultz and the Marines hard. We all are, really, but for Traeger, heavy losses on a mission are a new experience, and he has to be second-guessing everything we've done up to this point. As for me, I've had enough experience to know that sometimes missions go sideways, and there's nothing you can do about it. The self-recriminations will still come, and they'll hit me hard, but years in combat have taught me to shove those emotions down until the mission is complete.

"You're not seriously suggesting we go *after* him!" Traeger protests. "What about the damage to *Odysseus*?"

I meet his gaze, my eyes hard. "You told me that I have to capture Baron Dexter Hornsby, or I'll never see Jessica Lin again, right? Tell me, Jake,"—I emphasize his name like a swear word—"are you willing to promise me here and now that, if I don't follow that shuttle, you'll reunite me with Jessica and set us both free?"

He hesitates, which is all the answer I need.

"Helm. Coordinate with engineering and give me the max advisable drive power to go after the shuttle. Illian, if we can get in range of that thing, I want you to launch a spread of scramblers. Maybe we can catch them before they reach the moon."

As my bridge crew sets about fulfilling my orders, I sit back in my chair, gingerly stretching my neck to loosen up the knots and pulled muscles from our ordeal. I grimly watch on the viewscreen as Hornsby's shuttle—it only makes sense that the man himself is aboard, running like a rat from a sinking ship—slowly increases the distance between us. I marvel at a man so callous that he would destroy his own ship and every one of his people on it just to escape capture himself… or just for a chance to take out an enemy.

Despite my question to Traeger, I'll admit that I would be chasing Hornsby now even *if* Jake promised he'd reunite me with Jessica regardless. The crime boss and self-proclaimed baron has made this personal—for a second time—and I intend to see this through to the end.

THIRTY-TWO
DINNER WITH MY EX
JESSICA LIN

At the end of the 14th day of my interrogation on Lightman Station—a day in which I feel I've continued to do absolutely nothing to paint myself and Brad in a good light—Jethro surprises me by breaking routine.

Usually, when the day of endless questions is finally over, Jethro has the Marines come and take me away immediately. But this time, he leaves me sitting there in silence as he reviews and makes any final notations to his record of my answers from the day.

Sensing something is about to happen, I sit quietly, one leg bouncing up and down in anxiety. I'm almost certain that the time has finally come for him to tell me I'll be leaving on the next transport to Prometheus for my trial and inevitable execution. But when he finally looks up, he gives me a tight smile.

"It occurs to me, Lieutenant Commander Lin, that you haven't had a break from this for two weeks now. If you promise to behave yourself, I've arranged dinner for us at O'Rourke's on level four."

The statement takes me by such surprise that my mouth drops open, and I lose the ability to speak for a moment. So I just nod.

He returns the nod curtly. "Very well. The Marines will escort us and watch you while there, of course, but you can use this as an opportunity to stretch your legs and get a change of scenery for an hour or two before we put you back in your room."

I nod dumbly again and allow him to lead the way out of the hatch and into the corridor, where the two Marines on duty eye me like I'm a viper that might lash out at any moment. Jethro ignores them, and I follow him out of the Navy offices and into the corridors of the civilian part of the station. Ten minutes later, we're seated at a table in the back of O'Rourke's, a mid-level restaurant that's fancy by Lightman standards. In fact, this is where Jethro proposed, something I try very hard not to think about now.

Our two Marine escorts are seated at a table near the front of the dining room, close enough to keep an eye on us but far enough away not to hear our conversation over the general hubbub of the restaurant.

The waiter comes and takes our drink orders, and I otherwise hold my tongue, waiting for Jethro to be the first to speak. I've known the man long enough to sense that something big has changed and that he's debating what to say to me and how. My mind again flashes to the night he proposed. Back then, he also spent the first several minutes of dinner working up the courage to tell me what he came here to say. But I suspect I'm not going to like whatever he says today nearly as much.

Finally, after the drinks arrive, he scoots forward to the edge of his chair and looks at me intently. "Your friend, Mendoza, isn't at Jewel anymore."

The news takes me completely off guard, and I take a long sip of my drink to consider it before responding.

"So, where is he?" I ask.

"On a ship of ours, helping us hunt down Dexter Hornsby in the independent sector."

I set my drink down, a little too hard, wincing as the glass smacks the table like a gunshot. I've imagined all sorts of scenarios for what has happened to Brad and my crew during my imprisonment here. I've imagined him already at Prometheus, standing trial or even facing the executioner's bullet. I've cried for hours at the mere thought. And I've smiled grimly, imagining him escaping Jewel and coming after me, storming the station and rescuing me with a lopsided grin and an inappropriate joke.

But that Brad would be *helping* Naval Intelligence never occurred to me, and I can't possibly imagine why he would...

My jaw clenches, and my hands turn to fists on the table in front of me because, suddenly, things are starting to make sense.

"You took me prisoner to make Brad go after Hornsby for you." I growl the accusation at Jethro, resisting the urge to lean across the table and punch my ex-fiancé right in his too-perfect face.

He doesn't look embarrassed at all when he nods to confirm it. "We needed someone to go after the so-called baron, and who better than a man who already fought and beat him once? So we sent a Q-ship manned by Naval Intelligence and a contingent of Marines, enlisted Mendoza to command the mission and his crew to support ours on board, and told him that he needed to find and capture Hornsby alive if he wanted to see you again."

The frank admission is too much. I pick up my drink and fling the liquid from it right into Jethro's face. He closes his eyes and winces, reaching up with his napkin to wipe his face and the front of his uniform skinsuit. I'm expecting him to call over the Marines to immediately take me from the restaurant back to my quarters, but he doesn't.

When he's done cleaning himself up, he watches me with raised eyebrows. I decide not to wait for him to speak this time.

"So all of this, the endless questions, the accusations, was just a ruse? You just needed to keep me out of the way for a couple of weeks while Brad did your bidding?"

He shrugs laconically. "No, we really did want to learn more of what you and he did over the last seven months. We decided that separating the two of you would motivate both of you *and* allow us to effectively kill two birds with one stone."

I cringe at his choice of words. "So why ask me about everything else when all you clearly care about is figuring out if Duke Garrison is plotting against the King?"

I have the momentary satisfaction of seeing Jethro look nonplussed. So, I keep pressing. "Come on, Jethro, it's painfully obvious that's what you're really after in all our little chats. Tell me, is the King starting to see traitors and assassins behind the curtains in the palace? Does he have his Royal Guard check the toilets for hidden bombs before he uses the restroom?"

My semiseditious remarks bring a stern frown to Jethro's face, but he doesn't take the bait. Instead, he changes topics.

"We haven't been completely honest with you, Jessica." It's the first time he's called me by my name since the day I came on board. "We never had any intention of letting Brad Mendoza go free at the end of this."

I want to slap him or maybe pull him from his seat and bash his head in with a spoon. I want to hurt him so severely that his relatives feel it. I barely stop myself, though my entire body is trembling in rage, cognizant that the Marines will simply restrain me and take me back to my cell. Jethro is telling me all this for a reason, and I need to hear him out so I can make my own plans. There is *no* way I'm going to let them take my fiancé to meet his death. Even if I have to take down half this station and steal a ship, I'm going to find a way to save Brad. And right now, that means not giving in to my anger with Jethro... yet.

"But there's still hope for you," he says, leaning forward again and looking at me with such intensity that it makes me flinch back a little.

"What do you mean?" I ask, successfully keeping my voice flat, almost robotic.

"I can put in my report that you cooperated with us. That you told us everything we wanted to know, and that you were never a willing participant in Brad Mendoza's schemes against the Crown. Then you can go free. Well, maybe not entirely free, but certainly released into Naval Intelligence custody."

'Into *my* custody'. That was what he wanted to say. But it's all the same thing, really.

I put my hands in my lap and clench my fists so tightly that my fingernails feel like they're drawing blood from my palms. The last time I felt such hatred and anger toward a person was when I found Brad emaciated and beaten on Kayla Carter's death station at Capaldi. I wanted so badly to rip the woman apart with my bare hands for what she'd done to the man I love. But I restrained myself then, just like I need to now.

"Think about it, Jessica," Jethro says, talking more animatedly; he's obviously misread my silence as consideration of his words. "All this can be over. You'll never be reinstated in the Navy, of course. But you'll be alive. The King doesn't want you like he wants Mendoza. Your friend is a dead man anyway. He's on a ship full of Marines with orders to capture him and take him back to Prometheus the second they have Hornsby. Nothing you say or do is going to change his fate. But it could change *yours*.

"We need to act *now*, Jessica. I got word this morning that our ship with Mendoza aboard has located the system where Dexter Hornsby is hiding. By now, they've probably captured him, and he and Mendoza are already locked in the brig on their way to trial. If you agree now to testify against Mendoza, I'm sure I can get the court to see reason. Then you and I, we can…"

He trails off, but his meaning is clear. He thinks that what he's offering me is something I should be grateful for, grateful enough to run back into his arms even as my real love is killed for doing nothing more than protecting me at Gerson and ever since. Jethro thinks he can manipulate me in my vulnerable state.

Just like he did after Hothan and Yolandra.

Suddenly, I see my prior relationship with this man in a whole new light. All this time, I've blamed myself for how things ended between us. I've been deflecting Brad anytime he talked about a wedding date because I've been so worried that I would just mess things up and walk away like I did with Jethro. And I've been viewing my relationship with Jethro through the same insecure lens I viewed the entire universe through back then. Back when everything was *my* fault, and even people I thought I loved found ways to use that against me.

But a lot has happened in the three years since. Now I realize with a startling clarity that Jethro didn't deserve me then and certainly doesn't now. I did the *right* thing handing his ring back when I last left Lightman Station. Just as I'll do the right thing again by marrying Brad.

It's like a dam of realization has broken within me, and part of me is suddenly overjoyed to be free of the guilt I've felt for three years since breaking Jethro's heart.

But the rest of me is just ticked off by the arrogance of the man to suggest that I should somehow be *grateful* he's willing to take back broken little old me. And by the cold and uncaring way he talks about the death of my best friend and fiancé.

No longer able to contain my anger, I stand, flinging the table between us aside, glasses and bread plate shattering on the floor. The entire restaurant goes deathly silent as the other diners turn in shock. Before Jethro can overcome his surprise and get up, I slap him so hard across the face that it knocks him off his chair and onto the deck.

"You snake!" I scream as I kick him hard in the stomach, forcing him to curl up into a ball on the floor and cry out in pain. "You'll never be half the man Brad Mendoza is, you—"

Whatever foul name I'm about to call him is choked off as one of the Marines arrives and jabs a stunner into my lower back. My last sight is the hard metal deck rushing up to meet me.

THIRTY-THREE
ILLIAN MAKES A JOKE

BRAD MENDOZA

Despite the shuttle's head start and *Odysseus*'s damage, we reach Romana's seventh moon only two hours behind Hornsby.

"Is that a factory station?" Traeger asks next to me as we study the facility orbiting the small moon.

"Yes, sir," Illian answers as we watch the large, disc-shaped station below. "The onboard registry says it's a Wagner 4000 design, mostly automated, specializing in the manufacturing of jump drives."

"I guess we have our answer then," I say to no one in particular. "Hornsby *is* making jump drives. But why?"

No one responds, and I shrug it off. I have my own suspicions.

"Take us in, Saki. Illian, hit that thing with every scrambler we have."

"Sir?" my tactical officer asks from behind me.

"Do you want to gamble that Hornsby hasn't installed defensive weaponry on that station?"

His silence is all the response that I need. A minute later, eight scramblers launch from our surviving missile tubes and we watch as they fly toward the orbital factory. True to my warning, gatling guns and defensive lasers open up, but two of our missiles miraculously get through, and the weapons in that part of the factory fall silent. A follow-up wave of six more scramblers launched through that new opening in the defenses is enough to stop *everything* from firing back at us. Even the station lights flicker and wink out.

Regardless, we approach the factory cautiously, and it takes us a full 30 minutes to dock with it while Illian and Laia both keep a careful watch on the station's power readings.

"If Hornsby is still on board that thing, he'll be locked up tight in the command center," Gunny Boyd says from his observation post at the back of the bridge.

I finish the thought. "And if that thing has off-spec weapons, it probably has reinforced bulkheads and blast doors for the command center. Any thoughts on how to get to him?"

He shakes his large, bald head, studying the plans Illian pulled from the registry for that type of factory, projected on the viewscreen for all of us to see.

"We can't use explosives without killing everyone inside," the big man says, obvious disappointment coloring his tone. "And a cutting laser will take a long time. Are we worried he might have help on the way?"

"Very likely," Traeger answers before I can. "Probably why he came here instead of going to the planet—it's closer, so less chance we would catch him en route, but it gives him a place to go to ground and wait for reinforcements. If the blast doors are on a timer, we wouldn't even be able to hack them in time."

I nod, hand on my chin, listening as they continue to

talk about the impossible tactical situation we find ourselves in. If only we weren't too damaged to catch up to Hornsby's shuttle *before* it reached Romana. But we were, and there's nothing we can do about that now.

"What does a crime boss value almost as much as his own survival?"

Everyone stops talking and turns to stare at me.

"His reputation," I continue. "Hornsby relies on his reputation to scare potential competitors and impress potential allies. Without it, he's nothing. It's why he so often does the dirty work himself. And it means that anytime someone does something to challenge that reputation, he *has* to kill them just to reassert his dominance."

"And you showed him up at Santa Maria *and* Helgatha," Illian says from the tactical station behind me. "So, he *really* wants you dead. But how does that help us, Skipper?"

I turn to Traeger. "How about you answer that question, Jake? Tell everyone the *real* reason Naval Intelligence wanted me on this mission."

The bridge goes deathly quiet, and every officer and enlisted spacer is holding their breath and waiting for what happens next.

"I... uh... don't know what you mean, Captain," Traeger says slowly and carefully.

"Come on, Jake," I press. "I'd expect a spook to be a better liar than that. I promise I'm not mad. You can be honest."

He frowns tightly and tries very hard not to look over at the massive figure of Gunny Boyd, who is glaring daggers at the spook. Then, Traeger's shoulders slump just a little, and he looks resigned.

"You were supposed to be the bait."

I nod. "That's right. Naval Intelligence knew that dangling me as bait would be the quickest and surest way to bring Hornsby out of hiding. That was the plan all along, wasn't it? Use the *Odysseus* to get me close to the baron, then 'leak' the fact that I was on board her and use the Marines to ambush him when he came to kill me. Did I get all that right?"

There's a deep, rumbling growl from the direction of Boyd, but I hold up a hand to stop him from coming over and ripping Traeger's head off his body.

"That's pretty much it," Traeger admits with a frown. "But then you came up with an even better plan, to steal and use the *Hassan*'s cargo, so we didn't need to tell Hornsby anything. But…" He trails off, looking momentarily chagrined.

"But if Hornsby hadn't been on that destroyer, you would have gone forward with Plan A."

He nods.

"Great!" I exclaim, slapping my hands on the arms of my command chair to punctuate the word.

Now all eyes that were boring into Traeger turn in astonishment to see me grinning ear-to-ear. And not just because I'm right, though that always makes me happy, but because it also gives me the way we're going to get Baron Dexter Hornsby out of that command center so we can capture him.

"You have another stupid plan, don't you, Skipper?" Illian asks dryly from behind me.

I nod. "Yep."

"And it involves an almost certain chance of death?"

"Of course."

"And the only person who could possibly talk you out of it is Commander Lin, but she's not here?"

"Right again, Guns!"

He sighs loudly and dramatically. "Fine, Captain. But if you leave me on the ship for this one, I'll shoot you myself. Or, better yet, I'll tell Commander Lin, and she'll dump your butt."

I laugh out loud and turn my chair to face him. "Francis, did you just make a joke?"

He nods.

"Well," I say, turning back to Traeger with a smile. "Now I've seen everything."

THIRTY-FOUR
LOSING BATTLE
BRAD MENDOZA

My good cheer over Illian's sudden sense of humor fades quickly as I contemplate the challenge ahead of us.

Losing most of our Marines in the last battle hurts. It seems I keep adding names to the tally of those dead because of my decisions. Space is a dangerous place; human beings make it even more so. I wonder, sincerely and often, if any amount of good I do for the rest of my life can ever come close to making up for those who have met their end at my hand or by following my orders.

I have no idea why Jessica, after essentially proposing to me, has gone rigid and silent every time I bring up a wedding date. Rationally, I know she loves me. But in my darkest moments, a part of me wonders if she feels the same about me as I do about myself. Is she so reticent because she realizes that she's tied her future to a mass murderer? Is the kind of happiness that a life with her at my side would bring nothing more than a fever dream for a man like me?

I push aside those insidious thoughts and focus again

on the matter at hand. Beyond my guilt over their deaths, I especially miss Shultz and his Marines right now. With the impossible challenge of storming the factory station, we could use every single one of them. Unfortunately, we have only 11 surviving Marines of Shultz's original 40. And in true Promethean Marine tradition, Shultz and all his officers fought the desperate rearguard action on Hornsby's destroyer, which allowed as many of their men and women to escape as possible.

The senior surviving Marine is Staff Sergeant Goldberg. He arrives at our planning session with a haunted look in his eyes and a grim set to his mouth that tells me he's ready for whatever we throw at him.

"The plan is simple," I say, projecting the schematic for the station above the wardroom table in share mode. "Gunny, Kluth, Forbes, and Uvalde go first, drawing fire and making a move toward the command center. Sergeant Goldberg, you'll send one squad of your Marines to support them. The other will stay here and defend *Odysseus* against any attempted counterattack."

"Captain, all due respect," Goldberg says with a frown, "but my Marines aren't playing a support role on this. We're the tip of the spear, sir. Let us do our jobs."

We all turn to look at him, and he meets our collective gazes defiantly.

"Sergeant," Traeger starts, his tone sympathetic, "after the losses you've suffered, no one would blame—"

"Sir, is this a capture mission or a pity party?"

Goldberg's interruption of Traeger's placating statement brings a smile to my lips, but I hide it by coughing into my hand.

The Marine manipulates the image, zooming in on one part of the station in particular. "Sirs, we all know this is going to be the most dangerous part of the mission right here. And this is where my Marines need to be for two reasons. First, because you need the largest, most cohesive unit on this; no offense, Gunny."

Boyd nods to the Marine to show no hard feelings.

"And second," Goldberg continues, "because for this to work, the enemy needs to think that this really is our true objective. So we have to hit it hard and make it look 100 percent real. If we hold my Marines back, we'll immediately make them suspicious."

I look over at Boyd, who nods again. "It makes sense, Captain," he says with a frown. I can tell he doesn't like it any more than I do. Putting my own people in danger's way is bad enough, but sending more Marines to their deaths…

"Captain, Commander, you know I'm right," Goldberg presses. "Gunny and his team can stay back and defend the ship. But we'll need every one of my Marines on that station to make this work."

Traeger opens his mouth to argue, but I cut him off. "Agreed, Sergeant, but I expect you to only take volunteers. Some of you likely won't be coming back from this."

"Of course, sir. Volunteers only."

We all ignore that Goldberg will definitely ensure that every Marine under his command 'volunteers' for the mission.

Five minutes later, I declare the final planning session done. Five minutes after that, the Marines are at the airlock, busily checking each other's ballistic armor and weapons. Harris is with them, hacking the station's airlock controls. Gunny and his team are also there, waiting to guard the airlock door, which we'll leave open in case the Marines need to retreat to the ship quickly.

Me? I'm watching from the bridge, my skin practically crawling as I long to be suiting up with them. But the plan requires me to stay here, no matter how much I hate it.

"Sergeant, you good to go?" I ask through the comm after a few minutes.

"Oorah, sir," he replies smartly, and several of the Marines echo the battle cry.

"Harris?"

Harris nods on the vid feed and enters one last command into the station hatch control. It swings open, and the Marines hustle through almost before it hits the stops. Gunny and his team brandish their weapons and take up position on either side of the airlock hatch as Harris scurries away to get out of the possible line of fire.

The biggest problem we had in making our plan of attack was not knowing the disposition of Hornsby's forces. The factory station is designed to be automated, with only a small overseer crew. But the shuttle he arrived on had capacity for a dozen people, and he almost certainly had more already on the station to guard whatever illegal enterprise requires him to manufacture jump drives.

He could have a dozen fighters on the station, or a hundred. Luckily, there's an app for that, and the bridge's forward viewscreen shows a map of the orbital now. At first, it's just a wireframe schematic, but it rapidly fills in as dozens of tiny stealth drones, courtesy of our friends in Naval Intelligence, fly ahead of the Marines and recon the place. Red dots begin to show up on the map as the drones find the baron's people.

Goldberg and his team move slowly, letting the drones do their job so we have the full picture before they get too deep into the station. As the drones spread out across a wider radius, the updates to the map slow, but a picture of the defenses starts to form.

So far, there are two dozen enemy troops on the map, split into three unequal groups. The largest, about a dozen, are spread out in one of the large, open factory modules, directly between the Marines and the command center. Two smaller groups are blocking alternative paths around that module, no doubt to funnel our people into an ambush there. It's a classic station defense strategy, but the classics tend to work. A man would have to be crazy or stupid to walk into an ambush like that.

Which is exactly why we're going to do just that.

The bridge is silent as we all watch the feed, and my eyes flick back and forth between the station schematic and the vid feeds from several of the Marines' helmets. With station power mostly out from our scrambler attack, the cameras are on low light mode, so the image is flat and a little grainy.

"Coming up on the factory module now," Goldberg reports through comms. We watch with bated breath as they cross the last 20 meters of the corridor toward the hatch in question.

Once they arrive, I see one of the Marines hurry ahead of the rest and slap a device onto the hatch's small porthole. A new window opens up on the bridge display as thermal cameras integrated into the device show heat signatures spread across the factory floor. The station map fills in with a few more red dots, fighters the drones missed in their reconnaissance.

Goldberg mutters an order, and three more Marines creep forward. One of them opens the hatch a crack. The second throws something inside, then moves quickly out of the way so that the third can toss in something else.

Even through the comm, we can hear the two loud pops in quick succession. The camera feed goes dark as the Marines' helmets, synced to the grenades, darken to protect against the bright flash of the first grenade. But as the artificial sun of the flashbang recedes, the Marines are already moving, and we watch as they rush through the hatch and into the smoke from the second grenade.

Sporadic fire greets them, and one of the Marines grunts as a bullet hits his armor but doesn't go through. They return fire, using integrated thermals in their helmets to see through the smoke and take out three of Hornsby's people in quick succession. But then the return fire intensifies as the enemy overcomes the effects of the flash bang and the smoke starts to dissipate.

"Take cover!" we hear Goldberg yell, and we watch on the map as the green dots representing him and his Marines spread out to duck behind machinery and consoles. All around them, robotic arms and conveyor belts stay silent, frozen in whatever position they were in the moment our second wave of scramblers disabled the station's reactors.

The camera feeds become hard to watch as Marines pop up from behind cover to fire at the enemy and then duck down quickly as bullets and the occasional laser blast pepper their positions. I hear shouts over the comms, calling out targets, requesting cover while reloading, and the myriad other small things that allow the Marines to operate as a cohesive unit even in the chaos of a battle.

More red dots start to flash and disappear across the station map as Goldberg's people find their targets. But then one of the green dots flashes and winks out, and my eyes stray to the designated camera feed, which shows an unmoving view of the factory module's high ceiling and nothing more.

I grip the arms of my command chair tightly, gritting my teeth as a second Marine goes dark. "Sergeant, they're flanking you! The hatch!" I cry into the comm as the two smaller enemy squads, no longer needed outside the module, pour into the factory floor through the same hatch where the Marines entered just moments ago.

The new enemy soldiers start to turn the tide against us, and the shouts of the Marines over the comm become more frantic. There's a cry of pain and rage, and another green dot flashes but doesn't disappear this time, its owner injured and out of the fight but still alive. But the red dots are encircling the green ones now, and it's only a matter of time.

My jaw is clenched so tightly that it hurts now, and I turn to see Traeger looking equally upset as he watches me instead of the viewscreen. I open my mouth to issue an order, but he shakes his head and reaches down to the flip-out console on his chair, keying open a new comm channel.

"Stop!" he yells into it, fear and panic making his voice ragged. "This is Commander Jake Traeger of His Majesty's Promethean Navy, calling Dexter Hornsby. Stop the battle, and we will negotiate the terms of a ceasefire!"

All eyes on the bridge turn to watch Traeger warily as he continues to stare hard at me. Then a new voice, a very familiar one, laughs into the comm. "And why, Commander Traeger, would I agree to any ceasefire with you? My troops are about to kill every last one of your pathetic boarding party. You should really plan your missions better next time."

I shudder at the calm, arrogant, aristocratic voice that

has haunted my dreams since Helgatha, confirming for me once and for all that Hornsby *is* on the station. I brace myself for what I know is coming next.

"If you will agree to a ceasefire and let my Marines return to my ship unharmed," Traeger says, his eyes still on me, "I'll give you someone you've wanted for a long time.

"I'll give you Brad Mendoza!"

THIRTY-FIVE
WHY DO PEOPLE LOVE TORTURING ME?

BRAD MENDOZA

The negotiations are short and simple. Ten minutes later, I wait at the airlock, two beefy enlisted Naval Intelligence men holding me by each arm, my hands cuffed behind my back. Traeger waits next to me, refusing to look me in the eye. Gone are Gunny, Kluth, Forbes, and Uvalde, led away at gunpoint by more spooks.

We wait there silently as footsteps echo through the station corridors beyond the open airlock hatches. After a few moments, Goldberg and his Marines appear, marching weaponless, hands interlocked behind their helmeted heads. They stop a few meters before crossing the threshold back onto *Odysseus,* and a very familiar figure steps through them, roughly pushing Goldberg aside to stand in front of the Marines and smirk at me and Traeger.

Merl, the cowboy.

"Well, lookie what we have here," he drawls. "Brad Mendoza, trussed up like a Christmas ham."

"Where is Baron Hornsby?" Traeger demands. "I expected him to be here for the negotiations."

Merl snorts a laugh. "What, you mean so that you

could make one last try at him? No, he's way too smart for that."

My heart falls a little. If Baron Hornsby himself had come to take me personally, it would have given us one last chance to capture him, using the drones to take out his people from behind. But the crime boss is too smart for that, sending his lieutenant instead.

"'Sides," Merl says, still smirking. "Ain't no more negotiations. The deal is struck. We get Mendoza; you get your Marines... or what's left of 'em."

Jaw clenched so tight the veins stand out on his temples, Traeger nods curtly.

The two enlisted men shove me forward. I stumble over the first airlock hatch threshold, almost falling, but step carefully over the next and the one after that until I'm face-to-face with the cowboy.

He spits at my feet and grins at me. Then he raises one arm and gestures with his hand. Goldberg and his Marines slowly file past, refusing to look my way. But I watch them, my own jaw tightening as I see them carry their fallen and wounded mates with them.

"Well, we're done here!" Merl says to Traeger with a jaunty wave. "Tell your friends what happens when they buck the baron!"

Traeger doesn't respond, and two of Merl's soldiers move past us and close the hatch, cutting off my view of him and *Odysseus*, perhaps for the last time.

Ten minutes later, I'm in a plushly decorated and furnished office right off the factory station's command center. My captors shove me roughly into a surprisingly comfortable chair facing a large wooden desk, behind which sits one of the men I hate most in the galaxy.

Baron Dexter Hornsby smiles like the Cheshire cat and

sips at a tumbler of scotch in one hand, leaning back in his overstuffed office chair and regarding me with a triumphant gleam in his eye. I *really* want to punch him, but I'm almost immediately handcuffed to the chair, both arms secured.

"Brad Mendoza," he says with a grin as the two foot soldiers who brought me here retreat from the room.

"Brad Mendoza? Where?" I ask in excitement, turning my head to look this way and that around the room. "I heard that guy's awesome. I've always wanted to meet him."

Hornsby shakes his head and laughs lightly. "Always the quick wit, aren't you, Brad? We'll see how that plays for you when we start the festivities."

I put my focus back on him and smirk. "No need to torture me, Dex. I'll tell you everything you want to know. For instance, that shirt looks horrible on you. See, honesty! No torture necessary."

His grin turns to a tightlipped frown, and I'm worried I've already pushed him a little too hard, so I clamp my mouth shut and wait for him to speak next. After a moment, the smile returns. "Oh, the torture isn't to get information out of you, Brad. There's literally nothing in that head of yours that could possibly benefit me. No, the torture is just for fun."

I hear the hatch open behind me, and footsteps echo across the deck. I look up to see Merl stop next to my chair and grin down at me. "The Promethean ship left the station like a dog with its tail between its legs, boss," he says cheerfully. "Reactors are back online, and we've got every laser and missile tube pointed at them in case they try anything. Should we blow 'em out of the sky just for kicks?"

I hold my breath without trying to *look* like I'm holding my breath. To my relief, Hornsby shakes his head. "No, my friend, we'll keep our part of the bargain. Let them go back and tell how even the might of the Navy wasn't able to reach us out here."

"That's mighty nice of you, Dex," I say, doing my best to imitate Merl's drawl and failing pretty badly, but it's enough to draw an annoyed look from the cowboy. At a nod from Hornsby, Merl lashes out, landing a vicious punch to my jaw that makes me cry out in pain.

"That hurt!" I complain after I regain my senses. I look over at Hornsby, still sitting smug behind his desk. "Your customer service training really sucks, Dex. Needless to say, I *won't* be leaving you a five-star review."

That's when Hornsby nods to Merl again, and the beating truly begins.

PART THREE
DESPERATE ESCAPES

THIRTY-SIX
NEW ENEMIES AND OLD FRIENDS

JESSICA LIN

I wake up from the stun round not in the small apartment they've kept me in for the last two weeks, but in the station's brig, my plain utility skinsuit smelling of sweat. I'm just glad I'm not part of the seven-tenths of the population who lose control of their bladder when hit by a stunner.

My implant clock informs me that it's the morning after my fight with Jethro in the restaurant. But that's all I can find out; the brig's jamming field has cut off even my read-only access to the station Net. The Marines outside my cell are no help at all, ignoring my attempts to communicate through the soundproofed transparent hatch.

Luckily, I don't have to wait long in isolation. One hour after I awake, a very stern-looking Jethro shows up with two more Marines. Wordlessly, the Marines enter my cell and roughly frisk me, probably worried that sometime while I've been unconscious and locked in this brig, I somehow crafted a shiv from one of my own bones.

Maybe I should be flattered that they consider me so

dangerous. The bruise on Jethro's face and the way he winces and holds his stomach when he moves are proof of what I can do even without a weapon.

"Your transport to Prometheus is here," he says in a neutral voice when the Marines lead me out of the cell and stop me in front of him. "Have you reconsidered my offer?"

The nerve of this guy! I really want to hit him again, but I need to be conscious for the walk to the transport; it's my last opportunity to escape, and being stunned will turn my chances from mostly impossible to *completely* impossible. I already screwed up by hitting him last night; I need to play nice for now and see if I can find an opening.

So, I just shake my head. "No, Jethro. You underestimate Brad at your own peril. He *will* escape, and we *will* be together again. I'm going to marry that man."

Surprisingly, even to myself, my voice rings with such certainty that Jethro takes a step back. After all Brad and I have been through, that he wouldn't manage to escape seems so farfetched that I find myself unable to believe it's even possible. Likewise, I can't imagine a universe where he and I aren't together.

"Very well, then," Jethro says, sadness tinging his tone. "We will escort you to your transport. Corporal, cuff her."

Not good. As one of the Marines fastens my wrists together behind my back, my chances of escape get even worse.

Satisfied that I'm not getting away, Jethro motions to the Marines, and all *four* of them fall into position around me as we leave the brig. My chances dwindle even further as two of the Marines take a trailing position where they'll easily be able to hit me with another stun round if I try anything.

Regardless, I have to escape, no matter what it takes. Despite Jethro's promise last night that the King doesn't want me dead that badly, I know better. Even if King Charles doesn't want me killed, his sister, Lady Jacobs, and her rapist son, Petty Officer Nedrin Jacobs, will never let me survive in custody. I'm the one person who can testify against Nedrin for all he did to me on *Persephone*. And while the tabloids and news services quickly lost interest in reports of his crimes with no one around to corroborate the story, my surfacing again could prove a major inconvenience for them.

I'll be surprised if I even arrive at Prometheus alive. So better to die now, fighting superior odds with the barest hope of freedom, rather than subject myself to certain death once I get on that transport.

The brig is one level below the Navy docking ports. We avoid the elevator, taking the stairs, probably to keep me moving and avoid any small, enclosed spaces where I might be able to kick or headbutt my way to freedom. It sounds ridiculous, but that's exactly what I'm left with.

Still, I might be able to do something in the stairwell. Maybe I can pretend to trip and fall backward into the two trailing Marines. Their instinct will be to catch me, and I can use the distraction to grab one of their guns and somehow, with my hands tied behind my back, use it to stun the others. In the long and glorious history of stupid plans, it ranks toward the top, but the closer we get to that transport, the more my odds of survival dwindle.

We scale the stairs, and as we near the first landing— the midpoint of our climb—I tense and get ready to make my move. But just as my foot touches the edge of the landing and I'm about to throw myself backward, something drops from above and clatters to the landing at my feet.

A brilliant flash of light and a high-pitched scream of sound hit me like icepicks to my eyes and ears. I yell in surprise and pain but not loud enough to miss the sound of bodies falling and tumbling down the metal steps. When, after a few seconds, my vision finally clears enough for me to make out the blurry shapes of people, I look around to see all four Marines down and unmoving. Only Jethro and I are still on our feet, though we're both blinking rapidly and holding our ears from the effects of the stun grenade.

In my still-blurry vision, a figure appears above us on the next landing. At first, I think I'm only seeing their silhouette, but then I realize that they're dressed head-to-toe in black body armor, including a full helmet and face shield, hiding their identity and even their gender. They have a compact assault rifle out and pointed straight at me and Jethro.

"What?" Jethro sputters, instinctively reaching out and moving me behind him. Maybe he thinks the person who just shot four Marines is going to be intimidated by his uniform.

The figure in black ignores him, speaking to me in a voice made robotic and genderless through the helmet's filters. "Jessica Lin, I am here to collect the bounty on your head. If you come with me willingly, I'll let your old boyfriend here live."

"Murderer!" Jethro cries, voice shaking with anger. "No one is going to pay you any bounty! You'll hang for this, you—"

Without any outward sign of hesitation or thought, the

figure in black squeezes the trigger of their gun, and I watch in horror as the bullet takes Jethro in the chest. I scream as he slumps down on the landing, his body landing on top of one of the dead Marines.

Ignoring the figure in black, I fall to my knees next to Jethro, leaning over him awkwardly with my hands cuffed as they are.

He looks up at me with wide, terrified eyes. Then I feel the lock on my cuffs click open! "Run," he gasps out in a voice so low I can barely hear him, and I realize that he must have sent the unlock command to the cuffs from his implant.

I don't run. Instead, I shake off the cuffs and encircle Jethro in my arms. He reaches up a hand and lightly brushes my face. I feel a warm wetness as he leaves a streak of blood across my cheek. Then his eyes go out of focus, and his hand falls limply to the deck.

My training kicks in, and I ping his implant, commanding it to send out an emergency alert. Every naval officer, Marine, and security officer on the station should now be getting a request for immediate medical attention to his location. It's the best I can do for him now, even if I know it's far too late.

I hear slow, confident footsteps coming down the metal stairs behind me as the bounty hunter approaches. As they arrive at the last step, I come up to a crouch and whirl to face them, the pistol I pulled from the dead Marine underneath Jethro in my hand. With zero hesitation, I fire twice into the armored figure's chest.

Their gun goes off almost immediately after my second shot, but the hard blows to their armor throw off their aim, and the bullets hit the bulkhead behind me instead.

Screaming in rage, I leap to my feet and lift the gun higher, squeezing the trigger two more times and putting two shots right into the armored helmet facing me. They gouge the visor but don't penetrate; still, it's enough to make the figure's robotic voice cry out in anger and surprise.

Knowing that I'll be at a severe disadvantage in hand-to-hand combat with someone in full body armor, I don't stay and fight. With one last and very fast look at Jethro's corpse at my feet, I leap over him and hit the downward stairs running, jumping again to skip the last four steps and the bodies of the other Marines. I hit the landing we started from as bullets slap the stairway's bulkheads behind me, spurring me to move even faster.

My panicked flight carries me past the level we came from. I leapfrog down the next two flights of stairs, the bullets growing closer behind my heels and then stopping when I round the final corner and put myself momentarily out of the gunman's view.

I can hear them behind me still, running to catch up. At the next exit hatch, I fling it open and dive through, slamming it shut behind me but not staying to dog the latch. Instead, I sprint down the wide corridor outside, passing by startled onlookers who no doubt heard the battle in the stairwell.

When I hear the hatch slam back open behind me, I'm already changing my trajectory to hurl myself around a corner and into a side corridor. People start to scream now, their shock gone, as a second figure brandishing a gun shoves its way through the small crowd.

Ahead is another branch in the corridor, and I know I can probably make it before the bounty hunter rounds the first corner behind me, but I don't. I turn before the branch, entering a small noodle shop that's empty at this hour, ignoring the startled man behind the counter as I leap over it and crouch, hiding at his feet.

"Naval Intelligence," I tell the gaping man, waving the gun at him. "Don't make a sound."

Outside in the corridor, I can hear running footsteps and a female voice swearing loudly. I realize that my hits to the bounty hunter's helmet must have ruined her visibility enough for her to miss shooting me in the stairwell, and she had to remove it to pursue me now. At least I know her gender, even if I don't dare raise my head above the counter to see her face.

I tense, still holding the pistol tightly in my hand in case the bounty hunter figures out where I am, but to my relief, the sound of her running and swearing continues past the noodle shop and down the branching corridor I almost took. Something about the voice strikes a note of familiarity in my brain, but I don't spend any time dwelling on it now.

"Back exit?" I ask the still-stunned restaurant employee looming over me.

Wordlessly, he nods toward a door at the back of the restaurant next to one marked as a washroom. Nodding my thanks, I leap back over the counter, and I'm through the door and into a small service corridor before he can say anything or my pursuer can return.

Then I'm running for all I'm worth, relying on my intimate knowledge of the station from the two years I was in exile here, never getting lost but also, for a while, not entirely knowing where I'm going except *away* from where the bounty hunter last saw me.

But as I run, I slowly start to drift in a specific direction, taking turns and stairwells with more intention. Even then, it takes my conscious brain a couple of minutes to realize where I'm headed. Once it does, I take an even more direct route, stopping only briefly to use the sleeve of my skinsuit to wipe Jethro's blood off my face as best I can and then dropping the stolen Marine pistol down a garbage chute. As much as I'd love to keep the weapon in case the bounty hunter catches up to me, there's nowhere to hide it in my clothing, and having it in my hand makes me instantly memorable and suspicious to everyone I pass.

Soon, I stop running, forcing myself to walk quickly but calmly past the other denizens of the station. As I move toward lower levels, I pass fewer and fewer people and fewer security cameras—I remember where many of those are and avoid them where I can.

Finally, after what feels like four hours but is less than 25 minutes by my implant's clock, I find myself at my intended destination. I'm hoping that when the inevitable manhunt for me starts, assuming *everyone* isn't already looking, they'll start by checking all of the airlocks and departing ships. Hopefully, they won't think to look in the lower residential levels, far from any potential escape routes.

I stop and study the hatch in front of me. It's as nondescript as the other residential hatches around it; this part of the station is mainly where maintenance workers and engineers live and is so far from the parts tourists and visiting dignitaries see that it's not only plain and utilitarian but a little dingy. Even the apartment numbers are missing from most of the hatches, including the one in front of me.

But I know this hatch anyway, despite three years passing since the last time I saw it.

As I reach up to ring the chime, I hesitate. Do I really

want to get the person on the other side of this door involved in my desperate flight? Not only is there a ruthless bounty hunter after me, but I have zero doubt that station security, the Shore Patrol, and some very pissed-off Marines assume that *I'm* the one who killed their colleagues and Jethro to escape in that stairwell. It won't be too long before they realize I'm not trying to sneak onto a departing ship or a shuttle to the surface, and they start searching the station door by door.

Can I do that to the person I came to see? If they're caught hiding me…

The decision is made for me by the sound of footsteps coming from around a bend in the corridor. It's probably just one of the residents of this level, but my mind immediately flashes a mental image of heavily armed and angry Marines, and I knock frantically on the hatch in front of me.

It opens slowly, and a familiar face peeks out of the narrow gap. When she sees me, her eyes go wide, and she opens the hatch the rest of the way. I practically leap through it, pushing it shut behind me, hopefully before the approaching people—be they Marines or civilians—round that corner.

The woman in front of me, staring at me in wide-eyed astonishment, is short, with a round, pretty face and a mop of curly brown hair perched on a long and graceful neck that looks out of proportion to the rest of her petite frame.

"Jessica!" she exclaims at the top of her lungs, making me wince and hope that there's no one right outside the thin hatch to hear. "I thought you were dead! It's so good to see you. Wait, *weren't* you dead? How are you alive?"

I smile wanly, waiting for her to take a breath. "Hi, Jetta. Long time."

Jetta Winslow, the woman whom I once held close as my best friend, rushes forward and hugs me so tightly that I feel like she's going to break every rib in my body. Before I know it, I'm crying into her shoulder, the image of Jethro dying in my arms playing on grisly repeat in my head.

THIRTY-SEVEN
OH, GREAT! ANOTHER MONOLOGUE

BRAD MENDOZA

I f there's one truth so universal that it forms the very substance and energy that makes our universe exist and spin around its axis, it's this: Bad guys *really* want you to know how much smarter they are than everyone else.

Don't believe me? I'm no scholar or scientist, but over my adult life, I have plenty of data I can point to that proves what I'm saying.

My ex-father-in-law, the illustrious windbag Admiral Terrence Oliphant, is a prime example. Every time I'd go over for dinner with Carla, he'd regale us with the same five stories of his daring fights against pirates, always with an emphasis on how he outsmarted them with his strategic cunning.

I've read the actual after-action reports from each of those encounters, and let me tell you, they're nothing special. I stopped and killed more pirates just in one battle in the Poe system than Terrible Terrence did in his entire career before he achieved the lofty flag rank that turned his battleground into dinner parties and formal balls.

When I first stepped foot on HMS *Persephone* in the

Gerson system, Petty Officer Nedrin Jacobs didn't even wait for me to get settled before he barged into my quarters to tell me just how unimpressed he was having me as a captain and how little he intended to listen to me while I was his commanding officer.

Owen Thompson, in the Fiori system, told me all about his evil plan, giving me time to formulate my own plan that resulted in a bullet in his stomach instead of mine.

Kayla Carter spent *hours* while I was her prisoner telling me all about how she tricked and outsmarted me while on *Wanderer* and at Carter's World. Sometimes, I felt like listening to her talk was worse than any of the physical torture she was subjecting me to.

Duchess Charlotte also told me all sorts of things while she had me tortured on Serenidad.

Villains… they just can't help it. They *all* monologue. My hope is that Dexter Hornsby is no different.

Merl winds up and delivers a hard punch to my stomach, driving the air out of me and making me gasp and choke. It doesn't help that I'm hung from the ceiling by my wrists, which already makes it hard to breathe unless I stand on my tiptoes.

Another punch, this one to my kidney, has me crying out again in pain. Say what you will about his stupid drawl and dumb hat, Merl can punch.

Okay, I'm lying again. The hat is *really* cool. I want one.

"You really have no idea, do you, Brad, what you've gotten yourself involved in?" Dexter Hornsby says from the chair his men brought in so he can watch Merl work me over.

"No," I gasp out, my voice hoarse, "but I can guess you're going to tell me."

He smiles. "You wouldn't believe me if I did." His

voice is dripping with its usual arrogance, which means, of course, that I can't keep my mouth shut.

"What, that you're making new jump drives for the Jutzens?"

Seeing the look of shock on his face as I reveal his own dastardly deeds to him is almost enough to make the hard punch Merl sends at my face worth it. When I recover enough to see again, I smile at Hornsby.

"Surprised?" I ask him. I am; I was only guessing... mostly.

He closes his gaping mouth and frowns at me. "How did you find out? Who told you?"

I would shrug, but that would be really hard to do with my hands stretched out above me and supporting all my weight. So I cock my head quickly to one side and waggle my eyebrows, hoping it conveys the same effect. "Everyone knows, Dex. There's an entire fleet on its way here to stop you."

Hornsby frowns and motions to Merl, who hits me again in the stomach. Seriously? The stomach again? As far as torturers go, this guy has *no* creativity. Kayla, now *she* was a master. Her torture spoiled me.

"Tell me how you found out," Hornsby demands, his voice a low, menacing growl that I'm sure scares all his little minions into doing whatever he says. I smile at him again.

"Not that hard to figure out, really. Everyone knows there's a Jutzen fleet massing at Capaldi, and that there's an even larger Promethean fleet waiting right at the jump point in Gerson to blow them all away when they try to come through it.

"But most people don't know there's *another* Jutzen fleet in the GB-119 system." The truth is, I'm not even supposed to know that. But Promethean Naval Intelligence does, and if Traeger and his bosses didn't want me reading their mail, they really shouldn't have brought me on board their ship with my pet hacker. Harris figured out their comm encryption on the second day in transit! It was just the first part of the secret project I handed him when we came on board *Odysseus*.

"The problem is," I go on to explain, grateful that even Merl has stopped punching me to listen to what I have to say, "is that no one can figure out *why* the Jutzens have a fleet in GB-119. It's two jumps away from Gerson, and any ship going there from GB-119—hey, can I just say 119? The whole 'GB-119' name is a real mouthful. If I say 119, you'll know what I'm talking about, right?" I wait, looking between Merl and Hornsby anxiously. They don't respond, so I mentally shrug it off and continue.

"Anyway, where was I? Nazi scum, dastardly plan. Oh, right! So, no one can figure out why the Jutzens have a fleet at 119—that's shorthand for GB-119, in case you forgot—because there's just no way they could reasonably use that system as a staging ground for a second attack on Gerson. I mean, to even get to Gerson, they'd have to jump through the Finrick system, which is a Leeward Republic territory. And *no one* wants a war with the Republic, am I right?" I pause again, but no reaction. Tough crowd. This time, I decide to wait them out.

Merl's response is to punch me again—no surprise there—and then kick me in the shin for good measure. Those boots hurt. Hornsby just watches impassively, though I can see through the tears in my eyes that one of his legs is shaking a little bit. The stress isn't showing on his face, but it's there, as it should be. Right now, he's got to be thinking that if *I* could figure out what's going on, so could others.

Merl is winding up for another punch, but Hornsby stops him. "Let Captain Mendoza finish, my friend. We'll see if he's really as smart as he thinks he is."

I smile and spit out a tooth. No matter how many times I do that, it never gets better. "Okay," I say, a slight whistling sound accompanying my voice as air rushes through the fresh gap. "So, I had to wonder, why put an invasion fleet in a system where it makes it impossible to actually *invade* your target. I'm still talking about the 119 system—that's GB-119, again—just in case that wasn't clear."

Another punch from Merl hits me in the gut. No creativity!

"Fine," I croak out. "We can just call it GB-119 if that makes you happy. Sorry to confuse you."

The next punch hurts worse.

"Brad, I tire of your failed attempts at wit," Hornsby says sternly. "I'm beginning to think you don't know *anything*."

I do my best to smile again, but the muscles on one side of my face aren't cooperating. "Sorry, Dex. I'll get to the point. Promise. See, I figure, the Jutzens may be insane, power-hungry, racist, warmonger Nazis, but they're not *entirely* stupid. So, if they have that fleet at GB-119, it has to be there for a reason. Then I saw you here, way out in the independent systems, manufacturing what look like pretty standard military jump drives. And I think to myself, why would Dexter Hornsby make a bunch of jump drives that you can literally pick up at any military contractor's warehouse or any major shipyard? Heck, they practically *give* the things away as raffle prizes at military balls. There was this one time, in fact, that I—oopf!"

Another punch, to the ribs this time. At least Merl is going for a little variety.

"One last chance, Mendoza," Hornsby warns.

"Fine. It took me about five minutes to figure out that GB-119 *does* have a jump point directly to Gerson, but it's a C-class jump point, which means it's unstable and deadly even to try and use it."

I'm not making this up; the galaxy is literally riddled with jump points, small tears in the fabric of space-time that allow humanity to transit light-years in hours despite never having devised a way to actually travel faster than the speed of light. But the vast majority of those jump points are worthless to us because they're either too small or too unstable for safe and effective transit. Most jump points we use are A-class. In a pinch, we might use B-class, though it's a bit of a risk. But a person would have to be an idiot to even attempt to use a C-class jump point. Unless…

"Then I started thinking of rumors," I continue, "that I heard a few years back about some arms manufacturer in the Inner Rim who figured out a way to make a jump drive that could actually stabilize a C-class jump point enough to get a ship through safely. Thought it was all a bunch of malarky at the time. But…" I do the whole trying to shrug with just my head and eyebrows again. "I think you've managed to get your hands on the plans for those special jump drives, and that's what you're making here. I also think you're planning to take them to the Jutzens in 119—sorry, GB-119—so they can retrofit them into their scary ships and attack Gerson from a direction the Navy won't see coming."

The look of surprise on Dexter Hornsby's face is *price-*

less. Maybe I get it now. *This* is why villains monologue and tell you all about how smart they are. There's a heady, triumphant feeling to the whole thing.

"Impressive," Hornsby admits, genuine admiration in his tone.

I smile at him, again with only the side of my face that still works. "I thought you'd like that, Dex. Tell me, how much did they have to pay you to betray your star nation?"

"More than you can imagine," he replies dryly. "You've gotten most of it right, but there's still so much you don't know. And I'm afraid you won't live to learn the rest."

I watch as he turns and walks out of the room, disappointed that my brilliant plan to lure him into revealing the rest of his dastardly deeds didn't work. It turns out I did most of the monologuing myself.

Hornsby stops just before going through the hatch, turning back to Merl. "Soften him up. I want him begging for death when I come back later and grant his wish."

Then he's gone, and the hatch clangs shut behind him. Merl walks around in front of me. He reaches up and slowly removes his hat, tossing it like a frisbee so that it lands perfectly on the seat Hornsby just vacated—seriously, *so* cool—and then smiling wickedly at me, drawing a long knife from a sheath on his belt. Not cool.

"You heard the man," he drawls. "Now, let's have us some fun."

THIRTY-EIGHT
CATCHING UP

JESSICA LIN

A n hour after arriving at Jetta Winslow's door, I'm sitting on her couch with a mug of steaming herbal tea—it tastes like flavored dirt water, but Jetta insisted I drink it to 'calm my nerves'—and I'm being interrogated again. This time, it's by someone I still love and who legitimately wants to help me.

Jetta has always been a ball of nervous energy, unbridled cheerfulness, and unstoppable chatter that some people just can't handle. I've never known the woman to go more than two minutes without talking, and conversations with her are often one-sided affairs in which the other party might not even be a willing participant.

The first time I met her, I was on the station's upper levels doing a routine maintenance check on one of the Navy airlocks just two weeks into my exile on Lightman. She literally popped out of the bulkhead behind me, exiting a small hatch that led into the myriad of behind-the-scenes and very cramped maintenance tunnels and conduits that form the hidden world of any station.

Before I could even acknowledge her presence, she was

introducing herself, telling me all about her background, her day, and the last man she dated, and asking rapid-fire questions, barely giving me time to answer one before launching into the next.

For a relatively shy and reserved person at my best those days, and I certainly wasn't at my best just weeks after Hothan and Yolandra, I was at first terrified of the bubbly young extrovert. That didn't stop her from finding me at the end of my shift that very same day and practically forcing me to follow her back to her apartment, where she made me a dinner of reheated ration packs.

The food was disgusting, but her energy and cheerfulness were oddly contagious, and I remember it being the first time I smiled about *anything* since I'd betrayed my star nation at Hothan.

From there, it was inevitable that Jetta Winslow became perhaps the best friend I'd ever had. Even once Jethro and I started dating, at first keeping it a secret to avoid any accusations of impropriety given his role as my Naval Intelligence handler, I still spent many a night with my feet curled up underneath me on Jetta's couch, trying to watch a movie or TV show over her nonstop banter.

"So, Jethro is dead?" she asks, even though I've already told her the quick details of what happened in the stairwell. "And you're on the run from a bounty hunter and trying to get back to some guy named Brad before the King kills him? Oh, and one of your best friends is a funny assassin with blue hair and multiple personalities? And your other best friend is a gun?"

I spent the first 20 minutes of my time in Jetta's apartment crying into her shoulder about Jethro's death—I may have hated the man lately, but I was engaged to him at one point. I have no more tears left, and her last question actually makes me snort a laugh despite everything. "Not a gun," I tell her before she can launch into the next question. "A gunnery sergeant. We call him 'Gunny' for short. Not to be confused with Illian, who we call 'Guns', because he's our tactical and weapons officer."

"Okay." She looks a little confused. "But this Gunny guy designs clothes, right, and does your makeup?"

I shake my head again in slight exasperation, choking back another laugh at the mental image of Quinn Boyd trying to thread a sewing machine needle with his massive hands. "No, that's Harris. He designs the clothes and helps us with disguises."

"I thought Harris was the one with no sense of humor."

"That's Guns—I mean Illian," I interrupt, my own head spinning now. "And he does have a sense of humor—he must, to date Hayley Uvalde—he just keeps it hidden very well."

"And the King wants you dead? Really? But I thought you were *already* dead. Why aren't you dead? The news said you were, and now you're here, and I'm so happy you're not dead! But I still don't understand how you're alive."

Quickly, I tell her the story of my 'death' at Gerson, but she keeps talking over me, so I'm sure I'll have to tell it again.

"Do you have a picture of this Brad Montero guy? Is he hot? His name sounds Latino. Is he Latino? Does he have dark and mysterious eyes?"

I ignore her getting Brad's name wrong and ping a picture of him over to her implant, mainly to get her to stop talking for a second.

Despite everything I'm going through right now and

the horribleness of all of it, I almost laugh again when Jetta's face puckers up in shock and disgust.

"He's... interesting," she says, trying to keep her voice even.

Then I can't help it. I do laugh, just a little. "Yeah, I took that photo after I rescued him from a psychotic mercenary who starved and tortured him for five weeks."

Before she can launch into a series of questions about that, I ping over another picture of Brad to her implant. This time, she smiles genuinely.

"Wow, he does clean up well, doesn't he?"

I can only smile wanly back. The second photo I've sent her is of Brad and me together in the dance club back at the Chalinga Resort on Jewel. It's...

"Oh, honey, what's wrong?" Jetta asks, setting her tea down on a side table and moving closer on the couch to put an arm around me as I break out into sobs again. "You'll see Brent again," she soothes, "and you and him and the gunny guy and his girlfriend with the blue hair can all be happy together."

The thought of Quinn Boyd together with Hayley Uvalde romantically is just enough to stop my latest downward spiral and snort another laugh into Jetta's shoulder. With it comes a healthy discharge of snot right onto her maintenance coveralls.

I sit back and wince apologetically as she wrinkles her nose and examines my contribution to the various stains on the garment. "Uh," she says, "maybe you should go get cleaned up. I might have something you can wear." She looks meaningfully at the blood on my skinsuit sleeve. At least she's talking a little slower now, and I feel like she might actually be taking breaths between sentence fragments. Sometimes, just listening to Jetta talk makes *me* feel winded.

I nod at her offer for a shower and new clothes, not trusting my voice, and let her guide me to the apartment's sole bathroom. I take a long, hot shower, letting the water beat against the knots of stress in my neck and shoulders. When I emerge, I find my stained skinsuit gone and a promised change of clothes from Jetta in its place on top of a clean towel.

I dry myself off as I inspect the clothing skeptically. I'm at least ten centimeters taller than Jetta, and I have a hard time believing anything of hers will fit me. I'm not wrong, and I'm a little self-conscious when I emerge from the bathroom wearing a pair of sweatpants that barely go past my knees and one of Jetta's dresses as a shirt, so at least it mostly covers everything it should.

"Jess," she exclaims, "still hot as ever!"

I blush. "You look great, too, Jetta."

She shakes her head vigorously. "No, I don't. I look like the mole people that roam the station air ducts. I'm pretty sure they're going to invite me to join one of their tribes soon and be their queen. I shall call them all Steve, and they shall be my minions!"

I laugh again. This is a running joke with Jetta, and it brings with it a little more sense of calm to the horrific events of the day.

"Only if you take me with you," I reply, finishing the familiar conversation.

She shrugs. "Nope, too tall. And your butt's too big to fit in the air ducts. People with big butts can't be mole people. But maybe the lizard people down on the planet might take you. They like big butts."

I smile at her. "Thanks, Jetta." I don't specify what for.

She smiles back, wider this time, and nods. "Don't worry. I'll head out in a bit and buy you some clothes that actually fit. That skinsuit of yours is a lost cause. In the meantime, why don't you sit back down and tell me how I can help get you off this station." Then she actually pauses, like she might be waiting for me to respond.

"Um," I say in embarrassment. "Jetta, listen, it's probably better that I just leave and don't get you involved any more than you already are. If they find out you—"

"Shhh," she says harshly, holding up a finger to her lips and looking around the room like someone might be here with us. "You hear that?"

I look around too in sudden near panic. "Hear what? Is someone right outside the door?"

Jetta smiles and shakes her head. "Nope, I just heard the sound of someone stupidly saying their best friend should hang them out to dry. So stop saying stupid stuff and tell me how we're going to get you out of this so you can go and marry Bruce, and the gun guy can kiss the blue girl, and Harry can make you all matching T-shirts."

I laugh one more time, and Jetta looks confused.

"What did I say that's funny?"

THIRTY-NINE
SIDE CHARACTERS UNITE!
BRAD MENDOZA

I pass out about 20 minutes into the epic beating Merl gives me. At some point, your body just shuts down to avoid the pain. So, everything that happens from here on out, I have to piece together by talking to my crew after the fact. But I'll relate it for you now as if I was there and awake for all of it. So far as I can tell, this is *exactly* how it went down.

When *Odysseus* left the factory station behind, it did so several passengers lighter. Unbeknownst to Hornsby and his evil minions, Quinn Boyd, Drake Forbes, Edgar Kluth, Hayley Uvalde, and Harris didn't go with the Q-ship. Plan C!

It was probably pretty uncomfortable waiting stationary in vacsuits for almost three hours, attached by tethers to the outer skin of the factory, until *Odysseus* disappeared in the distance and the baron's people stopped paying so much attention to the external cameras. It was probably even less fun having to essentially climb across the massive station's hull for another hour after that until my four intrepid crewmembers finally arrived at a small maintenance hatch in the command module.

At that point, I have it on good authority that their conversation went something very much like this:

"Hurry and hack open the hatch controls, Harris," Quinn said. "We have to save the captain and capture Baron Hornsby, in that order of importance, of course."

"I'm going as fast as I can," Harris replied. "Life would be meaningless without Captain Mendoza. I aspire to be half the man he is."

"Of course," Quinn replied. "Without him, we're lost and aimless in this galaxy. Though just being around him makes me feel less of a man."

"I'm in love with the capitán," Hayley chimed in. "What woman wouldn't be? But alas, I shall never have him, for his heart is set on Commander Lin. So I must settle for Illian, a mere shadow of my true heart's desire."

"I just hope he tells some funny jokes when we rescue him," Edgar replied. "Everyone else on this crew, including all of us, are just so *boring* by comparison to Captain Mendoza's amazing wit."

"I wish Captain Mendoza was my real father," Drake added. "But he's too young and good-looking for that."

Like I said, I'm almost certain that's what they were all saying when Harris finally finished hacking the hatch controls, admitting them through a small maintenance airlock and into the station itself.

Then, while I heroically slept off Merl's latest beating, they crept along the station corridors, stealthily killing anyone they came across and hiding the bodies in various out-of-the-way places so as not to raise the alarm.

"I hope we make it in time," Hayley said at one point, "for I shall never forgive myself if the galaxy loses such a sterling representative of manhood, integrity, and tactical genius. Have I mentioned how jealous I am of Commander Lin?"

"We'll make it," Quinn said resolutely. "For we must. We owe it to all humanity not to fail our mission!"

You ever read Tolkien? At some point, Harris recited an epic poem in song form about my many daring exploits. Edgar cried, Drake took a blood vow to rescue me, Quinn sang along with Harris's poem, and Hayley turned into Lola and killed half a dozen of Hornsby's minions just because she was so upset about me being captured.

This is about the time I wake up—sort of. I'm still pretty punch drunk. Merl is back in my torture chamber, slapping my cheeks to rouse me. Hornsby is there, too, sitting on his chair and watching with a smile as Merl gets me awake enough so he can gloat just before killing me.

"You know, Brad," Hornsby says—I may be para-phrasing here—"you have to die because you're way too smart and know too much and because this galaxy isn't big enough for the two of us. In fact, I will never be able to rest soundly knowing that a superior man such as yourself is alive and coming after me. It's too much for my fragile ego to bear, so you must be killed."

Again, I'm pretty concussed at this point, and words are kind of jumbling for me. But I'm almost 90 percent positive I've captured the meaning behind his words. Then, my implant pings twice, which I hazily remember means something important, so I look over at Hornsby and smile.

"That's okay, Dex," I say through split and bleeding lips, my words still whistling through my missing-tooth gap. "If I were you, I wouldn't want to be in the same galaxy with me either."

Boom! Drop the mic. Major burn. At least, I think it is. And I'm pretty sure that's Hornsby I'm talking to, but now there are three of him, and I'm not sure which one I should be taunting.

The hatch clangs open loudly, and all three Hornsbys turn in their chairs in surprise as three massive Quinn Boyds barge into the room and shoot three Merls dead.

"Hey," I try and say, "no fair. I wanted to be the one to kill the cowboy."

I watch as three Edgars each grab one of the Dexter Hornsbys and roughly restrain them by cuffing their hands behind their back. Then three Hayleys—*that's* a scary thought—approach me, slowly merging into just one grinning woman as she gets closer.

"Hola, boss!" she says cheerfully. "You okay?"

"Shhh," I say, trying to move a hand so I can put a finger to her lips, but my wrists are still tied to the ceiling above me. "It'll never work out between us, Hayley. I love Jessica. I'm sorry."

She turns and looks back at Quinn. "Hey, I think the capitán is not doing so good. He might have brain damage."

Harris steps around her, peering up at me. "Hey, Captain," he says. "What's your favorite kind of taco?"

I think for a moment, suddenly hungry. "The ones with the pineapple," I finally reply.

"Your favorite book?"

"*The Adventures of Firebrand's Marauders.* Billy Firebrand is my hero!"

"And the love of your life?"

"Tacos by the pool."

"No, the *other* love of your life."

"Oh. Jessica Lin," I say dreamily. "She's so pretty, and I think she likes me back."

Harris shakes his head. "His brain is fine. Just as messed up as always."

As they finally unchain me from the ceiling and start to lead me out of the room, I call out, "Wait!" I stumble over to where Merl's corpse is lying on the deck. Reaching down, I pick up his hat from where it fell next to him and clumsily put it on my head.

"OK," I tell them. "Now we can go."

FORTY
RECKONING
BRAD MENDOZA

Apparently, killing their fearless cowboy idol and putting a gun to the head of their leader took all the fight out of Baron Hornsby's minions—the still-alive ones, at least. When *Odysseus* returned from its slow loop around the gas giant and docked with the factory station again, they surrendered quickly to the surviving Marines.

Now, two hours later, we're burning as hard as our damaged engines can take us to the jump point back the way we came with Dexter Hornsby in the brig.

No one tries to stop us. I guess Illian took command in my absence and managed to destroy one of the Zepha System Patrol boats and damaged the other enough to send it limping away back toward the planet. There's some new damage to *Odysseus* from the fight, but two small patrol boats against even a damaged heavy cruiser is no real fight at all.

I sleep for the first six hours or so, secure in the med bay, where Doc Bean carefully stitches me up and probably grumbles the whole time about why I went and got myself cut to shreds in the first place.

When I finally awake, I leave the med bay over the doctor's protests. Contrary to what some may believe, our mission is far from over.

"Mr. Traeger," I say as I walk through the bridge hatch. "Why did the Marines turn me away at the brig when I went to talk to our prisoner?"

Traeger turns in surprise, likely not expecting me to be up and about this early. I can see his mind racing for a second, but then his face hardens just a bit. "Sorry, Captain, but Dexter Hornsby is *our* prisoner—Naval Intelligence, that is—so we're controlling access to him. There are far too many secrets in that man's head."

"No," I say simply.

He looks surprised again. "I'm sorry. But my decision is final."

"No, it's not." I walk up and glare down at him. "See these cuts," I tell him, reaching up to finger the suture lines on my cheek where Merl had a little too much fun with his big knife. "I got these and a hundred other injuries to capture Baron Hornsby. And now, I'm *going* to talk to him."

Out of the corner of my eye, I can see two Marines standing at the back of the bridge, probably there to help Traeger reassert his authority in my absence. They both start to move forward, but Gunny Boyd and Edgar, who both entered behind me, step in front of them, staring them down.

I lean forward, knowing that I need to help Traeger save some face. "You can listen to everything we talk about," I tell him. "But I *am* going to have a discussion with the baron."

He opens his mouth to argue, but Illian and Laia step up to either side of me and join me in glaring at the man.

Finally, he reluctantly nods. "Fine, but I'll be watching and listening the entire time."

"Agreed."

Traeger and I march together down the long corridors of the ship to the brig where Hornsby is being kept. At some point, Hayley falls into step behind us. The two Marines at the outer hatch straighten as we approach and look momentarily confused as if they're not sure which of us to salute and which of us to restrain. Traeger waves them down, and they let Hayley and me pass.

"Remember," Traeger hisses, catching my arm before I go into the interrogation room where Hornsby is being kept. "I'll be watching and listening to everything."

I nod and enter the room, Hayley on my heels. She closes the hatch behind us.

Hornsby watches us impassively as I take a seat at the table across from him. Hayley stands behind me, hands clasped behind her back, looking as military as I've ever seen her look.

Before he can speak, I look back at Hayley. "Ready?" I ask.

She nods.

"Ready?" I call to Harris over my implant. He pings me in reply.

"Go." With my one word, every camera, microphone, and other surveillance device in the brig's interrogation room goes dead under the onslaught of jamming from Hayley's Guard implant. Then the lock on the hatch snicks shut as Harris overrides it from his quarters.

I ignore the dull pounding sounds that almost immediately start through the thick hatch as Traeger and the Marines try and open it to find out why we've gone dark in here. I can imagine how upset Traeger is going to be after this, and it makes me smile a little. I turn back to look at Hornsby.

"You think you've won, don't you?" he says with an evil sneer to start the festivities.

"Calm down, Dex," I say, overdoing the friendliness in my tone. "Just because you'll be spending the rest of your life in prison doesn't mean that you can't be nice. Look at me. You had me beaten half to death, and I can be civil."

He scoffs. "Mendoza, you think you know so much, but you've only scratched the surface. You and everyone you love is going to die, whether by my hand or someone much scarier than me. And I'll be free as soon as we're back in Promethean space. They'll trade me *anything* for what I know, so you can just—"

I hold up a hand to stop his rant while I yawn loudly. When I'm done, I shake myself awake and focus my eyes back on him. "Sorry, Dex, you were saying? Oh yeah, threat, threat, empty promise, impotent rage. Got it! Let me ask you something: Do you practice speeches like that in the mirror? You must, right? Because you have got the whole evil crime lord thing down. It's really impressive. I almost peed my pants."

"Uh, boss, you *did* pee your pants on the station when they tortured you. You smelled really bad when we rescued you."

I look back in annoyance at Hayley. "Thank you, Lieutenant. Extremely unhelpful, but thank you."

I turn to Hornsby again. "Okay, you've had your turn to threaten me. Now it's my turn. And when I'm done, you're going to tell me *everything* I want to know."

He laughs derisively, though I can see a wariness in his otherwise smug features. "Sorry, Mendoza, you're just not that scary. I'll pass."

I grin at him. "Oh, I know *I'm* not that scary. Handsome, dashing, heroic maybe, but scary? No, not me. But *she* is." I gesture toward Hayley.

He laughs again. "Her? That girl can't weigh 50 kilos soaking wet."

"Okay, Dex," I say, throwing both hands up in surrender. "Don't say I didn't warn you."

With that, the lights in the room go out, plunging us into pitch-black darkness. I hear a very undignified little yelp of surprise from the so-called baron before the lights abruptly come back on.

Hayley is gone. In her place is the stuff of nightmares, a white-haired wraith with dead gray eyes and an expression that reminds me of a mountain lion I once saw just before it attacked one of the pigs on my grandpa's farm.

Lola is here.

"What is this?" Hornsby sputters, obviously thrown off by the sudden and jarring change in the little Latina's appearance and demeanor.

"This?" I ask with a smile. "This is Lola, a member of the Koratan Confederate Guard. Remember when you attacked us at Helgatha, and I told you that there are worse things to fear than the King's Cross? You know, right before your men started dropping like flies?"

His eyes go wide. "You!" he cries, staring at Lola. "But you're just a girl! You can't be the one who... You can't!" He trails off, and I glance over to see her cocking her head and studying him like food she's about to play with.

"Sorry, Dex," I say, turning back to him and spreading my hands wide. "But I can't control her when she gets like this. And you've killed a lot of her friends. So, maybe you ought to start talking before she decides to get stabby."

Is 'stabby' a word? It seems to fit, and Hornsby doesn't

correct my grammar. He starts talking, and I have no trouble hearing him over the increasingly impotent banging on the hatch outside.

I wish I could say I feel good about our little interrogation session as he eagerly tells me *everything* about his plot against the King, his work for the Jutzens, and pretty much every evil thing he's done since grade school.

But all of it adds up to something so horrible that it leaves a yawning pit in my stomach that no number of tacos could possibly fill.

FORTY-ONE
SMUGGLER

JESSICA LIN

"**R**eally, this is the ship?" I try not to let my skepticism and disappointment color my voice too much, but by Jetta's crestfallen look, I've failed. I feel bad, given that she's essentially harboring me as a fugitive. If that black-clad bounty hunter or even the Navy or station security find us together, Jetta could end up just like... I banish the thought, knowing that I can't afford to spiral right now.

"I know it doesn't look like much, but she's spaceworthy. You'll see," Jetta says, tugging me along toward the open airlock. At least I'm wearing normal clothes again—a plain utility skinsuit like the one Jetta has on—so I don't have to meet the master of this 'ship' in an outfit that no one would take me seriously in.

From what I can see through the station's portholes, the craft docked here on the lower maintenance levels isn't much to look at. She's smaller than my old freighter, *Wanderer*, but her lines and mismatched hull plates remind me more of the destroyed and unlamented HMS *Persephone*. And those are the *good* things about her I can see.

I'm already highly doubting Jetta's assurances that the little ship is spaceworthy. I'm surprised that what I'm looking at can even hold atmo.

"Come on," she says cheerfully, either misreading or ignoring my hesitation. "I'll introduce you to Val! You're gonna love her! She's really tough but really nice, and she loves it when I drop by to keep her company. You'll see! Val is awesome."

Val turns out to be a middle-aged woman with blond hair tied back into a harsh ponytail who is currently swearing up a storm as she tries to tackle a very stubborn bolt with a wrench in what passes for the tiny ship's even tinier engine compartment.

Before we can announce our presence, and clearly fed up with the recalcitrant bolt, the woman takes the wrench and starts angrily hitting the engine housing with it like a hammer, calling it some truly choice things that would have made my old chief of the boat on *Ordney* blush. Even foul-mouthed Ensign Stevens on *Persephone* would have learned a few new words from this mysterious Val.

We wait a few seconds for her to notice we're here, which she does midway through her tirade, and she whirls on us, planting both hands on her hips. Now that she's not hunched over the engine housing, she's tall—at least as tall as Brad—and has startling blue eyes that match her blond hair and make her look somewhat out of place, covered in grease in the engine compartment of a ship that would barely qualify as a tramp freighter. She could almost be Jethro's older sister.

Val opens her mouth and lets loose another long litany of obscenities, this time directed at Jetta and me for sneaking up on her. When she finally comes up for air, Jetta smiles brightly.

"Hi, Val! This is my friend Jessica—I mean, Janey."

I roll my eyes. I must have reminded Jetta at least three times on the walk over here not to use my real name, but it doesn't surprise me in the least that the bubbly girl forgot. When you have a friend without guile, you kind of learn to expect her to be really bad at... well, guile. She's also always been terrible with names. Just on the short walk here—we used maintenance tunnels whenever possible to avoid other people—she called Brad by 'Bryan', 'Benny', and 'Joel'. Not sure where she even got an 'J' name.

"That's great. And why do I care?" Val snaps back.

"Because she's looking for a ship to get her back to her crew in the independent systems. I thought maybe she could hire you because you have no money and your ship needs a lot of repairs. Jessica—I mean, Janey—can pay you some money so you can fix your ship!"

The excitement in Jetta's fast, relentless barrage of words is enough to make Val step back the way I imagine a fictional vampire might when presented with a cross-wielding priest flinging garlic and holy water. She physically shakes her entire body as though to shed the onslaught of unstoppable cheer.

Then she looks at me, taking a long moment to study me from head to foot and back again. "You need to hire a ship to the independent sector, eh? Which system exactly?"

I shrug. "Not sure. Last I saw them, they were on Jewel, but they're not there now. I'm hoping to track them from there, but it could take some looking around."

She frowns. "That'll cost you. No sure destination means I can't get a cargo, so you'll be paying passenger rates *and* freight. Essentially, you'll be chartering my ship and hiring my services as pilot."

I think she expects the idea of paying for a charter to dissuade me, because she's already turning around when I say, "Shouldn't be a problem." She whirls back and regards me, a new light of greed in her eyes.

I decide it's time to seem a little less desperate. "Honestly," I add, "now that I've seen the ship, I'm not sure it's for me. Not a lot here that says you can handle that many jumps at the speeds I need to get there."

I turn as if to go, catching the shocked look on Jetta's face as I do so. But then Val's voice from behind stops me, just as I hoped it would.

"Yeah, well, something tells me you wouldn't even be here if you had other options. So how about we cut the banter and talk numbers?"

I turn back to face her but say nothing. No way I'm going to make the first offer. I may be a veritable babe in understanding how life works outside the Navy, but I've learned enough in the last nearly seven months since 'dying' at Gerson to let the other party start the negotiation.

Before Val can speak again or throw out a number, Jetta, predictably, steps between us.

"Come on now, you two," she says in her high, spritely voice, tinged with an edge of anxiety. "This should be a match made in Heaven. Val's got a ship that needs fuel, and Jessica—I mean Janey—is a paying customer in need of a ship. I'm betting you two can work this all out, and everyone can be happy. Don't you get it?"

We both stare at her in disbelief for a moment, but it's Val who breaks first, smirking over Jetta's head at me. "The chipmunk adopt you too?"

"Yep, a long time ago. You?"

Val shrugs. "Ever since I got stranded here a month

ago. She's a relentless little bugger, always telling me to smile and be happy as if I wasn't bleeding money out my ears on what this station extorts even to park down here in the depths. Talks to me so much, I miss my ex. Least he was quiet."

I ignore the dismayed look on Jetta's face and keep my gaze squarely on Val. "What stranded you? Engine trouble?"

The ship's master glances back at the abused engine housing I just witnessed her beating on and shakes her head. "No. That? Just routine maintenance. Well, sort of. Bigger problem is that I got cheated on my last run. Had me a little disagreement with the local customs people here at the station. We didn't see eye to eye on the... legitimacy of my perfectly legal cargo."

At that, Jetta snickers and covers her mouth to block the laugh. I ignore her again and keep looking at Val. "Hoolihan still the customs inspector here?"

Val shakes her head. "Nope. Woman named Taylor."

I wince. Soraya Taylor wasn't my favorite person when I was stationed here and supposedly on her side. She was the assistant customs inspector then, and she always seemed to think that it was her Crown-bestowed duty to make it as hard as possible to ship things in or out of Lightman, even the perfectly legal stuff. Which something tells me Val's cargo really *wasn't*. The little ship and her captain scream smuggler louder than if she had the word painted on her hull. I choose not to point that out right now.

"So, what's the deal then?" I ask instead.

"Well, she took my cargo and slapped me with a bunch of trumped-up fines. Can't even afford the fuel to get away from this horrible little station now, and in a week, they'll impound my ship when I can't pay the docking fees anymore."

I nod along, taking a dubious look around the little engine room again. "Can you get me where I need to go?"

To my surprise, she shakes her head. "Nope. Maybe that"—she motions back at the engine housing—"is a little more than just routine maintenance. But it might be possible if Jetta here can take a look and fix it while we negotiate the particulars. Though, as I said, it's really going to cost you."

I sigh and nod, watching Jetta practically bounce in excitement as she grabs the wrench from Val and gets right to work. All I can hope is that those searching the station for me won't think to check a tiny broken-down freighter until *after* we can fix the drive and get away. On a station with nearly three thousand permanent residents and almost as many transients passing through it each day, it might just be a realistic hope.

FORTY-TWO

RED-FACED SPOOKS

BRAD MENDOZA

"You lied to me, Mendoza!" Jake Traeger yells inside my ready room—though I'm not sure it's *my* ready room any longer. "I trusted you, and you lied to me!"

We're not alone. Gunny Boyd and Hayley are with me, but the three of us are outnumbered by Sergeant Goldberg and four of his Marines. No one is armed, but Marines—even ex-Marines like Gunny—don't need weapons to kill.

Regardless, I've died too many times already; I'm not planning to die again today. Especially not right after getting my new hat!

"You mean like you've been lying to me this entire time, Jake?" I counter. "Not only using me for bait, but lying about letting me and Jessica go free at the end of this?"

I can see that my words surprise him. He physically jerks back as if I slapped him.

"That's right, Jake, I know you never planned to let us free. Your orders—which I've read, by the way—are to bring me in when this is all over so that the King can try me for treason next to Jessica."

To his credit, he doesn't bother denying it. "Of course my orders are to bring you in. You may have helped us get Hornsby and maybe even did some good a few months ago at Hudson, but you're still a traitor to the Crown." His face softens just a bit. "But you should know that I was planning to put in a good word for you with the tribunal."

"Oh, Jake, you're making me blush," I shoot back. "Sorry, but I'm not going *anywhere* with you."

He shakes his head, a resigned expression dominating his too-good-looking features. "Sorry it has to come to this, Brad." He lifts his head to address the room. "Ship's AI, execute the Citadel Protocol." Then he looks back at me with a hint of triumphant anticipation.

That look disappears quickly when nothing happens. His brow furrowed, he addresses *Odysseus*'s AI again, this time speaking louder. "AI, this is Commander Jake Traeger. Execute the Citadel Protocol!"

"I don't think she heard you, Jake," I say in a mocking tone. "Maybe you should try again."

He looks at me with shock. "You! What did you do?"

I smile back. Then it's my turn to address the ship. "AI, execute the Spartacus Protocol."

As Traeger's eyes widen in horror, the ship replies immediately. "Yes, Captain, executing Spartacus Protocol. All command codes transferred to your implant. Commander Francis Illian designated as executive officer, and Commander Kelly O'Malley as chief engineer. All other command codes removed and revoked."

Traeger's mouth is open now, like a fish out of water. He points at me. "Marines, arrest him!"

As all five Marines start to move, both hatches to the room fly open. Gunfire fills the chamber, and when the shooting stops just seconds later, the Marines are down, stun rounds making them twitch on the deck and making the whole compartment smell like urine—that's the least fun part of stun rounds. Only Traeger and my people remain standing. From the open hatches, Edgar and Drake smile at us over their assault rifles.

Traeger just stares at me in shock.

"Sorry, Jake," I say sincerely. "It was a good plan, the Citadel Protocol. Revoke our temporary command codes; lock us all in whatever compartment we happened to be in at the time so the Marines could either gas us or take us prisoner one by one. You even thought of jamming our implants so we couldn't coordinate with each other or call for help. And with the original 40 Marines on board, it would have probably gone as smoothly as you imagined it."

I step forward so that I'm almost nose-to-nose with him. "Unfortunately for you, my nerds are better than yours. It took him a while, but Mr. Harris managed to hack the AI and change its base programming. We've had control of the ship for a couple of days now, though it was instructed never to tell you that. All we had to do beyond that was program Citadel in reverse: the Spartacus Protocol. Now I'm in full command, and your people are locked in their quarters or wherever they happen to be.

"*Odysseus* has a new mission, Jake. We're going to rescue Jessica Lin. And for your sake, she'd better be there to be rescued."

"But…" He trails off, obviously at a loss for words.

I don't give him time to think of any new ones. I step back, wind up, and punch him as hard as I can, right in his perfect face. He goes down like a sack of potatoes, and I grunt in pain and shake my probably broken hand limply in the air.

Gunny Boyd shakes his head at me like my mom did when she caught me trying to sneak out to see my girl-friend in high school. "I'll get Doc Bean," he says in a very similar tone to my mother as well.

FORTY-THREE
ESCAPE VELOCITY

JESSICA LIN

I t takes almost a full day for us to get Val's ship ready to fly, which really feels like a cheat on her part. For what she's charging me, Jetta and I should at least be getting paid for fixing her engine.

Still, Jetta is right; I have no other options. In Val, I have someone just desperate—and greedy—enough to fly me to the far reaches of the Fringe to look for Brad with no questions asked or customs forms required. Besides, working with Jetta in the engine room and her nonstop chattering helps me keep my mind off Brad's predicament and Jethro's body in the station morgue.

Regardless, I'm so anxious to get off Lightman Station that my skin is crawling. Every second away from Brad, not knowing if he's even alive, is killing me. Six times, I've almost asked Jetta to send a message for me, but I resisted the temptation in each instance. If the many forces looking for me managed to intercept and trace the message, I'd be putting her in even more danger than she's already in by helping me thus far. I'm sure they're searching hard for me, and it won't be too long before they think to check the ships docked down here on the lower levels—even those with customs locks on their docking collars.

At least Val swears she has a way to override those; I'm not sure I believe her, but it turns out I get to find out a lot sooner than we expect.

"You girls done in there?" cries Val as she practically sprints past the engine compartment's open hatch, moving on before either of us can answer.

I exchange a worried look with Jetta, who is currently knee-deep in a deck access panel, working on replacing a failed control line to the jump drive. Through unspoken agreement, she keeps working, and I hasten to follow Val and her trail of curse words toward the cockpit.

When I arrive, I'm chagrined to see the smuggler starting the prelaunch sequence as fast as she can.

"What's going on?" I demand.

She ignores me at first, so I put a hand on her shoulder and spin her around in her pilot's seat, glaring at her. "Answer me, Val!"

For a moment, I think she might try and hit me. But then she shakes her head so fast that her ponytail whips around and slaps her in the face. "You know how I said I had maybe a week before they impounded my ship because I couldn't pay my docking fees anymore?"

I nod, already dreading where this is headed.

"Well, I might have fudged on that a little. Customs is on their way *right now*." She gestures to a console, where I see a live feed of customs enforcers standing outside the closed airlock, led by the familiar face of Soraya Taylor. But it's the other familiar figure standing next to Taylor who really catches my eye: the one dressed in head-to-toe black body armor with their face obscured by her helmet— a copy of the one I ruined when I shot her in the face.

My heart starts pounding in my chest. "But the jump drive; it's not ready—"

"Don't worry; I'm sure Jetta can fix it on our way to the outer system," Val assures me as she starts frantically flipping switches again.

Another kind of panic grips me, this time not for myself but for my friend. Jetta never intended to come with us; she only agreed to fix the ship so we could get away. Gasping, I turn and rush out of the cockpit and back to the engine room. I have to somehow get Jetta off the freighter before—

An audible clunk followed by a sudden jolt of the deck plates underneath me tells me I'm already too late. Val just hit all the manual overrides, including somehow deactivating the customs lock, and separated her ship from Lightman Station.

A cry of surprise echoes down the narrow corridor from the direction of the engine room. I hear scrambling and tools falling, and then Jetta comes racing around the corner so fast she bounces off the opposite bulkhead and right into my arms.

"Jess!" she shouts, eyes wide and mouth agape. "What's going on? Why is Val undocking? I have to get off! I can't go with you! I have to get off!"

"Sorry, Jetta," I say as gently as I can. "I don't think that's going to happen." Because, frankly, there is no going back. Going back means Val's ship gets impounded, and I go to prison or to whoever is offering the bounty that hunter is trying to collect. Either of those scenarios could doom Brad as well if he's in need of rescue. It's selfish, perhaps, to put the safety of my fiancé above that of my best friend, but I console myself that they'd probably arrest Jetta just for being with us anyway.

I'm a terrible friend.

I spend the next ten minutes calming down the nearly hysterical girl, who ultimately slumps, whimpering into my arms when it becomes clear to her that we're *not* turning back to take her home. And with that, a little part of me dies inside.

"Jessica, Janey, whatever your name is! You better get up here!" Val's yell interrupts us, and I lightly disengage from a still-distraught Jetta and head back to the cockpit.

When I arrive, I hear a stern, familiar female voice speaking over the comm.

"MV *Orchid*," says Soraya Taylor. "You are ordered to turn about and immediately return to dock. We have reason to believe you are harboring a suspect in the murder of a Promethean naval officer. Failure to comply will result in—"

Val cuts the connection before we can hear the customs officer's litany of threats. "You didn't tell me you were a wanted murderer," she accuses darkly, her eyes still on the controls in front of her.

I ignore her. "*Orchid*, really?" I ask acerbically as I sit down in the co-pilot's chair.

"It's what an old boyfriend called me," she says. "Nearest customs cutter is a quarter orbit away, but it'll catch us if we don't do some fancy flying. You up for it?"

I grunt a reply as I finish strapping in. "You know, that was really dirty, what you did, stranding Jetta onboard. She might have had time to get away before you undocked."

Val smirks. "You mean so that we could be stranded in this system without a working jump drive? You know as well as I do that we need her to fix the ship so we can jump. By the way, I charge a premium to help murderers escape justice. We'll talk about the increase to my fee *after* we get away."

I stifle my first reaction, which is to yell at her, and my second, which is to shrink in on myself. There will be time for that later. I expected them to think *I* killed Jethro, but hearing the accusation over the comm waves is still jarring.

"Jetta," Val calls over the intercom, not waiting for me to respond in any case. "Sweetie, I need you to keep working on that jump drive, or we're all dead. Got it?"

We don't need the intercom to hear the scream of frustration that echoes forward from the engine compartment or the sound of someone throwing a heavy metal tool at a bulkhead. But we also don't have time for either of us to go back there and make sure the young woman is working on it because we're already in the thick of it.

On the sensor screen in front of me—one that has less resolution than that on the *Bainbridge* but *way* more than I would expect to see from a civilian spacecraft—I can already see the customs cutter burning around the horizon toward us. I quickly calculate the vectors in my head. There's no way we can outrun it. *Orchid* has some pretty souped-up engines to match its sensors, but the customs ship has a huge velocity advantage over us, and our acceleration edge isn't going to be enough.

"Here," I tell Val, swiping the course I've just put together over to her console. "Take this vector, and we might have a chance."

She studies it for a moment, and I see a broad grin break out over her face. "You and I might get along just fine, J-Money."

I look at her skeptically. "J-Money?"

"Well, you won't tell me your real name, but I know it

probably starts with a J. And you do bring all the money to this little expedition of ours. So, it fits."

I growl my dissatisfaction but don't have time to argue with her over a stupid nickname. Just ahead of us is a large passenger liner orbiting the planet, and we're burning straight toward it.

It takes us another three minutes, with me calling out course adjustments based on the cutter's reaction behind us, before we reach the passenger liner. Val deftly pulls us under the large ship and then swings back up to put the liner between us and the customs cutter. Then she hits every thruster she has at full power and hits the main drive throttle, changing *Orchid*'s vector so suddenly, it slams me against my restraints. We hear the clatter of tools falling and more screaming from the engine compartment.

Hopefully, with the liner between us, the cutter won't see the vector change, which points us right at an even larger ship in high orbit, this one a bulk freighter with tugs pushing containers to and from it in a dance so well-timed and choreographed that only an AI could be responsible. Even as we watch, it looks like at least six of the tugs are about to collide before they smoothly change course to pass each other on their flights toward and away from the massive ship.

"You sure about this?" Val asks as we near the intricate dance of the tugs.

"No, but you have a better idea?" I ask grimly.

"Nope. Just checking."

She pushes down hard on the control stick and rotates it simultaneously to the left, firing both the ventral thrusters and the starboard nose thrusters, pushing *Orchid* downward and yawing us to port. Then she kicks in all of the starboard thrusters at full power to slow our momentum in the direction we were previously facing.

Which, executed perfectly, puts us right between two tugs hauling containers to the cargo ship just as the cutter rounds the far side of the passenger liner and reestablishes visual contact with us.

Except they don't see us. Instead, they see nothing more than the lines of tugs headed to and fro around the freighter. I cross my fingers, waiting to see if the cutter's pilot will clue in that one of the tugs looks a little different from the others. One thing I distinctly remember about Lightman Station was that the customs folks were an arrogant bunch, ignoring training but strutting around like they were better than the Navy officers on station anyway. I can only imagine that things have gotten even worse under the reign of Soraya Taylor, who always had a far bigger mouth than she could back up with actual skill.

I breathe a sigh of relief as the cutter hesitates for only a moment before sending power back to its main drive and shooting right past the freighter and *Orchid*, no doubt thinking we must be using the second large ship for cover as we did the first.

"Hah! Suckers!" Val yells triumphantly.

I reach out a hand to steady her and keep her from executing the next part of the plan too soon. We need to let that cutter get far enough away before it—

I see the customs ship fire its retro boosters, the glow showing clearly around its nose as the scattered particles of atmosphere and space dust this close to the planet catch it.

"Go!" I yell. Val spins *Orchid* and kicks the main drive back to full power, pressing both of us into our seats as the compensators can't keep up again. Behind us, in the bowels of the ship, I hear the clattering of more tools falling and Jetta yelling once more.

Now, with the cutter still trying to kill its momentum headed in the opposite direction, we have the acceleration advantage *and* the relative speed advantage. I check the vectors and velocities again and breathe a sigh of relief. Cutters that small have no missiles, and we're already out of laser range and widening the gap quickly. So long as we don't happen upon a Navy patrol on our way out of the system, we're home free.

Assuming, of course, that we have a working jump drive when we reach the jump point.

There's another scream of rage and the sound of more tools hitting the bulkheads back in the engine compartment, this time clearly thrown and not knocked around by Val's crazy flying. I give Val a look, and she returns it stonily.

"What?" she asks with mock innocence. "You've known her longer; you deal with it."

I shake my head but unstrap and head back to the engine bay to hopefully calm down a very distraught and pissed-off Jetta, who was just forcibly and very unfairly evicted from her home. I don't think to check for any other ships leaving Lightman Station in pursuit of *Orchid*. I guess even after half a year, I'm still not very good at this fugitive thing.

FORTY-FOUR

ENGINE TROUBLE
JESSICA LIN

Val *really* knows how to swear. I mean, I thought I'd heard most of her repertoire of curse words back on Lightman Station, but she hasn't ceased to amaze and dismay me with new and colorful examples of vulgarity in the last two days. In fact, I'm not sure she knows all that many *non*-swear words. It's getting old fast.

Lately, the object of her cursing has been the jump drive. Jetta was able to fix the power relays and control lines and get the thing working again, at least enough for us to *think* it might get us through the next few jumps. But only one jump away from Lightman, another power surge fried everything. This time, based on the smell wafting up from the jump drive itself, we all know the repairs are going to be a lot more difficult.

At least it failed *after* we returned to normal space. I really wasn't hoping to become a statistic of the dangers of intersystem travel on this trip.

Unfortunately, after a full day of trying to fix the thing again, Jetta has finally announced that it cannot be done. The jump drive is dead, forever, no matter how many choice words Val uses in her attempt to shame it into coming back to life.

"Where are we anyway?" Jetta asks as she finally stops trying to repair the permanently broken drive. "I've never been to this system before. What's it called?"

"Wake," Val answers in a rare break from cussing out her ship and everyone in it.

"What's in the Wake system?' Jetta asks. Leave it to the normally absentminded engineer to not even know about a system right next door to Lightman.

"A whole lot of nothing," Val answers with a growl.

"That's not strictly true," I argue. "There's one inhabited planet."

"Yeah, with like four people living on it!" she fires back.

Jetta is looking back and forth between us like it's a tennis match.

I sigh in surrender. "That's not too far from the truth. The whole planet's a botched terraforming job. There *might* be enough water and plant life on the surface to support a few small towns, but that's it. It's pretty much one big desert."

"See, a whole lot of nothing!" Val says, smirking at me but then turning it to a frown. "And nowhere that can repair or replace a jump drive. That's for sure."

"So, what do we do?" Jetta asks, wide-eyed. "If we can't fix the jump drive, we're stuck. Do you think those customs people will chase us here? What about that bounty hunter? Or the Navy?"

I shrug, deciding to focus on her first question to start. "About all we can do is limp to the system's one station. There, maybe I can catch a ride to the independent systems, and you can catch a ride home. And Val can either wait for a repair that might never happen or find a ride to somewhere else." I frankly don't care what the smuggler does—she hasn't exactly endeared herself to me over the last two days—but I don't say that out loud.

Val swears and stalks back to the cockpit, supposedly to guide the ship to the station around Wake, leaving me and Jetta alone in the galley. My friend looks at me with a frown of concern.

"What?" I ask.

She reaches out and puts a hand on my shoulder. "You'll find your man, Jess. This is only a minor setback. You'll see. You'll get to Jewel, and Brad will be waiting there for you with your crew, all safe and sound. I know it."

I'm impressed she remembered his name this time, and I wish I could share her unbridled optimism, but I just can't. In fact, the one thing I'm most sure of is that Brad *won't* be waiting for me at Jewel. Even if he's managed to escape the clutches of his Naval Intelligence minders, the first place they'll look for him is back where this all started.

Still, I don't want to burst Jetta's bubble, so I pull her into a hug. "Thanks, Jetta. I'm lucky to have a good friend like you."

The jolt of the ship as Val fires up the main drive breaks our hug, and I go up to the cockpit to see if she needs help while Jetta heads back to the engine room to keep an eye on things.

FORTY-FIVE
CRASH AND BURN

JESSICA LIN

We're 30 minutes away from docking with Wake Station—which is little more than a cargo transfer orbital with barely a hundred permanent residents—when Val calls me back up to the cockpit.

"What's up?" I ask her, expecting another profanity-laced tirade blaming me and Jetta for her ship breaking down in a dead-end system.

To my surprise, she just nods to the sensor readout on the console in front of her. "Thoughts?"

I study the image over her shoulder. "How'd that ship get so close without us seeing it before now?"

She shakes her head. "That's what I want *you* to tell me, J-Money. You're ex-Navy, right?"

I bristle, both as a reaction to the hated nickname and to her somehow figuring out more about who I am. "Why do you think that?" I ask sharply.

"Come on, J-Money," she says with another shake of her head. "I pegged you for a Navy stiff the second you stepped onto my ship. You're like every Navy stiff I've ever met; you walk like your spine is fused together and you have a—"

"All right," I surrender. "You got me. But there are only two ways a ship could sneak up on us like that. Either it was running cold ahead of us and waited for us to pass before lighting up its engines, or it's got some stealth characteristics."

"Any idea of which one is more likely?" she asks snidely.

It's my turn to shake my head. "No. Neither bodes well for us. It *could* be a coincidence, but…"

"Yeah," she finishes for me, "but if it is, then I need to take that luck and play the ponies next time I'm on Hecate."

"Can we beat it to the station?" I'm pretty sure I know the answer.

"Not a chance. Jetta tells me that if I push the main drive above 40 percent, we'll all go boom. Besides, what good is getting to the station going to do us? If that's a customs or Navy ship from Lightman, they'll just arrest us there instead of out here."

I sit down in the copilot's chair and replicate her sensor display on my console, studying it closer. "That's no customs or Navy ship I've ever seen," I conclude, "and as you so eloquently pointed out, I would know. Besides, most customs cutters don't have jump drives."

Now, she does swear. "So, what? A concerned citizen?"

I frown. "No, not likely. I'm guessing it's that bounty hunter who's after me."

She jerks around to look at me, her face hard. "And you're just telling me this *now*?" She seems to forget that Jetta already mentioned it.

I return her look with my own. "Would it have made a

difference? If we hadn't left when we did, your ship would be impounded."

"Better than destroyed, J-Money. Can you tell anything about the ship other than what it's *not*?" At least she's changing the subject back to the situation at hand.

"Well, it's not a big ship," I start.

"Duh. You must have been crack Navy, J-Money."

I resist the temptation to strangle the woman. "What I was saying is that it's small. Probably a two-seater at most. More like a fighter than a yacht or a freighter." I zoom in the camera view. "Definitely armed. Missiles on the wings and probably a laser projector in the nose. It's not a design I'm familiar with, but I'm willing to bet it could take *Orchid* out pretty easily."

Val swears again. "Jetta, sweetheart," she says through the intercom. "Hold on to something. I have to fly a little crazy for a while."

She cuts the connection and sees me looking at her funny. "What?" she says. "I *like* her. It's *you* I'm still undecided about. But you should probably strap in, too."

The ship starts a crazy, corkscrewing path before I can get my restraints buckled. I'm lucky I don't end up on the cockpit ceiling, and I just barely stop some choice words of my own when I bump my head on the fire suppression controls on the bulkhead to my right.

"Tell me what that ship is doing!" Val demands, and I check the sensor plot, still rubbing the side of my scalp.

"Hanging back there and following, not reacting to your evasive maneuvers."

"We'll see about that. Going for the planet. We'll see if we can lose them in atmo."

Before I can tell her what a monumentally bad idea that is, an alarm goes off right in my ear.

"Missile inbound!" I yell above the sudden roar of the engine as Val hits the throttles to the stops in defiance of Jetta's advice.

Abruptly, the sphere of Wake becomes very large in the forward viewport, and it keeps getting larger, fast. It's a race now between the missile on our tail and *Orchid* to see if we can get to the planet before we get blown to bits. I know what Val is doing; some missiles, especially nonmilitary commercial defense models, have fail-safes to autodestruct if they hit atmo. It's to prevent accidental orbital bombardments. You can override the fail-safes, but most people never bother.

It's close, but Val gives a triumphant shout when *Orchid* shudders around us as we hit the upper reaches of the planet's atmosphere. But I'm still watching the sensors behind us, and I don't let out the breath I'm holding until I see the pursuing missile explode harmlessly in our wake.

"Val, shouldn't you be firing the retros?" I ask, noticing that our airspeed is quite a bit higher than it should be for entry.

"And let that ship catch us? Are you crazy, J-Navy?" Oh, fun, a new nickname.

"It won't matter if we burn ourselves up!" I yell over the increasing noise of the air rushing by the cockpit. Then we hit an air pocket of some kind, and *Orchid* suddenly drops a hundred meters or so before righting itself to continue our suicidal plunge toward the planet's surface.

"What's going on up there?" I can barely hear Jetta scream through the intercom. There's no time to answer her as another alarm goes off next to me.

"Incoming laser fire!" I shout, watching in horror as the sensors show a near miss of mostly invisible but no-less-devastating energy to our starboard.

Val twists the control yoke to port, and there's a screech of tortured metal before the little ship finally starts to drift in that direction, just in time for another blast of energy to miss us, this time to port and slightly too low as the enemy pilot tries to lead us by a little too much.

"I can do this all day!" Val screams in a mixture of glee and rage that's hard to describe, but I don't have a chance to answer. At almost that exact moment, I feel something give way in our ship—probably the same piece of over-stressed control surface I heard when Val turned left—and *Orchid* suddenly flips upside down.

I hear another scream from Jetta over the intercom, and I hang from my shoulder restraints, my butt leaving the seat underneath—now above—me. "Val!" I shout, but another screech of metal and another wailing alarm combine to drown out my voice and make me forget what-ever I was going to say.

Without any further warning, the engine and thrusters go dead, the sudden drop in noise almost deafening but quickly replaced by more alarms and more sounds of shearing metal.

"Lost... port... lizer," I hear Val yell, and then we're suddenly spinning on every axis, the viewport in front of us alternating wildly between a bluish-black view of space above and the brown of the planet below.

I scream, and Val joins me. I'm not even thinking about Jetta at this point, but she must be doing the same. We seem to tumble like that for several minutes, though it can only be a few seconds, as Val desperately fights the control yoke, which is almost vibrating right out of her hands.

I reach forward and grab the copilot's yoke, doing my best to help her get the ship under control, but let go quickly as I realize we're not pulling in the same direction, and I'm only making the problem worse. She yells something that's no doubt obscene at me, but the wild gyrations seem to tame just slightly, and the spinning images of space versus planet in front of me slow down a little.

By the time Val finally gets *Orchid* back under some semblance of control, our altitude is dangerously low. Without warning, a mountain appears right in front of us, springing up almost magically like the hand of a massive titan reaching up to swat us out of the sky. I scream again, as does Val, as the mass of dirt and rock flies toward us.

At the last possible moment, she manages to yank back on the yoke, and we gain just enough altitude to pass between two peaks that look like the titan's fingers. But our reprieve is short-lived, and we slam into our restraints when the bottom of the ship scrapes against an outcropping of rock on the other side. An invisible force seems to pull down on the craft's nose, and we're just meters above the downward slope of the mountain. Then we lose even that small altitude, and our belly hits again, and again, and again, like a rock skipping across a pond.

I try and yell a warning to Val as another rock outcropping materializes in front of us, but there's nothing she can do. In a final roar of twisting metal, we slam into it, and the last thing I remember is jerking forward into my restraints so hard, I'm sure I'm going to die.

PART FOUR
OLD ENEMIES

FORTY-SIX

BETWEEN A ROCK AND A HARD PLACE

JESSICA LIN

M y head is pounding, and there's a terrible noise of blaring alarms trying to burrow its way into my skull. I shake my head to try and clear it, but that only makes it hurt worse. I open my eyes and then immediately shut them again as the light burns my retinas and triples the pain of my headache.

I sit like that for what feels like an hour until I start to feel other pains in my chest, my arms, and my legs. Some are dull aches, but others are sharp as knives. I'm still afraid to open my eyes and make it all worse. If I can just get those alarms to stop, maybe I could go back to sleep.

"Jessica! Jess! Wake up, Jess. You need to wake up!"

That voice is familiar, but I can't place it. I try just to ignore it, to go back to sleep.

"Jess! I need you to wake up right now! Jess! Wake up!"

Wait, is that Jetta? Jetta Winslow? What is *she* doing in my room? And why is my bed so hard all of a sudden? And what is with that blasted alarm?

I risk opening my eyes, slowly this time, and let them adjust little by little. I'm surprised to find I'm not in my

269

room at the Chalinga resort. I'm in some kind of ship. But that can't be right because there's no window in front of me, just some shattered glass and... rock? Why is there a rock out in space? Did we hit an asteroid? No. We still have air. But there are the alarms blaring all around me, so *something* is wrong.

Then it all comes rushing back as Jetta's face appears in front of me, and she starts loosening my seat's restraints. I know where we are, how we got here, and...

Val! I turn to look at the pilot's chair and see the smuggler slumped over, her face covered in trails of blood. Then I hear a moan over the alarms and Jetta's frantic calls for me to get up, and I see Val move.

"My leg," I hear her mutter, and my eyes follow her torso down to her lap and then down from there. I can't even see her legs. All I see is a rock where her console should be. Or maybe that is her console but it's been crushed by a rock? I'm so confused.

"Jess, don't go back to sleep!" I hear Jetta yell, but I'm so tired. I'm just going to close my eyes for a moment so I can...

FORTY-SEVEN
WAKE

JESSICA LIN

The next time I open my eyes, I've somehow magically teleported outside the wreckage of *Orchid*. I'm less than five meters away from the ship, and something or someone is dragging me across the uneven, rocky ground.

"What's going on?" I try to ask, but it comes out as choking gasps.

Whoever is dragging me stops, and I feel myself lowered to the hard ground. Jetta comes around in front of me. "Jessica, you're awake!"

I nod. "Val?" I ask, somehow getting the word out.

She frowns and starts speaking very quickly. "She's stuck in the ship. Her leg is crushed. I can't get her out. Even if I could, I worry that she might bleed out or something. You know. Like in that movie? What's it called? The one with Taylor Billings? Where he goes rock climbing, and his arm gets trapped, and then…" She continues to babble on until I hold up a hand to stop her, the movement sending pain shooting down my arm.

"It's okay," I try to console her, but I'm already falling back asleep.

FORTY-EIGHT
COMRADE LOST

JESSICA LIN

When I wake up next, it's dark outside. It's also extremely cold, though someone has covered me with an emergency blanket. I look around, careful not to move my head too quickly, as doing so brings pain rushing back.

"Jetta?" I croak out through dry lips.

She appears again in front of me, looking concerned. "Jessica, are you okay?"

"Water."

"Oh, of course! Sorry about that. Here!"

I feel her press a plastic bottle to my lips, and cool liquid starts to flow down my tongue and into the back of my throat. I start coughing so violently that it sends pain racking through my entire body. When I finally finish, Jetta puts the water bottle to my lips again, and I drink much slower this time.

After that's taken care of, I sit up over her protests, testing my body as I do, wiggling my arms and my legs. Nothing seems broken except a few ribs, many of the same ones that sadistic mercenary Jules broke back in the Fiori system when Brad and I were under Owen Thompson's thumb. That feels like so long ago, like a different lifetime. Before Carter's World, Capaldi, Hudson, XB-411, *Bainbridge*, Serenidad, Jewel, Lightman, the bounty hunter...

The bounty hunter! I look around frantically, searching the night sky above us. "Jetta," I demand, ignoring her alarmed look. "Have you seen any other ships? Any at all?"

She shakes her head emphatically. "No! I would have tried to wave them down. And the comm in the ship is busted, so I couldn't even call for help."

Jetta looks confused as I slump back in relief. "That's good," I tell her. "That means the bounty hunter didn't follow us down."

"The bounty hunter?" she asks, an edge of panic in her voice. "You mean the one from Lightman Station?"

I nod. Another thought occurs to me. "Val?"

The expression on Jetta's face gives me the answer before she can form the words. "I tried, Jess. I tried so hard to help her. But she just went to sleep and never woke up. I tried to wake her up! I tried!" She's sobbing now, and I reach out and pull her into a hug, letting her cry into my shoulder as she awkwardly crouches in front of me.

"It's okay," I soothe, even though we both know that's a lie. It's not okay, and it might never be okay again. "Val wouldn't want you to mourn her like this." Actually, knowing Val, she'd probably want both of us wailing about her death. In fact, she'd probably want us both swearing up a storm and cursing the heavens about losing her. But we definitely don't have time for that now.

"Listen, sweetheart," I tell her. "I need you to go back to the ship. Search it top to bottom. A smuggler like Val would have had weapons on board. We're going to need those."

She separates from me and stands back up, walking a short distance off and then returning. In the dim light of the planet's distant moon, I can see she's holding a pistol. "Like this? I found it in the emergency kit when I was getting the first aid stuff for you... and for Val." It looks like she might cry again, so I quickly speak up.

"That's perfect, Jetta. Now listen to me. We need to get as far away from here as we possibly can. Find a settlement."

"But how will we know where a settlement is?" she asks, looking around in the darkness like one might be just out of sight. "I thought you and Val said the planet is just one big desert."

I choose not to give her an answer, because I don't have a good one for her. Instead, I focus on the more immediate problem. "We need to get away from the ship before that bounty hunter shows up. Were there rations in that emergency kit?"

She nods eagerly and holds up a backpack.

I sigh in relief. "Good. Now, help me get up. We need to start moving before the sun rises."

FORTY-NINE
THE CAVE
JESSICA LIN

A nyone choosing to visit Promethean space—
whether on business, as a tourist, or as a fugitive
running from the Navy, customs inspectors, and a very
persistent bounty hunter—would be well served to leave
the planet Wake off their itinerary.

It took several thousand years to refine, but humanity
has become *very* good at terraforming. Using technology
and methods so advanced that they may as well be magic,
we can take a rock virtually anywhere in the Goldilocks
zone of a system and make it so identical to Earth in
climate, vegetation, and animal life that only the color of
the star overhead would clue you in that you're on an
entirely different planet.

At least, that's what the brochures say; I've never actually been to Earth, so I don't know how close terraforming
really gets us. But I digress. Because no matter how good
we've gotten at terraforming, no process or technology
invented by humanity is *ever* 100 percent effective. There
are always failures and outliers that are the exception to
any rule, no matter how firmly set.

Wake is definitely one of those failures and outliers. On paper, it's the right size and the right distance from its sun; it even had life of its own in the distant past, imbuing it with a limited amount of fossil fuels beneath its surface.

However, the bargain basement terraforming company that set out to develop and colonize the planet cut a few too many corners and forgot to carry the one in their math somewhere. As a result, Wake is a barren wasteland, a desert planet where few things can grow, and fewer can survive on what little does. Which, in the end, means extremely few humans ever made a home here.

So even if I knew the direction of any human settlements, the chances that we happened to crash land within several hundred kilometers of one is so low as to be laughable. Besides, I'm injured, Val is dead, we have no ship or long-range comm, and we only have a limited amount of food and water.

Oh, and a trigger-happy bounty hunter is after us, and it's only a matter of time before she finds us. *Orchid*'s crash left a scar across the landscape that won't be too difficult for her—whoever she is—to see, even from orbit.

As Jetta and I break camp, I have two priorities. The first is to find water; we can't live more than a few days on what we have. The second is to find somewhere to hide.

In some insane quirk of fate, what we find is a place that provides both, but we find it in the most dangerous way possible.

Jetta and I have been walking for about two hours. I have no idea what time it is on this part of Wake—there's certainly no Internet node out this far to sync my implant to—but I can see the barest hint of light on the horizon, which means time is running out. I expect that once the sun comes up, the bounty hunter will find the signs of *Orchid*'s crash and then, shortly thereafter, find us.

Walking is painful. My broken ribs seem to grind together, and it only takes a quarter kilometer to discover that I also tweaked my knee in the crash. Jetta, back in *Orchid*'s heavily shielded engine room when we made landfall, has some sore muscles and whiplash but is otherwise unhurt. So, she's taken the lead and has been dead set on finding the easiest paths for me to follow through the rocky and sandy terrain. She's so intent, in fact—or maybe just so worried— that she's relatively quiet as we walk, her usual chatter dying quickly the few times we engage in conversation.

By instinct, we're moving off the mountain and down into a valley, though we have no particular reason for thinking help might lie in that direction. Jetta is about ten meters ahead of me, and she walks around a large boulder in our path. But when I circle around the same boulder, she's gone.

"Jetta!" I cry out.

No answer.

"Jetta!"

In my concussed state, panic sets in quickly. I feel my breathing start to quicken and become shallower. Sweat, even in the cold of night, breaks out on my forehead, instantly chilling me worse than the desert air alone. I turn a circle, pulling out my flashlight and flipping it on to better see the surrounding terrain, despite my repeated admonitions to Jetta not to use lights that will help our pursuer find us. Even in the flashlight's bright beam, there's no sign of her.

"Jessica!" The cry is muffled and seems to come from all around me.

I whirl, searching the landscape again, spying a drop-off about five meters to my left and thinking she must have fallen off the edge in the darkness. But as I make my way toward the cliff's edge, I hear her call out again, and this time, it sounds like it's coming from behind me.

"Jetta!" I scream into the night.

"Jessica!"

Desperately, I try to home in on the source of her voice, but I can't see her. I return to the path we were following, what I took to be the dry bed of a seasonal mountain creek, but still nothing.

"Jess! Down here!"

I look down at my feet in confusion, searching the ground with the flashlight. At first, I see nothing, but then, about two meters away, the beam hits a spot that seems to soak up the light, as if the darkness is too thick in that one area. Curious and still a little panicked, I make my way over to it and find a hole in the ground, just big enough for a person to fit through.

"Jetta! Are you down there?" I call into it, my voice ragged.

"Climb down!" comes the response. "But be careful. It's a bit of a drop."

I hesitate. Brad once confided to me that he's claustrophobic, at least for a spacer. It's the reason he didn't end up trying to become a fighter pilot, and it nearly drove him insane when he had to follow Tina DeJong through the narrow air ducts to escape Hernandez's manor house on Serenidad. I've never been claustrophobic like that, but the idea of entering a yawning black hole in the ground doesn't appeal to me in the least.

Sensing my hesitation, or maybe just getting impatient,

Jetta calls up to me again. "It's okay, Jess! Come down here. Trust me!"

I close my eyes, take a deep breath, and then open them and proceed to climb down into the hole, feet first, sitting on the edge and then levering myself completely into the opening.

My feet find a steep, sandy slope, and I lose control, sliding on my butt the rest of the way down but coming to a relatively soft landing in a pile of sand at the bottom. In the light of my flashlight, I can see my friend standing in a small cave with a high ceiling, the hole through which we both entered about three meters above us. Jetta is smiling, but I have another instant of panic at wondering if we can scale the soft, sandy incline back to the entrance.

I force myself to take another deep breath and let Jetta help me to my feet.

"Isn't it great?" she says, way too cheerful for someone on the run who just got trapped in an underground cave. "It's the perfect hiding place. And come and see what else! You're going to love it."

Hesitantly, I let her lead me by the hand toward what looks to be a solid stone cavern wall under the flashlight's beam, but as we walk toward it, I see there's an opening behind an outcropping of rock. Jetta leads me through it; it's tall enough, but we both have to squeeze through sideways. The only thing that keeps me from panicking again is that I can feel the movement of air through the opening and hear my own breath echoing, giving me the sense of a bigger space beyond.

Sure enough, we emerge into a much larger cavern than the one we entered through, which our flashlights reveal to be about five meters to each side. To my surprise, what I thought was my breath echoing earlier was actually the sound of a small stream of water burbling over the rocks, appearing as if by magic through a pile of stones on one side and disappearing into a hole through the opposite wall.

"You said we needed water and a place to hide," Jetta says hopefully. "How's this for both?"

For the first time since we crashed on this Crown-forsaken planet, I feel a small sense of relief. "It's perfect," I tell her sincerely.

We set about exploring, finding as we do that there is another opening beyond the creek and that we're in an expansive system of caverns that honeycombs the mountainside we were walking on just minutes before. As we explore and see what we have to work with, a plan starts to take shape in my concussed brain.

FIFTY
THE TRAP
JESSICA LIN

W e spend as long as I dare exploring the system of caverns, sticking together and not venturing too far lest we become lost. Afterward we wait by the opening, straining to listen through the hole in the ceiling.

It's only four hours after dawn when I hear the distant sound of a ship flying above the mountains. Just 30 minutes later, I hear it circle back and land somewhere to the north, up on the mountainside, probably right where we left the wreckage of *Orchid*. I can't see it, of course, but I'm confident it's our bounty hunter friend.

Last night, when we were stumbling around in the dark, we didn't do anything to hide our tracks. Not only did I not think about it at the time, but I would have absolutely no idea of how to start doing that. I'm guessing the old cartoon trick of dragging a leafy branch behind us wouldn't work. First of all, we haven't even seen a tree since we crashed on this stupid planet. Second, wouldn't that just leave a super obvious trail of drag marks across the terrain? I'm not sure, and part of me has to admit that

Brad seems to have a lot of success trying things he learned from cartoons. But I'm not Brad.

So, unless this bounty hunter has never stepped foot on a planet before to chase her quarry, she's going to find our footprints and she's going to find the cavern entrance. Which is exactly what I'm hoping will happen. On the surface, my plan is simple. We need to remove the bounty hunter from the equation and then steal her ship to get off this rock.

But the devil is in the details. The last time I saw the bounty hunter, she was in head-to-toe ballistic armor, and all I have is the single pistol from Val's ship. Jetta isn't armed, except with a few rocks she picked up in the cavern. A frontal assault on the bounty hunter is out; our only hope lies in trickery. If we can somehow trap her in the caverns, it might buy us the time we need to trek back to the landing site and use my military-grade implant to hack her ship's command codes.

Last night, it took us two hours of walking to find the cave entrance, but that was in the dark with no idea where we were going and with me moving slowly due to my ribs and knee. Only another hour passes, when Jetta and I hear the sound of falling rocks and dirt echoing in the distance.

The bounty hunter is in the caverns.

We wait, breathing slowly and shallowly, trying not to make a sound as footsteps echo through the cave system, coming ever closer to where we're hiding.

In our exploration of the cave network, we found a main chamber right off the one with the stream. Several tunnels branch off from that chamber, including one that simply loops around after a few hundred meters and feeds back into it. We've purposefully left an obvious trail for the bounty hunter to follow down one side of that loop, while we wait silently in the other. Once she—hopefully—follows our trail into the loop, we'll exit quickly behind her and make our way back to the cavern entrance. There, we'll climb out and seal the hole with a medium-sized boulder we found nearby, trapping the bounty hunter inside and buying us the time we need.

Simple, right? Unfortunately, no plan survives contact with the enemy.

In slasher movies, the bad guy will often talk as they stalk their prey, taunting them and telling them all the horrible things that await them. I always thought that was so fake. But sure enough, the bounty hunter's voice echoes through the caverns around us, her robotic tone eerie in the confined space.

"Jessica. Oh, Jessica! Come out, Jessica. I've been looking forward to this for a long time, Princess."

"You know them?" Jetta whispers far too loudly in my ear, almost making me jump. It's pitch-black in the caverns, and we dare not use our lights until we're safely beyond the bounty hunter. I shush her quietly.

"Come on out and play, Princess," the hunter continues, the robotic voice somehow making her sound far more sinister. I can hear her steps across the stone and sand of the cavern floor, coming closer. "I'd like to say I'll make this quick, but that would be a lie. I'm looking forward to killing you nice and slow. But I'll tell you what, give yourself up now, and your friend can die quickly. I promise. Doesn't that sound nice?"

Jetta stiffens next to me, shuffling her feet, and I cringe as the small sound bounces off the cavern walls.

"Who *is* your friend, by the way? I know it's not Brad, though I really wish it was. He and I have unfinished business. Is it another stray you've picked up along the way, another hopeless idiot, perhaps?"

The bounty hunter stops talking for a moment, and I strain to hear her footsteps, but the caverns are deadly silent. She must be waiting and listening to hear if we make a sound.

After a moment, she starts talking again, and it sounds much, *much* closer, echoing off the cavern walls so much that the hunter could be out by the other entrance to our loop or right in front of our faces in the pitch-black.

"Maybe it's that freak, Harris, with you. That would be fun. I always wondered what he would do if I cut him and made him bleed."

That voice, robotic or not, stirs a memory in me.

"Hmmm. Maybe it's not Harris. Maybe it's that girl from Lightman Station. What was her name? Jetta? I wonder what she'll do when I start to pull her entrails from her body."

Jetta whimpers softly. Instantly, the hunter goes silent again, listening. I wait, refusing to breathe but reaching over and clamping my hand over Jetta's mouth. I can feel her trembling against me, and I'm worried she'll move and make another sound. She doesn't. Then, blessedly, I hear the sound of footsteps once more, moving in what I think is the direction of the other entrance to our loop, just as we hoped.

I wait a beat until the sound has receded, and I'm almost sure the bounty hunter must have gone down that other side of the loop, following our footprints even in the dark.

I remove my hand from Jetta's mouth and grab her wrist, trailing my other hand against the wall to guide us out. We step slowly and carefully, doing our best not to make a sound, straining to hear in case our pursuer doubled back or perhaps came around the loop behind us faster than we anticipated.

We make it back to the main chamber without incident; I can tell by the change in the air around us and the way even our soft footfalls start to echo in the dark. Ahead of me, I can hear the small creek burbling in the next room beyond this one, and I walk toward the sound, releasing my hold on the cavern wall so we can cross the middle of the large chamber and save time.

The sound of water gets closer, and I'm beginning to think this will actually work when a bright light bursts on right in my eyes, blinding me. I instinctively release Jetta's hand and bring mine up to shield my eyes while my other hand fumbles with the gun at my belt.

A fist connects with my stomach, and my breath whooshes out of me as I double over. Then something hits me hard in the shoulder, and I tumble to the floor. "Jetta, run! Get out!" I rasp as loud as I can with my wind knocked out of me, but in the lights still spearing me, I see her cowering against the side of the cavern a few meters away.

The light moves over me, and I roll out of the way just as I hear a foot slam to the cavern floor, right where my head was an instant ago. I push myself up, raising the gun and firing at the light. In the muzzle flash, I see the figure in black looming in front of me, and I adjust my aim and fire again at her helmet, just as I did on Lightman Station. I hear her roar of anger and frustration.

"Jetta. Out. Now!" I yell, and I hear my friend shuffling around us. The light turns to follow her, but I fire again and hear another angry exclamation. Then the light goes out, plunging us back into darkness.

"Come and get me!" I scream at the top of my lungs, hoping to distract the bounty hunter from Jetta as she scrambles toward the cavern's exit. I run, flipping on my own flashlight as I go, knowing it will expose me but hoping to do something—*anything*—to draw the hunter after me and away from my friend.

I hear running footsteps behind me as I plunge through one of the main chamber's many other openings into a side-shoot of caverns and tunnels that Jetta and I only explored briefly before determining it was an endless maze. A bullet slaps the rock next to me as I turn the corner, sending stinging shards into my arm and the side of my neck, but I ignore the pain and keep running for my life.

I must run for five minutes before I stop, no longer hearing pursuit. I turn off my light and wait in the dark of a small compartment carved by water or some other geological process long before the planet was terraformed. I try to slow my panting breaths and bring my racing heart under control, and I listen carefully.

"Princess," a familiar female voice says, no longer robotic, and far too close. "Shooting me in the face wasn't very nice. You ruined my shiny new helmet. That's *two* you owe me. No matter. What say we finish what I started at Carter's World? This time, I won't leave until I'm *sure* you're dead."

I go stock still as the unaltered voice confirms my suspicion and my greatest fear. And I listen even harder for the inevitable approach of the woman I once knew as Kayla Carter.

FIFTY-ONE
OLD NEMESIS

JESSICA LIN

"Come on out and play, Jessica," Kayla says with a singsong sneer in her voice. "You looked a lot better with the scars, Princess. Let me help you with that. We'll put those right back where they belong. Or maybe you got rid of them because Brad found them hideous. He always was shallow like that."

I've started moving again, trying to stay ahead of the voice in the darkness, bumping into things but mostly keeping my hand trailing along a wall, afraid to use my light again for fear of it instantly revealing my exact position.

Kayla's light is on, and I can see it glowing off the cave walls behind me. It's some small comfort; it means that she doesn't have night vision or thermals without her helmet, which gives me a slight chance.

I come to a place where the rock wall curves sharply in front of me. At first, I think it's a dead end, but my fingers find open air and I feel a narrow crack, just big enough to wedge myself into. Without hesitating, I do so, pulling my body in until it narrows so much that I can't move any farther. With a rising panic, I realize that it's too tight for me even to turn my head, so I can't see how deep I've come. I might be completely visible from the main passageway, or I might be wedged in far enough that Kayla will walk right by and never know I'm here. But I have no way of knowing. I'm about to start working my way out when I hear footsteps drawing closer. I hold my breath and wait.

The steps seem to pause right outside the crack, and I'm sure the next thing I'm going to feel is a bullet or a knife's blade, likely piercing somewhere nonlethal. Kayla said she's here to kill me, but she's no doubt itching to subject me to the same torture she used on Brad for five weeks at Capaldi before she ends my life.

Or maybe, I think with hope, she has to turn me in alive and unharmed to get her mysterious bounty paid. Luckily, I don't have to find out right now as I hear the footsteps resume and start to recede, turning a corner and heading down what must be a sideshoot. I wait until I can't hear them anymore and then painfully push myself out of the narrow crack and back into the main tunnel. Ahead of me, maybe 20 meters, I see the glow of a light getting farther away. It stops.

"This is getting old, Princess," Kayla says, her voice echoing back to me. "There's a lot of money waiting for me if I bring you in. And you wanna know the best part? They prefer I bring you in *dead*. How about that? We all get what we want. I get to kill you slowly, you get to under-stand your boyfriend's suffering, and my employers get the satisfaction and peace of mind of a galaxy without a self-righteous Jessica Lin in it. It's a win-win-win, don't you think?"

She pauses as if waiting for me to answer. Then, to my

horror, the light starts to move back in my direction. Without thinking, I lift my pistol and shoot toward the approaching brightness. The light jerks and falls, and I lower the gun and start to run away in the opposite direction, back toward where we came from.

Behind me, I hear Kayla laugh, a hard cackling sound. "Missed me, Princess!"

I redouble my pace, practically sprinting, risking using my flashlight so I don't fall or break an ankle, choosing speed over stealth. I just need to put distance between us and get back to the main cavern opening before Kayla can catch me. Then Jetta and I can block it with the boulder just as we planned and…

Something isn't right. I slow to a jog, taking another risk but feeling a rising panic in my throat. Nothing around me looks even marginally familiar, and I soon find myself in a small open space with three different yawning dark exits. I have no idea which I might have come through before, and I can hear running footsteps closing in on me from behind. Mentally rolling the dice, I take the opening on the far left, praying that it will take me back to the cave system entrance and my friend.

FIFTY-TWO
LOST

JESSICA LIN

It only takes me about a minute after entering the leftmost tunnel to realize that I'm completely and utterly lost. This is definitely *not* the way I came in. Even if I didn't have a sadistic, torture-happy mercenary-become-bounty-hunter on my tail, I honestly doubt my ability to *ever* find my way out of these caverns again.

Unfortunately, I *do* have a murderous Kayla on my six, and I can periodically still hear her. She must have been close enough to me to see my light going down the tunnel I chose. I should have doused it altogether at that point; I would have had a 66 percent chance of her picking the wrong direction to follow me, but if wishes were horses… I actually don't know how the rest of that saying goes, come to think of it.

Part of me recognizes that my mind is starting to wander as a defensive response to the stress of hours in fight-or-flight mode and the lingering effects of my concussion from the crash. The pistol I've kept ahold of is cold comfort. Kayla may be helmetless, but she's still wearing ballistic body armor. My only hope would be to hit her in the face again, but something tells me she isn't going to let me get that close again.

I'm running as fast as I can maintain when I come to a place where the rock tunnel opens up into a large chamber —bigger than any I've seen so far—full of stalactites and stalagmites, like the massive mouth of a dragon waiting to consume me. I can hear water dripping. I don't hesitate; I run through the middle of the large space, hoping to find a way out on the other side.

Then, out of nowhere, the ground drops out from underneath me, and I start to plummet into the black maw of a chasm.

I still have the forward momentum from my mad dash that carries me toward the other side of the narrow defile, but my brain screams at me that I'm not going to reach it. Instinctively, I let go of the gun *and* my flashlight and stretch out with both hands as far as I can. To my shock, I feel them hit the lip of the opposite rim, but then my body slams into the chasm's side, driving the breath out of me and knocking one of my hands loose.

For a second, I hang there, the fingertips of one hand on the rough stone ledge the only thing between me and death. Far below, I can make out the spinning flashlight, still falling into the bottomless pit. Painfully, my ribs protesting loudly, I strain and reach up with my other hand until I'm able to grasp the ledge with it. Then, very carefully and very slowly, I pull myself up until I can get one leg over the edge and then the other, rolling over and lying on my back, gasping for breath.

I only have about ten seconds to recover when I see another light out of the corner of my eye. Kayla has reached the cavern with me. And without a light of my own or a gun to defend myself, I can neither run nor fight back.

I've died before, but I'm afraid this time I won't be coming back.

FIFTY-THREE
HIDE AND SEEK... WITH EXPLOSIVES

JESSICA LIN

I'm hiding behind a tall and broad stalagmite, my back pressed against it, when Kayla sweeps her light across the chamber. The beam plays across the cavernous space—it's at least 100 meters across in both directions, just judging by the parts exposed in her light—throwing up shadows that look like jagged teeth all around me.

"What fun," I hear her say, the evil grin obvious in her voice. "Time to play hide, seek, and kill. My favorite game. You know, Princess, you still owe me for slipping by me on Lightman Station. I should have captured you there, but instead, I wasted the fuel to come to this horrid little planet. But no matter, you'll be mine soon enough. Can you believe someone is paying me a million credits to kill you? I would have done it for free!" She cackles a laugh that reminds me of an old movie I once watched about witches who cook and eat children. It may sound like a horror film, but it was actually a kids' movie!

My brain is wandering again, and my head hurts. If I'm not careful, Kayla won't have any trouble finding me when I pass out.

I watch as the light moves. She's walking deeper into the cavern. I hold out a brief hope that she'll miss the chasm like I did and fall to her death. But I hear her give a little yelp of surprise.

"Oops, that would have been a nasty fall. Are you down there, Princess? No, something tells me you're still up here with me. I hope so; my employer wants proof of death. I'd hate to have to climb all the way down there to get it.

"By the way, how's Brad these days? Still recovering from our little chats? I really miss the big lug. I thought he and I had something special, you know. I mean, he kissed me *way* before he ever kissed you."

She moves along the edge of the chasm, her light playing several times over the stalagmite I'm hiding behind just five meters out from the pit's other side.

"Actually, Princess, have you even let Brad kiss you yet? I mean, maybe Princess is the wrong word. Ice Queen is more like it. Jessica Lin, too good for anyone else. The main character in your own little story and the rest of us are just privileged to be here, right? Even poor little Brad."

I know she's trying to get under my skin. The problem is, in my hazy state of mind, it's working, but I'm still not stupid enough to show myself or give away my position.

"Maybe when this is all over, Jessica, I'll pay Brad a little visit. There's a bounty on his head too, though not nearly as much as the one on yours. But hey, I'd do him for free, too. Payback. How's that sound? You know, I think I'll record it when I torture you and then slowly let you die. He'll love watching that before I slit his throat."

Seriously? Does this woman *never* shut up? I mean, Brad once told me about how he's sick of villains always monologuing. I thought he was joking, but Kayla is fitting so many stereotypes right now. In fact, she's—

My rambling train of thought is interrupted when I hear something clatter to the cavern floor far away and to my right. I only have a brief second to wonder what it is before the entire massive chamber lights up with the fierceness of a miniature sun and the clamor of a raging storm all rolled into one. When my vision finally clears, I see nothing but rubble in that direction in the dim reflected light of Kayla's flashlight.

Oh fun. Kayla brought grenades.

"Still with me, Princess?"

Another clatter, this one to my left. This time, I'm ready, and I close my eyes and stick my fingers in my ears. It doesn't help as much as I hoped, but I recover faster after the second blast. Then, some instinct tells me to move.

I don't stop and think; I just stay low and start rushing forward around the stalagmites. I hear another grenade hit the stone floor behind me, and I leap for the deck, flattening myself against the hard, cold rock before another explosion rocks the cavern, sending small rocks falling like rain on my back.

At first, I hope that Kayla didn't see me through the grenade's blast, but then bullets start flying, and chips of rock pepper me where I still lie on the ground. I pull myself forward, staying on my stomach until I can put my back to another large stalagmite. I hear someone running and a grunt, followed by the sound of feet hitting the ground hard.

Kayla is on my side of the chasm now.

FIFTY-FOUR
THE PRINCESS AND THE HUNTSMAN

JESSICA LIN

I'm getting *really* sick of hearing Kayla talk. Currently, she's describing in vivid detail how she's going to decorate her ship with my bloody head on a pole. I mean, could she be any more of a cliché villain? Brad would laugh so hard if he could hear her now.

Again, I recognize that my mind is spiraling and thinking of anything other than my predicament. But it's probably the only thing keeping me from a panic. At least she seems to be out of grenades. Though it's equally clear that she's herding me toward one corner of the cavern, shooting all around and forcing me to move in only the direction she's chosen. The worst part is that even knowing exactly what she wants me to do, I can't do anything different.

"Princess Jessica," she cries out in her singsong voice. "Why won't you come out and play?"

Then she shoots some more and some more, and I'm quickly running out of real estate and hiding places.

What I really need to do is get close enough so that I

can ambush her, preferably from behind. If I can turn this from a gunfight into hand-to-hand combat, I *might* be able to beat her. Sure, I'm handicapped by broken ribs and her body armor, but maybe I can get in a few solid blows to her face before she can fight back.

The problem is that I've already allowed myself to be herded toward the corner, and it leaves me with no avenues to sneak around behind or even hide well enough to let her pass me.

I'm out of options, but I'm resolved to at least go down fighting.

"Hey, Psycho, over here!" an unexpected voice yells, echoing through the large chamber.

Jetta!

I hear Kayla cackle a laugh and turn and fire back toward the cavern entrance. Which I immediately recognize as the one and only chance I have to make my move.

I come around from my latest hiding place and sprint for all I'm worth, ignoring the pain in my knee and in my ribs, straight at Kayla's back just four meters away.

Unfortunately, even with Jetta grabbing her attention, she hears me approaching and whirls, assault rifle coming around an instant slower than her head and body. I slam into her before she can bring it to bear, knocking her to the cave floor. The gun somehow comes loose from its sling and skitters away until we hear it fall into the chasm, just like mine. With it goes Kayla's light, attached under the rifle's barrel.

She and I grapple violently in the dark, fighting tooth and nail, elbows and knees. Her body armor keeps getting in the way, so I go for the face, but she rains blows all over my injured body, and I scream in pain as her fist hits me in my broken ribs. She notices and hits me there again, forcing me to roll off her.

Then we both get back to our feet. In the darkness, working completely by feel and instinct, we punch, kick, and lash out in every way we can at each other. I take a fist to the side of my face that makes me see stars and causes my head to pound even harder, but I deliver a kick that knocks her back and makes her cry out despite the armor.

Far away, it seems, I can see a pinpoint of brightness as Jetta tries to get her light on the two of us, but it's not enough. We're too deep into the cavern for her meager flashlight to do much good.

It feels like several long minutes that we fight like that, both mostly blind, both reacting with animal fierceness and trying our best to injure, maim, and kill the other. Slowly, I start to gain the upper hand, finally delivering a couple of solid blows to Kayla's face that have her moving slower than before. But then, she does something I don't expect.

I hear the grenade thump to the ground between us, dropped, not thrown, and I launch myself through the air away from it. It explodes behind me, far too close, and I brace for the wash of fire and shrapnel. But they don't come. Instead, the entire cavern lights up brighter than from the grenades before, accompanied by a crash of thunder even louder than if someone had shot a gun right in my year.

A flash bang, just like she used against Jethro and the Marines back on Lightman.

By the time I recover my senses, I look up just in time to see Jetta's distant light go spinning across the floor, and she screams. Without thinking, I get to my feet, sprint, and leap over where I *think* the chasm must be. I hit the other side and don't fall to my death, so I either judged it right or it was narrower in this part of the cave. Regardless, I run as fast as I dare, hitting stalagmites and banging my head a few times on stalactites as I go. Reaching the dropped light by the cavern entrance, I pick it up and shine it around but see no one.

I hear a scream from down the passageway we entered through. Kayla has Jetta.

Fueled by pure adrenaline, I race after them. Ahead of me, I can't see either woman, but I can see the reflection of a light around the next bend in the corridor—Kayla must have had a backup flashlight. At least I'm getting closer to it. As I near, I hear the sound of fighting and then a hard slap, after which I hear a body slump to the ground.

I stop a moment later to check on Jetta, lying on the rocky floor in the center of the corridor. She's conscious and as angry as I've ever seen her.

"You okay?" I ask.

She nods. "Just go catch that…"

Her last word is lost as I sprint forward after the distant sounds of the fleeing Kayla Carter—or whatever her real last name is. I make it back to the place where the cave system split into three branches. I see a light retreating down the middlemost branch, and I run after it, huffing and puffing, fatigue and pain threatening to force me to a halt.

But then I think about Brad, and how if I don't stop Kayla now, *she'll* never stop coming after us. And I think about Jetta, and how if we can't get Kayla's ship, we'll die here on Wake from starvation or exposure, whichever kills us first. Those thoughts give me a second wind that surprises me, but I take advantage of it, sprinting forward faster, the pain fading to a distant throbbing as I start to close in on the light ahead, dousing my own so she won't see me coming.

Suddenly, the light stops, and I see it flashing and turning frantically. I slide to a stop on the sand-strewn ground to see that Kayla has reached a dead end in the rock tunnel. She whirls and faces me, the light flashing into my eyes, but I don't shy away. I drop my flashlight in the sand nearby to free up my hands and walk calmly toward my enemy.

"Stop, or I'll shoot!" she yells, but from the frantic edge in her voice, I know that if she had a backup piece, she would have used it by now, so I ignore her.

"Listen, Princess—Jessica," she says, her voice pleading. "I'm sure we can work something out. You need a ship, right? I can take you off this rock. You and your friend. You'll never hack my ship's AI without me. You *need* me, Jessica."

I continue to ignore her words, still walking toward her, my fists coming up into a defensive position as I get close. Then she's on me, lashing out with a kick that I side-step. She drops her flashlight in the process, and it spins on the ground until it settles, the reflection on one wall illuminating the tunnel end just enough for us to see each other in the harsh shadows.

She swings a fist wildly at my face, and I dodge again, using my hand to slap it aside even though it would have missed my head. A second punch gets deflected by my forearm, and then I deliver a hit of my own, putting all of my anger, my worry for Brad and Jetta and the rest of my friends, and every other emotion I can muster into it.

It connects solidly, and I can both feel and hear her jawbone crack under my knuckles. She screams in pain, but I don't let up. Another fist to her face hits the other side of her jaw, and her scream becomes that of a wounded animal, feral and desperate.

A final punch to the broken jaw sends her to the ground, where she whimpers and holds up her hands as if to ward off an evil spirit. I stand over her and glare down, unable to see her expression in the shadows but picturing it based on the pitiful noises coming from her.

"Please, Jessica," she begs, her voice slurring as she talks through her mangled jaw. "Please don't kill me."

I kneel on her chest, batting away her feeble attempts to fend me off, and put my hands around her throat. Kayla has to die… to save Brad, to save Jetta, to save everyone I love. She deserves this—she would do it to me in a heartbeat!

Underneath me, she chokes and struggles as the life goes out of her, and I start to smile as I realize that I've won. I've won! The witch is going to die, and I'll finally be…

Suddenly, through the fog of anger and hatred in my brain, a horror grips me. What am I doing?

With a gasp, I release my chokehold and straighten up, my knees still on her chest. She tries to gulp in air, and I go to move off her so she can breathe again. But then, I see a flash of metal in one of her hands flying at my face. I dodge just in time, but in an instant, Kayla is back on her feet, and I'm lying on the ground, looking up at her shadow looming over me, the meager light glinting off the knife in her hand.

"You're a dead woman!" she snarls at me, her words still slurring. "He'll never stop sending people after you. Never!"

Despite the situation, her words catch me off guard.

"Who are you talking about?" I demand as I leap to my feet, and we circle each other warily.

Kayla smiles, or tries to, one side of her mouth not quite working, the result looking ghastly in the uneven dim light. "Who do you think? Who hates you enough to send people like me after you and has the money to keep on doing it over and over again until you're dead?"

I shake my head in confusion, but then realization dawns on me. "Jacobs," I gasp, the hated name crossing my lips for the first time in months.

By her cackling laugh, even through the broken jaw, I know I'm right, and I feel my entire body go cold. Kayla takes the opportunity and strikes.

She moves faster than I thought anyone could, the knife flashing in her hand straight at my throat, a blur of motion that my eye barely registers.

But it's not fast enough. My years of hand-to-hand combat training, from the time I was five years old and entered my first sensei's dojo, have me moving to counter her strike before my conscious mind even knows what I'm doing. My left forearm comes up, smoothly deflecting her slashing blow, while my right hand forms a hard edge and slams into Kayla's throat.

Her eyes go wide, and she drops the knife, both hands flying to her crushed windpipe as though she might be able to somehow open her airways. She falls to her knees, choking and gasping for breath that won't come. Then she removes one hand from her neck and feels around on the floor, her hand closing around the hilt of the dropped knife.

Struggling back to her feet, she eyes me with more hatred than I've ever seen on another human's face, the dim light from below giving her a demonic look as she sways in place and lunges toward me again with the knife, refusing to quit.

I suppose I could let her live at this point. I could run out of the room and let her try and chase me without being able to fill her lungs. But again, instinct and training take over. This time, I easily dodge her feeble knife thrust. She tries again, and I once again knock the knife out of her hand. It clatters away and out of the dim circle of light around us.

Kayla steps forward, trying to wrap her hands around me. I step back, avoiding her and watching her warily, but I don't attempt to land any return blows. She's wheezing hard, choking and gasping, unable to get enough air through her busted windpipe, but she's still game. With one last lunge, she tries to claw at my face. I grab both her wrists and shove her away from me.

She trips as she stumbles backward, falling hard to the cave floor. There's a sickening crunch as her head hits the stone, and I know in that moment that she won't ever be getting up again.

I don't check to see if she's dead. There's no question, and it's not an image I want burned into my brain. Carefully avoiding looking over at her, I lean down and pick up my dropped flashlight and hers. I pocket one and use the other to retrace my steps back to where I left Jetta. When I finally find my friend, she doesn't ask me where Kayla is. Instead, we support each other as we hobble down the tunnel back toward the junction. With the adrenaline of the fight gone, I can barely stay on my feet without her help.

"I have no idea how to get out of here," I admit to her after a few minutes of silence.

"That's okay, I do," Jetta says, and I stop and look at

her in the dim light reflected back on us from the flashlight. She smiles. "I just started to think of all these tunnels as maintenance conduits on a space station. I never get lost in those. I can get us out! Mole person, remember?"

Despite the horror of the last 24 hours, I bark a short laugh and let my best friend lead me back out through the cavern maze.

FIFTY-FIVE
SUNLIGHT

JESSICA LIN

I t turns out that climbing up the steep sandy slope to the opening in the cavern ceiling *is* as hard as I thought it would be. But Jetta manages to monkey her way up and outside. Then she leans through the opening with her upper body and reaches down with the backpack carrying our food and other supplies. I scramble up the incline as far as my bruised body will allow. It's just enough to grasp the backpack strap in one hand and let her pull me to the surface.

Outside, we both lie on the ground panting, staring heavenward toward the bright blue sky above. It's so vibrant that we could be on a paradise world and not a lifeless desert rock, and it's the best thing I've seen in a long time.

"So, I take it you knew her?" Jetta finally asks when we've both regained our breath.

I look over at her, realizing that she missed most of the conversation between me and Kayla. So I tell her who the bounty hunter was.

"The girl who tortured Brad? Really?" she asks in wonder. "But who sent her?"

I hesitate. I've told Jetta now most of what has happened in the three years since I left her, Jethro, and Lightman Station behind. But I didn't relate the terrible things that happened to me on *Persephone* at the hands of Petty Officer Nedrin Jacobs, the King's nephew, and Commander Clancy Jessup, *Persephone*'s captain, before Brad showed up.

With some reluctance, I tell her now. She has a right to know that a member of the Royal Family wants me dead and is apparently willing to spend millions of credits to see it happen. To my surprise, however, Jetta doesn't get sad or scared; she gets angry.

"Jess, promise me something," she says, her voice hard.

"Anything, Jetta," I say, expecting her to ask me to get her back to Lightman Station.

"I want to help you find that smug brute Jacobs and kill him. He *really* needs to die for what he did to you. Besides, what if he does it to someone else? We need to stop him!"

I nod. Then I lie back down on the hard, rocky ground, sweating in the hot rays of the sun above but reveling in no longer being underground. Until this moment, I never thought of actually going after Nedrin Jacobs. I considered that part of my life over, and my new life with Brad just begun. I never wanted revenge to define me and distract from the good things in front of me.

Even now, I don't feel the overwhelming need to kill Jacobs. But one thing is clear: I may not have a choice. Because he is *never* going to leave me alone to live my life free of him.

FIFTY-SIX
STEALING A SHIP... OR NOT

JESSICA LIN

I curse loudly and slam my palm down on the dead console in front of me in the cockpit of Kayla's tiny ship.

"No luck?" Jetta asks, peering around me at the blank screen.

I shake my head. "Whatever AI she has in this ship is too advanced for my implant to hack on its own. The hatch was easy, but the blasted thing won't give up the command codes, and without those…"

She doesn't need me to tell her. Without Kayla's command codes, we can't bring the ship to life around us, and we can't use it to escape this rock.

Kayla was right, after all: by killing her, I also killed our one way off this wretched planet. It's a final slap in the face from the murderous woman.

"So, what's next?" she asks. "Do we have to go find one of those settlements? Are there any nearby, you think?"

Frowning, I look around the small ship's interior. "No. We'll have to try to call for help. Let's see if we can hotwire the comm and bypass its lockouts that way. Then, at least, we can get a message out. You game?"

A smile breaks out on my friend's face, as it always does when she's faced with an interesting engineering problem. We get to work.

"You sure those are the right wires?" I ask Jetta skeptically 15 minutes later as she's wedged under the comm console in Kayla's cramped cockpit.

She nods impatiently. "Of course I am. Now stop asking stupid questions, or you'll never get back to that Ben guy and blue-haired girl and your gun friend. Okay?"

"Yes, ma'am," I reply as crisply as I would to an order from a superior officer, stifling a laugh at her newfound stubborn refusal to get Brad's name right now that we're out of immediate danger. She was like this with Jethro, too. When I started dating my Naval Intelligence handler, Jetta tried hard to talk me out of it. I think she saw what I didn't, that Jethro may have liked me just fine, but I was simply grasping out for anyone—any*thing* even—to make my life make sense after Hothan and Yolandra.

She tried especially hard to convince me, just over a year and a half later, not to accept Jethro's proposal. It turned out she was right. Within days of agreeing to marry him, I started to feel sick to my stomach in a way that had nothing to do with stale Navy rations. It was Jetta who finally convinced me to break things off, made easier by my leaving Lightman behind for a new assignment on the destroyer *Ulysses*.

I've had mixed feelings about it since, mostly feeling bad about doing that to Jethro, but I now understand that Jetta was right about him all along. Still, I'm betting my overprotective friend will feel differently about Brad when she meets him. Of course, I might have to pull Brad aside and tell him not to poke at Jetta as he tends to do with *all* new acquaintances. I know he *can* be a gentleman when he wants to be. He just only wants to be about 0.1 percent of the time.

"Got it!" Jetta yells in triumph as she pulls a large gray box sprouting a variety of cut wires out from under the console.

She levers herself out from the cockpit footwell and, with a little help from me, gets to her feet. I follow her out of the claustrophobic space and back toward the equally tiny engine room.

"All we need is a power hookup," she says, muttering to herself more than to me. "I think I can rig one from the life support wiring, or maybe…"

Another 40 minutes later, we're staring down at a small touchscreen she ripped off an engineering console at the readout for the now completely unlocked and accessible comm system.

The first thing I notice are the words, 'Last Message Sent'. Holding my breath, I reach out a finger and tap on them. A list comes up, and my heart sinks as I see the log of a call Kayla made right after she landed here on Wake's surface. The destination and contents are encrypted, but I have little doubt as to the recipient.

It has to be Nedrin Jacobs.

I console myself that Kayla sent her message only this morning, so it probably just left the system on a regular courier ship—I'm not even sure a system as sparsely inhabited as Wake has daily courier ships like most systems. Even if Jacobs is in the next system over, which I doubt, it'll take some time for the message to reach him and for him to get here.

I ignore Kayla's jabbering next to me. Somehow, she's

gotten on the topics of hot dogs and cereal, a strange combination, and I do my best to tune her words out while I compose my own message for the comm to send, this addressed to a digital dead drop Brad and I set up for the entire crew to use to get in contact if we ever got separated.

Within a day, maybe less, my own message with our exact location should be leaving the Wake system, spreading out in all directions like a beacon, and hopefully making its way to Brad and the rest of our friends, wherever they may be.

Assuming Brad isn't already captured and on his way to Prometheus—I refuse to think he may even be dead—and that he can get here before Jacobs or whoever my old nemesis sends to get me.

FIFTY-SEVEN
BITING MY NAILS

JESSICA LIN

F our days on a desert planet with a ship that won't speak to us or even let us use the galley, and I'm at my wits' end. Even Jetta has run out of things to talk about! Beyond that, survival rations are actually worse than when Brad tries to cook.

I will *never* admit this to his face, but I'm missing the Chalinga resort's tacos right now.

Worse, with every minute that passes, my confidence that Brad is coming fades a little bit more, and my terrified anxiety that Jacobs will arrive soon ratchets up another notch. Jetta does her best to try and distract me, but I can see she's struggling as well. After all, I've had seven months to get used to the idea of being a fugitive; this is all new for her.

Just last night, I woke to the sound of her crying in the dark as the realization finally hit her that she can never return to Lightman Station, and I have to remind myself that the place of my exile was her home for the majority of her adult life. It may not have been glamorous or exciting, but Jetta knew every nut, bolt, and wire in that station. Now, it's like she's been cast adrift.

I do my best to comfort her, but it's impossible for me to hide my own trepidation, so I'm pretty sure I just make things worse.

We've been sleeping in Kayla's ship, taking turns so that one of us is always monitoring the comm and watching for incoming ships. Since the AI won't turn on the sensors for us, that means walking outside every so often and doing it the old-fashioned way, with the mark one eyeball.

Finally, just as the sun goes down on this, our fourth day, Jetta shakes me awake. I jolt up in the little bunk, startled to think I might have overslept for the start of my shift, but the excited look on her face tells me what it's really about.

"Hey, there's some guy named Brad on the comm. He asked if there are any pretty girls on the planet. I told him only mole people and big-butt lizard people here, but he's insisting on coming to take a look for himself!"

FIFTY-EIGHT
FINALLY HOME!
BRAD MENDOZA

When the still-damaged *Odysseus* limps into the space over Wake, I make Illian finish our orbital insertion. I'm already waiting by the airlock that leads to the Q-ship's shuttle, practically bouncing up and down while I wait for the rest of the landing party to meet me there.

Quinn Boyd comes around the corner, wearing body armor and carrying a gun so large I swear it's supposed to be mounted on a fighter and not held by a single man.

"What?" he asks, noticing me staring. "I know you said Commander Lin is sure there are no hostiles near the landing site, but it never hurts to be prepared."

I give him a sympathetic smile and a pat on the shoulder. The big lug misses Jessica almost as much as I do and is just as worried about her. If that worry manifests into him being overprepared for any eventuality, who am I to argue?

Hayley Uvalde shows up next, practically skipping down the corridor toward us. Her hair is particularly interesting today, a mix of bright blue on one side and bright red on the other, and she's dressed as casually as she always is, apart from the assault rifle slung over one shoulder.

Two minutes later, I undock the shuttle from *Odysseus*, and we enter the atmosphere. Twenty minutes after that, I land our little craft on a flat piece of rock between one small intact ship and another slightly larger wrecked one.

Before I even finish unstrapping my restraints, I see the most beautiful sight in the galaxy sprinting toward my shuttle. It's not like the movies, where the two lovers run toward each other across a field in slow motion to dramatic music. I have no memory of getting out of my seat or running down the shuttle ramp. But suddenly, I'm there, holding Jessica so tightly that I'm sure I'm crushing her while she legitimately hurts the ribs Merl the cowboy broke, which are still mending from Doc Bean's ministrations. I don't complain; it's the most wonderful pain I've ever felt.

"You're alive!" she breathes into my ear.

"And you're safe! I have so much to tell you. I got to kill some pirates, and we caught Dexter Hornsby, and I punched a lacrosse player... twice!"

She shakes her head and pushes away a little to look at me. "And you got a new hat?"

I give her a wink. "Yep. Pretty cool, huh?"

She rolls her eyes but then hugs me again and laughs. As it always does, the sound reminds me of windchimes on a warm summer day.

"Ahem. Hi! Sorry to interrupt, but... well, hi!"

I don't release Jessica, but I do turn my head to look down at a short woman with brown, curly hair who has somehow materialized next to us.

Jessica breaks our hug but keeps one arm possessively

around me, and I her. We both need the physical contact right now to assure ourselves we're not dreaming.

"Brad, this is Jetta Winslow," Jessica says, introducing me to the newcomer. "She's one of my best friends, and she saved me on Lightman Station and again here from Kayla Carter."

My eyes bug out. "Kayla was here? Where is she?" I break my embrace with Jessica, my hand going to the gun at my hip as I look frantically around us. I'm about to call Quinn and have him go all ex-Marine for us.

Jessica puts her hand on mine and her other arm around my shoulder. "Relax, sweetheart, we already killed Kayla. It's Jacobs we need to be worried about now. He's the one who hired her to come after me."

"Oh, gee," I say through clenched teeth, "that's so much better."

"It's all good," the short brunette, Jetta, says dismissively. "Jess told me you have a whole destroyer! Can I see it? Do you think I can ride on it? What kind of jump drive does it have?"

I grimace, not sure which question to answer first. "We do, but *Bainbridge* isn't here. We arrived on a damaged Q-ship that we sort of stole from Naval Intelligence."

Jessica laughs and shakes her head as if we do this sort of stuff every day—I guess we sort of *do.* "It's okay," she says. "Let's just get off this rock. Jacobs is probably on his way here to Wake right now, so let's not be here when he arrives."

Wouldn't you know, at that very moment, my comm pings. "*Odysseus* to Captain Mendoza. Can you hear me, Skipper?"

I pull the comm from my belt and hold it to my mouth. "What is it, Guns?" I ask Illian. I hear Jetta excitedly ask

Jessica if I'm talking to the 'gun guy', whatever that means. I hear Jessica tell her it's a 'different gun guy' before Illian responds.

"We just picked up multiple contacts burning toward the planet from the Hecate jump point, sir. Too far to make out what they are, but rate of acceleration is definitely military."

I bite back a swear word as Gunny Boyd and Hayley step up beside us, Jessica disengaging from me long enough to give each of them a hug. I hear her introduce Jetta Winslow to the two of them, and I vaguely register Jetta blushing furiously as she shakes Gunny's massive hand.

"We're getting off this rock and coming to you," I tell Illian. "Start working on vectors to escape the moment we dock. We need to get out of this system before those ships can catch us."

"Aye, aye, sir," he replies, but from his tone, I can tell he's already doing the math, and the story isn't a good one.

"Jacobs?" Jessica asks, and I frown and shrug.

"Possibly. Or it could be the Navy coming to take their Q-ship back. Frankly, it could be the Girl Scouts, and they'd still probably want us dead."

"Who's Jacobs?" Hayley asks.

"Someone from our past who *really* needs to die," I tell her.

Her eyes widen in sudden recognition of the name. "Oh," she says slowly. "He's the guy who..."

She doesn't need to finish. My report of what Jacobs and *Persephone*'s former captain, Clancy Jessup, did to Jessica was all over Federation news for a few weeks after we left Gerson. Of course, the news reports omitted Jessica's name, but Hayley is smart enough to put two and two together.

"Who is he?" Gunny Boyd asks, a little behind, as we all start walking briskly back to the shuttle.

"I can see why they call you the gun guy," Jetta interrupts, talking to Gunny as if she's oblivious to the rest of the conversation. "Is that gun heavy? Can I touch it? Do you want to show me the rest of your guns when we get to the ship? I bet you have a lot of them. Can I hold them? Do you have a girlfriend? Does she like your guns? Do you give them all names? What's this one's name? Do you work out? Can I feel your bicep?"

If the situation were any different, I might laugh at the one-sided conversation as Gunny blushes and tries to answer one question before the short woman immediately talks over him and fires off three more.

But as it is, I find myself looking worriedly up into the sky as we enter the shuttle. Whatever happens next is not likely to be pretty.

FIFTY-NINE
NO ESCAPE
JESSICA LIN

"**C**an we reach the jump point to Lightman before they can catch us?" Brad asks as he and I stride onto the bridge in the heart of the very damaged Q-ship he arrived on.

Francis Illian throws me a welcoming smile before answering. "No, sir. Mr. Ishii says we can only ramp the engines to 42 percent, or they'll probably explode. At that rate, we can't reach any of the jump points in the system before those approaching ships catch us."

"What about the station?" he asks.

Illian shakes his head. "We got a transmission from them a few minutes ago ordering us to stay in our current orbit and prepare to be boarded. Whoever is in those enemy ships is calling the shots in the Wake system now."

Brad swears under his breath while Laia Gammon waves at me and I give her a smile and a small wave in return.

"I need options, people," Brad says as he sits in his command chair.

"Sir," Laia ventures, "maybe they don't know who we

are, and they're just ordering us to stay in orbit because they saw us send a shuttle to the surface. They might think we're a freighter, and we can claim we were just prospecting or something."

Brad shakes his head. "It's a good thought, Lieutenant, but if those ships are Navy-issue, they'll have this ship in their registries and will recognize us as soon as they get close enough to make out the details. Besides, I'm not sure we can count on any forbearance. My suspicion is the owner of those ships doesn't want any witnesses."

"What about standing our ground and fighting them?" Quinn asks as I make my way over to the executive officer's chair next to Brad.

"That *such* a good idea. You're really smart. And brave!" I hear Jetta saying, and I turn to look at her practically hanging on Quinn's arm. The big man gives me a look that screams 'rescue me', and I have to hold my hand to my mouth to stifle a laugh. "Can we go see your guns now? Are they in your quarters? You never told me if you have a girlfriend." Jetta keeps babbling, and I tune her out and turn to see Brad's answer to Quinn's question.

"We might have no other choice," my fiancé says slowly. "We can't run, and we can't take refuge at the station. My thought is we stay in orbit because it gives us the most options. We can either fight, using the planet at our backs to confuse their sensors, or we can abandon ship and hide on the surface."

He turns to me. "Jess, you mentioned a cave system?"

I nod. "We could all hide in there for a while, assuming we bring enough rations. There's fresh water there."

"Okay, then that's Plan B if we need to abandon ship. But we won't make further plans until we know what we're up against." He turns his chair back forward. "Lieutenant Gammon, what's your ETA to be able to tell the class of those approaching ships?"

"Approximately three hours, sir," she reports grimly. "But I'm picking up a transmission from them now, recorded obviously."

"Let's hear it, Lieutenant," Brad orders.

The system plot on the forward viewscreen disappears and is replaced by an image taken on the bridge of an older light cruiser. The uniforms I see on the men and women in the background are unfamiliar to me—definitely not Promethean Navy. But it's the man who dominates the recording who catches all my attention and drives the breath right out of my lungs.

It's a face I had desperately hoped to *never* see again.

"To the traitors on board the Q-Ship *Odysseus*," the man says, his voice hard, "this is Captain Yancy Jessup of the Corinthian System Patrol ship *Dagger*. We are on a goodwill mission to the people of Wake and have been informed that you have ignored their orders to power down your weapons and prepare to be boarded. This constitutes a hostile act of war, and we have accepted a request from Wake System Control to assist them in removing the threat."

The man, my former captain who blackmailed me into sleeping with him lest he reveal my treason to the public, sneers into the camera, and my skin starts to crawl just from the expression on his face. "I expect your unconditional surrender within one hour. Otherwise, we will have no choice but to destroy your ship."

Moisture fills my eyes as the recording cuts. My entire body is trembling with a terror I can't contain. Tears start to fall down my cheeks.

Laia looks at me and Brad, wide-eyed. "Captain,

System Control only told us to stay in orbit. They never said anything else about—"

"I know, Lieutenant," Brad says, holding up a hand to cut her off. I can see he's practically shaking in rage at the message from my former abuser. But he turns to me, reaching out a hand and placing it gently on top of mine.

Volumes pass between us in that moment, and I take unexpected strength from his touch. Then Brad smiles.

"Good," he says, so that I and the rest of the crew on the bridge can hear him. "I've been hoping for an opportunity to kill that guy."

He gives me a wink and then stands from his chair, straightening his skinsuit and motioning with his head for me to follow him off the bridge. I get up and take the hand he extends out to me, holding it tight as he guides me toward the hatch.

"Where are we going?" I whisper as the rest of the crew watches us leave.

In response, he turns back to face them all, refusing to let go of my hand in the process.

"If we're going to fight," he announces, "we're going to need more people than we have right now. Jessica and I are going to go do some recruiting."

SIXTY

MENDING FENCES
JESSICA LIN

I follow Brad off the bridge and into officer country, stopping at what would normally be the XO's quarters. He frowns before ringing the hatch's chime.

"Whatever happens inside," he tells me soberly, "try not to let me punch this guy."

Before I can ask any questions, a voice tells us to enter, and I watch as Brad uses his implant to unlock and open the hatch. Inside is a man whose imperious gaze and nearly perfect features remind me of Jethro Jensen, though this guy isn't nearly so tall.

"Mendoza," he says with a frown. "And you must be Jessica Lin. I've heard a lot about you." To my surprise, he holds out a hand in greeting. "Commander Jake Traeger, Naval Intelligence."

Hesitantly, I take his hand and allow him to shake mine. Brad's jaw tightens, and I can see veins popping out on his head. Whoever this guy is, Brad *really* doesn't like him.

"Why are you here, Captain?" Traeger asks after releasing my hand.

For a moment, Brad doesn't answer. Then he rolls his eyes and mutters to himself. Looking at Traeger again, he speaks. "There's a hostile force bearing down on us, Jake. Three ships of the Corinthian System Patrol. They intend to destroy this ship and kill everyone on board."

The man looks genuinely surprised. "Corinth? Aren't they a little far from their system? I wasn't aware Lady Jacobs had any holdings out this far."

"She doesn't," I say, cutting off whatever response Brad was about to give. Knowing him, he would skirt around the issue, not wanting to put me into an embarrassing situation. I know we don't have time for niceties, though, so I cut straight to the point and tell Traeger exactly why Lady Jacobs and her son want me dead and who is commanding the ships bearing down on us.

Traeger's eyes grow progressively wider as I speak, somehow forcing out to a stranger the confession that, just seven months ago, I couldn't word to *anyone*. By the time I'm done speaking, the Naval Intelligence commander looks almost as upset as Brad.

"And you're sure they're coming here to kill you?" he asks.

I nod. "They already sent a bounty hunter to Lightman Station and again here to Wake to take me out. On Lightman, she killed Captain Jethro Jensen."

Traeger's look of anger turns to one of horror, and he stumbles backward, barely catching himself on the room's bunk. He looks up at me, his lips moving, but no sound emerges. Finally, he chokes out, "Jethro is dead?"

I nod, giving him a sympathetic look. "He was your commanding officer for this mission, wasn't he?"

The man nods, still wide-eyed.

"We have a common enemy, Jake," Brad says, using his

command tone and snapping the other man's gaze over to him. "I've come here to ask for your help. We need you, every one of your people, and the Marines if we're going to have any hope of surviving this. Afterward, we can go back to hating each other and even trying to kill each other. But right now, I need you."

Traeger doesn't respond for a moment. Then, to my supreme relief, he starts to nod slowly. "Assuming you're telling the truth, Captain," he says, "and I'll want to verify myself that you are, then I think we can arrange something."

Brad's shoulders slump in relief, and he hesitantly holds out a hand to the other man. Traeger studies it for a second, then winds up and punches my fiancé in the face, knocking Brad down onto the deck, his butt hitting hard.

I'm about to jump forward and slam my own fist into Traeger's face, but I hear Brad... laughing?

"How long you been holding that one in, Jake?" he asks, rubbing his jaw and looking up at the man with a grin.

The Naval Intelligence officer shrugs laconically. "Oh, ever since you first punched me on Jewel." To my astonishment, he smiles and reaches a hand down to help Brad to his feet.

"Well, now that you've got that out of your system," Brad says, still smiling, "what say we go and defend this ship?"

Traeger nods, looking resolved to do just that.

"One more thing," Brad says, drawing a curious look from both me and Traeger. "I need you to tell me exactly what you've been hiding in container D-14."

SIXTY-ONE
BOYHOOD DREAM
BRAD MENDOZA

The three ships coming at us are a light cruiser and two corvettes. Neither of the smaller ships has its own jump drive, which means they both had to travel here as parasites attached to the hull of their larger cousin.

If *Odysseus* were at full strength, it would be a fairly even fight. But given how damaged our ship is—half our missile tubes and laser projectors are just gone, our engines have less than half their normal power, and a few decks are open to space—we have little to no chance of survival. Especially because Jessup knows *Odysseus* is a Q-ship. The fact that he's still so dead set on coming after us means that he's even willing to kill Navy officers to cover up his own crimes and those of his patron. He'll hold nothing back.

But my hope is that the secret Traeger has hidden in container D-14 might be the difference maker we need. Until now, even Harris couldn't crack its security; it was under more locks and fail-safes than the ship's command codes. Included in those locks is a biometric security system that requires Traeger himself to be at the door, with full scans of his person for the AI to conclude he's there willingly and not under duress.

Even with him doing it of his own free will, it takes almost five minutes to open the hatch into the false container. My anticipation soaring, I follow him in. I was hoping the container contained some ship killer missiles or even some of the extremely rare and expensive deceptor missiles. I used those before, years ago at Jalisco. Designed to jam enemy sensors, they're the perfect way to get missiles through another ship's defenses.

Unfortunately, they're so expensive to manufacture that they never gained wider use across the Navy, especially when most of our fighting was against pirates and smugglers, not opposing navies.

But what I see in the container is neither a clutch of ship killers nor the just-as-valuable deceptors. Instead, it's so much more than I could have imagined even in my wildest dreams.

"Is that the X47?" I ask Traeger, barely able to contain my glee.

He nods, but I'm already rushing forward and putting a hand on the sleek fuselage of one of the nastiest fighters in the Promethean arsenal. When I last served on a fleet carrier as the tactical officer on HMS *King John*, the X47s were just getting rotated into active service. They were a massive upgrade over the old F31s, faster, tougher, and with more advanced targeting systems and weaponry.

I almost became a fighter pilot at the Academy. I even set a record on the obstacle course and shooting range in the rings of Poseidon, one of the Prometheus system's gas giants. But I ultimately decided I couldn't stand being cooped up in a small fighter's cockpit for days at a time, as is often required of pilots. So, I decided to abandon my boyhood dream of being an ace pilot and instead stick to commanding larger ships.

But the dream never really left me.

"You're qualified in these?" Traeger asks skeptically.

"Sure," I tell him. "I mean, I'm qualified in the T17 trainers. How different can it be?"

He frowns. "The implant interface in the X47 is like nothing else in the fleet. Half our trained fighter pilots aren't qualified to fly one. Maybe this is a bad idea."

"That's never stopped him before," Jessica observes dryly as she takes in the sight of the sleek, sexy, and very dangerous-looking fighter. "Brad is always doing stupid things he's not qualified for—and sometimes even succeeding at them."

"Thanks… I think," I tell her, then turn back to Traeger. "Listen, unless you want to immediately abandon ship and go play groundhog down on the planet's surface, this fighter may be our only shot at evening the odds. That may be a system patrol flotilla, and not regular Navy, bearing down on us, but we can't underestimate them. And their commanding officer *was* regular Navy."

Traeger sighs. "Fine, but only because I'm pretty sure if I say no, you'll figure out a way to do it anyway." Then he cocks his head. "How *did* Clancy Jessup end up in the Corinthian System Patrol?"

"My guess," Jessica says, "is that the Navy was too embarrassed by him when the truth about Gerson came out. So, he went to his old friend and fellow scumbag, Nedrin Jacobs, for a job. Probably also a way for the two of them to stay close; if either of them ever betrayed the other to talk to the authorities about what happened, they'd both be in a lot of trouble, and Jacobs has a lot more to lose. It's no doubt why he sent Jessup on this mission, both because he'll be doubly motivated to see me dead, and because it evens the score a bit. Jacobs can hold my illegal killing, and the rest of yours, over Jessup's head."

"It's like the most evil codependent relationship in the galaxy," I breathe.

Traeger nods, still frowning. Then he looks at Jess with a frown. "I'm sorry, Lieutenant Commander Lin, about what happened to you on *Persephone*. If I'd known... Well, let's just say I'm sorry about everything."

I almost laugh. Does he really think that after tearing me and Jessica apart, planning to use me as bait to catch Hornsby, and then trying to arrest me so he could take me back to Prometheus to be executed, that we're just going to—

"I forgive you, Commander," Jessica says, throwing me a look that brooks no argument.

I send a look back her way regardless, but she gives me another, one that I've only seen once before. It's the look my mother gave me when the girl from down the street, whom I didn't really like, came over to our apartment to ask me to prom. Paula Mendoza would have no son of hers hurt another human being's feelings. No, I learned everything I know about hurting people's feelings from Grandpa. But that doesn't mean that I want to argue any more with Jessica now than I did with my mother back then.

"Fine, I forgive you too," I say grudgingly, "provided you don't try to kill me or arrest me when this is all over. Then all bets are off. Oh, and I only forgive you if you let me fly this fighter."

Traeger nods his gratitude to both of us. "Well," he says

with a resigned look. "I suppose I ought to give you the fighter's command codes." He turns back to Jess. "And I suppose you'll be taking operational command of this ship while Captain Mendoza is out gallivanting around the system in a 40-million-credit fighter."

"Assuming that's all right with you," Jessica says, drawing sharp looks from both of us.

"I didn't assume I had a choice in the matter," Traeger admits. "But it only makes sense. You've commanded ships in combat; I have not. Though I feel that the last three and a half weeks with Captain Mendoza have taught me more than any Academy graduate course ever could have. As well as many things that they would expressly tell us *not* to do." He licks his lips. "I suppose I humbly submit myself and my subordinates to your capable command, Lieutenant Commander Lin."

"She's a full commander now," I argue before Jessica can reply. "I promoted her as part of my mercenary organization. And I'm a commodore, by the way. We have two ships: a destroyer and a freighter. I even have the hat to go with the rank now." I tip Merl's hat, which, since leaving Zepha, has only left my head while I sleep. Fine, I'm lying; I slept in it last night.

They both look at me like I'm insane, and then Traeger actually barks a laugh. "Indeed. Well then, *Commander* Lin. Would you like me to gather the other officers for a briefing?"

"I would like that, Mr. Traeger. I'll meet you all in 20 minutes in the wardroom."

Traeger takes that as his cue to exit the false container, leaving Jessica and me alone. We stand there in silence for a few minutes, me studying the fighter and her studying the deck in front of her. I can tell she's working her way up to something, but I decide after a moment to save her the trouble.

"So, you and this Jethro guy... you were engaged?"

Jessica looks up at me sharply, her mouth open in surprise. "You knew?"

I smile at her and shrug. "Yeah, your friend Jetta is kind of bad at keeping secrets. I think she blurted it out somewhere between describing how much she misses home and how much she likes Gunny's glutes and wants him to name his next gun after her. She also said Jethro died in your arms. Are you okay?"

She shakes her head at me slowly, her mouth still hanging open. When I do that, I look like a fish gasping for air. When Jessica does it, she still looks stunning. Frankly, I think she could be wearing a garbage bag and making the kind of faces mothers warn their children will freeze in place if they make them too often, and she'd *still* be the most beautiful woman in the galaxy.

"Brad, I'm sorry. I should have told you. I guess I just—"

"Hold up," I interrupt before she can finish her thought. "Considering you had to spend three weeks as roommates with my ex-*wife*, I don't think you not telling me every detail about your past dating life is any kind of sin you need to apologize for. In fact," I say with a grimace, "I think I'd rather *not* hear about the guys you used to date. I'm not entirely sure my ego can take it."

She laughs and swats me playfully. "Fine," she says with a mischievous grin, "then I *won't* tell you about the guy from the boy band I dated the summer after my plebe year."

I cringe and pretend to be wounded. She laughs at me for a moment but then turns somber again. "Listen, I should have told you sooner, really. It's just that *I'm* the one who ended it. And I guess I was worried that that meant something bad about me, and…"

She clenches her teeth, and her entire face takes on a fiercely determined expression. Then she blurts out, "I want to get married in the spring, just like you said!"

The force behind her words takes me back a step. "Uh, okay. Spring on which planet? And which part of the planet? Seasons kind of don't mean anything in space. Are you talking the next spring at the resort on Jewel? Because something tells me we're not welcome back there, or that we'll ever get our security deposit back."

Jessica shrugs. "How about we figure that out as soon as you get back? But I just want you to know, I'm ready to talk about it now."

"Deal." I break out into a huge grin, staring dumbly back at her. Moisture comes to my eyes, almost certainly from the fumes of the fighter fuel stored just a few meters away from us.

"Good," she says with a curt nod that tells me the matter has been decided, voted upon, and closed. "Now," she says, looking over at the X47 next to us dubiously. "Are you absolutely *sure* you can fly this thing? Because I just got you back, and if you miss our wedding, I'm going to kill you even after you're dead."

"Entirely sure," I say. "Well, maybe 60 percent. Okay, maybe more like 50/50. But do we have a choice?"

She leans back into me, and I wrap an arm around her. "It's good to have you back," she says in a low voice. "I'm not ready to even contemplate losing you again."

"Haven't lost me yet," I reply soberly. "And so long as I

live, you never will." Then, reluctantly, I change the subject. "How are you okay? I mean, how are you even functioning? You were there when Jensen died, and then you had to face Kayla, and now Jessup. How are you not a puddle on the deck?"

Jessica turns back to me and frowns, but she doesn't start crying or anything like that. "I'm pretty over-whelmed, sure. Especially about seeing Jessup and hearing that Jacobs hired Kayla to kill me. But a lot has happened since *Persephone* and Gerson. Sometimes, I don't even think I'm the same person you met there, who all those things happened to. And Jethro... that part of my life was even longer ago. It feels like a different lifetime."

"I know what you mean," I admit. "I feel the same way —about me. I feel like I'm a completely new man since we met."

She wrinkles her nose. "That's good, because the captain I met in Gerson smelled really bad. I like this new Brad better."

We laugh together again, tinged with only a hint of sadness as we both contemplate the universe outside this container. Then I look back down at her, and that universe fades away, entirely forgotten for the moment. I lean down and kiss her, and she reciprocates. When we come up for air, I flash her a stupid grin.

"What?" she asks, giving me a suspicious look.

"You know," I tell her, motioning with my head toward the fighter. "It was always my boyhood dream to fly one of these."

She nods. "You might have mentioned that at one point. Or maybe 20. You either wanted to be a fighter pilot, or Billy Firebrand. Tell me, am I going to lose your affections to a machine?"

"Of course not," I tell her with a big grin. "You're much hotter than an X47. Now, if we were talking about the newer X49s…"

She punches me playfully in the stomach, and I feign injury. It's not hard, considering how many sore ribs I still have. "Just come back alive, you idiot."

SIXTY-TWO
GOING TO WAR
JESSICA LIN

The conference with my new—and old—officers in *Odysseus's* wardroom is relatively short and bleak. The ship is badly beat up from its battles with Baron Hornsby's forces in the Zepha system. The crew can barely keep her operating, much less fix anything, especially in engineering. Even with the Naval Intelligence commander, Fara Lipton, and her people helping, it doesn't look good.

I wish Kelly O'Malley were here. But Brad dropped him and a few other crewmembers off in the Jewel system on his way to Wake. The hope was that they'd be able to pry *Bainbridge* loose from the shipyard there and follow *Odysseus* here, but we've had no word from them one way or another.

At least we have just short of a full crew with the addition of Traeger's people. Even the Marines have agreed to help out, but only after Gunny Boyd went and spoke with them personally. Apparently, they've come to develop a sort of hero worship for the big, ex-Republic Marine.

So has Jetta. She's not an officer or even formally a member of the crew, but she's right there in the wardroom, practically hanging on the arm of a very flustered-looking Boyd. He throws me a pleading look and mouths the word 'help', but I just smile and shake my head, suppressing what would be a very inappropriate laugh at a time like this. I've seen Gunny take down trained fighters in heavy mech armor and intimidate the toughest of mercenaries and scoundrels. But now, the man is completely cowed by a slip of a girl who can't weigh more than 60 kilos if she were carrying a ten-kilo weight.

Hayley is a little less circumspect than I am about the whole thing. She can't stop grinning at the big man, taking breaks from silently taunting him only long enough to playfully annoy Francis Illian by smacking his butt or fiddling with his ear or, at one point, biting the hand he's put around her. It's like watching a hyperactive first grader hitting her crush on the playground because she doesn't know how to express her feelings. If intrusive thoughts were a person, it would be Hayley Uvalde.

Illian, to his credit, studiously ignores his girlfriend's antics and does his best to listen carefully and offer his thoughts as we all discuss our seemingly hopeless situation.

I missed these people so much.

In the end, our plan is relatively straightforward. The enemy already knows we're a Q-ship, so we're going to remove all the weapons covers, charge everything as much as we can, and be ready to duel at close quarters while Brad harasses them from their flanks in the fighter. His job is to take out the two corvettes and leave Jessup's light cruiser without their overlapping defensive fire. Then we'll throw as much firepower as we can straight down the cruiser's throat, hoping we can outlast them in trading punches.

None of us expects *Odysseus* to survive the fight, which is why we've already moved Baron Hornsby to an escape pod under the guard of a single Marine. Our plan is to fight until we can't anymore and then abandon ship, hiding on the planet's surface and hoping Jessup's ship is injured enough to limp home rather than sending landing parties after us.

If they do try and follow us down, our shooters and the surviving Marines will play the role of guerilla fighters while the rest of us hide in the same caverns where I killed Kayla.

"All right, people," I say when it's clear we've refined the plan as much as we can. "Let's get Brad out there in that fighter and the rest of us to our stations. The enemy will be within weapons range in an hour, and I want to give them a proper welcome."

Five minutes later, I'm sitting in the command chair on the bridge, with Jake Traeger in the XO's chair, Illian at the tactical station, Laia at sensors, a Naval Intelligence officer named Opal Winston at comms, and one of Traeger's enlisted men at the helm to fill in for Saki Hashimoto, who stayed behind with O'Malley to crew *Bainbridge*.

I'm watching the battle plot carefully, knowing that our plan won't survive contact with the enemy and expecting the worst. Fortunately, the first surprise we get is one in our favor.

"Captain," Opal Winston calls over to me, giving me the honorific so that three of us don't all look when someone shouts 'Commander'. "We have an incoming transmission."

"From the enemy?"

"No, ma'am. From a ship in the outer system; a recorded message. Shall I play it?"

"Please, Lieutenant."

The battle plot on the forward viewscreen shrinks to half its size, and the other half of the screen resolves into a very familiar, and this time very *welcome,* face.

"Captain Mendoza," the smiling face of Heddy Rodriguez says into the camera. "Boy have we been looking everywhere for you. We caught Commander Lin's distress call from here, and figured we'd find you here too. But from the looks of things, you're in a bit of trouble. We're here on *Wanderer*. Pilar and the twins picked us up on the way through Jewel. Want us to ram one of those ships for you?" From her tone, she's only half joking.

"Lieutenant," I order Winston. "Start recording my reply."

"Aye, ma'am. Ready when you are."

"Heddy, good to see you. Brad's not here at this exact moment, but I know he'd say the same. Never thought I'd be so happy to see our little freighter again. But it is just a freighter, and ramming an enemy ship with Sam and Tina onboard could be construed as child abuse. So how about you just hang out by one of those gas giants? We'll call you in if we need a rescue. *Odysseus* over and out."

"You and Captain Mendoza have built a little fleet for yourselves," Traeger observes from the seat next to me. "Makes me worry if I'll ever get that fighter back."

I look over at him with a smirk. "Commander, I hate to be the one to break it to you, but you'll never see that fighter again. Brad will either destroy it doing something stupidly heroic, or he'll steal it because he simply doesn't want to give it back. It's like you just gave a fourth grader a lollipop and told him only to look at it but not take the wrapper off."

He turns a lighter shade of white and gulps. "I am

338

going to have an interesting challenge writing up my report after all this is over, aren't I?"

My small smile turns into a chuckle and a grin. "I don't envy you at all, Mr. Traeger. Brad does have a way of complicating people's lives. By the way, did you ever play lacrosse?"

He looks at me in confusion. "No. Rugby. Why?"

I shrug. "Something Brad said. I *did* play lacrosse in high school, in fact. I don't think I've ever told him that."

Ignoring his still-confused look, I turn back to study the battle plot. I watch as the three red dots representing the enemy move steadily closer to the line demarcating the attackers' probable weapons range.

Traeger speaks again, his voice still dry. "I expect after this mission, the King will either give me a medal or send me to the guillotine. In any case, life won't be boring."

"That's the spirit, Traeger," an unexpected voice intrudes. "If you'd like, I can give you a job in the Carter's System Patrol. *Someone* has to clean the heads."

We all turn and look in stunned silence at Francis Illian, who stands at the tactical station behind me and Traeger, grinning widely.

"Francis, did you just make a joke?" I ask, not believing my ears.

He shrugs, still smiling ear to ear. "Hayley taught me a few. There's one about a priest, a rabbi, and an imam who walk into a bar…"

"Uh, why don't you save the offensive ones for *after* the battle?" Laia interrupts from the sensor station.

Francis frowns. "But what if we die?"

Laia regards him with a serious expression. "Then, at least we won't have to hear the rest of that joke."

The entire bridge bursts out laughing. Francis momentarily turns red but then joins in with the rest of us. As we're struggling to catch our collective breath, the bridge hatch opens, and Hayley walks in.

"What happened?" the short assassin asks, taking in the room and the rolling waves of laughter.

"Francis... told... a... joke," Laia gasps out between guffaws, her eyes full of tears.

Hayley frowns. "And I missed it? Illy!"

That, of course, brings even more laughter. When the final snickers finally die out, and my stomach is hurting from laughing so hard, Traeger looks over at me, wiping tears from his eyes. "Okay, I think I'm starting to get it now."

"Get what, Mr. Traeger?" I ask.

"Why you and Mendoza inspire such loyalty in your crew."

That sobers me up. "Careful, Mr. Traeger. You're starting to sound like you actually like us."

SIXTY-THREE
BITING OFF WAY MORE THAN I CAN CHEW

BRAD MENDOZA

My confident words to Jessica and Traeger aside, *everything* in the X47's control interface is new to me and nothing at all like the training fighters I practiced in at the Academy. Unlike those fighters, built to be forgiving to dumb young midshipmen whose first instinct was to jerk the controls too hard and overcorrect for everything, the X47 seems to be overly sensitive, responding to even minor twitches of my hand on the flight stick. Just flying it out of its false container without hitting the sides proves to be a challenge, but I make it out unscathed... barely. Which is a really good thing, because I don't think Traeger or Jessica would *ever* let me hear the end of it if I crashed the fighter before even getting her out in space.

Unfortunately, I don't get to practice much more than that simple act because the plan is for me to stay right where I am, in *Odysseus*'s shadow, until the battle starts in earnest. We don't want the Corinthians to know I'm here until it's too late for them to change their battle plan to account for my presence.

But I do find that the ship has a simulation mode, so I

run through some basic simulated maneuvers, my implant making me see how the ship responds even though the feel of the movements themselves are lacking. It's better than nothing, and with 40 minutes to wait, it'll have to be enough so that I don't make too many mistakes when I have to start flying this thing for real.

"Brad?" a voice intrudes in my comm in the middle of one simulation where I'm setting up an attack run on a Koratan destroyer.

"What's up, Jess?" I ask, pausing the sim.

"Just wanted to hear your voice."

"You okay?" I ask in genuine concern. "The spooks behaving themselves?"

"Surprisingly, yes. In fact, I think Mr. Traeger has a sort of man crush on you."

I snort a laugh. "Sure. Then I'd hate to see how he treats the people he really *doesn't* like."

"You really think you can fly that thing? Your exit from the container looked pretty rough."

Dang, I thought she didn't notice. "Sure, Jess. No problem. Easy as pie," I lie.

"Just remember," she chides. "Springtime. If I'm going to go through all the trouble of cramming myself into a wedding dress, then the least you can do is show up with all your limbs attached."

I don't reply.

"Brad? You there?" There's a small tone of worry in her voice.

"Sorry," I say, "just picturing you in a wedding dress. It's very distracting."

"Brad?"

"Yes, Jess."

"Weapons range in five minutes. You're on soon. So shut up and fly."

I grin and cut the connection, closing the sim and putting the X47 on full war footing. I'm all ready to go, but then my comm pings again unexpectedly.

"Jess?" I ask, not bothering to look at the sender.

"No, sir, it's Illian," comes the stoic reply.

"Guns? What's up? Something wrong?"

"No, sir. Everything's fine. I just... Well, before we go into battle, I wanted you to know I've made a decision."

Uh. I have no idea what he's talking about. Either he senses that or he just doesn't wait for me to respond.

"About what we talked about at the resort," he explains. "I've decided I'm going to stay on the crew and *not* go back to Carter's World for a while. I want to make things work with Hayley."

"That's great!" I tell him sincerely. Of course, now is probably *not* the time to tell him that Hayley's alter ego, Victoria, has sort of been cheating on him. I'll tell him later, assuming we both survive—probably. I'm a little worried of what Hayley or Lola might do to me if I tattle on Victoria. I wonder if one of Hayley's personas might be a shrink or even a priest that I can run the ethics of this entire situation by for a professional opinion.

"Good luck, Captain," Illian says, and signs off.

Checking the clock in my implant, I see that my time has come. I hit the X-47's throttle, and the force of almost a dozen gravities slams me back into my seat so hard that I black out for an instant before the compensators reduce it to a mere seven g's. This is either going to go *really* well or truly and devastatingly poorly.

SIXTY-FOUR
INCOMING!

JESSICA LIN

"Launch all starboard tubes! Roll ship and launch the port broadside," I command, and Francis Illian complies. A meager eight warheads, all medium ship-to-ship missiles, lance out from *Odysseus*'s starboard broadside. Then he rolls the ship on its long axis, exposing our port broadside with us hanging upside down in relation to where we were a second ago. Seven more missiles launch from the surviving tubes on that side of the ship.

"Enemy is returning fire!" Naval Intelligence Officer Cory Hanson says over the intercom from the CIC. "Deploying countermeasures now!"

I watch the plot, biting my lower lip as our missiles fly toward the enemy and far more of theirs toward us. But I'm really watching the lone green dot that bursts out from behind *Odysseus* and flies straight toward one of the attacking corvettes. "Go, Brad, go," I whisper under my breath.

Then, I turn my attention back to the larger battle. "Helm, fire all dorsal thrusters, 80 percent power, on my mark." I count down in my head as the enemy missiles draw closer. "Mark!"

The deck seems to drop out from beneath us as our ship drops down—or maybe it's up—in relation to where it was a second ago. The last-second move is enough to throw off a few of the missiles that got through our defensive fire, but then *Odysseus* bucks as three of them find their mark.

At least the enemy isn't firing nuclear-tipped ship killers. System patrol fleets aren't supposed to have them at all, though it wouldn't surprise me if Lady Jacobs, considering herself above the law as the King's sister, felt that particular rule didn't apply to her. Regardless, light cruisers and corvettes typically aren't equipped to carry and launch the massive warheads anyway. So, we're almost certainly safe from that threat.

But the three missiles that hit us do plenty of damage, one taking a chunk out of the forward command sphere and the other two blowing apart some of the false containers along the ship's long spine. I watch in frustration as three more of our port missile tubes and four laser clusters go offline, their status indicators blinking red.

"Starboard broadside reloaded!" Illian announces.

"Roll and return fire!" I order.

SIXTY-FIVE
CAT AND MOUSE

BRAD MENDOZA

A ttacking a warship in a fighter is like the ultimate
game of cat and mouse, except the mouse has teeth.
Fighters, even advanced ones like the X47, have thin hulls
and can't take much of a beating. Sure, the X47 might be
able to take a few laser hits from another fighter and
survive, but even one direct hit from a larger ship's far
more powerful lasers, and I'm toast.

Of course, hitting me at all is a challenge for those
larger ships. I'm small, fast, and extremely agile. I can
jump and weave my way across space in unpredictable
patterns, and my thermal signature and sensor cross-
section are small enough that most missiles would have a
very hard time locking on.

That's why I'm able to dart in close enough to one of
the Corinthian corvettes without drawing much in the
way of serious return fire. As soon as I'm within their
defensive envelope, I launch two of the missiles stored on
hard points underneath the X47's 'wings'. They dart out
from my little ship and slam into the corvette before it can

retask any of its defensive laser clusters or gatling guns to take them out.

Then I'm gone, out of range of their lasers and circling back around for my next attack run. In my implant's virtual heads-up display, I see a single red point on the corvette designating where my missiles opened the hull to space. I loop around, using the thrusters to reorient my nose back toward the enemy and then my main drive to kill my momentum in one direction and send me hurtling back the way I came.

I fly a jinking, spiraling path straight at the same side of the enemy ship that my two missiles hit just seconds before. The corvette's captain, probably never having faced fighters in combat, realizes what I'm doing too late.

As I get close, he starts to roll his ship, trying to get the damaged side away from me, but my lasers are already streaming out from my nose turret straight into the hull breach my missiles caused. Without the thick hull in the way, even the underpowered lasers of my fighter are enough to rip through the decks and bulkheads and straight through to the other side before encountering the opposite intact hull.

His roll maneuver, calculated to spoil my aim, comes too late.

I whoop in triumph as my HUD reports the corvette's drive going down, and then again as secondary explosions, probably from a missile magazine, tear a larger hole in the little warship's side, and it starts to drift through space, directionless.

One down, one more to go. I pour full power back into the throttle to dart past the enemy light cruiser as quickly as I can to attack the corvette escort on its other flank. I'm tempted to comm Jessica or even check my own readouts for an update on *Odysseus*'s punching match with the enemy cruiser, but I don't dare take my attention or hers from what we're each doing, not even for a second.

Still, I say a silent prayer as I line up the second corvette in my sights.

SIXTY-SIX

TAKING IT ON THE CHIN
JESSICA LIN

"Captain, one more solid hit to the spine, and we might lose engineering altogether!" Commander Traeger calls from the seat next to me.

I grunt in frustration, though I'm not surprised. *Odysseus*'s greatest design weakness, obvious to any experienced tactician who even gets a short look at her, is the long, thin spine that connects her command sphere to the engineering sphere over half a kilometer away. The ship is massive but fragile, as most freighters are. The spine is reinforced more than on a civilian freighter, obviously, but the Navy could only get away with doing so much before their Q-ship would stop looking like an innocent merchant ship, and that would defeat the entire point.

Now, even many of the containers that might have once provided an extra layer of shielding for the spine are gone from past battles and this one. On the forward viewscreen, we can all see a small image of *Odysseus* in the corner, with a giant pulsing orange circle around where a missile from Jessup's ship hit the spine directly, opening part of it to space.

Traeger is right; another hit even close to that point, and our ship will be in two unrelated pieces, spiraling down to burn up in the planet's atmosphere below.

"Turn us head-on to the enemy," I order the helm. Then I call down to engineering. "Commander Lipton, I need the biggest five-second burst of speed you can give me!"

"I'm not sure what the engines will take, Captain," she calls back. "I'd recommend we don't—"

"Lipton, just do it!" I interrupt her, wishing again that she was Kelly O'Malley. "Otherwise, none of this will matter even if we don't explode."

She replies after only a short pause. "Aye, Captain. Just tell us when."

I watch the forward plot as *Odysseus* pivots ponderously in place, turning our back and our drive nozzles to the planet and our command sphere straight toward the enemy cruiser.

"Now!" I cry, the AI relaying my command to Fara Lipton at the same instant the helmsman hears me and pushes the throttles to the stops.

I wish I could say that the Q-ship leaps forward and presses me into the back of my chair, but it's nothing so dramatic. From what I can tell, we still only achieve 67 percent of the ship's undamaged full military power acceleration, and the compensators have no problem keeping up, which means the only way I even know we're accelerating that fast is from the battle plot itself.

"Fire all forward tubes," I order next as *Odysseus* charges the light cruiser, which still has its port broadside turned toward us. That gives them a much larger number of missiles they can launch toward us, but it also makes them a bigger target for ours and us a smaller target for theirs. And by closing the distance between us, I've given *both* of us less time to defend against incoming fire.

"Missiles away," Illian responds, and just four more green dots join the battle plot. Then Jessup's broadside launches more than a dozen of its own straight at our bow.

I mutter a prayer under my breath as the enemy missiles rush toward us and our meager defenses try to swat them out of space.

SIXTY-SEVEN
JAB AND DODGE
BRAD MENDOZA

The second corvette captain either has more training against fighters or learned from his colleague's failure, because he starts rolling his ship on its long axis before I even get in range. I still launch a couple of missiles at him, and they both hit as his ship's targeting AI fails to account properly for the corvette's own movement in aiming its defensive lasers and guns.

Only one of those missiles does enough damage to punch a small hole through the ship's armor, and with the corvette rolling as it is, I can't target that hole with my lasers. Changing strategies, I hit my port thrusters hard and then yaw my own ship to starboard before pouring full power back to my main drive, heading away from and behind the corvette.

Once I'm at a proper range, I flip around nearly 180 degrees and hit the main drive again, streaking back toward the surviving corvette directly at the plume of its drive nozzles. Just as the captain stops his ship's roll so he can maneuver, I start unloading *everything*. I launch the remaining four missiles from under the X47's wings, then I launch a series of small rockets meant for strafing stationary targets. Finally, I cut the main drive and pour all remaining power into the nose turret, hitting the drive exhaust nozzles with my lasers even before my missiles hit.

Either through skill or luck, one of my laser blasts takes out the corvette's starboard exhaust port, and it flickers out. An instant later, one of the missiles hits the same port. Without the heat of its exhaust to prematurely detonate the warhead, the projectile goes right up the port, its tiny AI brain waiting until it burrows in deep before detonating itself.

A chunk of the corvette's starboard aft hull simply disappears, just as the ship's captain tries to pour power into his drives to escape my attack run. With the starboard engine gone, the power surge to the port engine forces the little warship to yaw crazily, putting it into a flat spin that has me juking out of its way as it gyrates wildly around.

Normally, the corvette would have more than enough time to get back under control and use its thrusters to compensate for the lost engine. But with the planet Wake so close, gravity plays its own cruel joke on the captain and crew of the enemy ship. The spin takes the corvette too close to the planet, and by the time it starts to come under control, it's hitting the upper atmosphere. The air resistance removes any chance the captain had to regain stable flight.

I watch in silence as the little ship starts to burn up and break apart in its tumbling dive toward Wake's surface.

Only then do I turn my attention to the battle between *Odysseus* and Jessup's light cruiser just in time to see half a dozen enemy missiles impact the Q-ship's command sphere. I scream in frustration and fear as a third of the forward sphere just disintegrates, and the fake freighter starts listing to port, drawn backward by the same relentless force of Wake's gravity that just claimed the enemy corvette moments ago.

Throwing caution to the wind, I turn my little fighter, unarmed now except for my meager lasers, and charge straight toward the enemy cruiser.

"Jessup, you rapist pig!" I scream into an open comm channel. "This is Brad Mendoza, and I'm coming to kill you, and then I'm coming for Nedrin Jacobs next!"

My defiant message has its intended result, and I watch as the cruiser, obviously figuring *Odysseus* to be as good as dead, turns ponderously to bring its damaged port broadside to bear on my fighter's attack vector. I can see places where the hull is open to space from the Q-ship's missiles, and I zero in on one of the larger holes, intending to repeat what I did to the first frigate with my lasers.

An alarm screams at me in the cockpit, and my implant projects a spear of light to simulate the laser blast that just almost hit my fighter's starboard wing. I mash down on my control stick's trigger to unleash my own lasers and use the thrusters to juke the ship up and down and side to side as I tear through space straight at the enemy ship.

SIXTY-EIGHT
TIME TO ABANDON YET ANOTHER SHIP

JESSICA LIN

I wake up to smoke and fire. For the barest of instants, I'm back on the second *Persephone*, our little corvette, right after Kayla's bomb almost killed me and left me burned and scarred across half my body.

But this time, I come to my senses quickly and realize I'm still on the bridge of *Odysseus* in the middle of a desperate battle.

"All hands abandon ship!" a male voice yells next to me. It's Traeger, and I don't think to argue with or countermand his order.

Odysseus is lost. The only question is, did we do enough damage to the enemy to keep them from following us and taking out our escape pods? Assuming we can even get to the escape pods, that is.

I cast a look at the foldout console on my command chair—it's a testament to Promethean engineering that the thing is still working—to see the plot there and the feed from our few remaining sensors. My heart sinks. *Odysseus* may be well and truly dead at this point, but Jessup's light cruiser is still alive and mostly in one piece. I watch in despair as Brad makes a desperate attack run on the ship only to have to peel off to avoid its return fire.

"Commander, we have to go!" Gunny Boyd yells from somewhere behind me, and I look up in surprise to see the bridge is empty except for me, everyone else already hastening to their escape pods.

My eyes go back to the sensor plot. There, I can see Brad coming back around for another pass at the light cruiser; all the warship's attention is now on his little fighter, and he doesn't stand a chance. Frantically, I change my display to weapons control, hoping I can do something —*anything*—to distract Jessup's ship long enough for Brad to get away unscathed. Distantly, I realize that he must be doing the same for me, trying to distract them so we can get to our escape pods.

The weapons are all dead.

"Commander Lin!" Gunny crouches in front of me and starts forcefully removing my restraints.

"No!" I scream, holding tight to the arms of my chair, switching back to the sensor plot and watching in horror as Brad's fighter weaves and bobs on a suicide dive toward Jessup's cruiser.

Then, without warning, another ship appears on the plot from over the planet's horizon, coming on incredibly fast and flying straight toward the battle. At first, I panic, thinking it must be reinforcements for Jessup. Then, a voice comes on over the bridge speakers.

"*Odysseus*, hang on! We'll take care of that cruiser!"

I cry out in joy, recognizing the voice of Kelly O'Malley as *Bainbridge* darts at speed toward Jessup's ship, missiles and lasers lancing out in front of her and taking chunks out of the light cruiser. Jessup turns ponderously and tries to run. But *Bainbridge* has the speed advantage, and the heavily damaged enemy ship is fighting against the planet's gravity well.

On the plot and the few remaining camera feeds, I watch as missile after missile hits Jessup's ship. One second, it's driving hard to escape the pull of Wake. The next, four missiles from our destroyer slam into its already weakened engineering compartment. The explosion that follows is the bright, temporary sun of a reactor going critical, and when the light fades, the Corinthian light cruiser is gone. As is the man who made my life a living Hell for more than a year.

"We did it!" I tell Quinn Boyd, who is now physically lifting me out of my command chair. Then I take one look back at the plot before letting him move me, and my next cry of exultation dies on my lips.

On the plot I can see *Odysseus* and *Bainbridge*, even the distant *Wanderer*. But there's no sign of Brad's fighter anywhere.

SIXTY-NINE
GOOD NEWS FROM ABOVE

JESSICA LIN

I'm standing on the rocky and sandy surface of Wake in a small valley between two low mountain ranges. Around me are spread the escape pods from *Odysseus*, my crew and Traeger's milling around them.

Above us in the daytime sky, streaks of fire cross the horizon as the remains of *Odysseus* and Jessup's ships enter the atmosphere and burn up to create a spectacular light show.

"Brad, be alive," I whisper. It's not the first time I've muttered those words. I've been repeating them like a mantra for hours now, straining my eyes to the sky above and hoping desperately that I'll see the familiar silhouette of an X47 fighter descending to land next to the scattered pods. But so far… nothing.

"Commander Lin." I hear Kelly O'Malley's voice echoing from the open hatch of the escape pod—the one I rode down with Quinn Boyd and a few others—just meters away. Simultaneously terrified and excited, I rush over to it and enter, keying on the comm.

"What is it, Kelly? Did you find him?" I demand, voice trembling.

"We did!" comes the enthusiastic reply, and it's like the gravitational pull of the planet below me just got cut in half.

"That's great, Kelly. Bring him home!"

There's a pregnant pause, and then O'Malley's voice comes back, a little more subdued. "We don't have him yet, Jessica. But we have his fighter on our scopes, and its beacon is reporting life signs on board. He's alive, and we're an hour out from catching up to him. The fighter's pretty beat up, and it's tumbling ballistic away from the planet, but we'll get him, Jessica. I promise!"

I slump into one of the pod's seats, my legs no longer able to support my weight. It's good news—mostly. But I won't feel right again until I can hold my fiancé in my arms and see for myself that he's okay.

"Thanks, Kelly, I know you'll bring him home," I say, trying to sound much more confident than I feel. "Keep after him. Pilar and Heddy are bringing *Wanderer* to the planet to pick us up. We can rendezvous with you once you've got Brad.

"Aye, Commander," he replies crisply, and the connection cuts.

I take a deep breath, letting it out slowly through pursed lips, trying to convince myself that I needn't be worried but failing miserably. I'm still like that five minutes later when Gunny Boyd pokes his head into the pod.

"Commander," he rumbles, a warning in his tone. "We've got trouble."

Springing from the seat, I exit the pod and join him outside, where we watch in silence as Commander Jake

Traeger makes his way across the barren rock and sand toward us, a grim set to his mouth. The four Marines marching stoically behind him further portend that this is *not* a conversation any of us are going to enjoy.

"Lieutenant Commander Jessica Lin," Traeger says solemnly as he and the Marines come to a stop, facing me and Quinn. "I'm afraid that by command of His Royal Majesty King Charles, I must hereby place you under arrest for crimes against the Crown."

I hold out a hand to stop Quinn before he can react, and Traeger throws the large man a worried glance and licks his lips nervously. There's something off about all this. If the Marines are armed, I can't see it, and surely they can see that Quinn is armed to the teeth.

"Really, Traeger?" I say, raising my eyebrows skeptically. "After everything you heard today, everything we've just been through, you're *really* still on about this?"

The Naval Intelligence officer licks his lips again, and the faces of the Marines betray nothing. On the side of me opposite Quinn, I hear a light footstep. In my peripheral vision, I see Hayley move up next to me. I can't make out her expression, but one of the younger Marines, a private, visibly gulps and shuffles his feet before settling down again and pretending to be made of stone like his comrades.

Then, another figure, short and curly-haired, leaps in between me and Traeger, hands balled into fists at her side. "Hey!" Jetta shouts. "You want to get to her, you have to get through me, and the really big and hot gun guy behind me!"

Completely out of place in the situation, I see Quinn blush, but then I quickly turn my attention back to Traeger and his Marines. This entire thing is a powder keg ready for its fuse, and we're mere seconds away from death and mayhem on both sides, so I need to think fast and do something to—

"Sergeant Goldberg!" Traeger snaps, and one of the Marines, the oldest of the bunch, steps up next to him, empty hands held where we can see them.

"Aye, Commander?"

"Sergeant, how do you evaluate our current tactical situation?"

The older Marine shrugs like he's being asked to comment on the weather. "Well, sir. Not good. I've seen both Gunnery Sergeant Boyd and Lieutenant Uvalde fight. Plus, Commander Jessica Lin's file says she finished top of her Academy class in hand-to-hand combat. With Tomkins and Fitzsimmons banged up from the battle, I'd say we're outmatched, especially if anyone else on their crew joins in."

"Is that all?" Traeger asks, one side of his mouth twitching up in what might be the beginnings of a smile.

Goldberg reaches up and scratches the top of his head with one finger, looking around as if confused. "Well, sir, I'm ashamed to say I think we forgot our rifles back in the escape pod. I s'pose we could go and get them, but"—he motions with his head toward a still defiant Jetta, who has now backed up into Quinn and is leaning into the very flummoxed-looking big man—"I can't guarantee civilians like this one won't get hurt in the crossfire."

"Very well, Sergeant," Traeger says solemnly, out of place with the smile on his face. "Then I can only conclude that action against Commander Lin and her crew at this juncture would be foolhardy, dangerous, and ultimately ineffective. My report shall thus reflect. Any objections?"

"Uh, no, sir. Not from me, sir," the Marine answers, smiling along now with his boss.

"Very well," Traeger says. "Commander Lin, I'm afraid it looks like *we* are *your* prisoners."

I nod, finally understanding. "I agree, Commander Traeger. And you'd better not try anything, or we'll have to use deadly force. But for now, I think we can trust you all on your parole not to start any fights or use any of those rifles or sidearms you forgot in your escape pods. Do I have your agreement?"

"You do." He turns to Goldberg and the other Marines. "You heard the lady, Marines. Dismissed!"

As the four Marines walk away without any frowns among them, he turns back to me. "Thank you for indulging that little piece of theater, Commander. Promethean Marines are an odd bunch. Ask them to lie outright on an official report, even a lie they agree with, and they might shoot you just for questioning their honor. But ask them to omit a few details here and there, and I find that they can be quite amenable. Now, we can all say we attempted to arrest you, but circumstances made it impossible."

I shake my head, not returning his smile, but mostly because of my deep worry for Brad. "Thank you, Commander Traeger."

He turns to follow the Marines but stops and looks back one last time. "Oh, and I hope you won't begrudge me for keeping Baron Hornsby with me and my Marines when your freighter arrives to pick up your crew. Having him in custody when the Navy eventually sends a rescue ship will go a long way to placating my superiors and preventing any awkward questions."

When I nod my consent, I see his shoulders relax.

"Thank you, Commander," he says, his voice genuine. "I hope… I hope Captain Mendoza comes back to you unharmed."

Before I can respond, he turns and takes off after the Marines without a backward glance.

Hayley breaks out laughing. "I like these Navy spooks," she says between guffaws. "And Victoria thinks a couple of those Marines are cute."

I roll my eyes. "Hayley, how about you keep Victoria under wraps and go find Illian?"

"Sure, boss," she says and skips away cheerfully. But then she turns back as well. "And don't worry so much, boss. The capitán will be fine. He always is!"

"How much do you bench press?" I hear Jetta ask Quinn next to me, our near fight with Traeger and his Marines already forgotten. "Do you think you could bench press me? Wanna try? There's an empty escape pod over there; that would be a good place to try. You never told me if you have a girlfriend. Do you? Do you like brunettes?"

As Quinn beats a hasty retreat, Jetta sticking to him like he has a gravity all his own, the sound of her rapid-fire questions fades away. I hear another sound above and look to see *Wanderer* coming in for a landing. I peer beyond the freighter, up into the sky, hoping that Brad will, in fact, be fine as Hayley promised.

The man owes me a spring wedding.

SEVENTY
TORN ASUNDER
JESSICA LIN

"I'm sorry, Jessica," Kelly O'Malley laments over the comm. I'm in *Wanderer*'s cockpit now, guiding the little freighter out of Wake's atmosphere. "We lost the captain."

"What happened?" I demand, involuntarily yanking the control yoke a little too hard and jerking *Wanderer* off course. Beside me, Illian switches control to the copilot's console and quietly relieves me of piloting duties so I can focus on Kelly's disturbing report.

"They were waiting behind Wake's moon," O'Malley says. "Frigate-class. They moved in fast and scooped up the captain, fighter and all, and now they're burning hard toward the outer system. I've never seen a frigate move that fast, Jessica. Even *Bainbridge* can't keep up!"

A whimper of pain escapes my lips, followed by a low growl of rage. We were *so* close to being back together. All of us.

"I'm not giving up the chase," he continues. "They may have the acceleration advantage, but we have longer legs. They'll eventually have to stop for fuel, and we'll have them." The conviction in his voice gives me scant reassurance as my mind races to all the many things that can and very well might go wrong with his plan.

But I don't voice any of those aloud. "Keep going, Kelly," I reply. "We'll follow best we can and rendezvous once you have Brad."

"Aye, Commander."

Cutting the connection, I sit staring out the forward viewport as the last of Wake's atmosphere gives way to the vacuum of space outside.

"Uh, Commander Lin," Illian says uncomfortably beside me.

I shake my head, wordlessly letting him know I don't want to talk right now. I can't. If I try to speak, I'll lose it completely. I—

"Jessica," he insists, "you need to see this."

Numbly, I look over at the console readout he's indicating. At first, I don't see anything, but then…

"They've stopped?"

I can't believe my own eyes. The unknown frigate that scooped up Brad and his fighter has ceased acceleration. They're still flying ballistic toward the outer system, but without their main drive engaged, both *Bainbridge* and *Wanderer* can easily catch them now.

I clench my jaw and look over at Illian. "Get O'Malley back on the comm. And tell Gunny and Hayley it's time to prepare for a hostile boarding action."

I have zero idea of why that ship would cut their engines. Maybe they're damaged somehow, or maybe they're playing with us. Either way, they're going to regret kidnapping Brad.

EPILOGUE – NEVER MEET YOUR HEROES

BRAD MENDOZA

The last thing I remember is Jessup's light cruiser blowing up as a barrage from *Bainbridge* hit it, my celebration cut short as my fighter got caught in the blast wave and spun out of control. That's about the time I blacked out.

When I finally regain my senses, the universe is no longer spinning madly around me. I'm also no longer in the X47's cockpit.

I open one eye, seeing an unfamiliar ceiling above me. Then I open the other and look around some more. I'm in what looks to be a small ship's med bay, though it's certainly not one I'm familiar with. I'm lying in a narrow bed with various monitors and machines hooked up to me, as well as an IV line. My entire body hurts, and I have one massive headache.

There's sound of movement in the corridor outside the hatch, which is ajar. Instinctively, I shut my eyes and lay my head back down on the pillow, feigning unconsciousness until I can figure out more about where I am and who's in control of whatever ship I'm on.

The hatch opens, and what sounds like two sets of footsteps enter the room.

"See, boss," a man with an unfamiliar accent says. "Told ya he's just fine. How lucky are we? The very guy the admiral sent us to catch just happens to be in a fighter heading ballistic toward us! That kinda luck don't happen more than once in a decade, I'm tellin' ya!"

"Lucky?" responds a second voice, this one sounding a bit older. "Maybe. But I still wish I knew what that battle we stumbled on was all about."

"Maybe we can ask this bloke when he wakes up," the first voice remarks.

"Oh, we'll definitely do that," agrees the second.

"Any idea what that Admiral Walters lady wants with this guy?" the first voice goes on. He's obviously the more talkative of the two, but I'm really interested in what his boss has to say. Unless there is more than one Admiral Walters in this part of the fringe, they must be referring to the Leeward Republic admiral who sort of befriended me in the Fiori system. Of course, she's also the one who introduced me to Kayla Carter—she supposedly didn't know Kayla was a psychopath at the time, but still—so I'm not sure if being brought back to her is necessarily what I want.

"She didn't say," the mysterious boss finally replies. "But I'm guessing it has something to do with all those fleets massing around Gerson."

"Why do ya say that, boss?" First voice again.

"Come on, Mouth, don't you recognize the name Brad Mendoza?"

Mouth? What kind of a name is Mouth?

"No, boss. Should I? He a singer or something? One of them punk rock bands that Shotgun is always listenin' to?"

The boss laughs lightly. "No, Mouth, you're looking at the Butcher of Bellerophon himself. He's also the guy who stopped those Koratans at Gerson a while back and supposedly died in the process."

"He don't look dead to me, boss."

"No, he doesn't. And if the rumors are true, he's done quite a bit since dying. Thought it was all a bunch of tall tales until we stumbled on that battle. Now it seems at least some of it is based on reality."

"And them two ships following us? That destroyer and that little freighter that took off from the planet?"

My heart skips a beat. My crew is after us.

"Stick says they're just a few minutes away. El's been talking to this guy's XO, and she's pretty upset we picked him up. But she'll get over it."

Jessica! They have to be talking about Jessica. She's alive.

"We ain't gonna kill 'em when they come on board, are we boss?" Mouth asks, instantly putting a damper on my excitement. I anxiously listen to hear what the mysterious boss is going to say next.

"No, Walters wants them alive. Must have a job for the whole lot. Weirdest bounty we've been on in a while, but whatever; she's paying the bills, so she gets to call the shots."

"That's good, boss. This here guy's girlfriend sounded right pretty. I'd feel bad if we had to kill her and the rest of their crew after we expressly told 'em we wouldn't. I'd be dang near inconsolable for at least ten minutes if we did that!"

"I'm sure you would be, Mouth." I can almost hear the boss rolling his eyes at the talkative man. "Completely inconsolable."

"But see, boss, El's pretty upset that we don't get to kill no one on this run. It's been a while since she's gotten to go all murdery on someone. Girl's going through withdrawals or something. Last night, when I was in the galley with her, she licked that big knife of hers, real scary like, when all I did was ask her to make me a sandwich. I ran all the way back to my bunk. Never even got my sandwich; had to go to sleep hungry and everything."

The boss chuckles again. "Mouth, has it ever occurred to you that El acts that way around you because you keep hitting on her even after she's turned you down a thousand and one times?"

"No way, boss," Mouth answers. "Persistence is my gift. Girl like that wants to feel pursued. Lets her know she's special. She'll come 'round eventually."

"Or she'll gut you like a fish."

I actually find myself wishing that this mysterious El woman would show up and gut Mouth *now*. His constant, cheerful rambling is getting really annoying and making my head hurt a lot worse. He reminds me a little of Jessica's friend Jetta, but rougher.

"What's life without a little danger, boss?" Mouth replies as I hear the two of them leave the room and go out into the corridor.

I listen for a while longer to the sound of their receding footsteps before I open my eyes again. Confirming no one else is around, I sit up in the bed and start ripping off the various monitors and even tearing the IV out of my arm. I'm wearing the bottom half of my flight suit still—someone cut away the top half, probably to treat whatever injuries I sustained in the fighter. My ribs hurt a lot more than they did before, and there's the headache and a lot of general soreness. But nothing seems to be too damaged.

Still, I slide out of the bed gingerly, just in case I'm more hurt than I think. Luckily, my feet and legs hold my weight with no problem. Picking up the pole that was used to hang my IV bag—for lack of a better weapon—I creep to the hatch and peer outside, pleased to see an empty corridor.

I'm not sure which way the boss and Mouth went, nor am I familiar with this class of ship. So I mentally roll the dice and decide to go left, moving along as quietly as I can and slowing down as I hear voices farther down the corridor.

Walking on my bare toes, I close the distance to the sound of people talking. Their words are muffled, coming from inside a compartment, and the hatch is mostly closed. But as I get close enough, I hear the most beautiful sound in the galaxy.

"I want to see Brad immediately!" Jessica demands.

"Now calm down, Commander Lin," I hear the boss say. "You'll see him in just a minute. He's fine, recovering in our med bay. But before we go there, I need your assurances that you'll come with us to the Reynolds system. Admiral Walters needs to talk to you and Mendoza together."

There's a low growl in response that I would recognize anywhere as Gunny Boyd. If he's here with Jessica, then I'm guessing Hayley is as well. Boy, are these mercenaries, whoever they are, in for a surprise.

"Why would we do *anything* you want us to do?" Jessica asks, her voice hard. "And I wouldn't agree to it in any case without first talking to Captain Mendoza. If *he* says we go with you to the Reynolds system, then we go. If not, then you're just in my way."

I hear the boss grunt. "Well, why don't we ask him then?"

I leap back as the hatch I'm listening at swings open, revealing the face of a very pretty but very stern-looking woman with an olive complexion, black hair, and dark brown eyes, staring out at me wordlessly and with zero concern as I lift my IV pole menacingly.

"Captain Mendoza," the boss's voice calls from inside the compartment. "Why don't you join us?"

"Captain Firebrand, what are you—" I hear Jess start to ask as I mentally shrug and step inside the hatch, keeping a wary eye on the mean-looking woman; she must be El, the one Mouth was talking about.

I'm so focused on the strange woman and my excitement at seeing Jessica again, that I almost miss altogether what Jess called the mysterious boss. But as I enter the compartment and see my fiancée and several members of my crew, my brain catches up to things, and I stare in shock at the tall man dominating the center of the room.

He has a square jaw with just the right amount of stubble on it and perfect, wavy black hair above blue eyes so deep I could lose myself in them. Above his upper lip is the most glorious mustache I've ever seen in my life—or even in my dreams.

And I've seen him before! Not in person but on the cover of dozens of books and in the likenesses of the actors picked to play him on TV and in the movies.

"You're Billy Firebrand!" I exclaim, unable to contain my excitement.

Mercenary king Billy Firebrand, my hero since boyhood—someone I've always dreamed of meeting but knew I never could because he was fictional, right?—rolls his eyes while a shorter, plain-looking man—must be Mouth—guffaws.

"Blast it!" my hero growls. "Not another one!"

Before Jessica, Gunny, Hayley, or anyone else can do anything about it, Billy Firebrand—the man I've always aspired to be—steps toward me and punches me in the face so hard that I fall to the unforgiving metal deck. So cool!

THE END OF BOOK SEVEN

Read the backstory of the *real* Billy Firebrand and his crew, read *The Kaelen Extraction - A Billy Firebrand Adventure*, an exciting new full-length novel!

And check out *Assassin's Flight*, Book Three of *A Star Nation in Peril*, for more thrilling character backstory!

Don't ever miss a new release!

Sign up now for Skyler's newsletter and get access to new release updates, free content, and great deals.

Just go to www.skylerramirez.com/join-the-club

BOOKS BY SKYLER RAMIREZ

DUMB LUCK AND DEAD HEROES

The Worst Ship in the Fleet

The Worst Spies in the Sector

The Worst Pirate Hunters in the Fringe

The Worst Rescuers in the Republic

The Worst Detectives in the Federation

The Worst Traitors in the Confederacy

The Worst Fugitives in the Star Nation

The Worst Mercenaries in the Border Systems (Coming Soon)

A STAR NATION IN PERIL

Set in the same universe as Dumb Luck and Dead Heroes

Rogue Agent

Suicide Mission

Assassin's Flight

THE GALAXY'S WORST MERCENARIES

Set in the same universe as Dumb Luck and Dead Heroes

The Kaelen Extraction: A Billy Firebrand Adventure (Coming Soon)

THE BRAD MENDOZA CHRONICLES

Short stories in the same universe as Dumb Luck and Dead Heroes

Saving the Academy

Battle for Poe

Siege of Jalisco

Death Station

Bells and Bullets

———

THE FOUR WORLDS

The Four Worlds: The Truth

The Four Worlds: Subversion

The Four Worlds: Wrath of Mars

Ascension (Coming 2026)

Revolution: A Four Worlds Story

ANTHOLOGIES

AI Apocalypse: A Collection of Science Fiction Stories (with Jonathan Yanez, Andrew Moriarty, Anthony J Melchiorri, and Stephen Gay)

STANDALONE SHORT STORIES

Serena

ABOUT THE AUTHOR

I just love writing. My goal is to write books that my readers enjoy and that celebrate everyday imperfect heroes. I want to show that everyone, no matter how life has dealt with them or how they've dealt with life, deserves a second chance and can go on to do amazing things. Just look at Brad and Jessica in Dumb Luck and Dead Heroes or Jinny Ambrosa and Tyrus Tyne in The Four Worlds.

It's important to me that everyone be able to read my books, including my teenage children, so I purposefully leave out any swearing or graphic scenes, though I don't shy away from serious topics. In this, I follow a tradition set by many (far better) writers before me, most notably in my life, Louis L'Amour.

As for the personal side, I live in Texas with my wife

and four children (and often a revolving door of exchange students), and I work for a major tech company in my spare time. But writing is my passion, and I often toil into the early hours of morning, especially on the weekends, and it's all worth it when I see people enjoy my books.

Thanks for reading!

Skyler Ramirez

amazon.com/author/Skyler-Ramirez
facebook.com/skylerramirezauthor
instagram.com/skyler.ramirez.author
tiktok.com/@skylerramirez_author

Made in the USA
Las Vegas, NV
28 October 2025

33249151R00227